PENGUIN BOOKS

the banksia bay beach shack

Sandie Docker grew up in Coffs Harbour, and fell in love with reading when her father encouraged her to take up his passion for books. Sandie first decided to put pen to paper (yes, she writes everything the old-fashioned way before hitting a keyboard) while living in London. Now back in Sydney with her husband and daughter, she writes every day.

ALSO BY SANDIE DOCKER

The Kookaburra Creek Café
The Cottage at Rosella Cove
The Wattle Island Book Club

sandie docker

the banksia bay beach shack

PENGUIN BOOKS

PENGUIN BOOKS

UK | USA | Canada | Ireland | Australia
India | New Zealand | South Africa | China

Penguin Books is part of the Penguin Random House group of companies
whose addresses can be found at global.penguinrandomhouse.com.

Penguin
Random House
Australia

First published by Michael Joseph in 2020
This edition first published by Penguin Books in 2021

Text copyright © Sandie Docker 2020

The moral right of the author has been asserted.

All rights reserved. No part of this publication may be reproduced, published,
performed in public or communicated to the public in any form or by any means
without prior written permission from Penguin Random House Australia Pty Ltd
or its authorised licensees.

Cover design by Laura Thomas © Penguin Random House Australia Pty Ltd
Cover illustrations: (banksias) Anastasia Lembrik/Shutterstock.com;
(van) krisArt/Shutterstock.com; (seashells) Jenny Klein/Shutterstock.com
Typeset in Sabon by Midland Typesetters, Australia

Printed and bound in Australia by Griffin Press, an accredited
ISO AS/NZS 14001 Environmental Management Systems printer.

A catalogue record for this
book is available from the
National Library of Australia

ISBN: 978 1 76104 546 2

penguin.com.au

MIX
Paper | Supporting
responsible forestry
FSC® C018684

For Chris

One

*L*aura rearranged the hydrangeas that adorned the end of each pew. They were supposed to be in alternating bunches of blue and pink down the aisle, but somehow the florist had missed that instruction. Lillian wouldn't be happy.

The guests would be arriving soon. Was 'guests' the right word in this context? It seemed too upbeat. Laura was feeling anything but upbeat.

She switched the second row pink with the third row blue and retied the pearlescent ribbon into a double-centre bow, just the way Lillian had taught her. Lillian was always showing her how to tie intricate bows – she said it was the special little touches that told people you cared. Down the aisle Laura walked, adjusting each of the bows. It was the least she could do.

From beyond the heavy wooden doors she could hear muffled voices. *Deep breath*. The moment she'd been dreading for a week was here.

She gave the usher at the entrance a nod, and they opened the doors. Slowly Lillian's friends from bridge trickled in, dressed in lavender and teal, and they came up to greet her. No family, though. Laura was all that was left of Lillian's family now. Unless you counted Donna, but she was unlikely to come. As the church filled and everyone took their seats, Laura focused on her breathing. In, out. She was determined not to cry. Lillian Woodhouse-Prescott would not approve, not even at a time like this. Maintaining a stoic veneer, however thin, was one of Lillian's great strengths. Something Laura had always admired.

Laura was a lot like her grandmother – organised, methodical. Unsurprising, given her upbringing. She even looked a lot like her, some people said. The thick dark hair that fell perfectly straight past her shoulders, though of course Lillian's was grey in her later years; the same high cheekbones; the same brown eyes. That was a small comfort to hold on to today, to feel close to Lillian still.

Men in flashy suits arrived next. Friends of the family going back generations. Lillian hadn't followed in her father's political footsteps – women didn't in those days – but the old connections were strong.

The ushers showed the suits to their seats, Laura breathing deeply as she offered them her condolences for their loss. Laura wasn't interested in receiving sympathy from anyone today, but it did seem strange to her that she should be offering it instead. It was backwards. Upside down.

Her life was upside down now.

Laura caught sight of her boss, Stanley Maher, slipping into the back pew with a slight incline of his head towards her, and was filled with relief. At least there was one friendly face among the crowd.

The priest gave a slight wave of his hand, indicating that he was ready to begin. Laura really should take her seat. But Mrs Duncan wasn't here yet, and they couldn't start without her. The home had promised they'd get her there on time.

Swallowed coughs and restless whispers wafted through the cavernous space of the church. The priest raised his eyebrows in question at Laura, and she gave him a pleading look, hoping he could hold off just a little longer.

Then, through the doors, Laura saw the home's minibus pull up out front. She raced down the aisle to help wheel Mrs Duncan into the church. There may not have been any family in the church today, but Mrs Duncan was there, and that was something. Lillian wouldn't have approved of the rush of affection that flowed through Laura as she adjusted the blanket over Mrs Duncan's legs – she was only 'the help' after all. But other than Lillian, Mrs Duncan had been the one constant in Laura's life, and even though the old woman was lost somewhere inside her own mind nowadays, she was the last tangible piece of home Laura had now that her grandmother was gone.

Laura settled Mrs Duncan and took her place at the front of the congregation.

The ceremony was long and dull. Old politicians talked of their enduring relationship with the esteemed Woodhouse family; old friends recounted stories of a fragile Lillian who relied on her faith in God to face the many trials of life. Their stories were cold, pale outlines of a woman they barely knew. Laura stared at the crucifix above the altar, holding in a groan.

This wasn't the real Lillian. Not the Lillian Laura knew, anyway – the grandmother who'd sat with four-year-old Laura in her lap reading her Dr Seuss; the woman who'd tucked Laura into bed every night until she was ten; the warrior who'd taught Laura how to be strong and independent. Her beloved Nan.

The priest called her up to speak. She would set the record straight. She would show them there was so much more to Lillian than they knew.

Laura stood from her seat in the front row and walked up to the lectern at the altar, beside Lillian's mahogany coffin, hoping nobody would see that her hands were shaking slightly. She cast her eyes over the crowd and saw a middle-aged woman in a poorly-fitting black dress fumble her way into the pew beside Maher. Everyone turned around at the kerfuffle. Laura stared at her icily. *How dare she?*

The priest stepped beside Laura and touched her hand gently. He offered her a tissue, which she brushed aside. She wouldn't cry. Especially now. She wouldn't give that woman the satisfaction.

It had been years since Laura had seen Donna, but there she was, hiding behind oversized sunglasses and dyed black hair with a fringe that fell across her face.

'Whenever you're ready,' the priest whispered in Laura's ear.

But all her words were gone. No one here deserved to know the real Lillian. All her life she'd been a fiercely private woman. Laura wouldn't betray that now in her death. Instead, she addressed the gathering with simple words and empty platitudes that carried no meaning. A throwaway anecdote about a loving grandmother. A quote from Lillian's favourite poem. Laura would keep her memories of Lillian to herself, deep inside her heart, where no one here could touch them.

She watched as Donna pushed her sunglasses to the top of her head.

Yes, no one here deserved to share in Laura's precious memories. Especially not her mother.

———

The wake was a far too extravagant morning tea in the hall next to the church. Laura supposed that was probably always the way with a family like hers. She'd never been to a wake before, not even her own father's. 'It isn't right,' Lillian had said, 'to have children at such occasions.' Or something like that. Laura was only ten when it happened, and her memories were sketchy.

Around the church hall people were sipping on cups of tea served in white bone china, pushing tiny silver forks through soft carrot cake. Some pressed her hands as they offered condolences, 'You were so close', 'She loved you so much'. Most didn't bother. She wished Maher could have stayed. Someone she felt comfortable with. But he had to go back to work. The news didn't stop for anyone. She was thankful he could attend the funeral at least.

Someone had wheeled Mrs Duncan into the corner of the room, slightly behind a ficus in a heavy grey pot. So many of the funeral-goers were only here because of Lillian's family, her father's legacy – the esteemed Senator Woodhouse. The only one who actually knew Lillian properly, had been there her entire life, was shoved out of the way.

Laura marched across the room and knelt beside Mrs Duncan. 'Can I get you a cuppa, Mrs Duncan?' She squeezed her hand. The hired wait staff had overlooked her, it seemed.

The old woman grunted. She rarely spoke these days, and often when she did, the words made no sense.

Laura wheeled her towards the trestle tables adorned with shiny white crockery and pressed linen serviettes, and silver platters laden with finger food the catering company had supplied. Yes, far too extravagant for Laura's liking, but it was what Lillian had wanted. Nothing but the best, even in death. Laura handed Mrs Duncan a cup of tea with an extra splash of water to make it weak, the way she liked it.

Mrs Duncan took a sip, her hands shaking slightly as she raised the cup to her lips.

Laura pulled up a chair and sat beside her and asked Mrs Duncan how she'd been, how the nurses at the home were treating her. She didn't expect an answer. But she didn't need one. She visited Mrs Duncan regularly at the aged-care facility and they couldn't be looking after her old governess better. 'Governess'. It was a silly word, and one that hardly did justice to everything Mrs Duncan had been to Laura and Lillian over the years. Besides, chatting to Mrs Duncan helped keep her mind off the unexpected appearance of Donna at the service.

The side door to the hall opened and Laura held her breath. Surely she wouldn't be so bold. Attending the church service was one thing. To turn up at the wake as well?

But of course Donna would be bold enough. Of all the adjectives Laura could use to describe her mother, 'bold' was most definitely near the top of the list.

Right under 'absent'.

A whisper went around the room. They all knew who she was – Lillian's outcast daughter-in-law. Even those who'd never met her had heard the rumours.

Donna sauntered towards Laura, who stood to greet her mother.

'I'm surprised to see you here.' Laura's tone was even, cool.

'I couldn't miss this.' Donna shook her head. 'Ding-dong, the witch —'

'Don't, Mum. Not today. Not here.'

Donna took a bacon-wrapped prawn from the waiter walking by.

Laura took in a deep breath. 'Mum, what are you doing here? Clearly you haven't come to pay your respects.'

'Respects?' she sniggered. 'Respect is the last thing I have for that woman.'

'Then maybe you should leave.'

'Your loyalty to your grandmother is admirable, darling.'

'She did raise me.' Laura looked her mother in the eye.

'Yes. Well, she didn't give me much choice in that.'

Laura had heard this before. The evil mother-in-law who'd never accepted her son's choice of wife, blah, blah, blah. All Laura knew, all she cared about, was the fact that Donna had left her after her dad died and had made very little effort to be part of her life in the two decades since.

'Mum, this is not the time or place.'

'It never is. It's amazing how you Prescotts and Woodhouses stick together. Circle the wagons against outsiders. Hide your dirty little secrets from the world.'

Mrs Duncan dropped her teacup and the bone china shattered on the wooden floorboards. Everyone turned their gaze to the trio. Laura bent down to pick up the pieces, but a waiter rushed in and assured her he'd take care of it.

Donna lowered her voice. 'That's the thing about coming from money. There's always someone there to clean up your mess for you.'

At this Laura stood and took a step towards her mother. 'Is that why you're here? You want money?'

'No, darling. It was never about money. Not for me. I came to give you this.' She handed Laura an envelope. 'Your father found it, not long before he died. I don't know what it means, but he and Lillian had a huge argument about it. You were so little, you wouldn't remember.'

Laura opened the envelope and inside was a photo of two young girls on a beach. Mrs Duncan began to mutter random words. 'No. Gigi. Bad.' Her entire body was shaking. 'Don't cry, baby girl.'

'Mrs Duncan? Are you okay?' Laura put her hand on the old lady's shoulder.

'No.' Her whole body trembled. 'No. No. No.'

Laura hushed Mrs Duncan and rubbed her back until her agitation settled. It was never nice seeing her upset like this.

'I think maybe it's time you left.' Laura turned to her mother.

Donna turned her back. 'I did try, you know. Many times. To see you. She wouldn't let me. Maybe, one day, now you're free of her, we can talk.'

'Leave. Now.' Laura felt tears well up. She'd held it together all day. She wouldn't let her mother be her undoing. She watched her mum walk towards the door and Donna turned back once, looked Laura in the eye and put her hand to her chest. As she stepped outside, the afternoon sun cast her figure in silhouette and Laura watched her disappear into a bright light.

In the late afternoon Laura padded barefoot around the lavish townhouse. She adjusted the paintings on the walls, a few millimetres up, a few down. She was alone at last. It had been a long day, the forced smiles exhausting, and it was good to be home. Memories of her childhood, sliding in socks along the marble floor whenever Lillian wasn't home, played through her mind. It hadn't been easy to move back in two years ago, when Lillian had fallen ill. Giving up her independence had felt so hard at the time. Now she wished she'd done it earlier, stolen just a little more time with her grandmother.

She looked up at the oil painting of Lillian that hung above the fireplace. Her grandmother's stern expression was so familiar, yet distant. Laura didn't want to remember her that way, despite it being an accurate likeness. She wanted to remember the look of peace that came over her as she read poetry in the conservatory on Sundays, the cheeky smirk that touched her lips as they snuck ice-cream in the middle of the night, long after Mrs Duncan had gone to bed.

She walked into the kitchen and opened the double doors of the freezer, pulling out the ice-cold tub of rocky road for old time's sake. Laura swivelled around on the black bar stool, using the white marble benchtop as leverage. 'Sit up straight.' Lillian's words echoed in her memory, and out of respect she obliged one last time.

'Oh, Nan.' Laura breathed out, allowing her shoulders to slump.

The phone in her handbag vibrated. She'd forgotten to take it off silent after the funeral. Reaching into her bag, she felt the envelope Donna had given her and pulled it out along with her mobile. A message from Maher wishing her a restful night.

She opened the envelope and pulled out the photo, taking a closer look. Two young women, teenagers, stood arm in arm on a deserted stretch of beach, the waves behind them thinking about teasing their ankles. She ran her fingers around the edge. The girl on the right wore a dress that seemed a little too small for her and her pale hair was in a perfect sixties bob. The girl on the left, dressed in a polka-dot swing dress, with long dark hair kept off her face by a bow, looked at the camera with a sweet, perfect smile – Laura had seen it rarely in her life but would recognise it anywhere. Lillian's smile.

Turning the photo over, Laura read the inscription on the back. 'Lily and Gigi. Sisters of Summer, Banksia Bay, 1961.'

What was the name Mrs Duncan had muttered? Laura had never heard Lillian mention a Gigi before, or any name like it. Nor had she ever spoken of a place called Banksia Bay. And one thing Laura was most certain of when it came to her grandmother was that Lillian never went to the beach. And she certainly didn't have a sister.

The next morning Laura stopped at the nursing home to visit Mrs Duncan before heading to work. She clutched the photo in the envelope in her hand. It was a long shot – longer than a long shot. Completely futile, really, but what was the harm in trying?

She let herself into Mrs Duncan's room quietly. Laura had moved Mrs Duncan into the best home money could buy after Lillian had signed over the family accounts into her name. It was the least she could do for her old governess. However long Mrs Duncan had left, Laura was going to make it as comfortable as she could.

Mrs Duncan was up and sitting by the bay window looking out onto a rose garden. She'd always been an early riser, thanks to a lifetime in the service of a wealthy, often demanding, family. Around the room were photos of Lillian as a young child, of Laura's dad at various ages, of Laura. Mrs Duncan had never had children of her own, widowed before she took her post with the Woodhouses. This was her family.

Back at home, there were baby pictures of Laura's grandmother in the photo albums, black-and-white vignettes of an impeccably dressed little Lillian with her thick dark hair. But nothing from her teenage years. Laura had asked her once about the gap in her pictorial history and she'd brushed it aside, mumbling something about them being lost in a move.

'Good morning, Mrs Duncan.' Laura sat on the padded bench under the window. 'What a beautiful day.'

Mrs Duncan blinked – her way of saying hello. They sat in silence and drank the tea Laura had made them, Mrs Duncan taking slow sips.

'Mrs Duncan,' Laura said, pulling the photo out of the envelope, 'can I ask you something?'

Mrs Duncan looked at the picture and her hands began to shake.

Laura placed it on Mrs Duncan's lap. 'Do you know who Gigi is? Do you know Banksia Bay?'

Mrs Duncan brushed the photo off her lap, letting it fall to the ground.

'Is she important? This Gigi?' Laura picked up the photo and went to hand it back to Mrs Duncan. The old woman growled at Laura, an indecipherable sound from somewhere deep within. Somewhere dark.

Tears fell down Mrs Duncan's cheeks. 'No. No. No.'

Laura had never seen Mrs Duncan cry. Not once.

'It's okay. I'm sorry.' She hugged Mrs Duncan, smoothing her hair. 'I didn't mean to upset you.'

As she pulled away, Mrs Duncan grabbed her hand. She nodded to her dresser in the corner of the room. Over the past few years Laura had learned to read the 98-year-old's physical cues – a wink of her left eye when she was cold and needed a blanket, her thin lips turning slightly up when she wanted Laura to fluff her pillow, a certain tilt of the head, a particular hand movement, a frown.

The nod towards the dresser now to let her know she wanted her hair brushed. Laura walked across the room and picked up the tortoiseshell brush. As she reached for it, she knocked a tiny silver jewellery box sitting next to it. She'd never noticed it before.

A short grunt.

'What is it, Mrs Duncan?' Laura spun round, her hand knocking the lid off the small trinket box.

A groan.

'I'm so sorry. It's okay. I didn't break it.' She looked inside as she returned the lid and saw a stunning pendant. Or rather, a half pendant. It looked like a delicate silver wing, each tiny feather that swept in an arc perfectly defined. Down one feather that draped to the tip of the wing were six blue sapphires. Laura may not have been interested in jewellery herself – she only owned one pair of very practical stud earrings, no necklaces, no rings – but you didn't grow up in a family like hers and not know the value of an antique. This piece was stunning. At the top of the rounded edge of the wing, near the first gem, the shiny silver was jagged, as if something had snapped off. Was there once another wing? Laura ran her fingers over the metal, from smooth to rough. Yes, there was definitely something missing here.

'This is beautiful. Did your husband give it to you? Or a long-lost lover, perhaps?' Laura found the thought of Mrs Duncan having a secret romantic past rather intriguing. She took the pendant over to her and Mrs Duncan started shaking her head.

'Mrs Duncan? Is everything okay?'

The old lady started rocking back and forth, her gaze on the photo of Lily and Gigi lying on the bay window bench seat.

Laura took a stab in the dark. 'Is it Nan's?'

She rocked harder.

'Does it have something to do with this?' She held up the photo.

Mrs Duncan closed her eyes, her shaking turning into convulsions. Laura called for a nurse and cradled Mrs Duncan in her arms. Laura rocked back and forth, whispering calming words, as much to settle herself as Mrs Duncan. She'd never seen her like this before and Laura fought to keep her worry pushed deep down inside.

Laura stared out the window of the newspaper office as the sun hit its midday peak, unable to concentrate on her article.

It had taken the nurse half an hour to calm Mrs Duncan down, and in the end she'd had to resort to using a sedative. Laura couldn't get the image of her seizure out of her mind. She'd rung three times since getting to work to check on her and had been assured that Mrs Duncan was now settled and resting well.

She would pop in on the way home just to check for herself.

Laura stared at the words on her laptop screen and tried to write her conclusion. She'd never missed a deadline. Never even cut it this close before. Maher would understand, of course. He knew how much Lillian meant to Laura and had suggested she take some time off to deal with her passing. But Laura had insisted she needed to keep busy. Taking yesterday off for the funeral was enough.

Except her fingers refused to move across the keyboard and her eyes kept dropping to her handbag, where the photo and the pendant were ensconced. She hadn't stolen Mrs Duncan's pendant. She'd merely borrowed it. For research purposes.

She'd tried to dismiss the photo as just some random black-and-white print capturing an unimportant moment in time, but she couldn't dismiss Mrs Duncan's reaction to it. Maher's third rule of journalism was *always trust your instincts*, and Laura's instincts were telling her it wasn't a random moment and it was anything but unimportant.

She'd tried to chalk up Mrs Duncan's reaction to the photo and then the pendant as mere coincidence. A sick old woman in her late nineties was bound to have turns. But rule number six, *there is no such thing as coincidence*, was at the forefront of her mind.

Words. Laura needed words. Any words to finish this article. She started to type. Who? What? Where?

Well, technically they were words. Just not the right ones.

Focus, Laura.

She took a sip of the strong black coffee she'd brewed. How hard could this be? She knew this piece inside out. Countless hours of research and undercover investigation had gone into it. All she needed was one magic line to tie it all together.

Think.

Lillian hated the beach, yet she looked so happy in the old photograph.

And that pendant. Her gut was telling her it wasn't just some trinket.

Focus.

An hour later, her deadline came and went and the words still failed her.

'Prescott.' Maher's deep baritone rang through the office. 'Come in for a minute.'

Laura drew in a deep breath and walked into her editor's office.

She sat opposite Stanley Maher in the green leather chair she'd first sat in as a cadet five years ago, so happy to have landed a job with the best news editor in the country. He'd treated her almost like family ever since she started at the paper, and he'd taught her everything she knew about being a reporter, about research, about protecting sources. He was the closest thing she had to a father-figure.

'It's nearly done,' she said. 'Really, it's all there. I just need to finish it off somehow.'

'Show me what you have.'

As he read through her article, he sat there and tapped his desk, once at the beginning, once somewhere in the middle. A tap was high praise from Maher.

'You're right. It needs something at the end. You're usually spot-on bringing these things home.'

'I'm sorry. It's just . . .'

He raised his hand. 'I know, Prescott. You have every reason not to be on your game. That's why I told you to take some time off. Lord knows you've got plenty of leave owing. When was your last holiday?'

Never. Laura hadn't taken a single day of leave since she'd started with the paper. She took in a sharp breath.

'Look. We could have pushed this back to next week. But now we're holding space for it.'

'Give me fifteen minutes. I'll get it done.'

He pushed his glasses up the bridge of his nose. Code for, *Do it now, don't let me down.*

Laura went back to her desk and read the last paragraph of her article, wishing the words would fill her mind. She closed her eyes and took in a deep breath. Never once had she failed to turn in an article. And she wasn't about to start now.

She opened her eyes and her fingers raced across the keyboard. Done. She saved the file to her laptop, backed it up on a USB like she always did, and printed out a hard copy, just to be on the safe side. No one else at the newspaper kept paper copies of their articles and stories, but Laura was nothing if not meticulous about backing up her work. Rule number five, *always back up your files.*

Maher stepped out of his office and put his hand on her shoulder. 'Go home. That's an order.'

Laura packed up her computer and put away her notes. She liked to start each morning with a clear desk and never left at the end of the day without tidying it. Outside the office she hailed a taxi, unable to face the press of an overcrowded bus.

She stopped by Mrs Duncan on her way home to find her sleeping. Laura stayed by her bed, reading the news on her phone. Usually she trawled through the pages of every major paper and network twice a day. But with the funeral she'd neglected to stay abreast of what was happening in the world.

An hour later a nurse insisted it was time for her to go home, that Mrs Duncan would be fine and they'd call if there was need.

Another taxi ride later and Laura kicked off her shoes as she entered the grand hall of Lillian's house. She fixed herself a quick dinner of cheese on toast and pulled out the photo and the pendant, turning each one over in her hands, studying every detail. She got her notebook out and started jotting down questions. Sometimes it helped her think better, to scrawl ink across paper.

Who was Gigi? Where is Banksia Bay? Why did the pendant cause Mrs Duncan to have a turn?

Perhaps there were other photos of this Gigi girl Laura had simply never paid attention to before. She went into the lounge room and pulled out the photo albums from a drawer in the heavy wooden coffee table. She flipped through page after page of Lillian's early life, the photo of the girls on the beach in her hand for comparison. There was no sign of anyone resembling Gigi.

At the back of the second album, Laura realised there were some pages missing. They had been cut out very carefully. So carefully that, unless you looked really closely, you would never have noticed. That was strange. She turned back to the last few pictures on the previous page. Lillian looked about twelve in them. She compared them to the picture Donna had given her. She was much older in this mysterious photo. Why were there no photos of Lillian in her teenage years, except this one? The one that had caused Mrs Duncan to have a turn. Hmm. Rule number six. *No such thing as a coincidence.*

Laura stood up and stretched her arms into the air. The base of her neck tingled, just as it always did before she chased down a story.

Yawning, she piled up the photo albums neatly on the coffee table. She would look through them again tomorrow. It had been a long few days. A long few weeks since Lillian's health had begun to deteriorate so rapidly.

With the 'Sisters of Summer' photo and the wing pendant in her pocket Laura passed Lillian's bedroom and paused at the door. The sage-green and white striped wallpaper hadn't changed in all Laura's life. Everything in the room was the way it had always been.

Everything except the tousled corner of the pink rose-petal bedspread where Lillian had collapsed.

That wouldn't do. Lillian always had perfectly pleated corners on her bedspread – it was Mrs Duncan's first job after breakfast. And once they'd lost her service to ill health, the maid Lillian had hired – or rather, series of maids, as none of them ever quite measured up and were fired after a few months on the job – had been schooled in how to make a bed properly. Laura had given the latest young maid time off since Lillian died. Had she left the bed like this?

Laura tucked the corner in exactly as she'd seen Mrs Duncan do it a million times and, as she did, her toe kicked something under the bed. She knelt down and pulled out an old shoebox, the corners of which had been eaten away by whatever little critter liked to munch on cardboard.

Opening the faded lid, Laura's hand began to shake. She looked at the keepsakes inside: a black-and-white postcard from Banksia Bay – she gasped and read the back, just two words, 'Forgive me'; a movie ticket stub for *The Musician*; a handkerchief with the initials RP, Richard Prescott, her grandfather, embroidered in the corner in navy blue. Underneath the handkerchief was a photo. Laura pulled it out. It was a wedding picture of her grandparents. She'd never seen a photo of their wedding before – another loss from the move. Supposedly. Lillian looked the picture of serenity in her white gown beside a very proud-looking Richard. Laura noticed something around Lillian's neck.

With the photo in her hand she ran into the kitchen and pulled out the magnifying glass she knew Mrs Duncan used to keep in the drawer. She pulled the silver wing out of her pocket and examined it. In the photo, the pendant around Lillian's neck was a heart shape. She moved the magnifying glass. A heart made of two wings: the right side an arc of sweeping feathers leading to a tip from which a dark teardrop-shaped gem hung; the left wing a mirror image but with six tiny sapphires embedded in one feather. Laura drew in a deep breath; there was no mistaking it. The pendant around Lillian's neck and the half in her hand were the same.

Two

*L*aura stood by the side of the road at what was supposed to be the interchange for the bus to Banksia Bay. This particular stretch of coastal road looked exactly the same as the rest of the fifty-odd kilometres she'd been travelling on since leaving the highway an hour ago. Just more patchy bitumen lined with gum trees. The only difference was the extraordinarily large tree stump that looked like it had been smoothed by many years of travellers resting on it. She sat down on its flat surface. There was no bus stop sign, no shelter, no timetable posted anywhere nearby. Nothing. Just Laura, her suitcase and the tree stump.

The afternoon sun beat down on her back as she sat there waiting for – what had the bus driver from Sydney called it? – the Bronte Bus? No. Bronte was a beach in Sydney. Oh, why hadn't she paid more attention? Something to do with surfing? Or a movie? *Well done, Laura.* Stuck in the middle of nowhere, at what may or may not be a bus stop, destined for a town she'd never heard of, waiting for a bus she couldn't remember the name of.

This was what happened when you abandoned all reason and didn't do your research properly. Rule number four, *always know what you're getting into*. Her sense had, apparently, taken a vacation. Is that what grief did? Take away your ability to think straight?

She pulled out her phone and snapped a selfie to send Maher. At least he would get a kick out of seeing Laura so far out of her comfort zone. As she went to send it, she realised there was no reception.

If she ended up in a ditch somewhere, it would be all his fault. He was the one who'd insisted she make the trip. Three days of subpar work from her, unable to focus or concentrate with so many questions running through her mind, and he'd called her into his office. 'Take a break, Prescott, and come back your usual self.'

She took in a deep breath. She wouldn't really end up in a ditch. Would she? Panic was not Laura's default mode. Panic was a waste of energy and completely unproductive. The driver who had brought her here had assured her that this was indeed the right place for her to change buses. What reason would he have to leave her anywhere else? Well . . . Laura's imagination began to tick over – setting her up to be robbed or, worse, the base of operations for a human-smuggling ring. She'd done a story on one of those early in her career.

Stop it. You're a journalist, not an author.

Stick to the facts. Rule number one, and the most important of them all.

And the facts were simple. She was at the right bus stop according to the driver and, according to the schedule the agent had given her over the phone, the bus to Banksia Bay would be along in half an hour.

Half an hour was a long time to pass alone, especially with no phone reception. She pulled out the novel she had in her backpack.

A story about a woman who goes missing in the bush wasn't the best choice of travelling companion, it turned out. After fifteen minutes, Laura stood and stretched her legs. No other vehicle had come past since she'd arrived, so she left her suitcase by the stump and strode down a little way into the tree line. It certainly was peaceful here. There was a whipping sound coming from somewhere deep in the bushland. If she'd had internet access she would have looked up what sort of bird made such an intriguing call.

A rustle in the leaves just off to her left made her jump back. Laura had no idea what sort of animals lived in a place like this. In the inner city there were no snakes or goannas or wombats, or any of the wildlife she knew was common in other parts of Australia. The wildest animal she'd ever seen was a possum (well, heard more than seen), or a huntsman spider hiding in the corner of the ceiling, which was no match for her extra-strength Mortein. She wished now she'd researched the area more. While she couldn't find much on Banksia Bay itself – just a few real estate listings, a holiday rental – surely if she'd looked harder she'd have found something on a neighbouring town. Breaking rule number four was never a good idea. Going into a situation blind and unprepared never ended well, yet here she was. Grief had a lot to answer for.

The rustling stopped, but she wasn't about to take any chances, so she headed back to wait on the stump. Before sitting down, she checked for any visible creepy-crawlies. Satisfied, she sat back down and waited.

Turning her face to the sky, Laura closed her eyes and breathed deeply, holding each breath for three seconds before exhaling.

She would put her momentary slip into chaos – if you could call a week 'momentary' – behind her and not allow grief to plunge her into any more rash decisions. She had something to focus on now. She would investigate Lillian's connection to Banksia Bay, the photo and the pendant. She would find answers and then get back to her normal life.

A very loud horn tooted through the silence as a vehicle came rumbling down the road towards her. It stopped right in front of her – a burnt-orange and white kombivan, in excellent condition, with the words 'Bodhi Bus' in the shape of a bright yellow wave emblazoned along the side. That was what the bus driver had said: Bodhi Bus. Was someone having a joke? Laura knew it wasn't going to be a big bus to take her to Banksia Bay. But she'd been expecting a minibus at least. Not some fifties relic named after a criminal surfer from a nineties movie.

The door swung open and out stepped a diminutive woman with a grey pixie haircut, wearing board shorts in a blinding swirl of psychedelic colour and an old T-shirt that looked like one more wash would probably send it to T-shirt heaven. Behind her Laura could make out the silhouettes of other passengers. The woman's eyes were kind and a smile spread across her face as she looked at Laura.

'You must be our pick-up.' She reached out her hand and shook Laura's vigorously. The slightest flash of something – recognition perhaps – crossed the bus driver's face. 'Um . . . I'm Yvonne. Let me help you with this and we'll be on our way.'

'Oh, no, it's heavy.' Laura went to stop the woman, but Yvonne was obviously stronger than she looked. She was at least 10 centimetres shorter than Laura, who only stood at 164 centimetres, but when Yvonne hoisted the suitcase onto the roof rack atop the van, Laura could see there was strength in the woman who she suspected was well into her late sixties. With one smooth movement Yvonne secured the case with an occy strap.

'Hop in, love,' she said, making a sweep with her arm. 'There's room in the middle. It's Laura, isn't it?'

'Ah, yes.' Laura waited for Yvonne to mark her name off a passenger list but there didn't appear to be one.

'Welcome aboard the Bodhi Bus, Laura. Next stop, paradise.'

Laura stepped into the kombivan and was greeted by the other passengers. The old guy up the back – bald head, white beard, skin like leather, no shirt – gave her a broad toothy grin and a welcoming hand wave (at least, she assumed it was welcoming). The middle-aged lady in the front seat – blue full-length kaftan smattered with sequins, long brown curls peppered with grey – said 'G'day'. The lady in the middle who looked around Laura's age, maybe just past thirty – long blonde hair, deeply tanned skin, small child asleep in her lap – nodded slightly in acknowledgement.

Slipping into the seat opposite the blonde, Laura leaned against the wall of the kombi and stared out the window.

'And away we go.' Yvonne shifted the van into gear and with a jolt they took off down the road at a speed Laura wasn't sure was exactly safe.

The music coming from the dashboard was loud and Yvonne moved her shoulders in time with The Beach Boys, singing along during the chorus. Yvonne might have been stronger than she looked, but she definitely couldn't sing. Kaftan and Leatherman talked across the empty space to each other, and Laura wondered why they just didn't switch seats.

The young boy in the blonde's lap sat up – no one could sleep through Kaftan and Leatherman's conversation – and Laura noticed the boy was older than she had first guessed. Six or seven perhaps. He was small, and his face still held some of the puppy fat that lingers in young children. His skin was the same olive colour as his mother's – she assumed they were mother and son – but his hair was jet black.

Laura pulled out her phone. Still no coverage. *Damn*. She'd been hoping to check her emails, read a text, anything to connect her with the civilised world back home.

Instead she pulled out her notebook and favourite pen and tapped lightly on the blank page. Yes, grief-imposed rashness had led her here but that didn't mean she couldn't prepare herself. If she applied rule eight – *start with one simple question and that will lead to others* – she might just have a chance of making this trip worthwhile.

Her pen floated across the page. *Who was Gigi? What was she to Lillian? Was Banksia Bay a large part of their lives?*

She didn't like not having even an inkling of what she might discover. What made her such a good reporter was her ability to research a story so thoroughly she often knew the answers before she asked the questions. How could she do that here? Small towns were often wary of outsiders, especially ones who hit the scene hard interrogating everyone. Many of her colleagues had told her that. If there was anyone in Banksia Bay who could help her, she didn't want to scare them off.

'Writing home?' the blonde asked, leaning slightly towards Laura.

'Ah, no.' Laura closed her notebook. 'Just doing a bit of work.'

'And what do you do? Not many people come to Banksia Bay for work, I can tell you.'

The question was bound to come up. Luckily, this was one thing Laura had prepared for, coming up with a cover story on the bus out of Sydney.

'I'm a travel writer. I'm doing a piece on city escapes.' *When you have to lie to protect yourself for a story, it is always best to remain as close to the truth as possible* – rule number two. Trying to pass herself off as a brain surgeon on holiday was too far from the truth to pull off. A travel writer chasing a story, on the other hand – that she could do.

'Nice to meet you, travel writer. I'm Charlotte.' She put her hand to her chest. 'Are you here for the Bee Festival? Outside of summer, that's the only time we see tourists.'

'Yes,' Laura lied. She'd never heard of their Bee Festival – it hadn't turned up in her Google search – but if there was something going on here that would help her cover story, she'd take it.

'It's not for another week, though, you know?' Charlotte narrowed her eyes.

'Yes, but that gives me time to check out the town properly.' Not a lie. 'A friend told me about this quiet little place and that it was a nice getaway.' Also not a lie, if you considered a mysterious old black-and-white photo of your grandmother on a beach a 'friend'.

'Does your friend visit often? Perhaps we know them?'

Oh no. Don't stray that far from the truth, Laura.

'Oh, Charlotte,' called Yvonne from the front. 'Leave the poor lass alone. We don't want to give her a bad impression, do we?' She looked in the rear-view mirror and winked at Laura.

'Sorry.' Charlotte raised her hand in apology. 'It's just unusual to have strang— tourists this early, as I said. I'm sure you'll love it. How long are you staying for?'

'Just a few weeks.' Not a lie. Not the truth. She had no idea how long her search would take. Or if there were even answers to find.

Yvonne looked in the rear-view mirror again but said nothing.

Laura had booked the holiday house she'd found online for a month, using her mother's maiden name, Hamilton. She wasn't planning on staying that long. But if her hunch was right that there was something to Lillian's past lurking in this nowhere town, then who knew how long it would take to discover the truth? And even if the black-and-white photo turned out to be nothing, Maher had insisted she take some time off. The cost of the accommodation was pretty reasonable, so an extra week or two wouldn't matter.

'How was the shopping in Ocean Heights, Charlotte?' Yvonne twisted in her seat quickly to look at the blonde woman and then turned back to the road. 'You didn't come back with many bags.'

The boy in Charlotte's lap wriggled and she stroked his hair from his brow. 'Couldn't find what we were looking for, could we, Aiden?'

'Oh well, maybe next week they'll have new stock.' Yvonne turned her head round quickly to look at Laura. 'I run this route with the Bodhi Bus every week to Ocean Heights. The bus stop where we picked you up gets pretty busy next week and in the summer.'

'And thank God you do, Yvonne,' Leatherman shouted from the back seat. 'An old salty like me would never get into Ocean Heights without you.'

Laura liked that – old salty.

'You're a blessing.' Kaftan reached forward and squeezed Yvonne's shoulder.

'All right, you lot. Now you're making me blush.' She turned the music up and started singing at the top of her voice.

Old Salty joined in the singalong and so did Aiden, who seemed to know all the words to 'I Get Around', and Laura wondered how many times the young boy had heard the song.

Trees flicked by the kombi windows as the van careered along the road. Laura stared out at the green flashing past her, unwilling to go back to her pen and paper for fear of being watched or questioned further by Charlotte.

It wasn't long before the road they were on melted into a narrow ribbon of undulating curves that hugged cliff edges jutting into the blue sea. Yvonne didn't slow down and Laura clutched Lillian's pendant hanging on a chain beneath her shirt, hoping her grandmother was watching over her at this moment, delivering her safely to Banksia Bay.

The road straightened as they started a steep descent and Laura began to relax. Below them the ocean crashed in a steady rhythm, pounding onto the long stretch of yellow-white sand that seemed endless from where Laura sat. She'd only ever been to the beach a few times as a rebellious teenager, defying Lillian's wishes for her to stay away from 'those devil traps of immorality', and only ever at a friend's urging. She'd never seen the appeal of beaches herself – stinking hot, crowded with noisy people, sand that invaded every crevice of your body, all for a few moments of cold relief only to return to your towel and find your wallet had been stolen. Okay, so she'd never actually had her wallet stolen at the beach, but she'd heard stories and was always worried that it might happen to her whenever she gave in to persuasion and headed to Bondi.

The beach they drove beside now, though, was deserted. No seething throng of barely clad humanity running in and out of the water; no radios blaring out rock and pop and hip-hop in competing disharmony; no brightly coloured umbrellas or tents dotted along the sand. Laura thought maybe she saw a lone figure in the waves, but it could have been a trick of the light.

She drew in a deep breath.

'Pretty, isn't it?' Yvonne smiled at her in the rear-view mirror as she slowed the kombi right down.

'Pretty' didn't even begin to describe it.

'I always know I'm home when we hit this stretch of road,' Yvonne said.

Aiden sat up straight for the first time all trip and stared out his window. Charlotte rubbed his back and Laura noticed the subtle tension the blonde had been carrying leave her shoulders. Kaftan started to apply lipstick and Old Salty raised his arms behind his head, leaned back and started to hum softly to himself.

They pulled into what Laura supposed was a car park – a large area of flattened grass alongside the beach. Aiden leapt out of the kombi and ran towards a tall man coming up from the sand dunes, surfboard under one arm. As the man rested his surfboard against the kombi, the boy threw himself into his arms. Charlotte got out of the van and the man gave her a hug and a kiss on the cheek. Laura guessed that was where Aiden got his dark hair from; the resemblance to his dad was uncanny.

Kaftan lowered herself out of the vehicle, spread her arms out wide and spun around three times. If she'd sung 'there's no place like home', Laura wouldn't have been surprised.

As Laura stepped out, Yvonne started unloading the luggage with the help of Aiden's dad. He had a scar that ran down the left side of his face, a red gash stark against his dark complexion. He handed Old Salty the surfboard that was on the roof rack and the old man thanked him.

'Be home by seven,' Kaftan called out. Laura hadn't picked Kaftan and Old Salty as father and daughter. Old Salty saluted his agreement before jogging towards the water with the longboard tucked under his arm.

'The place you've rented is just a short walk away.' Yvonne stepped up beside Laura. 'I'll just lock this old girl up and then I'll show you the way.'

'Thanks, but that's not necessary. I'm sure I can find it myself.' Laura picked up her bag.

'I'm sure you can too. But I have the keys, so I may as well.'

One street back from the beach, Yvonne led Laura through a picket fence and up the creaking wooden steps of an old house. There was a verandah out the front, painted a pale shade of blue, and the weatherboard that clad the walls of the small place was painted lemon yellow. It was peeling in places, but looked otherwise well-kept. A wind chime hung directly overhead as they climbed the steps – a piece of grey driftwood dripping with small glass surf-boards, each a different colour of the rainbow.

Yvonne opened the front door and stepped back to let Laura in. The living room was open and filled with an eclectic mix of fur-niture: an old whitewashed cane sofa covered with floral cushions of red and pink and lime green; a modern mirror, sleek and sim-ple, hanging on the wall; a rattan sideboard covered with trinkets. Laura could see a tiny glass flamingo, a green glass vase full of small mixed flowers, a stuffed elephant made of blue batik, a wooden sign saying 'Home sweet home', mismatched old photo frames.

'Are you the landlord?' Laura asked.

'Oh, gosh, no. An investor in Ocean Heights bought this place years ago. I do a few odd jobs around town. Managing this place is one of them. I decorated it myself.' Yvonne puffed out her chest. 'All the linen is fresh. The shops are just a short walk that way.' Yvonne pointed out the south-facing window. 'They're closed for today, but I've put milk and a few essentials in the kitchen for you.'

It was only five o'clock, but Laura supposed she couldn't really expect the same midnight opening hours she was used to in Sydney.

Yvonne turned to the sideboard behind her and fussed with the flowers and rearranged the knick-knacks and photos. 'There's a number I've written down here, in case you need anything tonight. Sleep well, love.'

'Thank you.' Laura walked her to the verandah.

Yvonne took her hand and squeezed it, smiling, though there was a touch of sadness in her eyes. 'Okay, then. Bye.' The little old lady waved as she headed down the path.

Alone in the house Laura made herself familiar with her home for the next . . . well, however long she'd be here. She found the bathroom first: small but serviceable. There were two bedrooms, a queen bed with a cheap surfboard doona cover in one, two single beds in the other. She put her suitcase in with the queen bed. There was a nook at the back of the house set up as a study and Laura put her laptop and notebooks on the old cedar desk. She ran her hands over the dark wood and the deep-green leather inlay. Laura knew her writing desks and this was a beautiful antique.

Yvonne had left some pasta and chicken in the fridge, and Laura took it out for dinner. As she passed the sideboard on her way back to the living room, her eye was drawn to the collection of photos on display. At the front stood a couple of small wooden frames with pictures of tree-filled hills and long stretches of beach, which Laura assumed had been taken locally. Behind them were some black-framed photos of what she assumed was the town centre, with various blurry figures in them, and a few shots of surfers bobbing in the ocean. She was about to head to the sofa when she noticed a small silver frame pushed to the back of the sideboard. She picked it up and her hands began to shake.

The photo, framed so beautifully by a silver filigree design, was of a group of people standing by a bonfire. A very short girl stood off to the side, as if she was watching the older kids, not quite sure she should be there. A group of boys stood near the fire, beers in hand, smiling, laughing. And just on the other side were two girls arm in arm. After studying her own photo so much in the last few days, the faces, though slightly older, were unmistakably familiar.

There in front of her again were Gigi and Lily.

———

All night Laura had tossed and turned. She'd stared at that photo for an hour, maybe more, and had opened the frame and turned the photo over, but there was no inscription on the back. She had no doubt now that coming to Banksia Bay had been the right move. There was, without question, more to Lillian's story and this place, and Laura was determined to find out just what that story was.

But she'd have to be careful. Lillian had come here more than once, it seemed, and had kept a mysterious postcard from Banksia Bay hidden under her bed with other special trinkets. Maher's rule number three, *always trust your instincts*, was one she never broke. And her instincts were telling her this story was more than just a few photos. How was she going to find the answers to questions she didn't know to ask, though? And how would this tiny town react to her probing?

With the morning sun just beginning to rise, Laura gave up on the hope of sleep. She crawled out of bed, got dressed and bent down and tied up the laces of her trainers. Pounding the pavement was just what she needed right now. She headed out the door and ran.

Half an hour later she'd pretty much taken in the whole town, as far as she could tell, and she slowed as she came back to the main street. At least she figured it was the main street, as it was the only one she had come across in her jog with any shops on it.

Wider than any road she was used to in Sydney's inner city, the west side was lined with small wooden and brick buildings protected from the elements by corrugated-iron awnings. There was a pub, of course – The Pioneer – rather grand for a small town, with its two storeys of taupe-painted rendering and upstairs verandah wrapped in a lacy white wrought-iron balustrade. Laura suspected you could see the ocean from up there. It was closed on Tuesdays. Shame. She'd been hoping to maybe start snooping there today. She figured all she had to do to begin with was find a quiet spot in the pub, settle in with a drink and just watch and listen. It might not give her anything specific, but if you paid attention, it was amazing what you could learn in a pub. Alcohol loosened tongues and often people believed they were hidden in dark corners that weren't as dark as they thought. A word here, a stolen glance there, a touch when you thought no one was looking, gave away so much.

She walked past the post office right next door, small and quaint with bricks painted white and a bright red wooden door, and then a general store that took up half the block. It was called The Saddler that Laura thought a strange name as she didn't get a sense this was a horse-type town. Next was a surf shop, which did make sense, with boards and wetsuits displayed in the window, and an ice creamery boasting forty flavours, which seemed to be tacked on to the surf shop. In the window of the ice creamery a hand-written sign hung: 'Open again December 1st'.

On the beach side of the street, right up the north end near the car park the Bodhi Bus had come in to, was a lone fish and chip shop, the walls painted in wide blue and white stripes, also not open until December. Charlotte hadn't been kidding. They really didn't get tourists here outside of summer. Laura put her hands on her hips and drew in deep breaths. She'd run hard. Fast. From behind the fish and chip shop she could hear the crashing of waves on sand.

She pulled out a drink bottle from her backpack and took a long sip. She was also carrying a notepad and pen inside the small running bag. Perhaps she could sit on a dune and formulate a plan.

The top of the deep-orange sun kissed the horizon as it climbed ever so slowly into the morning. The sea was cast in black and indigo, streaked with slivers of liquid-fire reflection. The rocks that framed the north end of the beach were dark and foreboding and the banksias reaching up from the hill behind them were just touched by the morning light.

Laura turned around and headed south along the beach. With only a few steps taken, she pulled her shoes off, tying the laces together and slinging them over her shoulder. The sand was colder than she'd expected, but it was soft and laid out before her like a plush carpet that had never been walked on. She had the whole beach to herself.

With feet bare, she inched closer to the water's edge as she ambled along. She breathed in a heady mix of salt and misty water, and the only sound was of the dark waves breaking white on the shore, their rushing in and slow retreat a haunting song of age and renewal.

Halfway down the beach she stopped and stood facing the sunrise, her ankles lapped by the cool water, and she took in a deep breath. What was the pose they'd been taught at work that time Maher had brought in a yoga instructor to increase productivity? Sun solution, warrior downward pony? Something like that. She hadn't really been listening. Yoga was for people who were stressed, and stress was for people who weren't in control of their lives. And she was always in control. Well, except for her decision to come here.

Laura stood on one foot, her other leg tucked up against her knee. That was right. Maybe. She straightened up, her hands above her head. Yes. That was it. And then a twist wasn't it? With a lean?

She overbalanced and, before she could stop herself, fell into a crumpled mess on the sand, splashed by the water, which seemed to be crawling further and further towards the dunes.

Laura laughed so hard tears fell down her cheeks. As her composure returned, she was left with salty teardrops at the edges of her mouth. She wiped them away, but more came. Was she crying?

She picked herself up and brushed the wet sand off her legs. Rash decisions and tears. When would grief be done with her? She didn't like it one bit. *Focus. You're here to do a job.*

Yes, think of it as a story, stay focused. She turned around to find a spot to sit and make some notes.

Walking towards her was Aiden's dad, a wetsuit covering his lower half only, surfboard under his arm.

'Morning,' he greeted her.

Up close she couldn't help but stare at the scar running down his face.

Move your eyes, Laura. Look somewhere else. Anywhere else.

Her eyes fell to his chest. His bare, broad chest.

Not there.

She looked up to his eyes, the palest blue she'd ever seen, the broad smile he wore reaching the corner of his gaze. Kind eyes. Knowing eyes. Eyes that looked into hers with a calm intensity she didn't know was possible.

Stop staring. Hair. Look at his hair.

He was a tall man – six foot, if she had to guess – the first hints of grey speckled in his black hair

'Sorry,' he said. 'Do you speak English?'

'What?' *Oh dear.* What an imbecile she must have appeared, staring at him like that. 'Yes. Of course.'

He held back a laugh.

'Did you . . . see . . .' Laura couldn't bear to ask.

'Not if you didn't want me to. I'm Heath.' He held out his hand. 'And you're the lady who came in yesterday on the Bodhi Bus.'

'Yes.' She shook his hand.

He raised his eyebrow.

'Oh. Yes. Sorry. Laura. My name's Laura. Nice to meet you.'

'Nice to meet you, Laura. Do you surf?' He pulled the top half of his wetsuit up and wriggled into it.

'Me? No. Not even much of a swimmer, actually.'

'That's a pity. One of life's true pleasures.' He strode off into the water, leapt onto his board and paddled out beyond the waves.

Laura watched him a moment, bobbing in the swell. She couldn't very well sit here and pull out her notepad now. She wandered further up the beach and found a series of dunes shaped almost like a horseshoe, which would protect her from view if anyone else joined Heath for a surf this morning. She nestled into the sand and started jotting down thoughts and questions.

Why is there a photo of Lillian and Gigi in the house? Does Yvonne know something? She underlined Yvonne's name and added two question marks. The woman had looked at her in the rear-vision mirror on yesterday's drive. A lot.

Laura looked up from her scribble and watched the waves rolling in and out. The longer she looked, the more colours she could see as the sun rose higher, lightening the morning. Black melted into grey, indigo blurred into teal, bright orange softened into lemon.

And she watched.

Voices dancing across the sand broke the silence and Laura realised she'd been staring into the ocean for half an hour. Heath was walking past with Old Salty, both of them carrying boards under their arms. Laura sank into the dunes, hoping they wouldn't see her.

A rumble in her stomach alerted her to the fact that she hadn't had a coffee yet this morning. Did surfers drink coffee after a morning in the waves? Maybe if she followed the men, they'd lead her to an open café. She slipped her sunglasses on and headed down the beach after them.

At the south end the men stopped at what looked to Laura like nothing more than a run-down wooden hut. But as she got closer she could hear voices, happy voices, coming from inside, and as she moved to the front of the shed, she could see a deck.

On the small deck were a couple of white metal tables and chairs. As Heath and Old Salty sat there, an old woman dressed in tattered denim overalls came out of the shack with a cup of coffee for each man. The front wall of the two-storey beach shack was painted blue, one side of the building was red, another yellow. All of the paint was flaking.

Inside, the shack was lined with shelves and Laura just had to take a closer look.

Heath waved to her as she passed inside, but she didn't respond, captivated by the sight before her. Against one wall, painted red, the same as the outside, the shelves were covered with books, second-hand books of all descriptions, from Tolkien to Jackie Collins, from instructional guides on building wooden bird houses to an unauthorised biography of Hugh Jackman.

Against the back wall, painted blue, the shelves were cluttered with knick-knacks – ceramic owls, glass ashtrays, carved wooden masks. There was also an impressive collection of shells, more than Laura had ever seen in one place before.

Hidden among the trash, Laura could see a few pieces of antique jewellery that looked like they might actually be worth a bit. In between the shelves was an old, comfortable-looking armchair and a small wooden coffee table covered with a pink cotton doily.

On the yellow side of the shack, a worn sofa sat in front of a counter stacked high with mismatched coffee mugs, some in bold plain colours of blue and red and green, some with brightly hued patterns. The woman who'd brought Heath and Old Salty their cups stood behind the counter watching Laura move around the shack.

'Can I help you with something?' She looked at Laura over her lime green glasses.

'Oh. No. I was just . . . Actually, a coffee would be good. Thank you.' *Play nice with the locals, Laura.*

'Well, first, you'll need to be taking those sunnies off. I don't like serving people if I can't see their eyes. You can tell a lot about someone by their eyes, you know.' The woman turned to the coffee grinder and set about making Laura's drink.

Laura pushed her sunglasses up her forehead and rested them on top her head. 'I'm Laura. I'm renting the holiday house one street over.'

'Welcome, Laura. I'm Virginia, owner of this little sha—' Virginia turned to hand Laura her cup and stopped, staring at her.

All the colour drained from the woman's face.

Three

Virginia's heart beat fast, her breathing quickened. What type of wizardry was this? The woman standing in front of her was the spitting image of Lily. Maybe she was having a stroke. Women her age did that. Had strokes. Or aneurysms. Did you hallucinate with an aneurysm?

'Hey, Virginia. You all right in there?' Ian called out from the deck. 'Are you going to give our visitor her coffee, squirt, or make the young lady beg for it?'

Okay. So if that old relic of a surfer could see the girl, then maybe she wasn't hallucinating. Though, given his misspent youth taking any number of hallucinogenic substances, coupled with the fact he was even older than her, maybe he couldn't be trusted either.

She turned to glance at the old man and saw Heath standing up.

'I got this.' Heath put his hand on Ian's shoulder and walked towards her. 'Gran? Is something wrong?' He took the mug from her hand and gave it to . . . what did she say her name was? Lauren?

Laura. He gave it to Laura. The woman really was there in front of her, now staring at her with a rather quizzical expression on her face. Virginia and Ian might be so old they imagined things, but not Heath. If Heath saw her too, she was real.

The young woman took the coffee with the slightest hesitation and stepped out of the shack, looking back once.

'Sorry, dear.' Virginia turned to Heath. He was a good kid. But not very adept at hiding his emotions and she could see concern looking back at her. 'Yes. I'm fine.' *Find your composure, woman.* 'I skipped breakfast this morning is all,' she lied. 'My blood sugar must be a bit low.'

Heath handed her a muffin from the glass cake stand. 'Why don't you sit down?'

'Oh, stuff and nonsense. I'm fine.'

'Sit.' Heath's voice was firm but his eyes were soft, and Virginia did as she was told. When that boy got something in his head he was as stubborn as they come. Just like his dad. Oh, how she missed her son, still, after all this time. There was no point arguing with Heath. She'd sit and eat her muffin and play her part, convince him she was fine, then he'd leave her alone.

Easing into the armchair, Virginia watched Laura out on the deck as she sipped her coffee, chatting with Ian. Who was she? And what was she doing here? Was she a mere coincidence, or was she an echo of the past?

Virginia would have to raise her guard. Not that she'd let it down in the last sixty years.

Not once.

Not ever.

She was always so careful.

It was only a matter of time, though, she supposed, that the ghosts of her buried yesterdays would come back to haunt her.

Not that they ever left.

Not once.

Not ever.

December 1956

Gigi looked at the girl standing on the dune, a floral summer dress with a wide full skirt dancing around her ankles. Her long brown hair stretched down her back, straight and sleek. Gigi raised her hand to the nest of sandy-coloured curly straw that crowned her own head and she wished she'd worn a hat to cover it up.

All her life she'd lived in Banksia Bay with its store workers, fishermen and, more recently, surfers. And none of the people in her tiny town were as glamorous as the girl standing on the dune. She was maybe two years older than Gigi, but she looked like she belonged to another world.

Gigi stepped towards the girl, mesmerised by the perfect smile that seemed to make her pretty face look sad. Well, no one should be sad when they were at the beach. Especially not her beach.

Marching up the sand, Gigi dug her hands into her overall pockets, the old pair with cut-off legs she'd been handed down from her mother. Not the best outfit to make a new friend in, surely. Especially a glamorous new friend. But, judging by the look on the sad girl's face, she needed a friend like Gigi, and needed one now.

'Hello. I'm Gigi.' She held out her hand. Did city girls shake hands, or should she curtsy?

The girl looked down the dune at her. 'Hello. I'm Lillian.'

Lillian didn't take Gigi's hand. Maybe she should curtsy. Or bow. Lillian looked away, so Gigi blurted out the first thing that came to mind. 'Are you here on holidays?'

Lillian nodded, but didn't say anything. She did look back at Gigi, though. And that gave her the courage to spill out more words.

'Have you seen the rock pool? It's just up there. I can show you. Have you ever seen a blue-ringed octopus?'

Lillian looked positively horrified.

'Come on.' Gigi stepped forward and took a shocked Lillian's hand. 'It'll be fun.'

'I'm not really dressed for . . .'

But before Lillian could finish, Gigi was dragging her down the dune and along the beach.

When they got to the rock pool, Gigi slowed down and dropped Lillian's hand. 'Be careful,' she whispered, and picked up a piece of driftwood shaped like a stick. 'They're pretty, but deadly.'

She poked around in the rock pool with the driftwood and found the tiny little octopus hiding under a rock. 'Watch this.'

She touched the top of the octopus very gently with the tip of the stick, and its skin changed from beige all over to beige with the brightest blue rings everywhere, like a polka-dotted skirt.

'But . . . how . . .' Lillian's disbelief seemed to be pushing her reluctance aside.

'They only colour when threatened. Don't touch it.' She pulled Lillian away just in time before her new friend reached out. 'Deadly, remember. Blue often is in nature.'

Lillian looked at her. 'Really?'

Gigi led her up to the granite rocks that overhung the beach and they sat down together. 'My grandpa, he loved nature. Taught me everything there is to know,' she said.

Lillian seemed interested, genuinely interested, so Gigi kept right on talking. About the octopi; the banksias that grew all around these parts – she thought the red ones that grew in other parts of the country were prettier, herself, but the yellow ones that grew here, with their soft spikes and silver leaves, were okay, she supposed; about the tides that came in every twelve hours, filling up the rock pools; about anything she could think of. She was a little worried she would talk Lillian's ear off – Mum was always warning her about that – but the more she talked, the more Lillian seemed to relax.

'You are a very strange girl, Gigi,' Lillian said when Gigi finally drew breath, but there was a smile on her face that Gigi was pretty sure was warm, not mocking. She'd been on the receiving end of her fair share of mocking from the kids at school – the girls who teased her for being a tomboy, and the boys who made fun of her when she tried to do the same things they did, like fish and climb rocks and jump off the jetty.

'Thank you,' she said. 'I think.'

Lillian laughed. It was the most angelic sound Gigi had ever heard. 'In this instance I definitely mean it as a compliment.'

The girls walked down the beach back towards the shack Gigi's dad and the other fishermen used to clean their catch in. Slowly Gigi angled her new friend towards the water. There was nothing like the fresh cool feeling of waves lapping your feet and she figured maybe Lillian might like it too.

The first wave kissed the girls' toes and Lillian let out a tiny squeal and ran up the sand. Gigi stayed put and started dancing in the shallow water. Lillian stepped closer. Gigi kept on dancing, splashing her small feet in the waves. Lillian inched towards her.

When the next wave hit her feet, Lillian didn't run away. She took in a bracing breath and did a little pirouette. Gigi had never seen anything as beautiful as that twirl.

Together the girls danced in the shallows and giggled and clapped their hands and the sun moved slowly across the sky.

And they didn't stop until Lillian's mum appeared at the top of the sand dunes, calling for her daughter to come in for supper.

'Lillian,' Gigi said. 'Do you think maybe we can play again tomorrow? If you want, that is.'

'I'd like that.' She walked towards her mother, but turned back after a couple of steps. 'You can call me Lily.'

She ran up the sand.

ↀ

It was a memory Virginia had pushed from her mind so very long ago. She stared past Heath and Ian and Laura and watched the waves tickle the barnacle-clad pylons of the small wooden jetty. Watching the ocean always helped calm her nerves. She was imagining things, surely. It was bound to happen, she supposed. As one passed into one's twilight, one's mind retreated to its dawn.

She just hadn't thought she was there yet. She'd become old without even noticing, it seemed.

Still, it was no excuse. She couldn't let her past encroach on her now.

It was buried for a reason.

She shook her head, hoping this nonsense would fall out of there somehow. Whoever this Laura was, she had nothing to do with that summer so long ago.

Virginia moved around the shack, tidying up shelves, sneaking glances at the newcomer here and there out of the corner of her eye. Her hair was almost the same colour as . . . *Stop it.*

It's just a coincidence. She kept repeating that over and over to herself. *You silly old fool.*

Ian was rambling on about who knows what, surfing probably.

Or fishing. Laura had the good manners to at least pretend to be interested.

As Virginia moved towards the coffee machine, Laura looked back at her, an obviously forced smile plastered across her face. Virginia gasped. She'd seen that look before.

No. This was no coincidence. The face, the hair, the expression.

All reminders of that summer when everything changed.

December 1961

'Hurry up, Lily. The fish won't wait forever.' Gigi banged on the window of the little wooden house her parents rented out to tourists every summer. Lily was always slow in the mornings. Definitely not an early riser like she was. Gigi had already had breakfast, done her chores, been for a long walk along the sand, collected twenty-seven seashells, picked up the bait from Ian, got their two fishing rods ready, stolen a fresh roll from the bakery while Mrs Andrews wasn't looking – the evidence of which she brushed from her overalls – and caught three sand crabs in her red plastic bucket and placed them as sentinels on her carefully constructed sandcastle. They'd abandoned their post as soon as she'd sat them on the battlements, though. Crabs could not be trusted.

And Lily still hadn't even got out of bed. That was a life of privilege for you. When your dad was a prominent politician and you had money to spare, Gigi supposed, you could get up whenever you liked.

Every summer it was the same. Gigi up before dawn, Lily bemoaning the fact she was on holidays and had a right to sleep in.

Gigi tapped on the window again. 'You know what my dad says. The best time to catch leatherjacket —'

'— is just before the breaking dawn.' Lily threw the curtains back and poked her tongue out at Gigi. 'And how many mornings have we got up early?'

'Five.'

'And how many fish have we caught?'

Gigi put her hands on her hips. 'That's not the point, Miss Lillian Woodhouse. It's an adventure. We won't have too many more summers like this one, you know?'

Lily smiled. 'I know, Miss Virginia Gilbert. That's why I got dressed fifteen minutes ago.' She climbed through the window, jumping down beside her friend.

Arm in arm they strolled down the beach to the rocks on the north side. They'd been fishing the same spot for five years, ever since Gigi had forced Lily to be her friend.

As morning gave way to day, they lay on the rocks, warming their bodies in the sun.

'Well.' Lily threw her hands in the air. 'Yet again we didn't catch anything.'

Gigi giggled. 'I know. But it was still fun.'

She rolled over onto her side and from far down the beach she could see a young man striding towards them.

Lily sat up straight when she saw him coming, and Gigi copied her.

He walked with an assuredness that Gigi assumed meant he was heading for them deliberately. He was good-looking, she'd give him that. And well-dressed. Maybe he knew Lily.

She turned to look at her friend for some sign of recognition, but there wasn't one. Just a strange grin plastered across her face. A fake smile she'd never seen her best friend wear before. Maybe that was just how one greeted a handsome stranger. She mimicked Lily – the expression, pushing her chest forward, crossing her legs. But she felt ridiculous. Besides, overalls and unbrushed hair hardly matched the forced façade. She slumped back down and fiddled with her fishing rod.

'Excuse me, ladies.' The man took off the straw pinch-front fedora he was wearing and bowed slightly in greeting. 'I'm sorry to intrude. I was looking for a Miss Lillian Woodhouse.'

Lily stood up and Gigi followed.

'That is I,' Lily said, in a voice so posh Gigi nearly spat out the gum she'd been chewing on.

'Ah. Wonderful. I'm Richard Prescott. My family and I are holidaying here this summer. Our fathers are acquainted and suggested you might be able to show me around town a bit.'

'Oh, I'd love to.'

There was no hiding the red in Lily's cheeks. Gigi coughed, rather loudly, just to remind her friend she was there.

'Oh. This is my friend Gigi. She's a local and I'm sure she'd be happy to accompany us too.'

Gigi tried to hide the horror she felt and hoped her eyes weren't as big as they felt. She absolutely did not want to show this intruder around. Besides, she had every moment with Lily planned out. When you only got to see your best friend for a few weeks a year, you made the most of it.

'Nice to meet you, Gigi.' Richard held out his hand and she took it. She might not be fancy like these two, but she wasn't rude. His skin was soft and his handshake gentle.

'Nice to meet you, too. Some of the boys are having a fish fry-up tonight. You could join them, if you like.'

'That sounds neat. Will you ladies be going?'

Gigi went every year. Alone. 'Lily doesn't like —'

'Yes. We'll be there,' Lily interrupted. 'And then we can discuss some other activities for while you're here.'

'Sounds great.' Richard winked.

Lily hit Gigi on the hip and Gigi gave Richard the details of the fry-up before he strode back down the beach.

'I've been trying to get you to one of Ian's fry-ups for the last three years. You said you hated the smell.'

'Well, that was before.' Lily's gaze was held steadfastly on the retreating Richard.

'Oh.' Well, if it meant getting Lily to the fry-up, then she supposed she couldn't complain. Ian, her dad's boat hand, was famous in these parts for his fry-ups. Best fish cook this side of Sydney. Even better than her dad. Not that she ever told either one of them that.

Gigi and Lily packed up their gear and walked back to the holiday house. As they approached the white picket gate, Lily turned to Gigi.

'Will you do me a favour tonight?' she asked.

'Of course.'

'Will you wear a dress?'

Gigi was pretty sure she'd jump into a volcano if Lily asked. Luckily there were none in Banksia Bay. But wearing a dress?

Gigi groaned.

'Please. I want to look nice tonight, but I don't want to look like I'm trying too hard. If you wore a dress too then I wouldn't stand out.'

Gigi knew that even if she put on her best dress and borrowed her mum's make-up and did her hair in one of those fancy beehive things – if it would even go into one – Lily, with minimal effort, would still stand out.

She drew in a deep breath. Lily stared at her with pleading eyes.

'Okay then.' Her shoulders dropped.

Lily threw her arms around Gigi's neck and kissed her on the cheek. 'Wait there.'

She ran inside and returned moments later. 'You can borrow these, too.' She handed Gigi a pair of delicate white gloves.

'It's a fry-up, Lily. Not afternoon tea with the Queen.' Gigi stroked the soft suede.

'Every girl should have at least one pair of gloves, Gigi. If you don't wear them tonight, there'll be other occasions.'

Gigi highly doubted that.

Lily hugged her again and disappeared inside.

At the fry-up, just before the late summer sun dropped behind the hills that surrounded Banksia Bay, Gigi fidgeted with the tight sleeves on the orange dress she wore. Why did women subject themselves to this level of discomfort? Give her overalls any day.

She'd spent ages brushing her hair into something resembling a bob, and held her head stiffly so as not to shake it out of shape. She'd left the gloves at home.

The smell from the open fire pit in the sand was divine and she couldn't wait for Ian to serve up his famous whole fish.

Richard arrived before Lily, looking less at ease than he had that morning. But once the boys turned around to see who was joining them, Richard's façade changed to one of oozing confidence. Gigi introduced him to Ian, Ian's summer girlfriend – there was no point trying to remember her name – and the others gathered around.

'You look gorgeous,' Richard said to Gigi, once the introductions were over.

'Squirt? Gorgeous?' Ian chuckled. 'Let me take a picture of this day for posterity.' He pulled out his camera and snapped a picture of Gigi poking her tongue out at him. She cursed her mother for giving him that wretched contraption last Christmas.

Gigi kicked Ian in the shin and stormed off down the sand towards to the water.

Richard caught up with her and stood a little to her side. 'Don't listen to that oaf. You do look beautiful tonight. I nearly didn't recognise you.'

Gigi spun round ready to take him on too, if she had to, but his face was kind, no hint of mocking to be found. 'Thank you.' She cast her eyes down. It was going to be hard to dislike him if he was actually nice.

When she looked up again, she saw Lily gliding their way, an absolutely stunning vision in a soft pink and white polka-dot swing dress with a scalloped neckline, a pink satin bow holding back her long dark hair.

Lily hugged Gigi in greeting and Ian ran over and took a photo of the two of them standing in the sand before he went back to the barbecue. A dumbstruck Richard escorted Lily towards the group, leaving Gigi on the beach by herself.

For the rest of the evening, Lily was locked in conversation with Richard. Gigi might as well have been invisible.

When the fry-up ended, Richard offered to walk Lily home. At least she had the decency to say goodbye to Gigi before going. Not that it made Gigi feel any better. Dragging her feet, she helped Ian cover the fire with sand.

'You okay, squirt?' He ruffled her hair with his big hand the way he always did. She batted him away. 'Sorry. I forgot you'd coiffed it.'

'I didn't coif it.' She smoothed her hair and poked her tongue out at him again.

'Is someone a bit jealous, maybe?' he teased.

'Of what?'

His blue eyes sparkled, and he went back to packing away his stuff.

Jealous? Of course not. She'd just wanted to spend time with Lily after finally getting her to a fry-up. Okay. So, technically it was Richard who'd got her there. But she was still Gigi's best friend, and they should have had a great night together, instead of Lily spending all evening with him.

Jealous? Okay. Maybe a little. Maybe it wasn't going to be so hard to dislike Richard after all.

'Do you want me to walk you home, squirt?' Ian put a kind arm around her shoulder.

She wriggled free of him. 'No. I'll be fine,' she grunted. Then she remembered her manners. 'Thank you.'

Ian headed into the shack, where he sometimes spent the night, usually on his dad's payday when the pub stayed open late.

Gigi took the long way home. There was only one way to get from the beach to their little cabin in the caravan park on the edge of town, but if she walked slowly and zigzagged through the side streets, she could make the short journey last at least twenty minutes.

The caravan park had been home since Gigi was nine, the year before she met Lily, when the fishing season had been sparse for three years running. Mum had taken a job running the park and that was when they'd had the idea to turn their two-bedroom house near the beach into a holiday rental. They'd moved out the summer of her ninth birthday and had never gone back. Gigi didn't understand that – why couldn't they at least live back home for the other nine months a year? – but when she asked her mum, she simply said it was easier. Sometimes one of the bigger dairy farms in the area would rent it out for itinerant workers, and when that happened, Mum would look in Gigi's direction with a raised eyebrow – louder than any 'I told you so' could be.

Gigi didn't mind living in the caravan park. It gave her permission to be outside as much as she liked, free to roam until dark sent her home.

As she wound her way through the last of the side streets, she noticed the lights on in the old Parsons place. It had been empty for at least six months now, ever since grumpy Mr Parsons had passed on. She'd heard rumours someone had bought it.

She slowed down to take a sneaky peek to see if she could catch a glimpse of the new family. Maybe they had a daughter her age who would be starting school next month. Oh, she didn't dare hope.

The curtain in the front room was open. Inside there were a few small boxes waiting to be unpacked, an armchair and a small dining table with four chairs covered in some sort of blue fabric. She couldn't see anyone, but a delicious aroma was wafting out onto the street. Meat, lemon and some sort of herb that she'd never smelled before. She stood out the front and closed her eyes, taking a deep breath.

A cough from behind made her spin around.

'Sorry,' she said, before she laid eyes on the person who'd caught her snooping red-handed.

'Can I help you?' A boy, around her age, she guessed, maybe a little older, was staring at her. He had skin a different shade of dark than the surfer boys from school, and dark, warm eyes that were large and kind. And sad.

'Can . . . I . . . help . . . you?' He repeated the question more slowly.

Gigi just stared at him.

'Why are you peering into my living room?'

'Oh.' Gigi pushed past her embarrassment. 'Sorry. I was walking by and . . . what is that smell?'

'My ma's lamb kleftiko.'

'Lamb what?'

'Greek lamb. Sorry. I'll tell Ma to close the windows.' He looked down at the dirt road beneath his feet.

'Why would you do that? It smells delicious.'

The boy narrowed his eyes. 'Not everyone thinks so.'

'Well, I'm not like everyone, and I do like the smell.' Gigi put her hands on her hips. 'I'm Virginia. Gigi for short.' She held out her hand but the boy didn't take it.

'Nice to meet you, Virginia. My name is Costas.'

'Costaki? Agapi-mou?' a voice called from inside.

'I have to go,' he said.

'Nice to meet you, too.' Gigi held out her hand again, and this time Costas shook it gently.

A tingle ran up Gigi's spine and she pulled her hand back.

Costas lowered his gaze and headed inside. 'Sorry. Goodnight.'

Gigi stood in the middle of the road watching Costas open his door. A woman came to the window, looked straight at Gigi and with a flourish closed the curtain.

The rest of the way home Gigi fought the butterflies in her stomach, trying to understand what on earth they were doing there.

Four

*L*aura sipped her coffee, only paying scant attention to whatever it was Old Salty – what had Heath and the old lady called him in that confusion? Ian? Whatever Ian was prattling on about – surfing, or tides, or waves, or some such nonsense. It was not interesting enough for Laura to take her focus off the woman in the shack.

Because the woman kept looking at her. *Really* looking at her. Every time Laura looked up, Virginia was sneaking a glance at her. From behind the stacked coffee mugs, from around the shelves, from over the counter as she bent down pretending to pick something up. And the way she'd turned a sickly pale colour when Laura had ordered her coffee was just unnerving.

'Hey.' Charlotte came up the sand, greeting the space rather than anyone in particular. Ian stood and gave her a hug. Aiden bounced along beside her and jumped into Heath's arms as Charlotte kissed him on the cheek.

'How was your surf this morning?' The question was directed at Heath, but her gaze was firmly on Laura.

Why did everyone stare at her this way? Were they like this to all out-of-towners? Or had Laura grown a second head overnight? Under this much scrutiny, it was going to be hard to start asking questions.

She'd have to change her tack. Be a regular tourist, make 'friends', assimilate the answers instead of asking for them.

'So, have you?' Ian repeated the question she'd obviously missed, and she looked at him blankly. 'Ever been surfing?' he prompted her.

'Ah, no. I've never tried it.'

'Heath here could teach you.' Ian patted the younger man on the back. 'I taught him, way too many moons back now, and he's taught nearly every tourist who's visited these parts in the last ten years.'

Heath smiled fondly at the old man and looked at Laura. 'I run the summer surf school. Obviously it's not summer now, but I'm happy to do private lessons, too.'

'Thank you. But I'm not sure I'd make the best student.' Laura raised her hands in protest.

Charlotte shot her a look. 'Haven't you got too much work on, anyway, Heath?'

Laura had said no, hadn't she? Why was Charlotte being possessive?

'Never too busy to surf.' He winked and Charlotte glared at him.

'Well, some of us are.' She pulled her sunglasses down over her eyes and took Aiden's hand. 'I'll be by about four to do some work in the garden.' She looked at Laura.

'Sorry?'

'One of her many talents,' Heath said. 'Great gardener. She looks after a few properties in the area in her spare time. The house you're staying in, for one.'

Great. This was just what Laura needed. That prickly woman snooping around. Maybe she could go for a walk this afternoon and not be there when Charlotte arrived.

Virginia came past the table and collected the empty mugs. 'Can I get you anything else, love?' Her countenance completely different to ten minutes ago, all warmth and charm now.

'No. Thank you. That was a very good coffee, though.' *Play nice. Be sweet.*

'Now, if you're looking for something to pass the time while you're here, other than surfing lessons –' she pointed towards Heath – 'I do lend out the books in my collection. How long are you staying with us, dear?'

People kept asking that question. 'Just a couple of weeks.'

'Lovely. Actually, I have something that might interest you.' Virginia rushed into the shack and came straight back with one of the coffee-table books and a notepad. 'This is a bit of a must-do around here. If you've got the time, I'm sure Heath wouldn't mind taking you on a drive one day.' She handed Laura the book and looked at Heath, who simply smiled back.

Banksia Bay Bush Tracks was the name of the book. Laura flipped through the pages, which were full of stunning photos of landscapes, peppered with maps and notes about bush trails in the area.

'I'll just take down your name in my lending book, and you can return it once you've had a look. Laura, isn't it? And a last name?'

'Hamilton,' Laura lied, using her mum's maiden name again. 'Thank you. That's very nice of you.' Laura watched Virginia write her name in the book. There was a whole list of names and dates in there and Laura wondered if Virginia ever sold any books, or simply lent them out.

Ian stood up. 'One of our gems, is Virginia.' He went to pat her on top of her head, but she ducked skilfully out of the way.

'Get out of here, you salt-encrusted old buffoon.' She pushed him back, but Laura could see the kindness in the woman's eyes.

'On my way, squirt.' Ian scuttled down the sand just out of reach of the shoe that came flying after him.

'I'm off too.' Heath hugged Virginia. He turned to Laura. 'I'll walk you up the beach, if you like?'

There was no other word than 'awkward' for the silence as they walked side by side. Laura had no idea why Heath wanted to accompany her. It wasn't night-time. It wasn't far.

She stopped and turned to face him. 'Is there something I need to know about walking by myself in broad daylight?' The words came out harsher than she'd meant.

Heath stopped and lowered his eyes. 'Sorry. No. I was just being neighbourly. I didn't mean to upset you.'

The sun, now well on its ascent, sent shards of light through the clearing clouds, casting a shadow across half of Heath's face – the side with the scar. He frowned slightly, his pale blue eyes shading grey.

'No. It's me.' She shook her head. So much for making friends with the locals. She wasn't very good at this at all. 'This is a bit different to what I normally do.' Not a lie. 'So I'm a bit on edge, I guess.' Also not a lie.

'Ah.' He nodded. 'No worries. I have just the thing that might help with that.'

'If you're going to offer me surfing lessons again, you'd better have a pretty damn good argument. I don't do –' she waved her hands towards the water – 'the ocean.'

Heath's eyes lit up. 'Well, firstly, there's this incredible peace that comes over you when you're out there in the waves . . .'

Laura tilted her head. 'You did see my feeble attempt at yoga this morning, right?'

Heath laughed out loud. 'Yes. I mean no, remember? Okay, so the spiritual angle isn't going to sway you. What about health? It's a great work-out and exercise produces endorphins and they make you happy.'

'I run. Every day.' She could see him trying to come up with another reason, and if she hadn't been as entirely stubborn as she was, she would have admitted she was enjoying the challenge as much as he seemed to be.

Heath took a few steps back and forth, rubbing his chin. 'Hmmm.'

A cool breeze floated off the sea, sending a shiver up Laura's spine.

'How about fun?' Heath spun around and stopped just in front of her, so close she could feel his breath dance over her head. 'Surfing is fun. Surely you can't argue against having a little bit of fun.'

Stepping back, Laura drew in a breath. For the life of her, she couldn't think of any kind of coherent comeback. So she just looked at him. Possibly stared.

'Uh-huh. There you go.' Heath did a little victory dance and Laura's heart may have skipped a beat. 'At least think about it?'

'Okay. I'll think about it.'

With that, Heath bowed, shot her a grin and continued up the beach.

Back in the holiday house, Laura quickly checked her emails, the living room giving her the best reception. Nothing. Maher really meant it when he said take a break from the world. She sank into the soft sofa with the coffee-table book Virginia had lent her.

Green hills were accented with the yellow, red and pink of native flowers; small dirt roads wound their way through thick vegetation; deep-blue water framed the white coast line. The maps and bush trails held little interest for her. Wandering around the wilderness wasn't going to help her find the answers she sought. Though taking up Heath's offer of a drive would perhaps help her making-friends-with-the-locals plan. But then, so would learning to surf, and she wasn't too keen on that idea.

She turned over to the next page. There were photos of the town, tones of sepia and black-and-white predominant. From what Laura had seen on her run, things hadn't changed much. The streetscape remained the same – shops lining one side of the broad road, their corrugated roofs, the sign across The Pioneer exactly the same then as today. There were two photos in faded colour on the next page. One was a shot of eight men standing in a line at the water's edge, their surfboards rising tall beside them. The caption read, 'Banksia Boys, 1963'.

The other colour picture was, if Laura wasn't mistaken, of the holiday house she was staying in. She looked more closely. There was a family standing out the front with suitcases beside them. A short paragraph on the opposite page, above the washed-out photos of the town centre, gave a brief history of the village that had grown into a town after the war, with the influx of migrants and people looking for a better life out of the city. The word 'influx' was some pretty heavy creative licence, as the population only increased by a dozen or so at that time. The author talked about the importance of the surfing culture in the early sixties and the summer tourists who flocked to the Bay every year. Including the Woodhouse family from Sydney.

What?

No.

It wasn't an altogether uncommon name. But . . .

Rule number six, the extended version. *A coincidence is just a connection you haven't discovered yet.*

Laura pulled out her phone and opened the magnifying glass app.

The picture looked to be a few years earlier than the one she had of Lily and Gigi, but Laura was certain the young girl standing rigid and glum in front of her serious parents was her Lillian. She couldn't have been much older than eleven or twelve, and though the photo was blurry and faded, in her gut she knew it was her grandmother.

Right. Time for some positive action. She grabbed her pen and notebook.

What did she know? That Lillian came here for summer holidays. That her family rented this very house at least once for their stay. That some girl named Gigi was in a photo that Lillian had kept hidden until Laura's dad had found it and it was a source of tension between them, according to her mother.

What didn't she know? Well, that was an endless list. Rule number eight was important here: *start at the beginning with a simple question.* What was the simplest question she could ask in this mystery? How often did Lillian's family come here?

She turned to the back of the book. On the very last page were the photo credits. She looked for the listings for page ten. Most of the early photos of the town had been taken by the same person, a Mr J Taylor, spanning a period from the nineteen-twenties to the mid-sixties. The shot of the Banksia Boys was credited to an I Holland, and the picture of Lillian's family was taken by . . . who? Laura dropped the book and the corner dug into her thigh. *Really?* She looked at the name again. Mrs D Duncan. She let out a long breath. Mrs Duncan's reaction to the photo of Lily and Gigi, to the pendant, and now her name in this book. No. This was no coincidence at all.

She took note of the date: 1956. Yes, Lillian would have been twelve.

She pulled out her photo of Lily and Gigi on the beach: 1961. Lillian would have been seventeen. So, two photos of Lillian in Banksia Bay aged twelve and seventeen, and the photo on the sideboard with an even older Lillian in Banksia Bay, too. Was it reasonable to assume that Lillian's family had come here every year? Or at least frequently? And this house, was it significant too? The earliest photo taken out front, by Mrs Duncan no less, and the latest sitting inside on the sideboard, suggested it was.

Laura's pulse raced. Her instinct had been right. There was most definitely a story here.

She paced the living room floor. The photos, the pendant, this house. Yvonne had said this house was an investment property for someone in Ocean Heights, but she'd decorated it. That meant she'd put these photos here. *Wait a moment*. When she'd let Laura in, she'd moved the photos on the sideboard, hadn't she? Yes, she was sure of it.

Yvonne! What did she know?

Laura stopped and wrote the question in her notebook. She loved that feeling when one question led to the next.

Her phone rang and she smiled when she saw Maher's caller ID.

'Hey, Prescott. How's the holiday going? Or are you too busy snooping around?'

'A little.' Laura filled him in on everything so far, not that it was much.

'I thought you were supposed to be taking it easy.'

'I am. In fact, I might be learning to surf.' That was a lie. She had no intention of taking surfing lessons.

'You? Surf? He better be cute.'

Laura rolled her eyes. 'He's married. And has a child.'

Maher fired back, 'But you didn't deny it.'

'He's . . . all right. Nothing special.' Except when he smiled. Then his whole face lit up.

'Well, for what it's worth, I reckon you should still take him up on lessons. Might be fun.'

'That's what he said.'

'Well, he might not be cute, but he sounds intelligent.'

Laura could hear the smirk in Maher's voice.

'Prescott. Promise me you'll relax while you're away. I want my top reporter firing on all cylinders when you get back.'

'I promise.' Lie or truth? Laura didn't know.

She hung up and a sound from the front yard made her jump. *Shit*. Charlotte was here. Laura had forgotten to make herself scarce. She really didn't want to have to talk to her.

Peering through the curtain, Laura watched Charlotte weed around the lilly pillies and hydrangeas that hugged the front fence.

There was a look of contentment on Charlotte's face as she worked, humming to herself. Laura could hear the sweet tune floating towards her on the cool ocean breeze that had just started up. Maybe she should make a peace offering. She didn't know what she'd done to offend Charlotte, but the look the woman had given her both times they'd met spoke volumes.

Laura went into the kitchen and prepared a tray with iced tea and the chocolate-chip cookies Yvonne had left her.

Stepping onto the verandah, she cleared her throat. Charlotte looked up, her face falling from its happy countenance into the expression Laura was already getting used to.

'I thought you might like a tea break.' Laura held up the tray.

'Thank you. That would actually be lovely.' She came up the

steps and sat next to Laura at the white metal table. 'These are good.' She took another bite.

'Yvonne made them.'

Charlotte finished off the cookie. 'That makes sense. She's the best baker in the Bay.'

'A baker, a bus driver and a property manager?' There was more to Yvonne than met the eye.

'Yes, well, we all do what we need to, to make ends meet. Speaking of which . . .' Charlotte looked to her gardening tools lying in the grass. 'I should get back to it.'

Laura suspected there was more to everyone around here than met the eye.

As evening settled over the old house, Laura threw together a simple dinner of cold chicken and cheese and crackers. She would take a long bath and then go through the photo book once more. Just in case she'd missed anything. Rule number nine, *you never know where an answer will come from.*

Five

Virginia sat in her tiny living room perched above the shack, Yvonne watching her from across the dining table.

'You saw it too, didn't you?' Virginia looked at her old friend.

Yvonne closed her eyes briefly.

'And you didn't think to warn me?'

'Sorry.'

'I nearly collapsed in the shack, right in front of her. A heads-up would have been nice. More than nice. Necessary, wouldn't you say?'

Yvonne got up and walked towards her. 'I'm sorry, Gigi.'

Virginia shot her a look that would silence any mention of Gigi.

'Virginia, really. I thought maybe my eyes were playing tricks on me. I'm not as young as I used to be. I would have told you if I thought it was something.'

'Something? Something! This isn't something, Yvonne. It's everything.' She took a breath, trying to lower the pitch of her voice, which was far too high for her liking. 'What is she doing here?'

'I don't know.' Yvonne got up from the dining table and poured them both a stiff drink. Virginia kept the good single malt hidden in the top cupboard behind the biscuit tin but her friend knew where to find it. And when.

They only ever shared a glass together one day in January, every year in silent memory. But Virginia was glad Yvonne had pulled down the bottle today. She certainly needed it.

'Maybe it's just a coincidence,' Yvonne said. 'She just happens to look like . . .' Her voice trailed off.

'Just happens to look like her? And is here? And is staying in the holiday house? And has the same mannerisms?'

Virginia downed her whisky and poured another. 'She knows something.'

Yvonne sipped her drink slowly. 'How can she? You and I are the only two people who know the truth about that night. She couldn't possibly be here for that.'

'Then what?' Virginia didn't know, and she wouldn't be able to rest until she did. Her cheeks felt moist. Were those . . . tears? She hadn't cried since . . . Well, since. And she wouldn't have a bar of it now.

'Oh, sweetie.' Yvonne wrapped her hands around Virginia's, but Virginia slipped free and walked around the dining room, four paces taking in the entire space.

It was silly calling it a dining room. There weren't any actual rooms in the loft above the shack. There was an open kitchenette, a dining table in front of that, and a single bed behind a bamboo and rice paper partition screen at the eastern end. Washing facilities were downstairs in the shop.

She'd moved in here once the caravan park had got too much for her. Maybe she could have bought a small place with the money she'd got from selling the holiday house, but what would she be living off now? The pension? A pittance. What she made from the shack? A labour of love. Not that she minded. She'd always loved the shack. It felt more like home than anywhere else. Even though it was filled with memories.

So many memories.

'I don't know why she's here.' Yvonne stepped closer to her. 'Or who she is. But I have to believe it is an innocent coincidence.'

Poor Yvonne. She'd kept Virginia's secret for so long. This whoever-she-was who'd hit town would affect her life too. And that wasn't fair. Virginia had to hold it together for Yvonne's sake. Whatever this girl was doing here, Virginia wasn't going to let it undo her. Nothing had undone her in sixty years.

Nothing could after that day.

This wasn't an innocent coincidence. It couldn't be. This Laura woman was connected to Lily somehow. She felt it in her bones.

They drank one more whisky in silence before Virginia put the bottle away and Yvonne washed up the glasses.

'Do you want me to stay?' Yvonne asked.

'No.' *What good would that do?* 'Thank you, though. You go home and rest. We'll talk more tomorrow.'

Yvonne stood at the door. 'Virginia. Listen to me. Even if Laura is . . . somehow related, which I doubt, we will face this together.'

Virginia rushed over and hugged Yvonne tightly, quickly, then pushed herself away.

'Go.' Her voice was gruff as she held back the flood of tears she'd been keeping inside for so long.

Ever so long.

Under the cover of darkness, Virginia slipped through the night. She wasn't going to sit back and wait for coincidence or fate or whatever was at play here to come crashing through her life. If Laura was connected to her past, to Lily, then she had to know – know why she was here, what she wanted, what she knew. If she knew something, anything at all, Virginia had to be prepared. But how? She'd buried that summer in the darkest reaches of her mind so long ago, nothing could help her if it resurfaced now.

She slunk along the beach, her breathing becoming heavy as the holiday house came into view. There was a light on in the living room, the curtains were open.

Virginia snuck along the side of the house until she was under the smaller of the two living room windows. She inched her head up, stealing a look inside.

Laura was sitting on the sofa, her back to the window. In front of her was a laptop, the screen ablaze with light. Virginia was too far away and her eyesight too bad to make out what was on the screen.

Who was she kidding? What could she possibly discover peering through a window at night-time?

Silly old fool.

Laura stood up and Virginia dropped down into a crouch. Her heart beat heavy against her chest.

Gentle mumbling reached her ears. Was there someone else inside?

She had to risk another look, so she popped up. Laura was still facing away from the window. No one else was there.

Virginia stretched up to see better. The girl was scribbling something on paper, her shoulders slouched over. She stopped, threw a pen onto the coffee table, and tore the page out of her notebook. With a quick flick of her wrist, she flung the piece of paper behind her and Virginia fell to her aching knees as the flash of white flew towards her.

She held her breath. If Laura fetched that piece of paper, she'd be discovered. If Virginia ran, she'd be discovered.

She waited.

A door thudded shut, the old pipes that ran beneath the home hammered.

The bathroom. Laura was in the bathroom. This was her chance.

Slowly she stood up, careful not to make a sound. She dared to look inside. The paper Laura had thrown had landed on the sideboard. It was covered in thick black question marks, large enough for her to see.

Another thud of a door.

Virginia stepped back into the shadows and hurried out of sight as quickly as her old bones would let her.

What did those question marks mean, she wondered as she raced back home. Simple doodles of a curious mind? No. Those dark inky scrawlings were the marks of frustration.

Laura had some questions she clearly wanted answers to. Questions about her? Virginia's stomach tightened.

She climbed the spiral stairs of the shack and entered her flat. Without turning on a light, she found the whisky bottle and took a long swig. And another before crawling into bed.

The only light penetrating her darkened world came from the bright moon sending cruel silver shards through the window that looked out to the ocean.

The ghosts would return tonight.

She knew that without doubt.

January 1962

Gigi waited outside the holiday house for Lily to come out. Dressed in her trusty overalls, she was ready to go hiking in the hills that surrounded Banksia Bay. It was their tradition on the second-last day of summer to take a picnic and sit among the wildflowers.

And Gigi waited.

She never wore a watch, instinctively knowing by the height of the sun in the sky, or by the rumble of her tummy, approximately what time of day it was. Dad always said it was the generations of fishermen's blood that ran through her veins. Mum always said it was because if she didn't eat every hour she'd implode.

Gigi preferred the romanticism of her father's explanation. And she knew Lily was late.

Just as she was about to give up, Lily emerged from the house, dressed in what was, for her, a 'roughing it' outfit, but what to Gigi seemed a bit too fancy for what they were going to do. Still, she knew by now not to question it.

'Sorry. I tossed and turned all night, and then I slept in. Mother thought I was sick. She nearly didn't let me come.'

Gigi took her friend's hand and led her down the path before Mrs Woodhouse changed her mind and stopped them.

They hiked until Lily started to complain – which was never as far as Gigi could walk on her own – and then they laid Gigi's picnic blanket in a clearing. They could see the beach from here, though it wasn't the breathtaking view from Gigi's favourite spot in the hills. She'd never been able to get Lily to hike that far.

They ate their chicken sandwiches and scones and Lily let out a most out-of-character burp as she sipped the lemonade.

'You'd better not let Richard see you drink like that.' Gigi snorted.

Lily looked around as if she were expecting him to turn up right behind them – the mere mention of his name summoning him somehow.

'Oh, Gigi. Isn't he dreamy?'

Gigi tilted her head. He was certainly handsome and seemed nice enough. Shaking his hand hadn't sent a shiver up her spine the way touching Costas' had, though.

'When we met him the other day . . .' She didn't quite know how to ask Lily if she got all tingly. That seemed like something you should probably keep to yourself.

'Oh, I thought my knees were going to crumble and you were going to have to carry me home.'

Gigi conjured the image in her head and tried to imagine Mrs Woodhouse's expression as she lugged a semiconscious Lily through the gate. She giggled and Lily's face fell.

'Oh, no. I wasn't laughing at you, Lily. Just the thought of me trying to carry you home.'

Lily hugged her. 'These summers with you have been the best, Gigi.'

'Do you want to make this one even better?'

'Oh no, Miss Virginia Gilbert.' She put her hand on her hip. 'Every year you try to talk me into it and every year I say no.'

'Please, Lily?' Gigi got on one knee and clasped her hands in front of her chest. 'You said you'd do it one day. And I declare that day to be today.'

Lily stood and put her hands on her hips, which looked quite ridiculous in her pretty little shift dress. 'You can't make me.'

'And I never would.' Gigi grinned. 'But I can try to persuade you. Do you think Richard would like a girl with a bit of daring?'

'That's not fair.'

'You could tell him all about it when you see him next.'

Lily shot Gigi a look but Gigi maintained her pleading expression. This time she was going to wear Lily down. 'I reckon he'd be impressed.' She put as much singsong into her voice as she could.

Seconds ticked by. Minutes?

'Oh, all right then.' Lily gave in. 'We can stop by home and I'll get my swimming costume.'

Gigi jumped up and twirled around.

Standing on the small jetty that jutted into the south end of the bay, Lily stepped forward and back, looking over the edge and then up to the sky. It wasn't that high up. Gigi had done it heaps of times. She knew Lily would be nervous, though. That's why she'd brought the old life-ring from the shack. Not that Lily would need it. But maybe it would make her feel better about jumping into the sea below.

Gigi took Lily's hand. 'You don't have to do this.'

Lily was shaking. 'No. I want to.'

'What if I go in first, and take this?' She held up the life-ring. 'And then you can jump and I'll be there to help you.'

Lily nodded.

'You count me in.' Gigi smiled at her friend.

'One, two . . .'

With a big splash Gigi entered the cool water below. She let it take her down, just for a second, before bursting through the surface. Normally she would stay under longer, but she didn't want to frighten Lily.

'It's beautiful,' she called up to her friend.

Lily peered over the jetty. 'Okay. Just give me a minute.'

Gigi lay back in the water waiting, not wanting to force Lily. The sun was warm on her face and she skulled the water with small movements of her hands so she didn't drift away on the tide. The world was quiet with her ears below the surface as she bobbed up and down with the gentle undulation of the sea.

She closed her eyes and allowed the weightless freedom to wash over her, taking in deep salty breaths. When she was younger she'd wanted to be a mermaid, to live like this in the ocean her whole life. Losing such childhood fancies to growing up made moments like this so special.

A large swell lifted her up and as her head rose above the water's surface she could hear giggling.

She dropped her legs and sat higher in the water. There on the jetty was Lily, talking, giggling, twirling her hair, with Richard standing beside her.

'Are you coming in?' Gigi shouted, and they turned towards her.

'Hi!' Richard waved. 'I was out walking and saw Lily up here. I thought I'd see what was happening. This looks like fun.'

He stripped off his shirt and took off his shoes. Standing there in just his shorts, his pale torso muscled, he looked over the jetty.

'What do you say?' He turned to Lily.

She took his hand and Gigi felt a stabbing pain in her heart.

As Richard leapt off the jetty, Lily let go. He shouted with delight as he entered the water and when he came back up for air he beamed at Gigi.

'That *was* fun. You've got nerve, I'll give you that.' He winked.

On the jetty, Lily looked down, hands on her hips.

'Did you forget something?' Gigi whispered to Richard, pointing towards Lily.

'Oh, damn. We'd better go up.'

They climbed the wooden ladder back onto the jetty and Richard stepped in close to a less-than-impressed-looking Lily.

'Do you want to go back to shore?' he asked.

'You two are having fun. I don't want to ruin it.' She pouted.

'It's okay if you want me to stop.' He took her hand in his.

'No, it's fine. I don't mind.' Her pout gave way to a sweet smile. 'Really.'

Gigi wasn't sure what was happening. Clearly Lily didn't want Richard jumping in the water without her. Why didn't she just say so? If he didn't like it, tough.

Richard, though, didn't hesitate.

'Why don't you sit down?' He guided Lily to the edge of the jetty. 'And Gigi and I can have a few more jumps and then we can all head into town for a milkshake?' He touched her cheek gently. 'Maybe I can impress you with some fancy tricks.'

Lily raised an eyebrow. 'They'd better be good.'

'All right, then. Gigi, let's see what you've got. Can you do this?'

He flung himself off the jetty and did a somersault midair before splashing into the sea.

Gigi rubbed her hands together and shot him a look that said, *Oh, just you watch*. At least she hoped that's what her expression conveyed. She jumped and did a somersault, finishing with a salute before going under the water.

Three more times she and Richard jumped, each time him daring her to do a trick – jumping off backwards, backwards with a somersault, a double somersault. She didn't quite land the last one and hit the surface with a painful thud that knocked the air out of her lungs.

But she wasn't going to let it show and she climbed back up, ready for the next dare. She looked at Lily, who moments ago had appeared merely bored. Now she looked angry with Gigi.

Message received. 'I think I might be done for the day.' Gigi wrapped her towel around her shoulders.

'Let's go get those milkshakes, then.' Richard helped Lily to stand and put his shirt back on.

Lily shot Gigi a look.

'Oh, um, I have some chores to do at the shack,' Gigi said. 'Dad's heading out this evening and could do with my help getting the boat ready.' She may not have had much experience in this area of boys and hearts and feelings, but she was pretty sure Lily wanted some time alone with Richard.

As she watched the two of them walk down the jetty, Lily turned around and mouthed 'thank you' over her shoulder.

The feeling of knowing she'd made her best friend happy didn't quite push aside the sense of loneliness that enveloped her. And worse. She was actually hungry after flinging herself into the ocean that many times. She really could have done with a milkshake.

Oh well. She walked barefoot along the old jetty, expertly avoiding the cedar planks with thick rusting nails poking out.

On her way home she stopped by the bakery rather than the milk bar – no point rubbing salt in – and bought an iced bun. Well, she promised Mrs Andrews that she'd come back and pay for it later. There was no room in a swimsuit for a purse. Mrs Andrews' iced buns were sticky and sweet with their pink icing, and so soft Gigi could never resist one. She owed that woman quite a bit of money by now. For the buns she knew about and the ones Gigi snuck when she wasn't looking.

She might be on her own for the rest of the day – Mum would be at the caravan park, Dad had actually headed out on last night's tide – but she could still look forward to tomorrow and spending the last day of summer with Lily. It was always deliciously bittersweet, saying goodbye for another year, drinking in the day with a swim in the sea and chips on the jetty and a bonfire at night.

And then she'd start the countdown to next summer.

Gigi wiped the icing from her lips and licked the dripping stickiness from her fingers as she finished the bun. She passed the old Parsons place – she'd have to call it something else now – and saw

Costas in the garden with his mother. Gigi wasn't sure what they were building, but there were wooden planks and wire and long stakes. Mrs Andrews had a vegie garden in her front yard, but this was much bigger than that.

She waved to Costas as she walked by and he waved back, only to receive a clip over the ear from his mother. She must really want whatever it was to be built fast.

Gigi turned back to look at Costas, bent over the wooden planks, his mother waving a finger in his direction. He looked up briefly and smiled and Gigi grinned.

All the way home.

Six

*L*aura had googled late into the night until her eyes were strained by the bright light of her laptop and she rose early to continue the search. It was easy enough to find the photographer of the early pictures of the town from *Banksia Bay Bush Tracks* – turns out Mr Taylor was a prolific photojournalist in the twenties and thirties, though they might not have called it that back then, and his archives of work were all over the internet. He had lived in nearby Ocean Heights but had long since passed away. So that probably wasn't going to help her solve the mystery of Lillian.

Rule number nine, *never discount a lead*. She jotted this information down, just in case.

Mr I Holland was proving harder to track down. She couldn't find a reference to a photographer of that name with any connection to Banksia Bay. At least not in cyberspace. Laura would have to resort to some old-fashioned sleuthing. At the library, perhaps. Did Banksia Bay have a library? Laura made a note to check. Actually, a local library could be very useful. Archived newspapers, town meetings, death records – it was surprising how much you could find out from death notices. Yes. Her next priority would be to investigate the nearest library.

She stretched her arms behind her back, and rolled her neck round three times. The sun was rising and her stomach was groaning. A quick jog, some breakfast, and then she'd get back to it.

There was no one in town. Laura supposed it was too early, though there was a light on in The Saddler. She ran through the empty streets and then ventured further afield into the hills that hugged the edge of Banksia Bay. There were a lot of paths crisscrossing the green slopes covered in spindly yellow flowers. Some of the paths were marked with little brass plaques on short wooden stakes – 'Wanderers Way', 'Banksia Bash', 'Lookout Trail' – and were clearly used often. She even recognised a few of the names from the photo book. Some of the paths were barely worn, and were perhaps not even tracks.

She ran up the hill where the banksias thinned out, turning her mind to what she'd learned and what was still left unanswered. Normally when she was chasing down a story, she carried within her a confidence that she would succeed. This was different.

Was she going to find the answers she was looking for here in Banksia Bay? Were there actually any answers to be found? Was she on some sort of wild goose chase that, in the end, would mean nothing?

She took a left turn.

This was not like her. Usually running stopped her tumbling thoughts. She sucked in a few deep breaths, slowing her stride as she did.

Hmm. Where had the track disappeared to? She found herself in a clearing of grass that swayed in the breeze but saw no evidence of which way she'd come through the trees. That was just what she needed. To get lost. And no one would know where to search for her. No one would think *to* search for her, probably.

She looked about. From the top of the hill she could see Banksia Bay below, its broad main street cutting a gash through the landscape. Behind the strip of shops were a few rambling streets where blocks of houses nestled in under the banksia-clad hills. She could see the jetty stretching into the ocean and the empty caravan park on the town's edge. Okay. So she wasn't totally lost. Though she didn't fancy having to navigate her way back to civilization down that rugged drop. She took a step back away from the edge and tripped over something in the grass. She tried to stop herself from falling backwards, her arms flailing about in a vain attempt to keep herself upright, but all she managed to do was throw herself forward instead and she hit the dirt hard, her knee scraping on a rock as she went down.

'Damn it.' She cursed under breath and held her leg. She'd torn a great big hole in her mauve running tights and a huge gash in her knee that was bleeding profusely.

'That was rather spectacular.' A deep voice, a mocking voice, came from behind.

She twisted to see Heath striding towards her, and she shot him a look that she hoped conveyed her lack of appreciation for the humour he saw in the situation.

'Are you hurt?'

As he circled around her he saw her leg and bent down beside her. 'Well, you did a good job of that.'

Without asking, he grabbed her drink bottle and poured water over the wound. She winced.

'Sorry. We've got to clean it up a bit to see how bad it is.'

He washed it again and she held her wince in that time.

As the blood thinned out with water, sending pink floods down her shin, she dared to look more closely. It was a big gash, wide and deep.

Heath took off his T-shirt and soaked it with what was left in the water bottle. 'Don't want this to stick.' He wrapped his T-shirt around her knee. 'Can you stand?'

He held out his hand and she looked at it there in the air before realising that she might need some help, just to steady herself, as she stood on legs that felt just a little wobbly. As he helped pull her to standing, pain shot up her leg and she buckled over.

Heath caught her. 'I've got you. Take it slowly.'

Laura drew in a deep breath and tried to put her weight on her leg again. She leaned on Heath quite heavily, but could manage it. Just.

'Okay,' he said. 'Now let's try walking. That's it. Slowly. Use me to take the weight.'

Laura took a few steps around. It hurt. Like hell. But she could just about bear the pain. The alternative was to have him carry her down the hill and she certainly wasn't about to let herself become a hopeless damsel in distress in the arms of a bare-chested hero.

'I can manage.' She winced.

'Uh-huh.'

Come on, Laura. Hold it together. It's just a grazed knee.

They hobbled back to the path she thought she'd been following before getting herself lost, to where it took a turn down the hill.

'Just give me a minute.' She stopped and took in some desperate breaths. How was she going to negotiate the way down? Even with Heath's help?

'No hurry.' He stood beside her and waited.

As she gathered her fortitude Heath pulled out his phone and sent a text.

'Calling for reinforcements?' She looked up at him. 'Or are you calling the local paper for a story about the useless tourist who had to be rescued from the mountain top?'

Heath's eyes crinkled around the edges.

'Okay. Hill, not mountain. But a journalist will embellish the details to make it more dramatic.'

'Just as well I didn't text a journalist, then. What were you doing up here anyway, off the path like that? More of that special falling-over yoga you like?'

'That you never saw happen, remember.' Laura hit him in the arm. 'I was running and got lost.' She squared her shoulders and lifted her chin. Time to get moving. 'What were you doing up there?'

She didn't particularly care what he'd been doing, but she figured if she kept him talking, she'd distract herself from the descent they'd started on.

'I sometimes go up there to sit and watch the water. You know, away from the bustle of town.'

'Bustle?'

'Well, our version of bustle. It's such a peaceful spot. The waves were pretty pathetic this morning, so I wasn't in the water long.'

'I thought you surfer dudes hung ten any chance you got.'

'"Surfer dude"? "Hang ten"?'

Heath was polite enough not to laugh, though Laura could feel his amusement as she clung on to him and they slowly limped along the steep track.

'Sorry. I don't mean to offend,' Laura said through gritted teeth.

'You didn't. But I am thinking the sooner I get you out on the water and teach you some basics, the better.'

Laura stopped. 'Um. You have witnessed firsthand twice now my complete lack of physical coordination. I can fall over on dry steady land perfectly well without any help. Trying to balance on a surfboard? In moving water? I'm thinking that's not a very good idea.'

'Nah. You'll be right. It's easier than it looks. Especially if you have a good teacher.'

'And you're a good teacher?'

Heath shrugged, but didn't answer. Silence fell between them and Laura felt the pain in her knee getting worse. She had to distract herself, keep him talking.

'How many people have you taught?'

He couldn't give a number. He'd been teaching every summer since he was eighteen. Twelve years now. He loved teaching the kids, the joy on their faces was priceless, but his favourite students were the reluctant ones who think they're too old, or unfit, or uncoordinated. Teaching them to love surfing was his greatest joy.

'People like me?'

'I never said you were old.' There was a glint in his eye. 'Or unfit.'

Laura hit him in the shoulder with the hand that wasn't hanging on to him with a death grip.

As they reached the edge of town and the smooth flat roads, the pain in Laura's leg eased slightly, but she didn't let go of Heath's arm. While the pain wasn't so bad, the wobbly feeling after the exertion of climbing back down to civilisation was a lot worse.

'Dr Lapsley doesn't open till ten, but I'll get you to the shack and we can look at patching you up good enough there.'

'The shack?'

'It's close and it'll be open.'

That might be so. But Laura didn't recall seeing anything there that would be useful in 'patching her up'.

Limping through town they fell into silence. Laura didn't mind the quiet so much now. She just counted steps in her head and made a little game out of it. One step, two steps, Laura takes a breath. Three steps, four steps, she lets it out again. Okay. Maybe the pain was worse than she'd realised.

They finally reached the beach and she hesitated as they took their first step onto the soft sand and she felt her leg give way. Heath stopped beside her.

'Do you need a hand with this bit?'

'No.' She couldn't let him pick her up and carry her. She'd rather cope with excruciating pain than that kind of abject humiliation.

He looked into her eyes and his gaze softened. 'What about just an arm around the waist? So I can take a bit more of the weight?'

Hmm. A compromise. She could cope with that.

She let him slip his arm around her, trying to ignore the tingle it sent up her spine.

It wasn't far to the shack, thankfully, and he helped her into one of the chairs that was basking in the morning sun on the deck.

'That's odd.' He frowned. 'Gran should have opened by now.'

He stood up and was about to leave when Charlotte arrived, carrying a bag. Aiden ran from her side and into Heath's arms.

'Hey, buddy.' He kissed Aiden on the forehead. 'Thanks for coming,' he said to Charlotte. 'Here's the patient.' He tapped Laura on the arm. 'I'm just going to go check on Gran.'

He left with Aiden on his hip and Laura sat there looking at Charlotte, who was eyeing her with . . . well, the only word Laura could come up with was 'suspicion'.

'I was out running through the bush and tripped.' Her words came out fast, which did nothing to soften Charlotte's expression. 'Heath found me and got me back here. Really. I'm okay. You don't need to . . .'

Charlotte knelt beside her and unwrapped Heath's blood-stained T-shirt with such a gentle touch that Laura didn't even notice it was gone until she looked down.

'Hmm. That's going to need a stitch or two.' Charlotte opened her bag and Laura realised it was a first aid kit. Charlotte took out some sort of solution to clean the wound. Antiseptic? Alcohol? Anaesthetic? Laura had no idea.

'Oh. What time does the surgery open? Or the hospital?'

Charlotte shook her head. 'It's not worth making the journey to Ocean Heights to the hospital for something like this. Dr Lapsley opens at ten, but he's one hundred and thirty years old and doesn't have the steadiest of hands anymore. I'll do it here.'

'What?' Laura tried to stand up, but Charlotte's hand on her good leg held her in place. 'I, um, I'm happy to wait to see the doctor.' She wriggled in the seat.

'Does it hurt?' Charlotte looked her in the eye.

Laura nodded.

'You can wait to see Dr Lapsley, but he'll only call me in to do the stitching anyway. I'm the local nurse.' She held Laura's stare.

'Oh. Maybe you could have led with that.' Whatever Charlotte's problem with her was, Laura had done nothing wrong and she wasn't going to be intimidated.

'Okay. Fair enough.' Charlotte dropped her gaze. When she looked up again, the hostility had faded away and in its place was the comforting look of a seasoned medical professional. 'You're right. I'm sorry. If you'd rather wait for the doctor, I understand. If you'd like me to stitch you up now, then I'd be happy to do that for you.'

Laura really didn't want to wait, so she took in a deep breath and gave Charlotte the go-ahead.

Charlotte worked quickly and efficiently. Laura had never had stitches before, but she was pretty confident the job was rather excellently done. As Charlotte finished up – dressing the stitches, giving instructions on how to care for them which Laura was only half listening to, telling her to get to Dr Lapsley at some point today to get a script for antibiotics just in case – Heath returned with Aiden.

He pulled Charlotte aside and whispered in urgent tones. Laura couldn't help but try to listen in.

All she could make out was 'unwell', 'never seen her like that', 'but I have work'. Whatever the problem was, the looks of concern on both Heath's and Charlotte's faces were intense. They stopped talking and just looked at each other.

'Is, um, is there something I can help with?' Laura piped up.

'No. This is a family matter.' Charlotte waved her hand in dismissal.

Aiden came and sat next to Laura. 'Does it hurt?' He pointed his finger so close to Laura's leg she was worried he was going to poke her.

'A little. Your mummy was very gentle, though. She's an excellent nurse.'

Aiden's pride was written all over his face. 'Gran isn't feeling well. Mummy has to work today, so she can't open the shack.'

Heath swooped in and picked Aiden up. 'And I've got an appointment in Ocean Heights that I can't miss. We'd just leave the place closed, but Yvonne's bringing a bus group by later today.'

Charlotte shot Heath a look. 'Seriously? We do not need to discuss family business in front of a stranger. Yvonne can open the shack when she brings the group by.'

Laura watched the two intently. Heath's shoulders were relaxed, his face calm, a picture of serenity. Charlotte was clearly agitated, and Laura suspected there was more to it than just the fact they were having this spat in front of her.

'Yvonne doesn't know how to use Gran's fancy new coffee machine.' Heath looked at Laura.

She cleared her throat. Perhaps this was her way in, a chance to build some trust. She had no idea who in this town had the answers she was looking for, but she had to start somewhere.

'I know how to use it.'

Charlotte turned to face her, anger in her eyes. 'What?'

'The coffee machine. I know how to use it.'

They had a similar one at work and she virtually lived off strong coffee when working on a difficult story. She and the coffee machine had become very good friends over the years.

Charlotte took a deep breath. 'Thank you, Laura. But we can't exactly leave Gran's business in the hands of a stranger.'

Heath stepped forward. 'What if she came only when Yvonne was here? Yvonne could open up, be in charge, and Laura could just make the coffees.'

Charlotte looked at Heath and then back to Laura. It was a simple solution. A logical one. Laura looked her in the eye, almost daring her to find a good retort.

'You'll be in too much pain.' She put her hands on her hips.

'Not once I get some painkillers. Besides, I owe you for treating me just now.' She rubbed her leg just above her knee.

'Sounds like it's settled to me.' Heath looked right at Laura and she felt the heat rise in her cheeks.

Charlotte's hands stayed on her hips, and unless she was blind she would have seen the red flush that came over Laura. Oh dear. Laura didn't need to find herself in the middle of that. She averted her eyes and made preparations to get up.

Heath came to her side and helped her.

Good God, man, that is not helping. No wonder Charlotte was prickly towards her. She thought Laura was trying to steal her husband.

Charlotte sighed. 'Okay. As long as Yvonne's here. Come on, Aiden. We have to get you to school.'

She grabbed her son's hand and turned to go. Heath bounced two steps towards her, whispered something in her ear to which she just grunted in answer, and he kissed her on the forehead.

'I'll help you home and get you those painkillers,' he said, coming back to Laura.

'No, really. I'm fine.' She walked forward and winced.

'Really. You're not.'

'Okay. But I don't want to get you into more trouble.'

'What makes you think I'm in trouble?'

Laura paused and tilted her head.

'Okay. But I'm always in trouble with Charlotte.' He laughed.

Well, each to their own, Laura supposed. Though she did wonder if that was any kind of way to live a marriage. Not that she'd know.

Heath helped Laura settle onto the couch in the holiday house, set up her laptop for her, and popped out, returning shortly afterwards with medicine to help her with the pain. 'When I get back from my appointment this afternoon, I'll take you to the doctor and we can sort out those antibiotics.'

Laura tried to protest that he'd already helped her so much, but he wouldn't hear of it.

'I guess this means I have a good excuse not to take you up on the surfing lessons,' she called after him as he headed out the door, relieved she'd found something he couldn't counter.

'Only for a week.' He winked and walked out the door.

Her cheeks burned again. *Seriously? Stop it.* It must have been some sort of delayed shock from the fall, or the stitches, making her all woozy like this.

Get a grip, girl. You have a job to do.

Adjusting the pillow under her knee – keep it elevated, Charlotte had said – she took a big gulp of water to help the painkillers down. In the grand scheme of things her injury was relatively minor, but boy, it still hurt.

The alarm on Laura's phone chimed and she opened her eyes. The laptop was lying on the sofa, her notebook on the floor. She must have fallen asleep. As she moved to get up her knee was stiff, but she had to get to the shack to help Yvonne.

She hobbled over to her handbag and pulled out Lillian's pendant. Hanging the chain she'd placed it on around her neck, she felt the weight of unanswered questions pressing on her.

'Tell me, Nan, why am I here?' she asked into the void. 'What am I going to discover?'

She pushed the pendant inside her simple white shirt and did up the top button so no one could see the necklace.

It would take a few minutes to get to the shack, so she made her way down the steps and headed towards the beach. Her knee was hurting a little, and a rather angry-looking bruise was already forming. But the painkillers were doing a good job and she could put enough weight on it to make walking, or at least limping, a possibility.

There was no one at the shack when she finally got there and she was a little relieved. A few moments to rest before anyone arrived would not be unwelcome.

She sat in a chair on the deck and looked out to the ocean. There was no one else around, just a long stretch of deserted beach and waves crashing into the shore. They were bigger than yesterday. And louder, the sound pounding in her ears.

As she watched the waves, her tumbling thoughts stopped and she sat, mesmerised.

She wasn't sure how long she'd been there before a gaggle of noise behind her broke her trance. She turned around and saw Yvonne leading a group of eight elderly tourists towards the shack.

Standing with most of her weight on her good leg, Laura waved in greeting.

Showtime.

'Heath rang and told me you'd be helping out today,' Yvonne shouted across the sand. 'Let's open up then, shall we?' she said, more quietly as she got closer.

The group she'd brought with her were like a flock of scavenging birds, going through every shelf in the shack, turning over trinkets, rearranging books in an effort to find something that struck their fancy, chattering without end. From behind the coffee machine Laura looked on, not quite believing what she saw, as they piled knick-knacks and novels into bags they'd brought with them.

'Did you get that?' Yvonne asked.

'Sorry. No.' Laura picked up a pen and a scrap piece of paper.

Yvonne repeated the order she'd taken on the bus – two lattes, one skim cappuccino, four teas, a hot chocolate and eight slices of carrot cake – and Laura got to work.

As Yvonne rang up the till one customer at a time, Laura prepared the drinks and cake and started ferrying them out to the tables on the deck. She hoped everyone was too busy bustling about in their frantic little shopping spree to notice the three mugs of mistakes she'd had to throw down the drain.

Light, happy voices floated on the air as the group drank and ate and showed off their purchases. Laura set about cleaning up the insane mess making eight cuppas had somehow made. Well, she could rule out becoming a barista if her journalism career ever got boring.

'Thank you.' Yvonne patted her on the arm after tallying up the takings. 'This crew come twice a year and it's a huge day for Virginia.' She tapped the bag she'd put the money into as she put it in the tiny safe under the bench. 'It means a lot that you'd help out.'

'Any time,' Laura said, feeling just a little guilty that her motives weren't entirely pure.

Yvonne rounded up the group with shouts of 'Next stop, home', and they picked up their bulging bags and drained the last sips of coffee from their mugs.

As Laura cleared the tables, Yvonne grabbed her arm. 'Do you mind locking up? We have to get back on the road, and there's still the washing-up to do.' Her eyes were wide with pleading.

'Of course.'

It didn't take long to clean and put away the mugs and saucers, and when she was finished, Laura hobbled around the shack, rearranging the shelves where Yvonne's horde had left great big gaps among the chaos. They had, in particular, made a rather large dent in the piles of books.

Laura restacked the ones that had fallen down, fighting her urge to alphabetise the titles as she went. That crew of vultures may be some of Virginia's best customers but they hadn't exactly been respectful of her property.

Behind a pile of how-to manuals, two thin books were jammed between the shelf and the red wall of the shack. Laura wiggled them free and wondered where she should put them, given the lack of order. Did the tattered old illustrated copy of *Pinocchio* go with *Car Racing in the Twenties*, or next to the raunchy novel with a half-naked man splashed across the cover?

The second book was covered with dust and Laura sneezed three times as she brushed it clean. How long had it been stuck there?

She lowered herself into the old armchair, realising as she sank into its soft comfort just how much her knee was hurting now. She considered the book in her hand, but it wasn't a published work at all. It was a scrapbook of sorts. The pages were yellowed and, as Laura turned them, she could feel how brittle they were. Ever so slowly she looked through history.

There were newspaper clippings from the late fifties and early sixties – an eclectic mix of stories and snippets from the Vietnam War and the death of Marilyn Monroe to the winning catch at the 1958 Ocean Heights Fishing Classic. Interspersed with the clippings were a movie stub from the picture palace in Ocean Heights, and faded black-and-white photos of wildflowers and waves and surfers. The next two pages were stuck together. Laura tried to separate them, but they started to tear, so she stopped. Maybe she shouldn't be looking through this. But then, rule number nine did say *you never know where you might find an answer*, so Laura always looked hard at everything.

She turned the next page and found herself looking at a school photo. It was a small group of twenty-one kids ranging in age from five to late teens. The little blackboard in front of the group read, 'Banksia Bay Central School, whole school, 1962.'

The students' heads were held high and they all wore smiles, except the boy with dark skin in the second-back row, standing just off to the side.

Under the photo someone had handwritten all the names in very neat script. Laura read through them and stopped when she got to Costas Tinellis, not just because the name stood out among the Jacks and Todds and Michaels that surrounded him, but also because the name was circled in pink pencil.

She counted the names and then the faces in the photo. Costas was the boy standing just a bit away from the others, his skin dark, his face sad.

Running her finger along the names, she kept reading until she got to 'me'. Again she counted and stopped on 'me' – a face that was now familiar to her, a face she had looked at so many times standing next to Lillian on the beach. The girl had the same mischievous eyes and unruly hair.

'Hello, Gigi,' Laura whispered.

Stuck onto the next page was a collage of cut-up photos. Most were either too blurry or the figures too tiny to make anything out other than basic shapes, a building in the background, or the beach. She brought the scrapbook closer to her face to try to see some detail.

'Can I help you with anything?'

A croaky voice from behind startled Laura and she dropped the scrapbook, fumbling it with both hands to stop it from falling to the floor. In what she was sure was hardly a graceful move, she managed to catch the scrapbook, spin around and put one hand on the armchair for support, looking ever so casually back at Virginia.

'Oh. Hi. Are you feeling better?'

'Much. Thank you. What have you got there?' Virginia pointed to the scrapbook in Laura's hand.

'I was tidying up after Yvonne's bus load came through. Man, do they know how to decimate shelves. Anyway, I was restacking all the books they'd knocked over and found this stuck behind the shelf. And –' she turned and pulled out the *Pinocchio* book – 'this too. They were stuck together.'

Virginia stepped forward, ignoring *Pinocchio*, and took the scrapbook in both hands. She let out a long breath. 'I haven't seen this in . . .' She looked up to Laura and her expression turned hard. 'Thank you for tidying up. And for helping today.'

'That's okay. It was kind of fun.'

'Would you like to help out tomorrow, too? If I have a turn like this, it can take me a few days to recover.'

Laura stared at Virginia, who was holding the scrapbook so tightly her knuckles were turning white. She wasn't sure what the old lady's true motive was, but she was absolutely sure she'd stumbled on something – rule number three, *trust your instincts* – and she couldn't say no.

'Of course. I'd be happy to help out, if I can.'

'Great. Swing by at nine, then. If that suits you.'

Laura agreed.

'Virginia Gilbert, what are you doing out of bed?' Charlotte's shrill voice cut through the shack.

As Charlotte felt her forehead, Virginia pushed her away, insisting she was fine.

'Thank you.' Charlotte turned to Laura, her face softening slightly. 'We really do appreciate you helping us out today. Yvonne said they all loved your coffee and she couldn't have done it without you.'

Laura wondered how Charlotte had had a chance to get a report from Yvonne already, but she supposed one would have called the other straight away. That was how small towns worked, wasn't it? The 'bush telegraph', they called it. She'd done a story on it early in her career. More effective than any postal service or spy organisation in the world.

Surely that would make finding out information on Lily and Gigi easier. Perhaps . . .

'I'll see you tomorrow, Laura,' Virginia said and waved as she headed up the spiral staircase. 'You'll lock up, Charlotte, won't you?'

'Tomorrow?' Charlotte looked at Laura, her eyes wide.

'Virginia asked if I could help out again. I'm not doing anything else, so I figured I may as well.'

Charlotte huffed. And then actually puffed.

'Laura.' She lowered her voice. 'I'm going to be frank with you. One of my things, my special talents, is reading people. I sense you're hiding something. And every time I turn around, there you are with my family. With Heath, with Gran. I don't like it when people mess with my family.'

Laura looked Charlotte in the eye. 'I assure you, I am not here to harm your family.' She thought about adding more – reiterating that she was just here to write a travel piece. But if Charlotte was a good reader of people, she'd see through that. If Laura stuck to the simple truth, and it was the truth that she had no intention of hurting anyone, maybe Charlotte would believe her.

'Okay, then.' Charlotte seemed to accept her word. 'I'd better go up and check on the old duck.'

'Something tells me Virginia isn't going to take too kindly to that.' Laura smiled and Charlotte let out a little snort.

I can read people too, thought Laura as she left the shack. And she just knew Virginia was an important piece of the puzzle. The way she held on to that scrapbook. What if . . . No, that couldn't be. But maybe . . .

Laura picked up her pace, cursing the fact she couldn't jog with her injured knee. Damn. She wouldn't be able to go for her usual morning run for a few days either. She hobbled as quickly as she could back to the house and pulled out her laptop as she flung herself onto the sofa.

Google to the rescue again – nicknames for Virginia.

Gin.

Ginny.

Geena.

Vivi.

And there it was.

Gigi.

'Yes!' she shouted. Virginia Gilbert of the shack was Gigi of
the photo.

Seven

'You did what?' Yvonne's voice rang through her kitchen, much louder than Virginia was expecting.

'I asked Miss Laura to help me today,' Virginia repeated.

'No. The other bit. You spied on her the other night?'

'Close your mouth, Yvonne. I think we can both agree now that her being here is no coincidence. The way she was studying this . . .' She handed the scrapbook to her friend. 'I think it might be safer if you hang on to this while she's here.'

Yvonne stroked the cover. 'Maybe. Or maybe she was just fascinated because it's really old. But if she's here to . . . well, you know . . . then why do you want her in the shack? Shouldn't you be keeping your distance?'

Virginia took her old friend by the shoulders. 'You know what they say. Keep your friends close —'

'— and your enemies closer. I'd hardly call her an enemy, though.'

Beautiful, sweet Yvonne. She never wanted to see the bad in

anyone, even after everything she'd witnessed, everything she'd been through in her life.

'Maybe not. The truth is that we don't know.' Virginia eased into the dining chair, in front of the tea and toast Yvonne had made her for breakfast.

Yvonne sat beside her and Virginia took her hands, their contrast stark. Yvonne's so tanned from decades in the surf, so strong still. Unlike hers, so weak and frail. Wrinkled hands. Pale hands.

Haunted hands.

'Virginia?'

Virginia forced her fear aside. 'It will be all right, Yvonne. Whatever she's here for. It will be all right. We've carried this with us for so long now.' She reached out and stroked Yvonne's hair. 'And it was a burden you should never have had to carry.'

Yvonne squeezed her hand. 'It's never been a burden. A secret held in love never is.'

Virginia hugged her tightly. She didn't deserve a friend like Yvonne.

Pulling herself together she broke away and nibbled on the toast and marmalade.

'I'd better figure out what I'm going to get that girl to do though, or she'll know something's up.'

'How's Charlotte going to react to her helping in the shack? You know what she can be like.'

Oh yes, Virginia knew all too well. A tyrant when it came to looking out for her family; 'overbearing' wasn't too harsh a word.

'She's already had her say about that. But when I pointed out that if Laura's helping me, she won't be bothering Heath, well, that shut her up pretty quickly.'

Everyone knew that after Aiden and Virginia, the only person Charlotte was more protective of was Heath.

'Touché. Family, huh?' A hint of sadness rang through Yvonne's voice and she drank her tea.

Virginia smiled at her friend. She'd never come out and asked, but she'd always wondered if events sixty years ago had had anything to do with Yvonne staying single all this time.

Possibly. Probably.

They ate the rest of their breakfast in silence and afterwards Virginia made her way through the streets just as the world was about to wake. As she turned onto the beach, a figure cast in shadow walked towards her. Laura was early. Virginia didn't know why she was in Banksia Bay, but she would find out.

She did know that the past reached into the future and manipulated it, twisted it, changed it. You could bury it deep. Hide it away.

But it was always there.

Always.

February 1962

The first day of the school year started out as dreary as always. Gigi had patched up her uniform from the previous year and it would serve for another few months yet. She trudged into the playground, looking at all the familiar faces, bussed in from all the tiny towns around Banksia Bay. She knew all twenty-odd kids from year one to sixth form. The handful of kindy kids, identifiable by the huddle they stood in, were dressed in pristine uniforms. She would know them by name by the end of the day.

There were no new kids in her form. No new girls. That wasn't going to do much to improve the ratio. There used to be three girls in Gigi's form, but one by one they'd left school as their parents decided it wasn't as important as running after the men on the dairy farms that surrounded the area. Gigi was thankful her parents wanted her to finish school. Not that school was great. Or exciting. Or fun. But it was better than the alternative. She'd tried to convince her dad to take her out on the boat with him, but he wouldn't have it. 'It's no life, Gigi. I want better for you.'

She lined up with the all the other students as the bell rang, signalling the start of the day. They filed into the large classroom and Miss Smith, back for her sixth year at Banksia Bay Central School, greeted each of them.

The kindies took the front few seats that were empty. Gigi sat in the chair in the far left corner, the same seat she'd sat in for the last few years. Behind her was Todd, in front of her was Sam, two seats over, Darren. The same old faces. Beside her the empty chair that Rosemary used to sit in, before her parents called her back to the farm.

Miss Smith started her lesson and Gigi gazed out the window, answering correctly every time she was called on. The hours ticked by.

Just before recess was due, Miss Smith let the whole group out early. 'Sam, can you stay back a moment, please?'

It wasn't unusual for Sam to stay in during break time. He often did extension work then.

Gigi went out into the playground and sat under the twisted gum tree by the fence to eat her banana. In the middle of the playground the boys played marbles, and the few younger girls pulled out their elastics. Gigi took out her pen and paper and started writing Lily a letter.

'How is Sydney? I miss you already. Next summer . . .'

The bell rang and all the students lined up again. As they entered the classroom, Sam hung back. He was always the first in. Gigi looked over her shoulder. What was going on?

Miss Smith settled everyone down, and still Sam didn't take his place. Five minutes into the lesson – Shakespeare for the older kids like Gigi, *The Wind in the Willows* for the younger ones – Sam came back inside.

With Costas walking behind him.

Gigi stared at them as they walked to the front of the room.

'Eyes forward, class.' Miss Smith's call for attention wasn't necessary. Everyone's eyes were already fixed on the newcomer. 'We have a new student. This is Costas Tinellis.'

Quiet giggles reverberated around the room.

'Costas and his family are new to the area. I hope you will all make him feel welcome. Sam will be able to show you the ropes.'

The only spare seat was beside Gigi and Sam showed Costas to his place.

Gigi could hear whispers and everyone was staring at the new boy. They didn't often get new kids at the school, so it wasn't altogether unusual that Costas' arrival would create interest.

Miss Smith banged the yard-long ruler on the chalkboard, silencing everyone, and went back to teaching.

Costas sat tall and proud, eyes on the teacher. Everyone else's eyes were on him.

At lunchtime, Gigi sat in her customary spot under her tree, eating her cheese sandwich.

The form five and six boys gathered near the water tank and spoke in hushed tones. When Costas emerged from the classroom, they turned their backs to him. He approached Sam, his supposed helper, and Sam pretended not to see or hear him.

For the briefest of moments, Costas' shoulders dipped, but he righted himself quickly and looked around the playground for a place to sit down. As he headed towards the seesaw that no one really used anymore, the pack of boys turned as one.

Todd, the youngest in the group, was urged to the head of the pack by the others and caught up with Costas first. Ever so deftly, in a movement Gigi nearly didn't see, he put his right foot out and Costas went crashing into the dirt, his lunch spilling out onto the ground.

'Sorry.' Todd smirked. 'Let me help you up.' He reached out his hand.

No. Gigi stood up. She'd seen Todd use this trick before. But before she could get to the other side of the playground, Costas had taken Todd's hand.

He nearly made it to standing before Todd loosened his grip, sending Costas backside first into the dust.

'Stay in the dirt where you belong, you dirty wog,' Todd growled.

The pack of boys moved away, stomping Costas' lunch into the ground. They knew not to push things too far, though. If they actually hurt Costas, Miss Smith would know and she'd have to intervene.

Gigi walked up to Costas as he hauled himself to standing, brushing the dirt off his shirt and trousers.

'Are you okay?' Gigi asked.

'Yes. Thank you.' Costas' eyes remained downcast.

'They're just trying to let you know who's on top. Thugs, the lot of them.'

Costas smiled, and Gigi's breath caught in her throat. 'I think we both know there's more to it than that. But thank you.' He looked Gigi in the eye, and she had no response. She simply handed him the half of her cheese sandwich she hadn't eaten yet.

The bell rang, and everyone lined up as if nothing had happened. Gigi wanted to pull Miss Smith aside, dob on terrible Todd and his awful gang. But she knew that would only make things worse.

When she was in first form, Todd and his cretins had put a worm in her sandwich. After she'd dobbed on them, they spent two weeks putting all sorts of things in her schoolbag – a handful of dead cockroaches, a rotting dog bone, a decapitated rat. Miss Smith had known about all of it, but had done nothing. The son of the local sergeant, Todd Broadbent could get away with just about anything.

Gigi had learned rather quickly that one had to stand up for oneself.

So she went into the classroom, took her seat, and said nothing.

'Costas? Did anything happen at lunchtime?' Miss Smith asked him when she saw the state of his uniform.

'No, ma'am.' He cast his eyes down. 'I fell over one of the benches.'

Miss Smith raised an eyebrow, but took it no further.

Gigi let out a slow breath of relief.

In the afternoon heat Gigi walked home, avoiding the main street. Todd and his gang would be at the milk bar and she really didn't feel like having to deal with them. On their own, none of them were too bad, she supposed. It was when they got together that they seemed to forget how to be . . . human.

'Wait up,' Costas called from behind her as she turned the corner into his street.

'Hi,' she said, as he fell into step beside her.

'Thank you for today, Virginia.'

'I didn't do anything.' She kicked the footpath. 'I wish I'd stood up to them.'

Costas stopped and Gigi turned to face him. 'Discretion is the better part of valour,' he said.

'Shakespeare?' Gigi asked.

'Yes. And you did plenty. You showed me kindness. Which is more than most people do.'

'I take it this isn't the first encounter you've had with idiots like Todd?'

He cocked his head to the side. 'I may have lived in this country most of my life, but I'm still an outsider.'

'Well, that's stupid. The outsider bit.'

He shrugged.

'You can sit with me tomorrow at lunch, if you like. Safety in numbers.' She looked into his dark eyes and forgot, just for a moment, her own name.

'Thank you. But that will just make you a target, too.'

Gigi laughed.

'What?'

'I learned a few years back how to deal with that pack of animals. When your dad owns a fishing boat, there's all manner of ways to exact revenge.' She smirked. 'They don't come near me anymore.' Not since she'd filled Sam's schoolbag with fish guts and hooked Darren's trousers to his seat with a rusty old lure one day at the milk bar so that when he got up they tore. Right in front of everyone. Granted, that was a few years ago, right after the decapitated rat incident, when Gigi still had the advantage of height over them. Before they started to grow and fill out and change from boys to young men. But now, other than some harmless insults every few months to remind her of her place in the food chain, they pretty much left her alone.

She wasn't sure they'd give up on Costas so lightly, though, and if she could help simply by association, she was happy to.

'I think maybe I wouldn't be surprised by that.' Costas peeled off to the side to head into his yard, where his mum was working under a broad-brimmed hat.

'Hello, Mrs Tinellis,' Gigi called out and waved. 'I go to school with Costas.'

Mrs Tinellis shouted something back in Greek. Gigi had no idea what she was saying, but she wasn't sure it was a polite hello, judging by the tone and gesturing. But she'd never met any Greeks before, so perhaps she was being greeted warmly.

Perhaps.

Costas waved his farewell and Gigi skipped the rest of the way home.

The next day at lunch, Costas sat near the seesaw. Not with Gigi, despite her invitation, but within sight of her. The boys stared at him across the yard, but left him alone. Maybe some of them had done some growing up over the summer and yesterday was just a glitch. It was about time.

That afternoon Todd separated himself from the herd and walked with Gigi a little way home.

'So, Gilbert. How was your holiday?'

She'd known Todd all her life and he'd never once asked her about her holiday. 'Um. Okay. I guess.'

'I saw you jetty-jumping that day. It looked like fun.'

'It was.' *What is going on?*

'Maybe one day we could do it together. I mean, get a group of us together and stuff.'

Gigi dropped her schoolbag and Todd picked it up.

'There you go.' He handed it to her. 'Anyway, I'll see you tomorrow.' His cheeks had turned red.

Is this what happened to boys when they matured? They turned into someone else? Todd – sweet and charming? Well, that was just plain confusing.

Gigi turned down the road. She liked it better when boys were enemies and she knew what to expect from them.

One cold day in June, as Gigi ate her lunch, Sam spat on the ground next to Costas as he passed him. Darren did too. Todd stood there, hesitated and then followed suit. Gigi abandoned her spot under the twisted gum tree and plonked herself down next to Costas.

'What are you doing?' he whispered, as eyes turned their way and hands were raised to hide flapping lips.

Gigi squared her shoulders and shot a look at the gang of boys across the playground. They remained where they were, unmoved, but Gigi could see their expressions. Todd was shocked. Darren confused. Sam angry.

As the long silence was broken by the bell, Gigi stood up, feeling rather pleased with herself.

After school, she was on blackboard duty. Apparently, telling Miss Smith that it would be a nice change to look at history from the side of both the victors – or oppressors, as they rightly should be called – *and* the losers was not appropriate. Maybe it was the phrase 'for a change'. Or the choice to throw 'oppressors' into the sentence. Whatever it was, she was stuck beating chalk dust out of the dusters and washing down the board.

The winter sun hung low in the sky as she left school, dragging her schoolbag behind her. The streets were nearly empty; a storm was coming in. She stopped by the milk bar and bought a chocolate milkshake and ambled home.

A block from the school, which sat at the northernmost part of town, she heard a clanging sound behind her. She turned around to see Sam hitting an empty can with a stick. He was alone. And for some reason that frightened her more than if he'd had his gang backing him up.

'Are you in love with that wog?' Sam sneered, closing the gap between them. 'Off to see your wog boyfriend, then?'

'Go away, Sam.' She wouldn't let him hear the nerves in her voice. She just wouldn't.

'Why? What are you going to do about it?' He stood an inch away from her but she wouldn't back down.

'Nothing. You're not worth my energy.' She put her hands on her hips.

Oh shit. She should run. But she couldn't. Firstly, everyone knew that bullies only understood strength. Secondly, her legs felt like they were made of jelly. Heavy jelly. And she knew they wouldn't actually obey her command to get out of there.

From behind a nearby tree, Todd emerged. 'What's going on?' He put his hand on Sam's shoulder.

'I was just asking Gigi about her wog boyfriend.'

'Nah, Gilbert's just being polite.' Todd looked at Gigi. 'Isn't that right?'

'I don't have to explain myself to you.'

'Ha.' Sam sniggered. 'That's what you get for sticking up for Fish-Girl.'

'I thought you were a mate, Todd.' Darren appeared. Gigi hadn't seen him coming. 'One of us.'

Gigi had to find a way to get out of there.

'Of course I'm one of you.' Todd looked to Gigi and then back to Sam. 'Go home, Gilbert. Now,' he barked.

Gigi turned and ran.

She ran so fast she took the corner too sharp and fell onto the edge of the gutter. She took a great big gash out of her shin, but she got back up and kept hobbling.

Around the next block she stopped and closed her eyes. When she opened them again, Costas was standing in front of her. She looked around. She'd stopped in the middle of the road, right outside his house.

'Come with me.' He led her inside.

A man, she assumed Mr Tinellis, came into the living room, took one look at Gigi's leg and disappeared, returning shortly after with a bag full of gauze and iodine and bandages.

He tended Gigi's leg with a gentle touch – cleaned the wound, disinfected it, bandaged it up.

'Thank you.' Her voice was weak.

Mr Tinellis squeezed her hand.

'He was a doctor. Back home,' Costas said as he helped his dad clear away the bloody bits of cotton wool. 'After the war, their village was in ruins. Then the civil war hit Greece. They lost everything. We came out here once the civil war finished. Back in 1949. But he isn't allowed to be a doctor here.'

Gigi nodded, as if she understood what Costas was saying. Civil war? What civil war? His dad was a doctor? But wasn't?

Ouch. The pain was too much.

She was about to stand up when Costas' mum burst into the room. Her arms were flailing about, words coming out of her mouth at an alarming pace.

Costas spoke to her in Greek. His voice was calm, as if he was explaining something to her. Gigi suspected Mrs Tinellis wasn't all that keen on his explanation.

After some more gentle words from Costas, Mrs Tinellis stood quiet. She looked at Gigi and said a broken 'Thank you', before bowing and leaving the room.

'Why is she thanking me?' Gigi looked to Costas.

'I was telling her who you are. I told her about today. Am I right in guessing this is the fallout?' He pointed to her leg.

She looked at the floor and nodded. 'They didn't do it to me. I slipped when I was running away. Sam just frightened me, is all. And then Darren turned up. And then I ran.' She pushed her hands onto her hips and raised her gaze. 'Todd was nice. At first. Then he wasn't.'

Costas was looking at her with the kindest expression she'd ever seen. 'You are one in a million, Virginia. Can I help you home?'

'No. I think I'm okay. Please thank your dad again for me.'

Staring up at the night sky through her tiny window, Gigi lay in bed that night unable to sleep. She didn't *think* the boys would actually hurt her. They were just trying to scare her. It had worked. And she hated herself for it, because that meant they had won.

And what about Todd? Had he actually saved her? No, that couldn't be right.

Gigi was confused. Life was taking turns all over the place and she couldn't keep up. First, the whole Lily and Richard thing. Now Todd was saving her from bullies, sort of. And every time she spoke with Costas, a tingle tickled her spine.

She threw her arms above her head and longed to be ten again. Things were simple when she was ten.

The school year dragged on and everyone fell into a sort of routine. Gigi sat with Costas at lunch throughout winter, and once a week Sam or Darren would walk past them and make some unsavoury comment about Costas' stinky lunch, then knock it into the dirt. But never more than that. As the warmth of spring pushed the colder days aside, Todd would watch and mock with his mates, his glare hardening with every week.

'Would you like to try it?' Costas held out his lunch to Gigi one day in October when it was clear no one was coming past to ruin things.

'What it is?'

'Lamb kofta.' He held out the meat shaped a little bit like a sausage.

Gigi took a bite. It was delicious. She swapped her cheese sandwich for it and devoured the whole thing.

After school, they walked along the beach together. 'Have you ever fished off the rocks?' she asked, as they headed north along the sand.

'Nope. Never fished.'

'Wait here.' Gigi ran to the fishing shack and grabbed a couple of rods.

When they got to the rock pools, Gigi showed Costas how to bait his hook.

'You're very clever, Virginia.' He seemed genuinely impressed.

'It's just fishing.'

They threw their lines in, and within seconds Costas' was being pulled down. Gigi showed him how to reel it in.

On his hook was a large snapper.

'Not bad for your first time.' Gigi was a little jealous, to be honest, but the feeling soon dissipated at the look of joy on Costas' face. 'I'll show you how to clean it up and you can take it home for dinner.'

At the fishing shack she stepped Costas through scaling and gutting the fish. It wasn't a job she ever enjoyed, more something you got on with. She was used to the smell by now, but she could tell by the look on Costas' face that he was having trouble with it.

'I know it isn't a pleasant aroma,' she said. 'But even fish guts can come in handy every now and then.' She told him about the guts-in-the-schoolbag incident.

'You didn't!'

She gave a sly grin.

He bent over laughing. 'I wish I'd seen that.' He waved the fish's insides in the air.

'Don't forget the high-pitched scream.' She imitated the sound that had come out of Sam's throat when he'd discovered the stinky mess in his bag.

They both doubled over until tears fell down their cheeks. Gigi's stomach ached.

'Remind me never to get on your bad side, then, Miss Virginia.' Costas threw the guts away and they finished cleaning the fish.

Outside the shack, Gigi said goodbye.

'Thank you, Virginia. This has been the best afternoon I've had since moving to the Bay.'

'Really?'

'Even with the smell.' He smiled.

'Do you want to go digging for crabs tomorrow?' Gigi asked.

He nodded. 'That sounds like fun.' Costas headed home, catch in his hand.

Gigi stayed behind to meet Ian. She'd convinced him to teach her some boxing moves, having a session with him every time he and her dad came back in from a long-haul fishing trip. Of course she told him it was for fitness. Of course he didn't believe her, but he didn't say anything. If anyone knew her, it was him.

Ian, who was four years older than Gigi, had been a part of her family's life for as long as she could remember. They'd virtually grown up together. Though when he was fourteen he had basically ignored her for two years. Which was fine by her as he'd been smelly and generally not very nice for those two years. When he finished school two years ago, he started working for her dad on the boat full-time.

Gigi was glad Dad had Ian to help him. She didn't like the idea of Dad out at sea for long stretches on his own.

After their boxing session, Ian turned to her, concern across his face. 'Squirt, if anyone's, you know, bothering you, you'd tell me, right?'

'Yeah.'

He took her by the shoulders. 'Seriously. No one messes with my little sister.'

Gigi really liked it when he referred to her as his sister. Which he didn't do nearly often enough.

She assured him she was perfectly fine, and he let it slide. Gigi didn't think the boys would ever actually come after her. But she also wasn't going to take any chances.

On a nondescript day in November, when the sun had burned off the morning cloud and the afternoon heat was beating down on her as she walked home from school, Gigi stopped by Costas' house. She hadn't seen him for a few days and was worried.

What if one of the boys had escalated things?

She walked past the large vegetable gardens that now bore cucumber and peas in large quantities. There was another plant growing that she didn't recognise – a small green bush with tiny leaves that grew in pairs opposite each other. She touched the leaves and as she pulled her hand away the most delicious whiff met her nose. She sniffed her fingers, then the plant. It was that same aroma from the first time she'd met Costas outside his place. What was the name of that dish? Keftikis? Klefto? Something with lamb.

She walked up to the front door and raised her hand. Drawing in a deep breath, she tapped the wooden frame lightly.

Mrs Tinellis answered and didn't look too thrilled when she opened the door and saw Gigi standing there.

'Good afternoon,' Gigi said, not knowing how much English, if any, Costas' mother understood. 'I just wanted to check on Costas, as he hasn't been at school. Is he okay?'

Mrs Tinellis shut the door.

Gigi stood there, not sure whether to wait or leave. She heard voices inside. Raised voices. The only word she could pick out from the commotion was 'xenos'. It was said numerous times.

As the voices raged on, Gigi started to rock back and forth. *No. You shouldn't be here.* She turned and walked up the path.

'Virginia. Wait.' Costas stepped up behind her. 'Sorry.' His hand went to his stomach, a grimace of pain flashing across his face before composure returned.

Gigi smiled at her friend and saw his mother standing at the window with the curtain pulled back, watching them.

'I just wanted to check on you. You haven't been at school.'

'I've been sick. Flu. I'm sorry you worried about me.'

Gigi wasn't sure she believed him. 'Are you feeling better now?' She'd never had flu herself. Not proper flu. Did you get stomach cramps with flu?

'Yes. Thank you. Much better.'

'When will you be back at school?' Gigi knew – well, Lily had told her – that you shouldn't let a boy know you were keen; they liked to figure that out themselves, and besides, you didn't want to come across as a hussy. But she missed the quiet, gentle company of her friend.

'Next week.'

A noise from inside rang out into the evening.

'Does your mother not like me?' Gigi asked.

Costas shook his head. 'It's not you. She doesn't know you. And she knows you've been a good friend. She's just . . . a little . . . wary of foreigners.'

'Xenos?'

'You heard? Sorry. That wasn't very nice.' He looked at his feet. 'Ma just needs time. To get to know you. To get used to this place. They haven't had it easy since they came to Australia.' His voice was heavy with sorrow.

Gigi understood. Look what Costas had to put up with at school.

'Okay.' She smiled. 'I'll see you next week.'

On Monday, Costas didn't sit with Gigi at lunch. Or Tuesday. He was polite. As always. But the distance was undeniable. When she asked him about it, he simply explained it away as trying to get to know the other kids, trying to fit in more.

Except he didn't speak to any of the other kids.

At the end of the week Gigi sat with a pen and paper on the swing her dad had hung from a large gum tree up the back of the caravan park. In just a month, the park would be full of vans and tents and her peaceful perch would be overrun with pesky little kids. It was only a month now till Lily was back and there was so much to say. She scribbled down all her news – or what accounted for news around here, which was school, milkshakes, and boxing lessons (about which Lily had expressed her horror in her last letter) – and told her how much she couldn't wait for the summer holidays to start. Writing to Lily once a month always made her feel better. Then she went inside and helped Mum prepare dinner.

With the days getting longer, it was still light by the time they'd finished eating and Gigi excused herself from the table, promising to do the washing-up after a quick walk.

'I'll get them tonight, squirt,' Ian said. At some point in the last few years he'd taken to joining them for supper every Friday night he and Dad weren't out on the boat.

Gigi gave him a quick hug and headed off into the hills. She climbed till she got to her favourite spot among the banksias and lowered herself into the long grass. The setting sun cast long shadows down the hill and bathed the ocean below in a soft pink glow.

A small group of surfers gathered at the north end of the beach, where the waves broke best. Gigi recognised Ian among them, his height making him easy to spot.

Mum must have let him off the hook for the washing-up. She always did let him get away with anything. The son she never had, Gigi supposed.

It wouldn't be long now till the handful of locals out for a sunset surf became a horde of tourists splashing in the waves, dropping their ice-cream scoops into the water – Gigi's sleepy little town disrupted for the holidays. But that also meant the return of Lily.

Gigi lay back in the grass and looked up to the rising moon, dreaming of all the fun summer would bring.

Eight

*L*aura spent three mornings helping Virginia in the shack, mostly cleaning and dusting and tidying. The woman wasn't much of a conversationalist, but if Laura had learned anything during her time as a reporter, those who were hiding something usually weren't.

On the third day Laura suggested they have lunch together on the deck before she headed off.

With a raised eyebrow, Virginia agreed.

'I don't know how you get any work done in there.' Laura pointed behind her shoulder to the shack. 'When this is right at your feet.' She looked out to the ocean.

Virginia smiled, for the first time that Laura had seen. At least, the first genuine smile.

'Confession time. Some days I do just sit out here and stare into the sea. Especially in winter.'

Laura could certainly understand that. 'Have you lived here all your life?'

Virginia's expression hardened. 'Yes. What about you? You're from Sydney, aren't you? Been there all your life?'

'Yep. I don't have views like this where I am, though.'

'I dare say.' Virginia leaned back in her chair.

'This really is very peaceful.'

'Well, not for long. The Banksia Bee Festival starts in three days and then you'll see this place in a whole new light.'

'The what now?' A memory of something Charlotte had said on the bus her first day here teased her mind.

'The Banksia Bee Festival. Every autumn, the Bay celebrates the honey industry we have in these parts. Did you know we had a honey industry? It's very big. The festival.'

Surely it couldn't get that busy.

'Shame you didn't bring your family. Kids love the festival.'

Laura stared out to the ocean. 'Oh. It's just me.'

Virginia looked at her.

'Not married.' Laura held up her left hand, showing no ring.

'Any other family?'

'Dad died when I was young. Mum's been kind of in and out of my life since then. Mostly out.'

'I'm sorry, dear.'

Laura couldn't believe she'd told Virginia that. Her mother's absence had always been a topic she didn't like to talk about. At least she hadn't slipped up and said anything about Lillian. 'It's kind of nice having some time to myself, away from the office.' And that was the truth.

'Well, make the most of it. This place will be overrun before you know it.'

Laura huffed.

'Ah, you don't believe me. You'll see.'

A mischievous look crossed Virginia's face, but she said no more.

Seriously? How big could a honey festival be in a town no one had heard of?

'Famous last words' came to mind as Laura walked through the packed main street of Banksia Bay three days later.

Paper beehive lanterns were strung from every lamppost and power pole, and lining both sides of the street were marquees showing off local wares, all with some sort of bee theme – cheeses infused with honey, honey-scented candles, paintings of bees, honeycomb-shaped jewellery, hexagonal chopping boards made of local wood, and jars and jars of honey.

Laura wandered the stalls, the sweet aroma filling her nose as she walked. She snaked her way through the throngs of people, smiling at the children wearing bee antenna headbands.

In one tent, Kaftan bustled about between racks of loose flowing dresses, which had sequins and beads sewn around the neckline to look like tiny bees.

'Good morning. Laura, isn't it?' She waved, and Laura stopped to say hello.

'Yes. Hi.'

'Welcome to your first Bee Festival.' She spread her arms out wide.

'Thank you, um . . .'

'Trish. Sorry. We met on the Bodhi Bus.'

'I remember. This is quite something.' Laura indicated the festivities behind her.

'Isn't it?'

Three people walked into the tent.

'Customers.' Trish sashayed forward. 'Will we see you at the bar-bee-cue tonight?' She accentuated the middle of the word.

Laura nodded, not sure what Trish was talking about. She left the tent and was jostled by a family carrying yellow and black striped bags, stuffed full of goodies.

Off to the side was a tent selling cold drinks and Laura ordered a honeycomb milkshake. She took a moment to sit and watch the passing crowd from within the relative quiet of the tent.

Children skipped by with faces painted, either done up as actual bees, or with bee motifs on their cheeks. Even some adults were sporting face paint.

A child with a bee mask bounced up to her.

'Hello,' Laura said.

The boy removed his mask. 'Hi.' Aiden's sweet face stared back at her.

Heath came in after him. 'I told you not to run off,' he reproached Aiden, but there was only gentleness in his tone. 'Hey, Laura. Enjoying the festival?'

'Yes. It's different.'

'Ah, but different good, or different bad?' He pulled a face.

'Good, I think. I'm not sure I understand it, though.'

Aiden pulled Heath's arm.

'Okay, buddy. We're going.' He looked at Laura. 'Have you been down to the beach?'

'Not yet.'

'There's stuff for the kids down there. Walk with me, and I'll try to enlighten you about the festival.'

On the beach a huge obstacle course stretched a hundred metres down the sand, away from the jetty. Aiden ran through the blow-up beehive entrance, waving to Heath as he threw himself onto the honeycomb-shaped climbing wall.

'Is Charlotte here?' Laura asked, looking around.

Heath shook his head. 'She had to work. This is the first

festival she's ever missed. I'll buy her one of those giant blocks of chocolate-covered honeycomb to ease her disappointment.'

Laura had seen that tent. She had no idea how anyone would ever be able to get through that much chocolate honeycomb, but plenty of people were buying the huge chunks of confectionary to try.

'She's always had a sweet tooth,' Heath said.

'I've never seen this much honey-ness in one place before.'

'Ah. And you probably never will. It's Banksia Bay's only claim to fame, this festival. It started in the seventies. A local apiarist realised that because the banksias around here bloom best in autumn, his bees had access to good nectar all year round. Then a lot of the dairy farmers got on board, caring for their own hives, and we became one of the biggest honey-producing areas in the country.'

Not once in Laura's life had she ever wondered where her honey came from. Actually, she never gave much thought at all to where any of her food came from.

'A couple of local guys,' continued Heath, 'started the festival back when I was a kid, and now that "artisanal" is back in fashion, the festival has become huge.'

Laura couldn't argue about the size of the crowd that had invaded the town. She wondered why the festival hadn't come up in her Google search. Now there was a missed opportunity.

Aiden waved to them from the top of the climbing wall and Ian walked by, camera in hand, taking photos of the festivities.

'Lovely day for it.' He stopped in front of Heath and Laura, and took their photo.

Laura put her hands up in front of her face.

'It's okay. Ian's a bit of a professional amateur with that thing. Only time he's without his camera is when he's in the water. Some of his photos will end up in the local paper. But most will go into his studio.'

His studio? Laura's mind began to tick over.

'Hey, you should check it out some day. It might help with your story.'

'What's Ian's last name?'

'Holland. But he's not famous or anything.'

Ian Holland. One of the photographers from *Banksia Bay Bush Tracks*? Laura nearly fell over.

She had to stop herself from demanding that Heath take her there right now.

'How long has he been at it?' she asked, ensuring her voice stayed neutral.

'Um, I'm not sure. Forever, I think.'

A tiny speck of hope crept into Laura's heart. She watched Ian pick out his next subject, a family eating honeycomb fairy floss. How could she snaffle an invite to his studio?

Aiden came running towards them. 'Can we go see the bees?' He pulled on Heath's arm.

At the end of the beach one of the local apiarists had set up a real live hive with real live bees, and was demonstrating how he extracted the honey. Aiden watched on, fascinated. So did Laura.

As the sun began to sink low in the sky, they headed past the obstacle course towards the shack, and the most delicious aroma wafted up the beach.

Along the jetty, a line of barbecues had been set up, and the sizzle of cooking meat and vegetables made Laura's stomach growl. Steak, sausages, fish, lamb, corn on the cob – every food that could be barbecued was being grilled.

Heath got himself and Aiden some steak and Laura tried the lemon honey fish, which melted in her mouth.

'You know,' Laura said as they finished their dinner, 'this could be so much more.'

'What do you mean?' Heath looked into her eyes.

'There are a lot of talented people here. The food, the art and craft – and, as you said, artisanal anything is back in fashion. This could be a real draw for the area. Outside of the festival, I mean.'

Heath's face lit up. 'I think we need to talk about this some more.'

Aiden took off down the jetty, running towards the shack. Heath and Laura followed, and as they walked through the crowd they were pressed together. Their hands touched, heat shooting through Laura. Heath looked down and his eyes bored into her.

Laura stepped to the side. What did he think he was doing? Had he forgotten he was married? No wonder Charlotte didn't like her. The woman's instinct had been right. Laura should have known. There was a universal truth about men and it wasn't what Jane Austen claimed, all that fortune and needing a wife nonsense. No. The universal truth was that they were all jerks who, given the chance, would cheat.

They reached the shack and Virginia was serving coffees. She looked busy, so Laura excused herself and went to see if she could help.

Fifteen mugs of caffeine later, Virginia turned off the coffee machine.

'Thank you, dear, for helping. You're a good girl.'

'It's fine.'

Laura started to clean up. As she bent over to pick up the bag of rubbish she'd dropped, her necklace popped out from under her shirt and she quickly put it back in. She heard Virginia clear her throat, but when she looked up she saw her on the sofa reading to Aiden. Heath was busy cleaning the coffee machine.

Laura said goodnight and took her leave. She sped home, glad to be out of there. Away from scrutinising eyes.

Away from Heath.

Nine

As soon as Heath and Aiden left, Virginia jumped off the sofa and closed up the shack.

She'd nearly blown it. Nearly let out a scream when she saw the pendant around Laura's neck.

All doubt was gone now.

Laura was here for her. To destroy her. How could this be?

A knock on the shack door made her jump.

'Need any help in there, squirt?' Ian let himself in.

The last thing Virginia needed was that old codger under her feet. 'I think I've got it all under control.'

'Another successful festival.' Ian lowered himself into the armchair.

Virginia knew what that meant, so she poured him a glass of beer from the stash she kept hidden at the back of the fridge.

'You look like you could do with one too,' he said.

He wasn't wrong. Virginia poured herself a glass and sat opposite him on the sofa. The silence between them was comfortable

and comforting. Ian had always been there in her life. A friend.
A brother. A constant.

'I saw Laura helping you again today.' He took a long sip of
beer.

A pest.

She simply nodded. Did he see it in her too? The resemblance?
Did he even remember Lily?

'Funny how life can throw twists at you.' He looked into the
distance.

Virginia sat up straight. 'What do you mean?'

He turned back to her. 'I just mean that she's a stranger, but
right when you need help, she happens to turn up. One of life's
funny coincidences . . .' His voice trailed off.

This had to end. Now. Ian may not be known for his insight.
Or intellect. But he could easily bumble his way into a conversation
Virginia wanted no part of. He knew her well, and if this continued
it wouldn't take long for him to figure something was up.

'I hear Farmer Clarke is selling up.' Virginia would try anything.

'I heard.' His eyes didn't leave hers. This was getting unnerving. She stood up and pretended to busy herself behind the counter.

When Ian finished his beer he walked over to her.

'Goodnight, squirt.' He raised his hand and she ducked her
head, expecting him to try to ruffle her hair.

Instead, he hugged her. He hadn't done that since . . .

She hustled him out of the shack with a goodnight and the
excuse of exhaustion.

Once he'd left, Virginia rearranged the cushions on the sofa
and wiped down the coffee machine again, her hands shaking the
whole time. She paced back and forth. She picked up the phone to
call Yvonne, then put it back down again.

Today was a busy day for her friend, running visitors back and forth between the Bay and Ocean Heights from dawn till, well, actually, she was probably still driving, taking the last of the revellers back to their hotels.

She wouldn't trouble Yvonne with this tonight. Lord knows she'd burdened that woman with too much for too long. Telling her about the pendant tonight would achieve nothing.

It could wait till tomorrow. Then she'd ask Yvonne if she could look up Laura Hamilton on that inter-spider-web thing. See what they could find out about her.

In the meantime, Virginia did a sweep of the shack to make sure there was no more incriminating evidence that could lead Laura to anything in her past. No photos, no local histories, no knick-knacks that could lead her to Gigi.

Virginia's past was most definitely here, and she needed to ensure Laura didn't find another piece of it.

December 1962

As the sun began to rise, the crunching of gravel on the road into the caravan park heralded the arrival of the first tourists of the season. Gigi jumped out of bed and pulled on her overalls, tied her ridiculously untamed blonde curls into a messy ponytail, and ran out the front door of the cabin. She wasn't excited about having to help her mum book visitors in – what sixteen-year-old would be thrilled about showing strangers to their sites, helping people who clearly didn't go camping often peg their tents correctly, unblocking the communal loos when some idiot tried to stuff too much toilet paper down the S-bend, or being called on to kill a huntsman spider who'd been innocently minding his own business up in the corner of the laundry block when the city slicker screamed blue murder at the sight of it?

But it was a distraction, at least, something to keep her busy – and it certainly did keep her busy – until teatime.

Teatime, when Lily would arrive.

As the midday sun beat down from its height in the clear summer sky, the gentleman from site number seven couldn't figure out how to use the washing machine and called on Gigi to help. It was a pretty basic twin tub, but the way he looked at it, Gigi wondered if he'd ever even set foot in a laundry before. Really, this was the last thing she wanted to do right now. She had at least four chores to do for Mum this afternoon before she could head off to see if Lily had arrived yet. What kind of adult couldn't figure out how to use a washing machine?

'Elaine always did the washing,' the man said, looking at Gigi with such sadness that she couldn't help but feel guilty for her uncharitable thoughts. 'Six months she's been gone. We'd always wanted to go round Australia in the van. Her dying wish was that I go ahead and do it. "Arthur," she said to me, "Arthur, you go explore this great big land." Oh, she was a peach.' He raised his gaze to the sky.

Gigi took him by his shaking hand and led him over to the machine. Slowly, simply, she instructed him on the mysterious ways of the twin tub. And she stayed with him to show him how to spin the clothes to get some of the water out.

Arthur thanked Gigi for her help and bade her farewell, but she couldn't just leave him there with a basket of damp clothes, even if it was only a few shirts. He'd probably never hung clothes out on a line either.

She showed him where the Hills hoist was and helped him peg up his laundry. Arthur insisted Gigi had done more than enough but she told him she had nothing better to do and pegged away.

'You might just be a peach, too.' Arthur patted her on the back.

Gigi raced through her remaining jobs at breakneck speed and by four her mum said she could clock off.

Back in the family cabin, she threw off her dirty overalls and changed into a slightly less worn pair. Then she ran a brush through her hair and headed off to the rental house. As she passed Costas' home, she slowed down, hoping he might be in the garden with his mother. But there was no sign of him. No sign of anyone. Had they gone away for the holidays?

He'd mostly ignored her for the last few weeks of school, though she did catch him once or twice glancing in her direction when he thought she wasn't looking. She was so confused by his behaviour. It made no sense. Boys made no sense.

She missed him terribly, though. School was bearable when he sat beside her, when they shared lunch. When he pretended that she didn't exist, school became even more of a drudgery. Despite their recent lack of communication, surely he would have told her if he was going somewhere for the summer.

The only way to know for sure was to stop by every day. Luckily, Costas' house was on the way to Lily's, sort of – at least, if she took a certain detour – so keeping an eye out for his return would be easy enough.

As Gigi wound her way through town, she started humming a tune by that new band Ian was obsessed with. The Beach Brothers, or Boys, or whatever they called themselves. He was always singing their songs at the top of his lungs. She had no idea what song she was humming. Or if it even was a tune, per se, and not some random amalgamation of the music that she simply couldn't get out of her head. That Ian had so much to answer for.

Still, it was a pleasant enough accompaniment as she walked – well, skipped was more like it – to go and see her best friend.

The Woodhouses' car wasn't in the driveway when Gigi reached the holiday house and her heart sank. The sun was low enough in the sky now. Lily should be here already.

There was a small stump along the path that lead to the house – an old gum tree Dad had cut down years ago – and Gigi sat herself down on it and waited.

And waited.

It was well and truly dark before the headlights of the blue EK Holden lit up the hydrangeas that lined the driveway. Gigi jumped off the stump and smoothed her overalls down. Pointless, she knew. But she also knew Mrs Woodhouse wasn't exactly enamoured of her, and she always made Gigi nervous.

Lily flung open the door of the car as her father slowed it to a stop, and she ran over and threw her arms around Gigi.

'Oh, you wouldn't believe the traffic heading out of Sydney. The whole city must have decided on an exodus. I thought we'd never get here.'

'Lillian, please.' Mrs Woodhouse frowned at the girls. 'Show some decorum.'

'Sorry, Mother.' Lily pulled herself away from Gigi and straightened her monogrammed shirtwaist dress. 'Would it be all right, Mother, if Gigi and I take a short walk, just to catch up? I really could do with stretching my legs after such a long drive.'

Mrs Woodhouse started shaking her head, but Senator Woodhouse interjected. 'Just a short one, Lily-pilly.' He stroked her hair and looked at her fondly.

'Thank you, Daddy.' She kissed him on the cheek.

Gigi grabbed Lily's hand and yanked her down the path, Mrs Woodhouse's words floating on the air behind them. 'Really, Michael. You'd let that girl get away with murder . . .'

Once on the beach, the girls sat in the sand, just out of reach of the receding tide.

'Oh, it's so good to see you again.' Gigi linked her arm with Lily's and told her all about the last few weeks since she'd written. Not that there was much to tell.

'He sounds lonely,' Lily said, when Gigi told her about Arthur and the washing machine.

'What about you?' Gigi turned to her. 'What's been happening in your life?'

Lily was no longer at school, at least not regular school. Her mother had enrolled her in something called June Dally Whatsit.

'Dally-Watkins,' Lily corrected Gigi when she repeated the name with a sharp intake of breath.

It sounded positively awful: walking straight, speaking well, sitting just the right way, and a whole lot of other really stuffy-sounding things. 'Deportment' was the word Lily used. Deportment didn't sound anything like fun to Gigi. Thank goodness they had the summer to knock some of that polished dullness out of Lily and remind her what it was like to be free and enjoy life. She started making a list of activities in her head – antidotes to the Miss June Dally-What-a-pain poison – that would unleash the Lily she knew was inside.

'Stop screwing up your face, Gigi. You're acting like I'm describing military school.'

Wasn't she? Only this one was wrapped in a perfect pink bow.

'Okay. Sorry. There must be something else going on in your life?'

Gigi regretted prompting her friend the moment Lily mentioned Richard's name, because once she started, she simply didn't stop. Richard this, Richard that. Blah, blah, blah. Calling on her for dinner. Taking her to university social events. Apparently, he was the brightest medical student ever to walk the halls of Sydney University.

Blah, blah, blah.

'It's been such a wonderful few months. Mother thinks he's a real catch, and now that I'm eighteen he's allowed to court me properly. Daddy's already talking about him joining the party. They always need intelligent young men in politics, you know. He's holidaying here this summer too. I think they arrived last night. I can't wait to see him again.'

Gigi could hear the giddiness in Lily's voice. She didn't need to look over to see the dreamy expression that was plastered across her face. And she knew what Lily's parents were thinking too, especially with sending Lily to finishing school – 'Dr and Mrs Richard Prescott', their daughter married off appropriately. Well, not yet. Adulthood be damned. At least for one more summer.

'Lily, will you promise me something?'

Lily rose up on her elbows. 'Anything.'

'That you'll keep coming back here for summer. Every year. Even as we get older and start our grown-up lives.'

'Of course.' Lily took her hand. 'You're like a sister to me, Gigi. My summer sister. Nothing can change that.'

Gigi swallowed the lump in her throat. 'Even if you go off and marry Richard and have ten babies. You'll still come back, right?'

Lily giggled.

'Lily?'

'Don't be silly, Gigi. You know I will.' She hugged her friend. 'I'd better get back before Mother sends out a search party.' She jumped up and ran down the beach.

Gigi watched her friend go, holding on to hope.

———

The first few weeks of summer holidays rolled by in a haze of heat, saltwater swims and ice-cream from the parlour that opened at the beginning of the season. Every day Gigi did her chores around the caravan park in the morning, spent the afternoon with Lily, and sat with Arthur after supper, helping sort out Elaine's coin collection.

'Never understood it, myself,' Arthur said as they sifted through another box of coins, these ones from Europe. 'But she loved friends and family sending her coins from their travels around the world. There's this great little coin dealer in the middle of Sydney, and every week she'd walk past the window and pick out the rare coins she wanted. Never could afford them though.'

Gigi and Arthur were sorting this box according to year. As far as Gigi knew, there were no rare coins in the collection. Still, it was fun going through them – the different designs and sizes and shapes. And she loved spending time with Arthur.

'Ha,' he said, pulling out a small coin with a hole in it. He passed it to Gigi, his eyesight not the best for reading the tiny words.

Gigi took a look. 'Norway.' She'd learned the native word 'Norge' from Arthur. '1927. That's very neat.'

Every day she went past Costas' house and he wasn't there.

The New Year was rung in and 1963 began as every other year before it, with fireworks on the beach. Bright and joyful, yet they filled Gigi with melancholy. The beginning of the New Year meant the beginning of the end of summer.

The last week of the holidays loomed and Gigi was, she had to admit, getting bored with her routine. She knew just the cure. It was Sunday, and that meant she had the day off from the caravan park.

Lily didn't seem too keen on the idea of heading up the north bluff and exploring the old cheese factory, but Gigi insisted. Yes, people said it was haunted. No, she'd never seen a ghost and they would be perfectly safe.

She didn't tell Lily she secretly hoped they would run into a spectre or spirit or ghoul. How exciting would that be?

Shards of morning sunlight shone through the bare wooden beams of what remained of the roof of the factory. Wind whistled through holes in the walls where stones had been dislodged. Fog surrounded the abandoned building and Lily clung to Gigi's hand as they stepped over a broken table and wove past a large copper kettle that had fallen into the fire pit below it. The kettle moved ever so slightly, releasing a metal groan into the air, and Lily jumped.

Gigi had always loved it here. She'd never seen an actual ghost, but didn't doubt for a second they haunted this space. Banksia Bay was surrounded by dairy farms, so it made sense to have a cheese factory here, too, but it had been deserted ever since she could remember. She'd asked Dad about it once. He said he couldn't remember what had happened, something about the family who owned it moving away, and then made himself busy helping Mum with the washing-up. He never helped with the washing-up. Gigi didn't believe him. No one else in town seemed to remember what had happened to it either, or why it hadn't been started up again.

So she made up her own story about a cheese maiden falling in love with the son of a rich dairy farmer. It was a forbidden love, of course, and one day, when the dairy son came to steal away the maiden, the cheese factory owner pushed the dairy son into the very kettle they'd just crawled past and cooked him alive. It was gruesome, yes, but weren't ghost stories supposed to be gruesome? And, of course, now the dairy son haunted the factory, preventing anyone from working it ever again as he wandered the forlorn ruins still looking for his maiden.

'That is not true!' Lily screeched, as Gigi finished telling her this theory.

'It could be.' Gigi giggled as she pulled her friend up onto the cart in the corner of the factory, which sloped to one side as it was missing a wheel. 'You should try coming up with a story. That would be fun.' She looked at Lily with pleading eyes.

'That's not fun. That's scary.'

'It doesn't have to be scary.' Gigi nudged her.

Lily tried her hardest – a story about love and babies and simply moving away – but clearly this wasn't her forte. And it didn't explain why the place was still abandoned today. Gigi was going to have to teach her how to better use her imagination.

Silence fell between them.

There was no point continuing to make up tales. Gigi had to find something else to talk about.

'Costas has gone away for the summer. I think.'

That did the trick. Tiny concerned wrinkles that Miss June Dally-What-a-bore wouldn't have approved of formed between Lily's eyes.

'We're just friends.' Gigi didn't know why she had to defend herself. 'Really. Around here, there aren't a lot of people my age to choose from.'

'What about Todd?' Lily's face again became a picture of serenity.

'Todd?' Gigi asked.

'Yes. You mentioned him a couple of times in your letters. Didn't you say he seemed to be getting better as he got older?'

'Maybe. I suppose.' He had been unusually nice to her lately.

'He's terribly good-looking. And comes from a good family. I saw the way he was looking at you at the bonfire last year.'

Gigi knew she wasn't going to win this debate. Good-looking, which he certainly was, wasn't enough for her. And despite his gentler disposition of late, he didn't make her spine tingle. She might not know a lot about that sort of thing, but she figured that was important.

'If you took a bit more care with your hair, the two of you would make a beautiful couple.'

Gigi pushed her wayward strands of blonde spiral straw behind her ears. There was only one way out of this. Lie.

'He has a girlfriend. From Ocean Heights.'

'Oh. Pity. Well, maybe once I've met more of Richard's friends, I might find someone suitable there who can court you.'

Court her? She wasn't interested in being courted. And she was fairly certain none of Richard's high-society mates would be interested in her. Time to change the subject again.

'I was thinking tomorrow we could go for a swim.'

Lily didn't answer, her mind clearly on other, courting-related matters. They sat back in the cart and listened to the breeze whistle through the building as the sun moved across the sky.

A crash and a guttural shout from behind made both girls jump, Lily throwing herself into Gigi's arms.

Gigi grabbed a rusted metal hook that was lying beside her. It was long. Long enough to keep a distance between them and the ghost that was about to attack them.

'Hoooo, hooooo.' An eerie sound echoed through the factory.

Wouldn't metal go straight through a ghost? Oh dear. Gigi's dream of coming face-to-face with an apparition might not be as romantic as she had imagined.

Behind her Lily started weeping.

'Come out!' Gigi shouted. 'I'm armed.' *For what good it will do me.*

A deep snicker came from the shadows of the upturned table in the opposite corner of the room.

It was a sound Gigi recognised.

She dropped the metal hook.

'Come out, Todd. You're not funny.'

'Well, I'd say it was pretty funny seeing the looks on your faces.' He stepped out from behind the table and doubled over onto his knees as he laughed.

'Grow up.' She scowled, gathering a shaking Lily in her arms.

He stepped into the light. 'Is she crying?' He inched closer. 'Oh, gee, it was just supposed to be a bit of fun. I didn't mean to make anyone cry.'

Panic spread across his face. Todd may well have been top dog around these parts, thanks to his dad's position as the local sergeant, but he knew just who Lily was, or rather, who her father was, and just what he was capable of doing to Todd's dad.

'Gee, Lillian, I'm really sorry.' He came over and knelt in front of the cart. 'What can I do to make it up to you?'

Lily took a few deep breaths and composed herself. She shot Todd a steely glare. 'Well, I'm going to have to think about that.'

'Anything.' He turned to Gigi and mouthed, *I'm sorry.*

Lily didn't answer. Not right away. Gigi was impressed with how quickly she went from blubbering mess to ice queen. Was that part of her finishing school training?

Lily raised a long, elegant finger to her chin. 'Hmm. Meet us tomorrow after lunch at the fishing shack and I'll let you know.'

Todd ran off, even faster than Gigi had seen him run that time there was a red-bellied black snake at school when they were ten.

'What are you doing? Why do we want to meet him tomorrow?' Gigi couldn't believe it.

'You'll see.' Lily smiled.

'Really, Lily. Maybe he hasn't changed at all. Look what he just did.'

'Boys will be boys.' She tsked. 'They all make mistakes. If we didn't forgive them, where would we be?'

Gigi didn't have an answer to that. She didn't seem to have any answers when it came to boys and growing up.

Later that night, Gigi ate supper with her mum in silence. Dad and Ian had sailed on the evening tide and it was just the two of them. After Gigi cleared the table, she took some leftover salad to Arthur's caravan and they went through the next box of coins.

'Is everything all right?' Arthur asked, not looking up.

She didn't know. She didn't know anything.

'There's something I have to do tomorrow. And I'm not sure I want to.'

'Ah.' Arthur slipped his hands into his pockets. 'I always find when I'm faced with a task I don't want to do, if I just get on and do it, it usually isn't as bad as I figured.'

Gigi smiled. '"The thought is worse than the deed". Mum always says that. Usually about my chores around here.'

'Your mum is wise.' Arthur tilted his head. 'I'm thinking this isn't about chores, though?'

Gigi looked at the silver coin in her hand.

'Something scary?' he asked.

'Maybe.' Anything to do with boys was turning out to be scary, apparently.

'Then here.'

He took her hand and slipped something into her palm. It was a small pendant made of two silver wings, each feather delicately moulded, lying against each other to form a heart. Down the inside curve of the left wing were studded six deep blue sapphires. Off the tip of the other wing hung another sapphire in the shape of a teardrop.

'Arthur, no.' She tried to give it back to him, her cheeks flushed with embarrassment. She'd never seen anything so beautiful. And Gigi and beautiful weren't two things that normally went together.

'It was Elaine's.' He pushed her hand away. 'She always said it was her guardian angel.'

Again Gigi tried to hand it back to him. It must be worth a fortune. Again he refused.

'If it wasn't for that little trinket, I never would have taken my first trip. If you need to borrow some courage, this might help. Just bring it back to me when you're done.'

Gigi looked at the angel wings again. She certainly would need some courage tomorrow. Maybe she could borrow it just this once. But she'd return it to Arthur straight after whatever it was Lily had planned. Lily wasn't usually one for coming up with schemes. But she was planning something that involved Todd. And that meant much courage would indeed be needed.

Ten

*L*aura strolled home past the bee-themed obstacle course as it slowly deflated. Most of the festival goers had left and the clean-up had begun. Heath had followed her out of the shack – the nerve – but she'd managed to escape him. She knew from personal experience that men weren't to be trusted. Rule number three, *trust your instincts*. Except in this case, her gut was telling her that Heath was a good guy. It must still be the grief, interfering with her usually accurate instincts.

She'd turned back once after she left the shack and caught Virginia watching her. Laura was more certain than ever before that Lillian's connection to this place was more than a random summer holiday or two. But her search was proving fruitless.

Over the past few nights she'd googled Virginia Gilbert (the only information related to the shack), Gigi Gilbert (a passing mention in a school newsletter archived on Banksia Bay Central School's centenary page) and Costas Tinellis (nothing at all).

What was she missing?

Something she hadn't given any thought to yet was actually searching Lillian.

She smacked herself in the head. *Idiot*.

Laura flipped open her laptop and googled her grandmother. There wasn't much there. Nothing that she didn't already know, anyway. Daughter of a politician, raised a young family on her own, lived in Sydney.

Okay. What else could she look up?

Her grandfather? There was probably no point. But how many times had rule number nine served her well in her career? Too many times to count, the answers had come from some unexpected lead.

She googled Richard Prescott. Married to the daughter of a prominent politician – she knew that already. Died young, before his son was born, in 1964 – she knew that too. *No, wait*. Laura's grandpa had died in Vietnam in 1965. At least, that's what she'd been told.

Another lie?

She read the article three times, looking for any further information, but the details were sketchy. The only other mention she could find of her grandfather was a snippet from a gossip column in the *Ocean Heights Chronicle* from 1961 about the Prescott family visiting Banksia Bay.

Richard had been to Banksia Bay!

She jotted a few thoughts down in her notebook for searching Trove tomorrow. She'd used the site many times in her career to look for historical information, particularly old newspapers. Whoever had spent hours upon hours digitising those documents was a saint, in her opinion. Knowing that Richard had visited Banksia Bay gave her something to go on. The date of his death would also aid her search. Knowing that Virginia Gilbert was Gigi, or at least strongly believing it, also helped. She had somewhere to start now. It was amazing what you could do with a few names and dates and some archived newspapers.

She'd dive in with fresh eyes in the morning. She curled up under the doona and closed her eyes. Images of bees buzzed through her mind, along with yellow fairy floss. She rolled over. Virginia's piercing gaze flashed into her head. She turned again and started counting sheep. One, two, three, a bee sat on a sheep's nose. Nine, ten, eleven, Heath's blue eyes and warm smile adorned a sheep's face.

Oh dear.

In the morning, cup of strong coffee in hand, Laura opened her laptop ready for a full day's research but a knock on the door interrupted her.

'It's only me. Don't hurry,' Heath's voice called down the hallway.

Damn it. She closed her computer. What was he doing here? Laura stepped through the house and let him in.

'You look like you're getting around much better. Stitches out soon, hey?'

'Not soon enough,' she groaned, and Heath gave her a sympathetic look.

He pointed to the scar on his face. 'At least it's not right up front for all the world to see.'

She felt bad for complaining and looked at the floor.

'It's okay. It was a surfing accident when I was young and thought I could conquer the world. I stayed out too late when a monster storm came rolling in and I got thrown against the rocks. I barely notice it anymore.'

Laura realised this was the first time she'd noticed it herself since their first meeting on the beach.

'Do you still think you can conquer the world?' Laura smiled. All sense had left her. *Send him home, Laura. To his wife.*

'Some days. Most days I'm just trying to get from A to B.'

'Just like the rest of us.'

He nodded. 'I had a night shift at the hospital, and just finished. I thought maybe we could go for that drive I've been promising you.'

'Are you a nurse too?' Laura asked. *Then why hadn't he patched her up?*

'No. Pathology. Not quite as glamorous.' He backed out of the door and led her to his car. 'Shall we?'

She should have said no. *Trust your gut, Laura.* But her gut said yes. Her gut was a traitor.

They wound their way along the dirt track that snaked over the hills surrounding Banksia Bay. Heath pulled off the track into a clearing and opened the car door for Laura to get out.

It was a lookout, of sorts, with a view to the south over the town.

'That's the caravan park Virginia ran up until a few years ago.' He pointed to an empty expanse of green grass just south of the beach shack, behind some trees. Laura could just make out a narrow path winding from the caravan park through the bush to the sand at the southernmost part of the bay.

'It was fun growing up with such a big backyard. I spent most afternoons after school there, instead of heading home.'

Laura turned and looked at him.

'Oh, nothing juicy. Home was fine. Just not as much fun as a caravan park. Gran grew up there too. It was sad when she had to leave. It just got to be too much for her, especially on her own.'

'Your grandfather?'

'He died in Vietnam.' He shrugged. 'She's never really talked about it. And never found anyone else.'

Laura's mind was buzzing.

Gigi grew up here. Lillian visited. Richard died in Vietnam. So did Heath's grandfather. Were they friends? Best mates serving together? Were they the same person? No. That didn't feel right.

Back in the car, Laura wished she'd brought her notebook with her.

Not much further down the track, Heath stopped the car again. This time they were outside an old stone barn, or farmhouse. At least, maybe it had been when it had actual solid walls and a complete roof. Now the old building sat sadly, sagging into the ground as if staying upright was just far too much effort.

'Now this, this is the most interesting part of town'. Heath led her around the building. 'Apparently, it used to be an old cheese factory. Like, a hundred years ago or so. But something happened, no one knows what, and it was abandoned.'

'Surely someone knows. I thought small towns were famous for everyone knowing everything.'

Heath nodded. 'True. Gossip spreads like wildfire. But when a small town wants to keep a secret, they can bury something so deep and rewrite their own history, until events, even people, are erased from collective memory. Trust me. I've tried to find out about this place. Nothing.'

He beckoned her to follow him around the other side of the building.

The view from there was the most breathtaking vista Laura had ever seen. The entire coastline was laid out before them, the rolling green hills framing the yellow sand that bled into the deep blue water. Banksia Bay, lying to the south, was almost hidden by a soft white haze that sat just off the hills.

'Beautiful, isn't it?'

Laura was spellbound.

'One day, I'm going to buy this place. Turn it into an artisans marketplace, where the farmers from around here can sell their produce. Cheese, pies, honey. There's even an olive farm outside Ocean Heights. You said yourself we could make so much more of the artisanal movement.'

Laura watched Heath as he walked up and down, his face animated.

'Artists could also sell their work. We'd have a small café in the corner, with a deck, just here jutting out over the cliff, taking in that.' He spread his arms out wide to indicate the view. He turned to Laura. 'What? You're looking at me funny. Oh God. I do carry on like a pork chop when I think about it.' He bowed his head.

Laura wondered what expression had adorned her face. She hadn't meant to upset him. 'I actually think it sounds amazing.'

He looked at her, his face open, hopeful, like a child's at Christmas.

'I just wasn't expecting it.' He'd painted such a vivid picture, Laura couldn't help but be swept up in his enthusiasm. She could imagine the transformation of the old cheese factory, and a flutter of excitement tickled inside her.

'What, from a boofhead surfer like me?' He raised an eyebrow.

'I suspect you are anything but a boofhead.' As the words came out of her mouth, her cheeks burned. *Stop that.* 'What does Charlotte think about it all?'

Yes, keep reminding yourself he's married. Keep reminding him.

'Charlotte?' He screwed his face up. 'She thinks I can't pull it off. But I'll show her. She doesn't think that much of my sculpting, either. I make things out of wood – driftwood, fallen branches, anything I can find.'

Laura remembered her own doorway. 'Like the wind chime at the holiday house?'

If Laura wasn't mistaken, Heath's cheeks reddened. 'Yes. That's one of mine.'

'It's beautiful.' *He'd made that?* She was impressed. And a little taken aback by how much.

'Thank you. I'm glad someone thinks so.'

Laura felt sorry for Heath, married to someone who didn't seem to support him. But that didn't give him the right to make her feel all wobbly and warm inside.

'Follow me.' He grabbed her hand and led her through a gap where the stones had fallen to the ground, leaving a space just big enough to step through. His touch caused her breath to catch in her throat.

There was debris and dirt everywhere and Laura was careful where she stepped. They moved past old equipment and tables, the sun shining spotlights through small and large holes in the mostly collapsed roof.

Heath pointed to a broken cart. 'That's where the produce would go.' He spun around and walked over to what had once, Laura assumed, been a table. 'Here would be where the art goes. And this copper kettle would be beautiful polished up and used as a display.'

He picked his way over the debris, describing every last detail. His passion was evident, his every word so clear, that Laura could almost see it take shape before her. It wasn't often in life she was dumbstruck.

'Oh–kay.' Heath said. 'I can see I've gone a little overboard and should probably stop now, before you run away.'

'Ah, but where would I go? I don't know my way around these parts, remember?'

'Good point.' He led the way back out. 'Still, best not to push things.'

When they got back to his car, Laura stopped and turned to him. 'Heath. I think it's amazing. I hope you can build your dream one day. I'd really like to see it.'

'I'd like you to see it, too.' He stepped towards her, then stopped.

Was he flirting with her? Damn her useless gut. She should never have come with him.

They headed back to Banksia Bay and Heath dropped her off on the main street so she could pick up some groceries for dinner.

'Oh, Heath?' she called before he drove off. 'Is there a library in Ocean Heights?'

'Yeah, not a bad one, either. They're open late tomorrow night. I could take you, if you like.'

The Bodhi Bus wasn't due for another run till next Monday. And while she had Trove to dig through, local libraries often had quirky collections that proved useful. It wouldn't hurt to have a poke around.

'Would you mind?' It was just a lift. Nothing more.

'Not at all.'

She waved as Heath's car pulled away and drove off down the street.

The following day Laura spent the morning pottering around the house, sifting through her questions and notes, trying to find the one thread that, when pulled, would unravel the whole story for her.

She trawled through Trove for hours, but to little avail.

She did find a piece in the *Ocean Heights Chronicle* about the school's honour list, 1963, that mentioned a Miss V Gilbert.

As much as Laura loved Trove, it could be slow going when you weren't sure what keywords you needed.

Stories like this – and she had to think of this as a story – were frustrating. So many pieces that didn't quite add up to a whole.

She knew exactly what the problem was. It was too personal for her. There wasn't enough distance for her to find the right perspective. The answer was probably there. She just couldn't see it.

Charlotte may well have given her strict instructions not to run, in case she burst open the stitches, but surely a jog would be okay. The stitches were due out tomorrow anyway. It would be worth the risk to clear her head.

She walked through town, oh so casually, just in case Charlotte happened to be around and caught her, but once she hit the hills, she picked up the pace. Her knee felt a little tight, but as she lengthened her stride, she got used to it. She resisted kicking into the next gear and did actually take it slow. Slow for her, anyway.

When she reached the hill that had attacked her knee last time, she pulled back to a walk. No point tempting fate. She carefully moved to the edge of the cliff.

With hands on hips, she drew in a long breath. It was a beautiful view, but not as stunning as the one from the cheese factory. If Heath could realise his dream . . .

The thought of him so animated as he told her about his vision made her heart beat faster.

No. Stop it. Think about the story. Always the story.

The sun bathed her face in autumn warmth and she lifted her arms. Was this warrior pose? Remembering her yoga attempt down on the beach, she thrust her arms back down. Falling here again was not a good idea. That blasted rock was still hiding some-where. She looked around, pushing her foot carefully through the grass. Ah, there was the nasty little sucker.

'You're not going to get me this time.' She bent down to clear away the growth that was protecting it from discovery by unsus-pecting joggers. 'No more stealth attacks for you.'

As she ripped the grass away, a carving appeared. Two sets of initials, shallow, jagged, etched into the rock.

'V.G', something that might have been a love heart, and 'C.T'.

Virginia Gilbert? Maybe. And Costas Tinellis? No. It couldn't be.

She may just have found one more piece of the puzzle, and she had to add it to her notes. She pulled her phone out of her back pocket and took a photo, before running back to the holiday house.

To hell with the stitches.

Back at the house, Laura waited for Heath to pick her up to take her to the library. She had her notes ready and couldn't wait to get started. She didn't know what she'd find, if anything. A small regional library might not have much information going back that far, or maybe it had a wealth of records. Hopefully there would be school archives, or a local history section, at least.

After she'd returned from her jog, she'd taken a quick shower and then started her internet search again. This time for Costas Tinellis. His name circled in the scrapbook, the carving in the rock. She had no idea if he was important or not – who didn't have a school-aged crush that was all-consuming at the time but insig-nificant in the grand scheme of life? But her gut was telling her to follow it through. Her instincts may have let her down when it came to Heath, but when it came to stories, rule number three had never steered her wrong.

She'd found an immigration record for a Tinellis family from post–World War Two, and a death notice for a Stavros Tinellis in 1970, in Melbourne. There was also a court report that came up in the search, but it was redacted. She'd never seen that before. She'd made a note of the reference number and would get a print-out at the library.

This Costas fellow might not have anything to do with Lillian, but there was definitely something more to his thread.

Of course, the easiest thing to do would be to come straight out and ask Virginia if she'd known Lillian. Ask her what had happened. But every instinct was telling her to hold off on that.

A car horn beeped.

She drew in a deep breath and went out to meet Heath.

The library in Ocean Heights was bigger than Laura was expecting and the librarian was extremely helpful. Once Laura had explained that she was doing a lifestyle series of colourful histories of small towns, including Banksia Bay, she took Laura into a private reading room and pulled out files that had old school archives and a folder with something called The Bay Bugle. Produced by the 'ladies' guild', whoever they were, it wasn't a newspaper as such – more like a local gossip newsletter.

Bingo.

Heath would be back in an hour to pick her up. She'd better get cracking.

The school archives had reports, Parents' and Citizens' Association minutes, and a few interesting articles from the local paper. No mention of a Lillian Woodhouse anywhere. Plenty of references to Gigi Gilbert.

There were some photos of the students, including the same

class shot from Virginia's scrapbook. Costas was there but there was no other mention of him anywhere else in the school archives. Laura circled and underlined his name in her notes.

The Bay Bugle, on the other hand, was a most entertaining read. It went as far back as 1920, and was full of salacious rumours and innuendo. Laura wished she had more time to pore over the publication for purely personal enjoyment, but she skipped the early years and found her way to the sixties.

In the summer of 1961, Dr Prescott, a renowned physician from Sydney, brought his family to Banksia Bay for the first time, and the ladies of the guild were beside themselves wondering which local beauty would garner the attention of his very eligible son.

By 1962, the guild were distraught that a young lady from Sydney, whose family were regular summer visitors to the Bay, had snaffled the affection of said Master Richard Prescott, and Miss Lillian Woodhouse had apparently broken the hearts of many, some might say more deserving, local girls.

'Yes!' Laura let out a loud cry.

'Are you okay?' The librarian came into the room.

'Sorry. Yes. Do you have a photocopier?'

The librarian looked down her nose, but led her to the copy room and set her up with an account.

'Thank you.' Laura copied the articles and scurried back to the reading room. It wouldn't be long now till Heath returned to take her home.

The next few Bugles had all the usual gossip – who was courting whom, how the local businesses were going, a scathing report on the hedonistic nature of the ever-increasing surf culture that was plaguing the Bay each summer, and perhaps Ian Holland would be better off catching more fish to serve a failing industry than teaching these hippie outsiders a pursuit that was, quite frankly, a waste of time.

Ian. Laura jotted his name in her notes, a reminder that she really needed to see inside his studio.

Laura was enjoying reading The Bugle. This Mrs Andrews who ran the newsletter certainly wasn't afraid to let her opinions be known.

'How's it going?'

Laura jumped. Heath was standing behind her, looking over her shoulder.

'Ah, The Bay Bugle. That's some interesting entertainment right there.' He put his hands on his hips. 'Though I'm not sure how much stock I'd put in the truth of their scandalous stories.'

'Well, no. I guess not.'

'Did you find what you were looking for?' Heath's brow furrowed as Laura scrambled to put her copied sheets into a folder. 'Anything I can help you with?'

'Thank you. I'm all good, I think. I might come back another day and keep reading.' She picked up her notes and folder and held them to her chest. 'Ready when you are.'

The drive back to Banksia Bay was quiet, and Laura didn't mind one bit. She turned today's findings over in her head. The Woodhouses and the Prescotts had holidayed in the Bay. That must have been how her grandparents met. How were Virginia and Lillian connected, though? The mysterious Costas existed, but there was nothing more on him. The Bugle was definitely a source she had to revisit. Even if, as Heath said, the accuracy of the pages was suspect, often truth lurked behind gossip. You only had to dig deep enough.

'Are you hungry?' Heath broke the silence.

'Actually, yes.' As if on cue, her stomach rumbled.

'Come over for dinner, then. Charlotte makes the most delicious cottage pie and there's always too much of it.'

'Oh . . . Umm . . .' Was he serious? Dinner with his wife? Maybe Laura was reading him all wrong. Maybe he hadn't been flirting with her at all. Perhaps he was just being friendly. Well, now she felt like a right donkey.

A starving donkey, truth be told, and back at the holiday house she only had basic supplies. A delicious home-cooked meal sounded wonderful.

'Go on. She's a pretty good cook.'

If Laura went to dinner, saw the two of them together, she could put these foolish feelings away.

'Sure.'

Charlotte didn't look too impressed when she opened the door, but she was polite enough not to come out and say, 'What on earth is this home wrecker doing here?'

Aiden came running to the door and threw his arms around Heath.

'Hey, buddy. How was your day?'

As he led Heath down the hall, leaving Laura standing in the doorway, Aiden launched into a complete retelling of everything he'd done, including exactly how he'd spread his peanut butter on his sandwich for lunch.

Charlotte put her hand to her chest. 'Sorry. My brother has a habit of forgetting his manners. And when he and Aiden get together, no one else exists.'

Wait, what?

'Brother?' Laura couldn't hide her shock. 'I thought you two were . . .'

'Oh God, no.' Charlotte made a retching motion.

Oh, how had Laura read it so wrong?

'Okay. I think we need to start over. Please come in.' Charlotte stepped to the side.

Brother?

Laura tried to process this new information as quickly as she could.

In the living room, Aiden had pulled Heath onto the floor, and they moved wooden trains around a wooden track, making 'choo-choo' noises. It wasn't a large room, but it was cosy and inviting, with two soft sofas and a gallery of photos on the wall: pictures of Aiden as a baby, of Charlotte and Aiden, of Heath and Aiden, of Virginia and Charlotte – the perfect happy family. Except there didn't appear to be any pictures of another man. A husband, a father.

Perfection was an illusion, after all.

Aiden stood up and plonked himself in front of Laura. 'Hi.'

'Hi yourself.' She smiled.

'Do you read?'

'I love to read.'

He took her hand. 'Come into Uncle Heath's room.' He dragged her down the hall before she could answer.

She could hear whispers behind her, but couldn't make out any words. She did hear a low chuckle, though, and her cheeks burned guessing what Charlotte and Heath were talking about. There were no rules on her list on how to deal with complete and utter embarrassment.

Uncle Heath's room was sparsely decorated. A blue striped doona on a double bed. A large photo of the surf on one wall. A picture of Aiden beside the bed. A surfboard in the corner of the room.

Aiden jumped up onto the bed and beckoned Laura over. She sat beside him, propped up on a mountain of pillows and cushions he had dragged in from other rooms. He handed her a book, opened it to a page somewhere in the middle, and said, 'We're up to here.'

Laura read aloud.

A few pages in, Aiden rested his head on her shoulder. She lifted her arm and he snuggled into her.

Laura didn't notice Charlotte at the door until she coughed lightly. 'Wash up, Aiden. Dinner's ready.'

Aiden jumped up and walked towards the door, but ran back and kissed Laura on the cheek. 'Thank you.' He ran off again.

'He's a sweetheart,' Laura said to Charlotte as she got up off the bed.

'I certainly think so.' Charlotte started putting Heath's bed back in order.

Laura helped. 'And he and Heath obviously have a special bond.' She reached out and touched the photo beside the bed.

'No denying that. My husband left. Two years ago. I can't afford the mortgage on my own, so Heath moved in to help out. I don't know what I'd do without him.' There was a catch in her voice.

Laura looked into her eyes and saw sadness there.

But in a split second it was gone. 'Shall we head to the dining room? I'm sure Heath has oversold you on my culinary talents, but my cottage pie is probably the best dish in a very small repertoire.'

'It'll be better than anything I can make.' The honest truth.

And it was. Not five-star – Laura had eaten in many restaurants in Sydney that were considered fine dining – but Charlotte's cottage pie was delicious and hot and comforting.

After dinner, Heath was dragged back to the train track and Laura helped Charlotte with the washing-up.

'I may as well have a look at those stitches while you're here.' She got out her medical kit.

'Oh, no. I don't want to ruin your night.'

'Nonsense. Save you coming back tomorrow.' Charlotte pressed Laura into a chair. 'Let me see.'

She pushed Laura's A-line skirt up just a fraction so she could get a good look at the wound.

'That's healed brilliantly. Let's take these out.' She slipped on a pair of gloves and in just a few seconds had removed the stitches. She wiped the wound, making sure it was clean. 'That looks pretty good to me. Rub this in every day and hopefully it won't get too itchy.' She handed Laura some aloe vera cream.

'Thank you, Charlotte.'

'Does this mean we can begin our surfing lessons?' Heath entered the kitchen.

'Oh, I don't know if that's a good idea.' Panic filled Laura.

'No medical reason why you can't.' Charlotte packed away her things. 'Just clean the area afterwards.'

'See?' Heath clapped his hands together. 'No excuses. It's Saturday tomorrow. Not much is open. Not even the library. What else have you got to do?'

Laura tried to think of an excuse, but came up blank.

'Besides –' he tilted his head and raised his hands – 'if you want to get a true taste of Bay life for your article . . .'

She knew she wasn't going to win this one. 'Okay. What time?'

'How does six-thirty sound?'

'It sounds early.'

'Great. It's a date.'

Charlotte pursed her lips.

'Can I come too?' Aiden came into the room. 'I'm a good surfer.'

'You're the best. But I think Laura might feel a bit self-conscious if she has an audience, buddy.'

Aiden pouted, but accepted his uncle's refusal. 'Are we still going fishing with Gran in the afternoon?'

'Of course. You don't think she'd let us out of that, do you?'

Aiden giggled. 'No way!'

'Of course I wouldn't.' Virginia came walking down the hall.

'Gran!' Aiden gave her tight hug.

'Now, isn't it your bedtime?'

He skipped towards his room and Laura looked at Charlotte.

'I'm on an early shift at the hospital tomorrow,' Charlotte said, hanging up her tea towel. 'Gran stays over to look after Aiden for me.'

'What about Heath?'

'No way am I getting in between Gran and her time with her great-grandson.' He threw his arms in the air.

'You do enough already.' Virginia patted him on the cheek and for a moment he looked like a little boy seeking his grandmother's approval.

It was getting a little too crowded for Laura. 'I should go.'

'I'll walk you home.' Heath said.

'No. It's not far.'

'Nonsense.' Virginia raised a finger. 'If I've taught my grandson anything, it's to be a gentleman.' She herded them towards the door.

The stars above were bright against a liquid black sky. Laura never saw skies like that in Sydney.

'It is something, isn't it?' Heath whispered close to her ear, his breath sending a shiver down her spine.

She nodded, hoping her sudden intake of breath had gone unnoticed.

'I've left the Bay. Three times now. But I always end up coming back.'

'You must really love it here.'

'Yep. Do you want to see something special?' He held out his hand.

Laura took a step back.

'It's not like that,' he assured her. 'Seriously. I bet –' he turned around to face her and started walking backwards – 'that you've never seen anything like it.'

'If that's a line, it's the cheesiest one I've ever heard.'

Heath stopped and Laura nearly ran into him. He put his hand over his chest. 'Scout's honour, this is totally above board.'

'Were you ever a Scout?'

'That's not the point.'

Laura laughed. 'Okay. But if I'm anything other than blown away, I'll never believe another word you say.'

'You can trust my word.' He started heading towards the beach and she followed.

They walked to the northern end of the long stretch of sand and Heath took a few steps up onto the rocks. He held out his hand, which Laura took, and he helped her to the top of the slippery black surface. For a moment neither one of them let go. In the dark, they stared into each other's eyes. Laura's heart raced.

'It's just over here,' Heath whispered. Using the torch on his phone for light, he led her to the edge of the rocks.

He manoeuvred into position, making sure his feet were on either side of a small crevice. He'd picked up a seaweed stalk from the sand and he lowered it into the space and very gently prodded. Holding out both his hands he looked at Laura. 'Hang on, and look down.'

Laura hesitated, just for a moment, and then took the offered support. She leaned over and looked into the crevice.

'Oh my!' Below, in the water between the jagged rock edges were dozens of luminescent shells, shining a bright green light into the rocky void. She looked up at Heath.

'What . . . how . . .'

And then she turned her gaze back down to the strange phenomenon below her.

She really hadn't seen anything like it before. 'Wow. All I have is wow.'

She looked back up at Heath, who indicated with a tilt of his head that they should move to somewhere with slightly better footing. They shuffled up the rocks to the highest point, where a sandy grass carpet met the hard shiny boulders, and they sat down.

'What was that?' Laura asked.

'They're sea snails. Clusterwink, they're called. Among other names.'

'Cluster-what?'

'Clusterwink. They love hiding in rocky crevices where the waves crash, but they don't like being exposed to the weather much. That's why they love that spot.'

'And the glow.'

'Yep. Scientists think it's a protection mechanism. So, how did I do? Have I lost all credibility, or is my word still good?'

Laura was grateful the cover of night meant he couldn't see the blush rising in her cheeks. 'Still good.'

'Phew.'

'I can see why you love this place.'

'And once you get to know the people, it's even more special.'

She didn't doubt that one bit.

'What you do for Charlotte is really sweet.'

'She's my big sister.' His expression was full of love. 'Besides, I've actually got the better end of the deal.'

'How?'

'Well, I get to spend a lot of time with Aiden, and I have a house in Ocean Heights I rent out, and I get a lot more for that than Charlotte charges me, so . . .'

'So it won't be long before you can afford to buy the cheese factory.'

Heath turned to look at her, his eyes wide, shining in the moonlight.

'I think it's a great dream,' she said.

'Most people mock me when I tell them.'

'Well, I'm not most people.'

'You certainly aren't.'

He stared into her eyes, thrilling, unnerving, so much depth. No one had ever looked at her like that before. For a moment she forgot how to breathe. At least when she'd thought he was married, he was safe. Now he was dangerous. Breaking eye contact, she coughed and wriggled where she sat.

'Right.' Heath stood up. 'I'd better get you home. Early start tomorrow.'

He walked her right up to the front door of the holiday house and held the screen open for Laura as she stepped inside.

'Thank you. For today. For showing me the cluster . . .'

'– wink.' His pale blue eyes looked into hers. 'It was my pleasure.' His voice was low, melodic. 'See you in the morning.'

She closed the door behind her and fell back against it, expelling all the air she'd been holding onto.

Trouble.

She was most definitely in serious trouble.

Eleven

Virginia stood looking out the window of Charlotte's living room. What was taking that boy so long? Always had his head in the clouds, that one. Always getting swept up in a dream. It was part of his charm. And she didn't begrudge him that. Not one bit. Her grandson had enough in life to challenge him. If dreaming, however impossible, gave him happiness, she wouldn't take that away from him.

She wished Charlotte could see that. Far too sensible for her own good. She interfered too much.

This time, though, interference was called for. Laura was trouble. Virginia was certain of it. All her doubts about the girl's purpose in coming here had been erased the moment she saw that pendant around her neck.

Where is he?

The front door opened and in he strolled. Not a care in the world. A silly grin across his face.

'Ah, there you are, Heath. I was just about to make some hot chocolate before bed. Care for some?'

'Sure, Gran.' He kissed her on top of her head and put his arm around her shoulders as they walked into the kitchen.

'I heard you took Laura to the library today,' she oh-so-casually mentioned as she put his mug on the table in front of him. It was Aiden's old Elmo mug, but Heath didn't object.

'Yeah. I drove her to Ocean Heights. She seemed excited by what she found.'

Virginia sat down beside him and sipped her hot chocolate. 'Oh? And what was that?'

He looked at her blankly.

Typical male – light on details.

'She was looking at The Bugle. And some old school archives. There was a photo of you at school.'

Virginia held on to the base of the chair to stop herself from sliding off. If Laura was looking at photos of her at school, that meant she most definitely knew something. But what?

If it was all perfectly innocent – if she was simply related to Lily and wanted to know more about her – surely Laura would come straight out and ask. Looking into Virginia's past was not innocent. It couldn't be.

She had to find a way to get a look at Laura's notes.

A plan – not a great one, mind you, but a plan nonetheless – began to form in her mind. And she'd need Yvonne's help. Tomorrow, when Heath took Laura surfing, she'd make her move.

'You were quite the looker in your day, Gran.'

All charm, that boy. 'Fiddlesticks.'

'No. Really. No wonder Grandpa fell for you. I wish I'd known him.'

'He would have loved you. Both of you grandkids.' She sighed.

'Why don't you talk about him, Gran?' He reached out and held her old hand. He had such strong hands. Just like his grandpa.

She stood up, clearing her mug away. Standing at the sink, she fought back the tears. She'd been doing that a lot lately. Holding back tears. Ever since Laura had turned up in the Bay. Nearly six decades of stoically burying one's memories undone, just like that.

'Gran? Are you okay?' Heath stood behind her, a hand on her shoulder.

'Yes, dear. Just old and weary.' Oh so very weary.

Heath frowned.

As well as charm personified, he was astute. And he knew her better than anyone. Well, the parts of her she allowed anyone to know. She'd been lying to him his whole life. If he ever found out, he'd be crushed.

'Don't you worry your handsome head about me.' She touched his cheek. 'When you get to my age, dear, old and weary are simply part of the game.'

He could never find out.

Heath turned her round and embraced her in his big strong arms.

Most days she wished he had less of his grandfather in him, the constant reminder so hard to bear. But every now and then she was grateful to hold on to a small piece of her past for just a little longer. Now that Laura was here to destroy her, memories were all she had.

January 1963

As the sun passed its highest point in the sky, Gigi waved to Arthur and headed off to the fishing shack.

'You're braver than you feel,' he called after her.

She fiddled with the pendant in her pocket, just in case Elaine was looking out for her.

Whatever Lily had planned, she'd figure out a way to get out of it. Gigi could be wily when she needed to be. A sudden stomach bug wasn't out of the question.

Gigi rounded the main street and took the few steps across the trodden grass to reach the beach. The fishing shack was just ahead.

So was Todd.

And Richard.

They were standing over a tartan rug laid out on the sand. Lily sat in the centre, the wide circle skirt of her dress spread around her like a blue gingham doily. Beside her were plates of food.

Gigi slowed right down. No one had seen her yet. She could back away, turn and run, and pretend she was never there in the first place. She could make up some excuse about Mum needing her at the caravan park.

She halted. Took one step back.

Then Lily saw her.

'Gigi!' she called out, and waved her white-gloved hand. 'Come. Come.'

Gigi cursed under her breath, but held her composure as she walked towards the picnic.

Richard turned around, looking her up and down. 'Nice to see you again, Gigi. You're looking well.'

She pushed her wayward hair, which she'd forgotten to brush, behind her ears. Lily was resplendent, as always, and Richard and Todd were in tailored trousers and button-up shirts. Gigi was in her work overalls.

'I thought a picnic might be nice.' Lily offered Gigi some home-made lemonade. 'Richard and Todd can get to know each other. It will be nice for Richard to have a man to talk to and not just us ladies.'

Gigi saw right through the scene in front of her, despite her naïvety. This was a double date. Todd stood up and offered her his hand to help her down onto the rug.

'Isn't this lovely?' Lily smiled.

'Lovely' was not exactly the word Gigi would have chosen.

Todd and Richard seemed to get on quite well, and Gigi sat back, saying very little, while Lily played hostess, serving the guys sandwiches and lemonade and scones to finish with. It was all terribly polite and Gigi hated every minute of it.

Lily packed up the picnic basket she'd brought with her and invited Gigi for a stroll down to the water.

'Well, that's gone very well.' She sounded rather pleased with herself.

'How is this punishment for Todd scaring us half to death yesterday?' Gigi stopped walking and spun around in the sand.

'It's not. Not really. I wanted to have a picnic with Richard, and Mother would only let me if it was with a group, now that we're officially courting. She has this archaic notion that because we are no longer just friends, and he's made it clear he is serious about pursuing me, we cannot be alone together.'

'That doesn't explain why you had to invite Todd. Don't I count?'

Lily linked her arm with Gigi's and dragged her further down the beach. 'More than you know. To me. But Mother . . .'

'Your mother doesn't trust me.' Gigi sighed. All these years of friendship and Mrs Woodhouse still couldn't accept Gigi.

'Well, it isn't that. If she didn't trust you, we wouldn't be allowed to see each other at all. It's just that Daddy knows Todd's father quite well and that means having you both here is extra . . . insurance. So to speak.'

So to speak. Gigi may not be destined for a posh life like Lily, but she understood how things worked. Alone with Lily she was a mere distraction for the Woodhouses' only daughter. A passing summer friendship that kept their little girl happy. But they also knew that the girls were as close as sisters. They assumed Gigi would lie for Lily if she asked. And they were right.

They also knew that Todd would never let anything improper happen to Lily, as he understood the world too, and he knew there would be consequences for his family, for his dad, if he didn't look out for her.

'You were wrong, you know. About Todd. He doesn't have a girlfriend at all.' Lily's voice was sickly sweet. 'You would make a lovely couple, Gigi.'

Gigi stopped in the sand.

'Couple?'

'Yes. Don't you see it?'

Todd was handsome, yes. And he seemed to have grown out of his childhood shenanigans. But that didn't mean Gigi was interested in him. They weren't even friends.

'No' was all she could say.

'Give it time. Often that's all these things need. Can you do me a favour?'

'Anything.'

It wasn't fair, what Lily asked. She knew Gigi wasn't interested in Todd. Gigi had just told her. She also knew that Gigi would never say no to helping her out, and she used that against her: could she distract Todd so Lily and Richard could go for a short walk up the beach together? Alone.

Gigi pouted at her.

'Please, Gigi. For me.'

That wasn't fair either.

'We won't be long. We'll just walk to the end of the beach and back. And we'll stay in sight the whole time.' She looked at Gigi with wide, pleading eyes.

And Gigi couldn't resist.

'Thank you.' Lily hugged her.

Todd stood up as soon as Lily and Richard took a few steps away from the picnic blanket and Gigi groaned to herself. There was only one way to stop him following them.

'So, Todd.' Oh God, she wasn't used to being fake. 'I hear this year you're going to be captaining the district football team.'

He turned around and flashed her a self-assured smile. 'You heard that, huh?' He folded his arms across his chest and leaned towards her.

Lord save me. 'Yes.'

Todd looked to the couple, their silhouettes getting smaller and smaller as they walked down the beach. He rocked back and forth – follow or stay?

'Yes. That must mean you're the best player around these parts.' Okay, now she was actually going to vomit. She touched the pendant in her pocket.

But at least that made him stay. And talk. About himself, without pause.

Gigi nodded and uh-huh-ed where she should as he rabbited on and on. She feigned interest and shock in the appropriate places. Every now and then she glanced up the beach to see if Lily and Richard were on their way back yet, picking their way past the families dotted along the sand with their buckets and spades and umbrellas. When they finally did turn around and come back, relief washed over her.

'I know, right? Amazing.' Todd mistook her sigh for a reaction to whatever it was he'd said last.

'You know what, Gilbert? This has been really nice.'

'It has.' *Not really.*

'And you're actually quite pretty, once you get past the gruff exterior.' He reached out and touched a strand of her wild hair caught on the breeze. 'I never noticed that before.'

She stepped back.

'Oh, here they come.' She pointed to Lily and Richard, walking along the beach, Richard, always the gentleman, walking closest to the lapping water, giving fair warning to Lily if a bigger wave rolled in.

Gigi's heart swelled at the look of sheer joy on Lily's face.

'Did you miss us?' Lily giggled.

'Absolutely.' Gigi hugged her.

'Richard has to go to some tedious family thing this afternoon.' Lily waved her hand dismissively. 'I think it's time to head home.'

They all walked the short distance to the holiday house, where Mrs Woodhouse was sitting on the verandah, so very obviously waiting for her daughter. A look of relief briefly crossed her face when she saw all four of them together.

'Todd, be a gentleman and walk Gigi home,' Lily said, after they had all bade farewell.

'Of course.' He bowed his head slightly.

Not wanting to make a scene in front of Lily's mother, Gigi said nothing and let Todd walk with her until they were out of sight. Then she turned to him. 'I think I can manage from here.'

'Ah, come on, Gilbert. We got on so well today.' He reached out to touch her arm.

'I did that for Lily.' She put her hands on her hips.

'What do you mean?'

'Todd, today was nice enough, but that's all it was.' She turned away.

He stepped in front of her, blocking her way. 'Gilbert?' His voice was low.

'Please, Todd. Can't we just be friends?'

She turned again but he blocked her. She squeezed the pendant in her pocket. 'Please?'

Todd shifted to the side as Gigi did. He shuffled back when she did.

'Is there a problem here?'

Gigi spun around to see Costas standing there. A taller, more filled-out Costas than he'd been at the beginning of summer.

'None of your business, wog.' Todd stepped towards him then hesitated. Costas was now much taller than him, and with broad shoulders he cut a rather strong figure, bigger than any of the boys in Todd's footy team. Gigi could see the conflict in Todd's eyes.

Costas didn't move, just stood his ground.

Gigi wasn't sure how this would play out. And she wasn't about to find out.

'Todd and I were just saying goodbye. Lily hosted a picnic we were both at.' She looked at Todd. 'Goodbye, Todd. See you at school next week.' She turned on her heel and headed towards home, hoping Costas would follow.

A few strides down the street he caught up, falling into step with her.

'You went away.' She didn't look at him.

'I did.'

'You didn't say anything.'

'I didn't.'

Silence. All the way back to the caravan park.

'And now you're back?' She turned and looked him in the eye and was met with sadness.

'I am.' He bowed his head. 'Good afternoon, Virginia.'

He strode off into the waning day.

———

Arthur was sitting in the shade under the awning of his caravan when Gigi walked into the park.

'Thank you,' she said, handing him back the pendant.

'Did it help?' He patted the deckchair next to him, inviting her to sit.

'Yes.'

From behind a forest of banksias, they couldn't see the ocean from the caravan park, but they could hear the sound of waves crashing into the shore. The soundtrack to Gigi's life. It was wild, and comforting; ever-changing yet perpetual.

They sat there listening to the sea as they sorted through coins spread across the vinyl card table.

'Thanks for your help with this,' Arthur said. 'Elaine, God rest her, was a beautiful soul. But she wasn't the most organised of people.'

'Tell me more about her.'

Arthur leaned back in his chair and told Gigi how they'd met. It was clear he'd loved her, every day of their fifty years together. Gigi let Arthur's tender words wash over her as they piled coins up. When they'd finished she sat forward as Arthur continued his love story, right up to Elaine's passing.

'I'm glad I found this little piece of paradise, Miss Gigi.' Arthur's voice floated into the cooling air.

'I'm glad you did, too.' Gigi pushed herself out of her chair, kissed him on the forehead and bade him goodnight.

With the midnight moon casting an ethereal glow over Banksia Bay, Gigi climbed down from her tiny bunk in the living space of the cabin, careful not to wake Mum and Dad as she pulled on her overalls.

She tiptoed through the caravan park and headed to the beach. Most of the tourists had gone now. In a few days the rest would disappear and she'd have her quiet stretch of peace back.

Kicking off her slippers beside the fishing shack, she let her toes sink into the damp sand and drew in a deep breath of salty air. It wasn't often she came down to the beach in the middle of the night – Mum would have a conniption if she ever found out – just every now and then, when she couldn't sleep.

She walked up the sand, jumping in and out of the tiny waves that lapped the shore, splashing around as she kicked off the white foam that stuck to her feet. She ran along the edge of the water, zigging in and zagging out until she reached the north end. The moon bounced silver light off the waves. Raising her arms in the air, she threw her head back to count the stars above. She always started the count right there at the Southern Cross, and she always gave up when she reached fifty-eight blinking dots.

A cold shiver ran up the back of her neck and she spun around, scanning the beach. There, over in the dunes, was a dark figure. There was enough distance between them that she could probably outrun whoever it was. She was fast when she needed to be.

She watched, for just a moment, before taking a few steps backwards. She was ready to run, but didn't want to draw attention to herself. The figure stood up.

Tall. Broad.

He hadn't seen her yet. She should run. Now.

Turn, Gigi.

She twisted her body, willing her feet to follow.

He started to walk towards her.

She stood still.

She knew that gait, despite the boy she knew turning into a man over summer.

He saw her, headed straight for her and stopped, just a few inches in front of her.

Gigi stared up into Costas' face. He'd been crying, the tracks of his tears still stained against his dark skin.

'Do you want to do something fun?' she whispered. She couldn't bear to see him looking so sad.

'Sure.'

She led him to the water's edge and drew a line in the sand with her toes where the waves stopped and returned to the ocean. It was a game she used to play with Ian, before he went and became an adult. You stood on the line, watching the waves, and waited till the very last minute before jumping as high as you could in the air. If you timed it right, you landed after the water had receded. If you didn't, splash.

'And you have to land on this side of the line.' Gigi tapped the wet sand with her foot. 'Or you're out.'

The first two waves, Costas jumped far too early and landed right as the wave crossed the line, splashing salty water all over his rolled-up trousers.

Gigi laughed. 'It's about timing. Watch me, and wait.'

Costas looked into her eyes and he twitched as the next wave came in.

'Wait.' Gigi's voice was low.

Costas rocked back and forth.

'Wait,' she said, as he bent his knees. 'Now!'

They jumped high into the air, landing just as the waved rolled backwards.

'And that's how it's done.' Gigi bowed.

Costas won the next two waves; the height he got on his jumps was seriously impressive.

On the next wave, Gigi lost her balance trying to stretch herself further and she fell into Costas, forcing them both to tumble onto the sand, rolling away from each other as they laughed.

Costas hauled himself to his feet. 'Thank you, Virginia. I needed that.'

He held his hand out to help her up. She took it and as he pulled her to standing they stared into each other's eyes.

Costas tilted his head towards the south, towards the fishing shack, as he angled his body away from her and she fell into step beside him.

In silence they walked, close to each other, his hands brushing hers briefly every now and then. She didn't dare look at him. Didn't dare reach out.

Outside the fishing shack, Costas waited for her to put her shoes back on and then led her to the road and walked her to the edge of the caravan park. He bowed and then tipped his imaginary hat, looking deeply into her eyes, before turning and striding into the night.

Gigi sucked in great gulps of air, her heart racing, as she watched him disappear into the dark.

Twelve

*L*aura was up before the sun, pacing the living room and waiting for the clock to tick over to six-twenty-five. She didn't want to appear too keen. She didn't want to be late. She didn't want to be seen in a pair of swimmers either, but there was no getting around that.

Six-O-five.

She checked her emails and fired off a quick note to Maher.

'Holiday doing me good. Very relaxing.' Lie. *'Start surfing lessons today. Send rescue helicopter.'*

She made a cup of coffee. How hard was this surfing thing actually going to be? Harder than she thought, probably. She tried to imagine jumping up on the board, catching a wave. What she mostly imagined was falling off. Heath having to catch her. His hands around her waist . . .

For goodness' sake, stop it.

He may not be married and off limits anymore, but he was the last thing she needed right now. Not that the thought of a brief hot fling wasn't appealing. It most definitely was. But he was Virginia's grandson and Laura was deceiving them all. There was no way that could end well. Rule number ten, *don't get personally involved in your stories.*

And this is a story, she reminded herself.

If only she could figure out a way to get out of what would surely be total humiliation today. Was that a stomach-ache she felt coming on? No. That would do her no good. Heath would be kind and understanding and simply postpone her torture to another day. And to maintain her façade about her fictitious travel article, she'd have to go through with it eventually. Surfing was part of the town's culture and history, after all. He'd played that card well.

There was nothing else to do but just get it over and done with. Maybe she'd be so bad that he'd give up on her altogether, suggesting she try her hand at milking cows or harvesting honey to get a dose of true local flavour.

Hmm. Now that was maybe worth angling for. Not that she'd have to fake incompetence on a surfboard. She was fairly sure that would come quite naturally.

Six-twenty.

A knock on the door.

'You ready?' Heath called from the verandah.

Laura walked down the hall, Darth Vader's march playing in her head.

'Ah, great.' Heath stood before her smiling, a wetsuit covering his lower body, the top half of the suit folded over, his chest and arms bare. 'Thought I'd better swing by on my way to make sure you were up. Which you are. Shall we?'

Laura took a deep breath.

———

She didn't know what she'd been expecting, but she had thought at least she'd get wet. Hence the swimmers – red polka dots. They had been a gift a few Christmases ago from Lillian. Polka dots were always her grandmother's favourite. Lillian had at least five outfits in different spotted colours. Laura's earliest memory of her grandmother was sitting in her lap as she read aloud, Laura joining the dots on her dress to make imaginary patterns.

Polka-dot swimmers seemed a waste right now, though, as she and Heath spent the first half-hour on the sand, lying on the board, Laura trying to jump up, keep her weight balanced and land both feet at the same time, in a smooth action, and not fall off the board straight away even if she did manage those first few steps. Which she didn't. Not even once.

Heath was patient and encouraging. She was doing well, he said.

No, she wasn't. She was all for charm, but outright lying to her was taking things a bit too far.

One more attempt.

She took a few deep breaths as instructed, raised herself up on her forearms, another couple of breaths, lift, pop, spread the feet, arms out wide . . . she did it! She landed both feet on the board.

And then she toppled over, ploughing face first into the sand.

'Oh God, are you all right?' Heath rushed to her side and put a comforting hand on her back. Her trembling back. 'Oh, Laura, you're crying. I'm sorry.'

She rolled over, giggling, tears streaming down her cheeks.

'Or laughing.' Heath sat back. 'Is that laughing?'

'Yes.' Laura could barely get the word out. 'Please tell me I'm not the worst student you've ever had,' she said between snorts.

'I don't want to ruin the trust thing we have going with a lie . . .'

She hit him in the arm. 'In this one instance, I'll allow a small fib.'

'You're not *the* worst.'

Laura stood up and swept the sand from her face and arms. Heath brushed it off her back. She froze at his gentle touch.

'Do you want to try again?' he whispered in her ear, his body behind her, almost touching her.

She stepped forward and turned around. 'Run the technique by me one more time.'

Again he showed her, making it look so easy. He broke the steps down and she repeated each one four or five times, before stringing them together.

Then she did it. And stayed upright. And she did it again.

She jumped up and down on the sand in a little victory dance.

Heath's expression was kind, warm. 'I knew you could do it. Now, we just have to do it out there.' He turned and pointed to the waves.

She fell to the ground, throwing her arms out beside her. 'You've got to be kidding. Can't we just take this as a victory and call it quits?'

Heath laughed. 'Well, not if you want to be able to say you learned to surf. Right now, you've only learned to stand up. On land.'

She shot him a look.

'On a board, yes,' he said. 'But that isn't surfing.'

'We could pretend it is.'

Heath pulled a wetsuit out of his backpack. 'You might want to put this on.'

She eyed the black rubber suit.

'It's Charlotte's. It should fit you. The water's pretty cold this time of year, and you don't want to chafe.'

Chafe? Is that a thing?

'Trust me.'

She did. Trust him. Turned out her instinct was right, and that's what worried her. There weren't too many people in her life she did trust – Maher, Mrs Duncan, and once upon a time Lillian, though that trust was now in question. Because her mother had walked out on her so young, trust was something that didn't come easily to Laura. That she trusted Heath, after such a short time knowing him, was new territory for her. New and frightening.

She slipped into the wetsuit. Well, wriggled and writhed and pushed her way in was more accurate. She'd seen surf movies. They made it look sexy. This was most definitely not sexy.

Heath moved behind her and pulled her zip up and then slipped his upper body easily into the top half of his suit.

'Ready?' he asked.

'No.'

With her surfboard under his arm, he took her hand and steered her to the edge of the water.

As she walked into the sea Laura stopped. The water was calm. At least she thought it was. In the time she'd been in the Bay, she had definitely seen waves bigger than this.

'You're not surfing?' She looked at him.

'These are a bit small. Great for you to practise on, though. The waves will be bigger tomorrow and I'll go out then.'

Laura bit her bottom lip. Part of her had hoped he'd be so busy catching his own waves, he'd forget all about her.

'No. This is a good thing. I can stay near you and you can practise getting up. And we don't have to worry about the hardest part.'

'This isn't the hardest part?' Fear rose inside her.

'When there are proper waves, we have to paddle out past the break to catch them.' He pointed out to sea. 'That's where the real work is.'

The real work? What had she been doing all morning? Knitting?

In the shallows he got her to practise getting up and standing on the board. The first five times she fell, crashing into the water. On the sixth go, she managed to stand for three whole seconds before falling. On the tenth she stayed up, and with a little push from Heath, she rode the dying wave in to shore.

'Great work. This time you're going to catch the wave yourself.'

She looked at him in shock.

'You can do it. Paddle then pop.'

Paddle then pop. Just like that.

Three times the little waves crashed over her head as she tried to paddle in front of them, not going fast enough. Maybe she should just drift back to shore. Call it quits. *No.* She'd come this far, surely she could take this step. She turned her board around and set herself up for the next one. This time she paddled as hard as she could. She set her arms right, pushed, slid her left leg forward and stood. She was standing. And the board was moving forward. On its own.

She let out a little scream.

'Bend your knees,' came a call from behind, and she did.

She rode the small wave all the way to the end of its life and then fell sideways into the water.

Heath came swimming alongside her. 'Did that hurt? Next time I'll teach you how to fall.'

'That was ... it ... I ...'

'You surfed.' He found her words for her.

She stood up and threw her arms around his neck. 'I surfed! Again?'

She caught five more waves, two ending with her falling off halfway through the run, three that she managed to ride in to shore.

And she was exhausted.

After the fifth wave she sat on the sand, surfboard next to her, just within reach of the lapping tide.

'Well?' Heath lowered himself beside her.

'It was more fun than I thought it would be.'

He bumped her shoulder with his.

'Don't you dare say I told you so.' She glared at him.

He zipped his mouth shut, his eyes glinting with joy.

She pushed him over and lost her balance, falling onto his chest. With one hand he reached up and brushed her wet, matted hair behind her ears. She stared into his eyes. His other hand pressed into the small of her back.

Oh God, what are you doing?

She pushed herself up. 'I'm starving. Maybe we should go get some lunch.' Starving – truth. Wanting to get lunch – lie. What she really wanted was to stay right there, in his arms.

'Good idea.' Heath stood up and helped her unzip her wetsuit and she stepped away from him as soon as he was done.

They walked into town to the bakery. Mrs Andrews' Finest Fresh Bakes.

'Hey.' Laura turned to Heath as he handed her a hot meat pie. 'Is Mrs Andrews any relation to the woman whose name is on those early editions of The Bugle?'

'Yep. Well, sort of. The original Mrs Andrews is long gone. But her family run the bakery now. They keep the name to honour their grandmother. It's hard to find anyone around here who hasn't been here for generations, or isn't related to someone who has. Kids move away all the time, for study, or work, or travel. But they often come back. It's always the same names you see popping up everywhere.'

Where had the Tinellis' name disappeared to, then? And why?

'It's not often, outside of tourist time, we get new faces around here.'

'And when you do?'

Heath looked her in the eye. 'Well, they are always noticed, often judged.' He raised a finger in the air. 'But they are usually interesting.'

Laura's cheeks burned when he looked at her that way.

They ate their pies as they sat on the small metal chairs outside the bakery. Heath said hello to everyone who passed, most people stopping for a brief chat.

'Do you know everyone in town?' Laura asked.

'It's hard not to.' He smiled. 'It's one of the things I love about living here. Even when I was living in Ocean Heights, I came home every weekend. Mind you, when I was a wayward teenager it wasn't such a good thing.'

'A wayward teenager?' Somehow Laura had no trouble imagining Heath as a cheeky youth.

'Some stories are better left in the past.' His eyes crinkled at the edges.

And some need to come into the light, thought Laura.

'So, tomorrow morning – lesson two?' Heath finished off his pie.

'Sounds like a da— a plan.' Yes, just a plan. Not a date. She wasn't here to date.

∽

Virginia rifled through the files on the coffee table in the holiday house.

Yvonne paced back and forth. 'We shouldn't be doing this.'

'Probably not. But we have to. We need to protect ourselves.'

'What are we looking for?'

'Anything? Everything.'

That wasn't much help, Virginia knew. They just had to go through whatever Laura had on them and figure out what to do next.

Yvonne pulled out some pictures of the Bay, of surfers. 'Maybe she is just here to do a travel story.' She held them up to Virginia.

'Keep looking.'

'Virginia?' Yvonne's voice was soft and she held up some copies of The Bugle.

Virginia took in a deep breath and searched more frantically through her pile. Then she came across a sheet of paper with names on it. Hers, Yvonne's, Richard's. There were questions on the paper too. But what caught her eye, what made the bile rise in her stomach, was seeing Costas' name in the middle of the page. Underlined. Surrounded by question marks.

'Yvonne.' Her hands quivered as she showed her.

'Oh, shit.'

The room began to spin and Virginia held on tightly to her friend. Laura may not know who Costas was, but she had his name and it was now only a matter of time.

The hinges on the picket fence groaned.

'Here.' Virginia pushed a cloth into Yvonne's hands and tidied up the files. She slipped out the back door and listened to make sure Yvonne was all right.

'Oh, hi.' Laura's voice filled the house. 'What are you doing here, Yvonne?'

'Just a bit of cleaning.'

Virginia was impressed how Yvonne held her nerve. But then, she had always been the braver of the two of them.

'You clean holiday houses?'

'Yes. Remember I said I manage this place?'

'On weekends?'

Virginia's heart raced.

'Whenever I can fit it in. I knew you'd be out and I didn't want to disturb you. How was the surfing lesson?'

Virginia let out the breath she'd been holding in. She hated asking Yvonne to lie for her. Again. She owed that woman so much. Her life, in fact.

Satisfied that Yvonne was safe, Virginia tiptoed away from the holiday house and once she was clear, she picked up the pace and made a beeline for home.

∽

As evening rolled round, Laura stepped away from her notes. She'd been poring over them, organising what she'd already discovered, writing out her next questions. Come Monday she would go back to the Ocean Heights library and resume going through The Bugle. She knew she'd find answers there. She just wasn't sure to which questions.

She was about to change into her pyjamas when there was a knock on the door.

Her pulse quickened at the thought it might be Heath. As she opened the door, though, her heart sank.

'Charlotte? What are you doing here?'

The woman stood before her, a baking dish in her hand. 'Sorry to bother you. I just thought you might like some leftover roast lamb.' She held out the dish.

Laura took it and invited her in.

'Is there something else?' Charlotte's demeanour wasn't sitting quite right.

'Actually, yes. I wanted to talk to you about Heath.'

'Heath?'

'Yes. Do you mind if I sit down?' She moved to the sofa.

Laura got her a drink of water and sat down next to her. 'What is it, Charlotte?'

'Heath. Well, he's not . . . like other guys. He comes across as charming and confident and strong, and he is. He's all those things. Stronger than anyone else I know.'

Laura had already ascertained all this herself. 'But?'

'Well, deep down he's actually more fragile than most.'

Laura was certain Heath would be mortified to know his big sister was going around saying that to women.

'He came home from your lesson, and he was . . . well . . . I don't want him to get hurt. He's had to deal with so much . . . pain in the past, so much uncertainty.' A look of sadness came over her face.

'We've all had our heart broken, Charlotte. Get to our age and it's inevitable.' She reached out and took Charlotte's hand. 'I'm not here to break your brother's heart.'

'Have you, Laura? Had your heart broken?' Charlotte looked her in the eye. The blue-green of Charlotte's gaze was the same as Virginia's.

Laura let go of her hand and looked down. 'Of course. We weren't married. But he left me. For someone else. After five years of lies.' *Hurtful, horrible, painful lies.*

'Why do men do that?' Charlotte hit her leg. 'If you don't love me anymore, then fine. But why have an affair?'

'If we knew the answer to that, we could start our own talk show.'

Charlotte laughed, a light, joyful sound, like Aiden's.

'I tried to figure it out when Bumfluff left me,' Laura said.

'Bumfluff?'

'Yes. Any time he tried to grow a beard, he could only manage this light, fluffy stubble.'

Charlotte raised her hand. 'Bumfluff.' Laura gave her a high five. 'Did you figure it out?'

'With him, I think it was because he didn't want to be the bad guy. If he broke up with me, he'd be at fault. If he never got caught, he'd stay a hero.'

'Men are stupid.' Charlotte sighed.

'A lot of them, yes.'

'I'm sorry I took up so much of your time. I just worry about Heath sometimes. He's got . . . I just worry.'

'You're a good sister.'

Charlotte got up and took her glass into the kitchen.

Laura scrambled to cover the notes that were strewn across the dining table before Charlotte saw anything. She wasn't sure if she'd made it in time or not. But her visitor didn't say anything, so maybe she was in the clear.

As she walked out the door, Charlotte turned around, gave Laura a look she couldn't decipher, and then headed down the path.

She turned back. 'You promised me you wouldn't hurt my family, remember?'

'I remember.'

Guilt tore through her.

Thirteen

The next morning Laura was down at the beach, wetsuit on, before Heath arrived. She was going to keep today's lesson strictly professional – teacher, student.

'Morning,' Heath called as he walked towards her, surfboard under his arm. He moved in to greet her with a kiss on the cheek, but she stepped back.

'Good morning.'

Heath seemed unfazed by her slight retreat. Perhaps Laura had imagined the heat between them yesterday.

'Are you ready for the hard work today?' He laid his surfboard on the sand.

Duck-diving was on the agenda today, the technique on sand to start, then some practice in the water. But before diving under the waves, Heath taught her how to fall.

'There's a right way to fall?'

'Always.'

Backwards, knees tucked in, arms around head.

She stood up on her board and prepared herself to topple into the water. A few deep breaths.

Heath tipped the board and in she went.

Splashing as she resurfaced, she wiped the salt water from her face. 'That wasn't very nice.'

'No time to prepare out there,' he declared.

'Oh, this is funny, is it?'

'A little.' His eyes sparkled. 'Yes.'

She hit the water with her arm, sending white spray into his face.

'Okay. I think you're ready.' He pointed out to the depths of the sea.

As he'd predicted, the waves were bigger today. A lot bigger. Here in the shallows Laura was feeling confident. Out there . . . the waves looked like mountains to her.

'There's a small rip just up there.' He pointed to the north. 'That will help us.'

She may not have known much, or anything, about surfing or beaches, but she did know you were supposed to stay out of rips. And she told him so.

'True. As a swimmer, absolutely. And if you were on your own, absolutely, again. But I've been surfing these waters all my life. You're in good hands. Surfers often use rips to help them get behind the waves.'

This required a huge leap of faith for Laura. Yes, she trusted this man, inexplicable as that was, but this was next level. The last time she'd trusted a man to this degree, it hadn't ended well. At all.

Her breathing became shallow.

'Hey.' He touched her cheek. 'It's okay. We don't have to, if you don't want to. We can do it the other way. Paddle out. Or not at all, if you want to stop.'

Laura looked into the aqua water, the waves foaming at their hips. Now that she was here, she didn't want to quit. But every fibre of her being, every instinct, rule number three, was telling her to stay away from the rip.

'Paddle?' Her voice was soft, unsure.

'Okay.'

Heath repeated his instructions on where to position her body on the board, and how to duck-dive. Pushing the nose of the board under a wave and following it down till you were completely submerged, to come back up on the other side didn't sound like too much fun to her.

'I'll be beside you the whole way.' He squeezed her hand and they faced the ocean.

On the board she kicked and dragged her arms through the water, like he'd taught her. She tried to push the board under the wave as it broke just in front of her, but she got dumped, tumbling inside the wave, not knowing which way was up or down. Fear raced through her. Panic.

Heath pulled her to the surface. 'That's what we call a wipe-out. Congratulations, you're now initiated.'

Laura coughed and spluttered and looked at him with wide eyes.

'Remember, push down with your arms, then one leg on the back of the board.'

Eventually, with lots of help from Heath, Laura managed to duck and paddle through the breakers. And she was absolutely exhausted. How was she going to catch a wave when her whole body felt like it had been hit by a truck?

She sat on her board, rising up and down with the swell. 'That . . . was not fun.'

Heath bobbed beside her. 'Paddling is the hardest part.'

'Which is why you use the rips.' She threw her head back.

'Next time.' He smiled.

Next time? It was going to take Laura a month to recover from this time.

With their legs dangling in the water, they sat out behind the break. The motion of the sea was rhythmic; the only sound was the crashing waves on the distant shore. Beyond them was nothing but the ocean. It was as if this was the entire world, just the two of them, the sea and the silence.

Laura raised her face to feel the warmth of the sun. She breathed deeply, the taste of salt on her lips. Exhaustion seeped out of her and energy filled her.

'Is it like this every time?' she whispered.

Heath paddled his board closer to hers. 'Yep. And there's nothing else like it in the world.'

As much as she could have stayed out there forever, she really wanted to catch a wave. With Heath's encouragement she turned her board around.

'This one,' he shouted to her, as the water heaved behind them.

But she froze, and the waved passed under her.

'That's okay.' Heath reached out and patted her leg. 'There's more coming.'

'I don't think I can.' She looked into his eyes. 'I mean, on the sand and in the shallows is one thing. This is real surfing. Proper waves.'

Heath's eyes were full of warmth. 'I know it's scary. But sometimes doing what scares us is a good thing.' He manoeuvred his board next to hers so he was facing her, his head just inches from hers. 'Besides, it's the only way back to civilisation.'

'Civilisation is highly overrated. I could become a mermaid.'

He laughed. 'I promise you you're ready for this and you won't regret it.'

She looked him in the eye.

'Have I lied to you yet?'

'Yes. You weren't a Boy Scout.'

'Technically I didn't lie about that.' Heath raised a hand to his chest. 'You've got this. I know you can do it. Here comes a good one. Ready?'

No. She wasn't ready. She would never be ready. So . . . if she'd never be ready, now was as good a time as any, she supposed. God help her.

She paddled hard. As she crested the wave she popped, putting out her arms to balance. She steadied herself, bent her knees. And she was surfing. For a few brief, terrifying, thrilling minutes she was actually surfing.

Before wiping out halfway through the ride.

She pushed herself to the surface and looked for Heath. He was coming in on the next wave.

'Did you see me?' she called out. 'I was surfing.'

As Heath's wave died, he slipped off his board and steered towards her. She threw herself into his arms. 'Did you see?' She hugged him tightly.

'You did great.'

She pushed herself back. 'Can we do it again?'

'Of course.' He looked rather proud.

Laura caught three more waves before the sheer exhaustion of paddling so much overtook the adrenaline pumping through her veins, and they headed back to shore.

'That was amazing. Thank you,' she said, as Heath helped her out of her wetsuit. The words so inadequate for the emotions raging inside her.

'Hungry?'

'Absolutely.'

In silence they walked to the shack at the end of the beach. Every now and then Laura looked up at Heath. Each time she did, he met her gaze, his pale blue eyes shining back at her. Every time her stomach tightened. Their pace was slow, their feet trailing through the water where the waves left the sand, their hands nearly touching.

'Here we are.' Heath's voice was low, rasping.

'Here we are.' Laura's voice was barely a whisper as she stared into his eyes.

'Successful morning?' Virginia shattered the moment.

Laura turned towards her and couldn't help but grin. 'I actually surfed.'

'She did well.' Heath said.

A scowl crossed Virginia's face momentarily, before she resumed her neutral expression. 'That's lovely. Can I get you something?'

They ordered a sandwich and a milkshake each and took their lunch down to the jetty to sit on the end with their legs dangling over the edge.

'So, do you think you'll get a piece out of your stay here?' Heath handed her a paper serviette.

'I think so.' She really hated lying. It was often part of her job – stretching the truth, obscuring vital information in order to coax a story out of someone – and she'd accepted that years ago. But she never lied in her personal life. Ever. And despite what she told herself, that this was just another story, it wasn't. This was as personal as it got. And it was getting more personal.

Poor Heath was an innocent bystander. He didn't deserve it. And Charlotte's visit last night didn't help allay any of Laura's guilt, either.

'How long did it take you to learn to surf?' She had to change the subject.

'Hmm, well, you'd have to ask Ian that. The way I remember it, he put me on a board before I could walk and I stood up first go. But I reckon he'd tell it differently.'

Laura could imagine.

'We're having a little party at the shack this afternoon, for Aiden's birthday. He told me this morning he hoped you'd come. Apparently your reading skills are second to none.'

Laura raised an eyebrow. 'Well, I did receive a sticker in kindergarten for exceptional reading out loud.'

'Impressive. Will you come? It's just family, a few friends. Very casual.'

Charlotte's words played in Laura's mind. *You promised me you wouldn't hurt my family*. Her guilt at lying to these people was heavy around her heart. But she didn't want today's feeling of joy and freedom to end. Since Lillian's passing, this was the lightest she'd felt. It was like a drug. She wanted more and she didn't care how she was going to get it.

'I'd love to come.'

Laura didn't know what to bring to the birthday of a seven-year-old boy, whose party you had been invited to at the last minute. The only shop in town other than the shack that was open on a Sunday, was the general store, so she had to improvise. She bought a block of chocolate, because who doesn't like chocolate, and a blue note pad.

Using the pages from the notepad, she designed an IOU for reading any book, any time. She hoped he'd appreciate it. She put on her blue A-line skirt and a loose white shirt, pulled her long brown hair back into a loose ponytail and set off along the beach to the shack, hoping Charlotte wouldn't be too upset that she'd come. She wrapped her teal cardigan more tightly around herself.

There would be other people there, so she probably didn't even have to talk to Heath, which would hopefully appease his sister. And help Laura keep a firm hold on her untrustworthy feelings.

As she neared the shack she could see everyone on the deck. Charlotte and Aiden, of course, Virginia handing out drinks, Yvonne following behind with a platter of nibbles, Ian at the barbecue with Heath standing beside him in a white linen shirt and dark denim jeans. He looked good. Really good.

Well, it wouldn't please Charlotte if Laura started to drool now, would it? She would have to situate herself anywhere but near him.

There were also two other people there who Laura hadn't met yet; both of them seemed to be around her age.

Aiden ran towards her when he saw her coming.

'Did you bring me a present?' he asked, looking at the gift Laura had wrapped in blue notepaper in her hand.

'Aiden. That's not polite.' Charlotte joined her son. 'Thank you. You didn't have to.'

'It's nothing. Just a token really.'

Aiden ripped open the present, his eyes lighting up when he saw the chocolate. Then he opened the IOU.

'Now?' He looked up at her.

'I don't have a book on me.'

He ran into the shack and grabbed three books off Virginia's shelves, handing all of them to her and sitting on the ground at her feet. She joined him down there and started reading.

Virginia whispered in Charlotte's ear, looking at Laura, a scowl on her face.

'Food's up!' Ian shouted. Trish, who'd been inside the shack, came out with some paper plates, her blue kaftan flowing behind her.

'Thank you, dear.' She kissed Ian on the lips.

'Anything for you, Trishy darling.'

Laura stared. That day on the Bodhi Bus when Kaftan told Old Salty not to be late, Laura had assumed they were father and daughter. But daughters didn't kiss their fathers like that. Ian and Trish were a couple? He had to be at least twenty years older than her. For someone who prided herself on being able to read people, she'd sure got some things wrong since landing in Banksia Bay. Could she still blame this on grief?

Everyone sat around the tiny mismatched tables and dug in to the sausages, steak and salad on offer.

'Oh, these steaks are the best I've ever had,' Laura declared as she finished off her serve. 'You have to tell me the secret.' She turned to Ian.

'Ask Heath. It's his secret. He won't even tell me.'

Heath put a finger to his lips and everyone laughed. Except Virginia.

After they'd all finished eating, Aiden asked Laura to read to him again.

'You know what time it is?' Yvonne said to the group, holding up two cricket bats and a tennis ball. Aiden dropped his book.

Everyone cheered. Except Laura. Cricket had never really appealed to her.

She stayed where she was as everybody took their places down on the sand, two bins in place to mark the wickets.

Heath ran back to her side. 'This is one of those not-optional kind of things.' He reached out his hand and pulled Laura up to standing. 'You eat at our table, you play beach cricket with us. No exceptions.'

She held her breath as he stood there, right in front of her, looking into her eyes.

'Uncle Heath,' Aiden called. 'We're ready.' He waved his bat in the air.

'We always open the batting together.' He turned and ran towards the wicket. 'Ready, buddy. Let's knock them for six.'

And Laura breathed out.

The next hour was more intense than Laura could ever have imagined. These people took their beach cricket very seriously. There were records that needed beating or defending, there were partnerships that needed to be destroyed, there were appeals to the umpire – Virginia – who sent Ian from the 'field' at one point for his refusal to accept he'd been run out. Laura was impressed that a man of his age still had it in him to run between the wickets at all, let alone with such determination. There was even a trophy – a big plastic model of Merv Hughes's head, which sat on one of the shelves in the shack – that was given to the MVP of the match. Yvonne had won it last year, apparently, for bowling out Heath and Ian in two balls, and she was determined to get back-to-back victories.

Trish had hiked her kaftan up into her knickers and took the bat from Kim, Charlotte's work colleague, who'd just got out. Trish stared Heath down as he prepared to bowl. She raised two fingers to her eyes and then pointed them at Heath.

Instinctively, Laura took a step back. She'd spent the match in the dunes, also known as the outfield, except for the brief few minutes when she'd batted, Yvonne sending down a few light balls that Laura actually hit. The only problem was, the third ball she'd hit sailed so high into the sky that she stood there admiring her own skill and forgot to run. Which was apparently against the rules of 'hit and run' cricket, and Aiden threw the ball at the wicket and ran her out.

Heath rearranged the field, moving Laura to the 'on side', which was just a fancy way of saying right on the shoreline. She stood where she was told, the waves lapping her ankles.

Heath's first ball was a wide, according to Virginia, who smiled sweetly at her grandson when he appealed the call. His second went straight through to the keeper, Charlotte's friend from school, Rod or Ron or Ryan.

Trish repeated her stare-down of Heath. He held her gaze as he ran up, bowled and grunted as he sent the tennis ball down the sandy pitch.

Trish swung the bat, connecting with a solid whack, and the ball rose high into the air.

Right in Laura's direction.

'Catch it,' Aiden called, and Laura realised he was yelling at her.

Oh, shit. She looked up, stepped back. The ball kept coming. She ran, deeper into the water, keeping her eyes on the ball.

Here it came.

She put her hands up, the ball fell into her grasp, she fumbled, someone gasped. She recovered, wrapping her fingers around the ball.

And she fell backwards into the ocean, her arm held aloft.

A cheer went up and everyone ran towards the sea.

Aiden threw himself into the water next to Laura. 'That was awesome.' He hugged her and together they stood back up to the applause of the group. They were soaked through, but Laura didn't mind.

'That *was* pretty awesome.' Heath winked at her, standing just a few centimetres away.

Aiden pushed between them and grabbed each by the hand and the three of them walked through a sea of pats on the back.

Back at the shack, Virginia brought out the Merv trophy.

'Ian, as the stalwart of the group, you get to choose the winner.'

He took the trophy with a reverent gesture. 'There is only one choice. Sorry, Yvonne.' She faked a look of disappointment, then smiled as he handed Merv over to Laura.

'You get to keep it for a week and then it comes back to the shack,' Virginia said.

As the sun began to set, Heath, Ian, Kim, Yvonne, Trish and Ryan – he was definitely Ryan – disappeared for a moment and then returned, each with their surfboard.

'Do you want to join us?' Heath asked Laura, his expression hopeful.

'I think I'll leave this one to the professionals.' She wasn't sure she had the strength to paddle any more today.

'Then take this.' He wrapped his large beach towel around her wet shoulders and a shiver ran down her spine. She pulled the towel tight and watched as he entered the water. In sync with the others, he paddled out the back and waited for the right set of waves. In pairs they'd catch one in, cutting through the water with ease, weaving out of each other's way. It was almost like a dance.

'They've been surfing together for years.' Charlotte stood beside her. 'Ian taught every one of them. Even Yvonne. She always says it saved her life. I have no idea what she means. Surfers can be a funny lot when it comes to their connection with the ocean. It's all very spiritual, I'm told. I'm just glad Gran doesn't surf. Otherwise I'd be the only one.'

'They're really tight, aren't they? Your gran and Yvonne?'

'I've never seen a bond like it.' She shrugged. 'They don't say much about growing up here. Not about themselves, anyway. The only thing she and Gran ever really talk about when it comes to the past is what Ian was like back then. They paint an interesting picture.'

'Did I hear my name mentioned?'

Laura turned around to see Virginia looking at her with raised eyebrows.

'Just . . .' she scrambled to cover her tracks, 'commenting on what a lovely group of friends this is.' Well, that was weak.

'The best.' Virginia looked out to the group surfing. 'We'd do anything for each other.' She looked back at Laura. 'Anything to protect each other.'

Aiden came up to his mum, bleary-eyed and yawning.

'Why don't you lot head off?' Virginia suggested. 'They'll be out there a while. No point standing around.'

Laura had been hoping to talk to Ian about his photography, but it was obvious she'd have to wait. She said goodbye to Charlotte and Aiden and walked up the beach. Halfway to the holiday house she stopped and sat on the sand watching Heath and his friends in the waves, her chin nestled in Heath's soft towel gathered in folds around her.

Fourteen

Virginia tidied up the remaining mess from the party, and then rearranged the books on the shelves inside. She paced back and forth, and eventually the surfers came in. She said goodbye to everyone and then grabbed Yvonne by the arm, dragging her to the side of the shack.

'My God, could you have taken any longer? We're heading back to your place. Now.'

Yvonne nearly fell as Virginia grabbed her hand. 'Why?'

'I need to use your inter-spider-web. We have to gaggle something.'

'You mean google?'

Virginia flapped her hand. 'I don't care what it's called. Let's go.'

When they got to Yvonne's cottage, Virginia didn't even let her get changed out of her surfing gear.

'Well, show me how this works,' she said, as she sat at the dining table, pulling Yvonne's laptop off the kitchen bench.

'Virginia, stop.' Yvonne sat down next to her. 'Don't you think this has gone far enough? We nearly got caught snooping around her stuff.'

Virginia rubbed her temples. 'I know. But we need to find out more. She was looking in The Bugle. The Bugle!'

'She won't find those pages. We took care of that decades ago.'

'I know. But this evening, when you were out having fun on the water, I overheard her asking Charlotte about you and me.'

'About both of us?'

Virginia rubbed her hands. 'About our friendship.'

'That can't be good.'

'Exactly.'

Yvonne opened up the computer, and with a few swift movements of her fingers across the keyboard, something opened on the screen.

'What are we looking for?' Yvonne turned to her.

'Anything we can find.'

'I googled her when you asked me to before. There's no Laura Hamilton that matches her.'

'Is that normal? For a young person like her these days not to be on the line?'

'Online,' Yvonne corrected her. 'Actually no. It is a bit strange.'

'Try something for me, Yvonne. Look for Laura Prescott.'

Yvonne gasped. Her fingers typed.

Virginia watched as a list came up on the screen. They scrolled through and every time Yvonne opened a new article, Virginia read with increasing horror.

Laura Prescott's name was everywhere, a small photo often accompanying the articles. And not one page they opened had anything to do with travel.

Yvonne pushed her seat back and Virginia stood up and paced the room.

She had trouble breathing.

'She's an investigative journalist.' The words barely came out of Virginia's mouth. 'She knows. She has to.'

'We don't know that for sure.' Yvonne stood up too. 'Maybe . . . maybe . . .'

Virginia waited. Sweet Yvonne, always looking for the good. She was unlikely to find any in this situation, though.

Her face fell. 'Shit, Virginia. What are we going to do?'

'We're going to have to do some investigating of our own.'

Virginia slumped into the chair and Yvonne put her arms around her. Normally she'd swat Yvonne away, keep her at a safe distance. But there was no safe distance now.

It looked like their past was about to catch up with them.

January 1963

In the early morning light, Gigi walked quietly around the caravan park, completing the chores she knew wouldn't disturb the guests – cleaning the shower block, picking up the litter left behind by those who'd moved on. She would empty the bins later, the heavy metal lids clanged loudly no matter how carefully she lifted them.

Out the front of his caravan, Arthur was bent over a small gas camping stove. Gigi put down her bucket and walked over to him.

'That smells good,' she said, and he stood up to greet her.

'Scrambled.' He stirred the eggs in the small frypan. 'They were Elaine's favourite. Would you like some?'

Gigi knew it would be impolite to impose on him, but she hadn't eaten breakfast, and after tossing and turning all night she was genuinely hungry.

'Oh, no, I couldn't.' Then a sound, something like a dog growling, came from her stomach.

'I think maybe you could. Please. I'd enjoy the company.'

The delicious smell of the eggs cooking did not, unfortunately, match the taste. They were like rubber and had a strange metallic flavour to them. Gigi didn't say anything, though. Arthur looked so proud of himself. She simply thanked him and told him how much she appreciated him sharing his breakfast with her. Which she did. The sentiment, at least.

'So tell me, Arthur. Where are you heading to after this? When summer ends?'

Arthur raised a finger, pushed himself out of his chair and disappeared into the caravan. When he came back he was holding a large, folded-up map. He cleared the tiny camping table and laid the map out, the sides spilling over the edge.

It was a map of Australia, with a long red pen line that looped its way all around the country.

'That is some journey.' Gigi put her hands on her hips, impressed.

'Now that I've started, I just can't wait to get all the way around.'

'How long do you think it will take you?' Gigi looked at all the towns and cities. Some she'd heard of: Melbourne, Adelaide and Perth, of course. Some she hadn't: Tanunda, Busselton, Woorim. She didn't count them, but there had to be at least one hundred stops marked along the winding route.

'I suspect many years.' His voice was wistful and there was a sadness in his eyes. 'I may not get to all of them, but where there's breath, there's hope.'

Gigi wondered if he had any intention of making it home at all, or if he would simply wander endlessly until the good Lord decided to take him. Perhaps it wasn't such a bad way to spend the last of one's twilight years.

'Will you do something for me, Arthur?' Gigi turned to him.

'Anything, love.'

'Will you send me a postcard? From every place you stop in?'

Arthur's eyes lit up. 'Of course. It would be my pleasure.'

There were still chores to be done, so Gigi excused herself. As the rest of the park guests began to stir, she put away her bucket and prepared to empty the rubbish bins. One day she would cast embarrassment aside and actually put a peg on her nose for the job.

Once her chores were done, Gigi cleaned up, grabbed her knapsack and filled it with the requisite supplies, before swinging by the holiday house to collect Lily. Together they walked up the beach, letting the waves splash their legs despite how cold the water was.

'You seem pretty chirpy this evening.' Gigi turned slightly to face her friend.

Lily's face went bright red. 'Do I? I don't know what you're talking about.'

'Don't play games with me, Lillian Woodhouse. I know you better than you think I do. And that silly grin across your face is a dead giveaway that something's happened.'

It didn't take a rocket scientist to figure out that whatever had happened had something to do with Richard. He was the only one who could cause such a tragic doe-eyed look like that.

And it was starting to get on her nerves.

There was no doubt he made Lily happy. Any fool could see that. And Gigi supposed he was an all-right bloke, as far as blokes went – though he was a little too self-assured for her liking. It wasn't him so much that upset her, but the fact that Lily spent so much time with him. Away from her. She was jealous.

'Okay. Yes, Richard came over this morning. He took Daddy and me over to Ocean Heights for morning tea. It was really quite lovely, and he and Daddy got on so well.'

Gigi changed the subject. 'Are we still on tomorrow? For our walk along the south track and a picnic?'

Lily nodded.

Gigi didn't think Lily would back out. But it seemed Richard was escalating things. Taking out Senator Woodhouse? Why couldn't Richard and the Prescotts holiday somewhere else? Anywhere else.

Still. She wouldn't let thoughts of that man ruin tonight. The most special night of all summer nights. When Lily's stuffy parents let her stay over at the fishing shack.

They strolled arm in arm up the sand towards the weathered hut, sleeping bags and pillows under their arms, a stash of popcorn and chocolate in the hessian knapsack Gigi carried on her back.

Gigi's dad had left the wooden pallets out the front of the shack as their makeshift deck. As good a job as he always did cleaning the fishing shack before the girls had a sleepover, he couldn't ever quite eliminate the smell completely, so Gigi and Lily chose to sleep outside, using the shack to wash up in if needed. They also stored their food on the benches in there, making it harder for the crabs that liked to scuttle up the sand and steal their supplies when the tide turned.

Ian had also left a few lanterns out for them so they'd have some light during the night.

They ate the popcorn as soon as they set up their sleeping bags, and lay back against their pillows watching the sky over the ocean begin to fade from white-blue to soft orange.

'Should we try to catch our supper?' Gigi leapt up and headed into the shack to grab their rods.

'Is there any point?' Lily groaned.

'Always.' Gigi dragged her down the beach.

An hour later and the fish still weren't biting. Gigi's tummy was beginning to rumble and Lily was shuffling in the sand next to her, clearly not happy about their situation. Giving up, they headed back to the shack.

As they got closer, Gigi could see a familiar figure standing on the deck waiting for them. Her stomach tightened.

'I won't intrude.' Costas bowed his head as the girls hung up their rods. 'I was just out fishing before and caught way too much for just my family. If you want them . . .' He held up two large snapper. 'They're cleaned and ready to go.'

'You are a lifesaver.' Gigi took the fish from him. Their hands touched briefly as she did and her cheeks burned red. Thankfully the light was all but gone and they hadn't lit the lanterns yet. 'We were facing the very real prospect of chocolate for dinner. Not that that is an entirely bad prospect.'

Costas laughed and Gigi had to turn away.

'Thank you, Costas,' Lily said, maintaining a certain yet polite distance.

'Rightio, then. Enjoy your evening, ladies.' He bowed and walked off into the dark.

'I guess he returned,' Lily whispered, as she stepped up beside Gigi.

Gigi hadn't mentioned to Lily that Costas was back. She felt awful, keeping it a secret, but it was better that way. Really.

'Please don't tell me you're harbouring a silly schoolgirl crush for that . . . boy, Gigi. You cannot possibly be flirting with the idea that he's an acceptable suitor.'

Gigi turned around and put her hands on her hips. She knew what was coming next and she really didn't want their night to be ruined.

Lily took in a deep breath, but her voice faltered. 'It's just . . . well, you know. He's . . .'

'Don't half-say it, Lily.' Gigi wouldn't let her get away with that. She would force her to confront her ugly thoughts.

'He's Greek.' Lily whispered the word like muttering it would invoke a curse. 'An outsider.'

'Yes. He always has been. Ever since I've known him.' Gigi would not take this. Not even from her best friend. 'And he's been my friend since then, too.'

'I know that. And I'm not a bigot. Really. He does seem like a lovely chap. For a foreigner. I just think, maybe you can do . . . better. Like Todd.'

Oh, here she goes again. Gigi knew that if they discussed this any further, she was risking her friendship with Lily. She also knew that if she could only get them to spend some time together, Lily would see that Costas was a great guy and didn't deserve her mis-informed opinions. What did her dad always say? 'You can't change people's minds by beating them over the head. You have to change their experience, and that will change their mind.'

But how did she make that happen?

She turned back to the barbecue and emptied the bag of saw-dust into the bowl below the grill plate. Ian had taught her how to stoke it just right to get it to burn properly. Then she added a few sprigs of oregano that Costas had snuck her from his garden to infuse a delicious flavour into the fish.

'Costas doesn't like me like that, anyway,' Gigi said, as she put the fish on the barbecue. It hurt to admit it out loud. The truth often did. Every time she thought they were getting close, he pulled away. Still, she had to try to come up with ways for Lily to get to know Costas. He may not like her in *that* way, but he was a friend, and would always be part of her life. Just like Lily would be.

'Are you sure you're just friends?' Lily stepped beside her.

'Yes.'

Lily raised her eyebrows, but didn't say whatever she was thinking. Which was probably just as well.

'Let's go for a quick swim before we eat.' Gigi had to salvage their night. She jumped up and stripped off her overalls, her old swimsuit underneath.

Lily stood and removed her dress, revealing a brand-new costume.

'Race you.' Gigi giggled, and they ran towards the sea, laughing all the way.

The water was cold as they splashed in the waves and Lily stopped when it reached her knees. Gigi kept going until she was so deep she couldn't touch the bottom.

'Come back,' Lily called. 'Don't leave me.'

For a moment Gigi hesitated, wishing she could float out to sea, where life was surely simpler than here on land.

'Gigi!' Lily's voice carried across the waves.

Gigi took a breath and dived under the water, where it was silent and dark and nothing else existed. She pushed her way through, staying under as long as she could, popping back up right next to Lily.

'Don't ever do that to me again. I thought you'd drowned.' Lily hugged her tightly. 'I don't know what I'd do if I ever lost you.'

Gigi laced her fingers with Lily's and they walked back up the sand. 'You'll never have to find out.' She bumped Lily's hip gently. 'Sisters of Summer, remember?'

Dried off, they lay under the stars with bellies full of delicious fish, and just a little chocolate. Gigi looked up to the moon, which was now directly above them. She'd sleep outside every night if her parents let her. The air was warm and heavy, and the cicadas droned on. She didn't mind their noise when she was out here under the stars.

'You know,' Lily said, 'this old fishing shack could be so much more.'

'What do you mean?' Gigi turned onto her side.

'Well, look at this location. What if it were a restaurant?'

Gigi snorted. The only restaurant in town, if you could even call it that, was the pub. Banksia Bay wasn't really a restaurant sort of place.

'Okay.' Lily realised her mistake. 'What about a book store? We could run it together.'

The thought of running a business with her best friend sent goosebumps pricking all over Gigi's tanned skin. 'Or a milk bar? Aren't they all the rage these days?'

Lily clapped. 'Maybe when your dad retires, we could turn this into a milk bar and sell milkshakes to the tourists and we could put a pinball machine in the corner.'

Gigi could see it now, the two of them running The Milk Shack. They could even put chairs out the front. There was only one problem.

'Dad's going to fish till the day he dies, and then Ian will probably take over the boat.'

'Hmm. We might have to give this some more thought. Maybe I can ask Richard tomorrow. He's so smart. I'm sure he can think of something. Wouldn't it be fun to have a little summer business together?'

Okay. There were two problems. Richard didn't seem like the kind of guy who'd think this was a good idea at all.

The cicadas continued their evening song, long after they

should have gone to bed. It was going to be a hot night, so Gigi threw open her sleeping bag.

'I think I love him, you know,' Lily whispered into the night.

Gigi had figured that out ages ago. 'And does he love you?'

'I hope so.'

'Me too.' Gigi let out a long silent breath and Lily reached across the dark and took her hand.

Dawn broke and Gigi stirred. Quietly she started rolling up her sleeping bag. Lily always slept longer than she did.

She tidied up their rubbish and packed down the barbecue. Perched against the shack wall, she watched the sunrise while she waited for Lily to wake. All night she'd dreamed of what they could do with this place one day – some brightly coloured paint, chairs out the front, a milk bar or a gift shop selling Banksia Bay key rings – and the thought filled her with joy. Even if there were two rather significant potential issues with the concept. Gigi just knew that if they really put their minds to it, they could come up with a solution.

The first of the morning surfers hit the waves as she watched on, Ian among the group.

Lily began to stir. 'Morning.' Peeling herself out of the sleeping bag, she stretched her long, slender arms.

'The weather looks perfect for our trek today.' Gigi handed her a vegemite sandwich she'd packed yesterday. They always had a vegemite sandwich for breakfast when they camped out.

She helped Lily pack up their things and they headed back to the rental before setting off for the day.

Even though it was technically her house – well her parents' at least – Gigi never went inside when renters were holidaying there. And the Woodhouses never invited her in. She knew how Lily's family felt about the tomboy daughter of the local fisherman. And while they never once stopped Lily from spending time with her – she suspected they were secretly happy she was occupied for the summer, leaving them to do whatever rich adults did when they didn't have a kid in tow – they also never extended anything other than the civility of practiced politeness her way.

She stood at the bottom of the path, waiting for Lily to come out. And she waited. And waited.

What was taking so long? Even Lily didn't need this much time to get ready. They really should get on their way before it got too hot.

She took a step forward, then stopped. She could just knock on the door, softly, and ask if Lily was ready. But she didn't want to intrude.

She turned around. Three times. Stepped forward. Then back. And she waited.

After what felt like hours, though the sun was nowhere near its peak, the door opened and a resplendent-looking Lily stepped out onto the verandah. There really was no other word for it. Resplendent. She was wearing a teal and white polka-dot swing dress with white gloves and a teal headband. Her hair was perfectly turned under and she had little white heels on. Heels!

She wiped away a stray tear and walked towards Gigi.

'Oh, Gigi. You won't believe what's happened. Richard is here. He came by this morning to ask Daddy for my hand. We're heading off now to meet his family for tea and he's going to propose.' Tears, happy tears, fell from her eyes.

'Stop that. Or your make-up will run.' Gigi handed her a handkerchief.

Lily giggled. 'I'm so sorry, Gigi. We won't be able to go trekking today after all.'

Gigi threw her arms around her best friend, and then released her, afraid she was going to crumple her perfection. 'Don't be silly. This is far more important. Congratulations.' She squeezed Lily's gloved hands.

'Thank you. I knew you'd be happy for me. And this afternoon, when all this is over, we'll catch up and I'll tell you all about it.' She air-kissed Gigi's cheeks and spun around at her mother's call.

Gigi walked through the main street of town, hands in her overall pockets, kicking pebbles along in front of her. She really was pleased for Lily. Still, that little green-eyed monster was pricking at her. She didn't want it to get the better of her, though, she wouldn't be that type of friend. No. She would distract herself until she could shake the jealousy building inside her.

She turned off the main street and headed up over the green hills, thick with banksias and undergrowth, to find the hidden track she liked to tread when she needed to be alone.

Married people had friends, didn't they? Of course they did. It was ridiculous to assume that just because Lily was going to get married, they couldn't be friends anymore. They would continue on as normal, writing to each other through the year, and every summer Lily and Richard would holiday here and nothing would change.

Nothing.

Fifteen

On Monday morning Laura rose bright and early and waited for the Bodhi Bus at the post office on the main street. She gave a small wave to the people walking past, most of whom were now used to seeing her around town. Some of them even knew her name and she wasn't sure how she felt about that.

Yvonne pulled the van up and Laura got in. She was the only one heading to Ocean Heights today, it seemed.

'Good morning, Laura. How are you?' Yvonne's voice was rather high-pitched.

'Morning. I'm a bit sore, actually.' She rubbed her shoulders.

'Well, learning to surf can be hard. You're probably using muscles you haven't used before.'

That was true. Laura ached in places she didn't even know she had. 'Is no one else coming today?'

'There were a couple of people who were supposed to come, but they . . . um . . . cancelled . . . at the last minute.' She fidgeted with the collar of her tie-dyed T-shirt.

'Oh. Well, you don't want to make the trip just for me.' Laura started to back out of the van, upset she'd have to wait to get back to the library.

'Nonsense!' Yvonne shouted. 'Really.' Her voice returned to normal. 'I make the trip regardless of whether I have passengers. I always have errands to run myself.'

Laura was relieved. She had so much more digging to do.

'What are your plans today, then, while you're in the big smoke?' Yvonne looked in the rear-vision mirror as they pulled onto the road, and smiled. Not her usual easy grin, though. This one was forced.

The big smoke. Laura held back a giggle. 'I'm going to the library. More research for my travel piece. Then I might take a look around the town.'

'Oh. Great. You know, if you're looking for information, or funny anecdotes, or, well, anything really, speaking to the locals is probably a better way to do it.'

Laura didn't doubt that if she interviewed the people of Banksia Bay, the stories she'd hear would be entertaining, but she did doubt that they would share what she was looking for.

'That's true. And when I'm looking to fill in the colour of the piece, that's exactly what I'll do.' It was frightening how easily lying was coming to her now. 'This is just the boring background stuff. Population over time, the history of local industries, that sort of thing.' Oh so easy.

Yvonne's forehead crinkled in the middle. 'And how's the story coming along?'

'Slowly.' Truth.

'Any particular angle you're taking? Articles are all about angles, aren't they?'

They were indeed. 'I haven't found the right angle, yet. But I think I'm getting closer.' Also the truth.

'Have you unearthed anything . . . surprising?' Yvonne's voice went high again.

'Not yet.' Lie.

Maybe it was because Laura was the only passenger and Yvonne was simply passing the time with idle chatter, but there were a lot of questions today. All about Laura's article. Time to turn this around.

'You looked like a real pro out on the water last night, Yvonne.'

'Thank you. I've been surfing since I was kid. It always feels like home when I'm out there.'

'Not a late learner like me, then.'

'Nope. Ian taught me in my teens.'

'And you were hooked straight away?'

'Oh, most definitely. I fell in love with it. Ian was a great instructor. He had me surfing in no time at all, and that really helped me when . . . um, well, anyway, you know what they say about the healing power of nature. I should stop talking your ear off.' Yvonne leaned over and turned the radio up.

Laura sat back in her seat, her mind ticking over with new questions. Yvonne was hiding something. Was there anyone in Banksia Bay without a skeleton in their closet?

She couldn't wait to get to the library.

The librarian showed her to the same room as last time and Laura dug straight in to The Bugle. There was a lot of random gossip in those pages, but Laura was looking for specific names. Gigi, Virginia, Lily, Costas, Prescott, Woodhouse, Gilbert, Tinellis. She added Yvonne to her names to look out for. Hmm. She didn't know Yvonne's last name. She scribbled a note on her paper.

Mrs Andrews certainly had her nose in everybody's business.

She even knew when someone called Henry hung his washing out and, in June 1963, reported that he had, for the first time in thirty years, changed his washing day from Wednesday to Friday, could anyone believe it. It must have been a slow winter that year.

In November of 1963, the entire Bay was looking forward to the return of the newly wed Mr and Mrs Prescott to their shores – Laura scribbled in her notebook that her grandparents returned to Banksia Bay after they were married – and Mrs Andrews was extremely put out by the planned renovations to the pub. Apparently the owners, Mr and Mrs Beaumont, were taking far too many modern liberties with the work and perhaps, rather than commit the terrible sin of ripping out some of the hundred-year-old period pieces, they really should concentrate on trying to get their painfully shy daughter, Yvonne, to socialise like a normal girl.

Yvonne? Laura did the maths. She would be about the right age. But she wasn't shy. Far from it. Yvonne Beaumont. Laura wrote down the name and put a question mark next to it.

She looked at the next Bugle. March 1964. Hmm. Where were the summer editions? Laura flicked back through the past Bugles. Not a single month was missing, as far as she could tell. She read the March issue. Nothing terribly interesting. Until she got to one line, the print so small she almost missed it, running along the bottom of the second page, hidden underneath an ad. *I retract my statements from the previous editions of The Bugle. We all know what happened, and I shall not speak of the incident again.*

Laura pushed her chair back and put her hands on her head. That was the summer before her father was born. What happened? She knew she was on to something now.

She trawled through the next few months and there was only the usual gossip about this person's dog defecating in front of the post office *again* and surely there was a need for Sergeant

Broadbent to intervene; about the dance held at Ocean Heights and which local girl looked loveliest; about someone putting up posters around town protesting Vietnam without permission and what was their town coming to.

No mention of whatever had happened that summer.

Laura stood up and stretched her arms, rolled her neck. To be this close! Not that there was any guarantee that whatever happened that summer had anything to do with Lily or Gigi, but in all her years of journalism, rule number six, *there is no such thing as a coincidence*, had been the one that proved true time and again.

Her eyes were getting tired, and she knew she had to take a break. There was a café just near the library. She asked the librarian if she could leave her things where they were; she'd be right back. Apparently that was no problem.

The main street of Ocean Heights was significantly more populated than Banksia Bay's. And there were shops. Actual shops – clothes stores, more than one grocer, three proper restaurants as well as the pub, two gift shops, a book store and four cafés, which seemed a little excessive for the size of the place, but she wasn't about to complain as she ordered her skinny cap.

Laura entered the bookstore with her takeaway coffee, which was too hot to drink just yet. Browsing the shelves, she was impressed by the extent of their titles. All the latest fiction, the healthy food-fad diet books you'd expect to see, and children's books too.

As she looked through the nonfiction section she saw a book called *The Art of the Artisan: The Rise of Artisan Popularity*. She pulled it off the shelf. Inside were the most beautiful photos of crafts and food and art and produce, and studios and converted barns that sold these artisanal wares. She purchased the book and headed back to her research.

'Oh, hi.' She nearly bumped into Yvonne as the old surfer left the library.

'Laura? Hello. Hi. I was just returning some books. Back to it.' She waved and hurried down the street.

Laura returned to her table and looked at her notes. Had they been moved? She looked around the library. There were a couple of teenagers, a mother with a toddler, an elderly couple sitting on the sofas reading. No. She must have been imagining things.

The next December, The Bugle was thrilled to welcome back the Bay's favourite son, Todd Broadbent, now a junior officer in the police force, following in his proud father's footsteps. The beach was overrun with tourists again, worse than any other year, surprisingly, some people might say, given, well, you all know what – *What had happened?* Laura took in a deep breath – and the surfers were flocking to Ian's surf school, though it baffled Mrs Andrews as to why.

The following January's edition was missing. So was February's. March 1965 continued on in its usual gossipy fashion.

Missing pages of a newspaper or gossip column, especially one that was so regular, usually added up to something significant. There was no further mention of the Woodhouses or the Prescotts. Laura flicked back through the past Bugles. Yes, the Woodhouses had been mentioned every summer since 1956 and the Prescotts since 1961. She rummaged through the next few summers as well. No further mention.

Question mark, question mark, question mark.

Laura filled her notebook pages with question marks.

She was close. She knew it. She just wasn't sure *what* she was close to.

The alarm on her phone trilled. If she was going to catch a ride back to the Bay on the Bodhi Bus, she'd better pack up.

She met Yvonne outside the bank.

'All aboard.' The old lady chuckled to herself, and Laura climbed into the back of the van. 'Did you have a good day, love?'

'I did. You?'

'Just a lot of running around. Not very fruitful, actually. Did you find what you were looking for?'

Laura noticed the way that last sentence went up in pitch. *Yes, Yvonne Beaumont, who is clearly no longer shy, you know something, don't you?*

'I was reading today about how surfing was a big thing here in the sixties. They must have been fascinating days. My grandmother used to tell me stories of that era all the time.' Complete and utter lie. Lillian never spoke about that time in her life. Ever. Laura always thought it was just too hard for her to talk about life with Richard after she lost him in the war. That's what people did when they lost someone they loved – they split their lives into two distinct parts. Life before, and life after.

'What was it like here, Yvonne, in the sixties? I bet summers were a riot.'

There was a long pause.

'Oh look, there's Trish.' Yvonne opened her window and called out. 'Hurry up there, Trish, we're waiting on you.'

Laura recognised a lie when she heard one. There were still ten minutes before the Bodhi Bus was due to depart.

Trish climbed aboard and started telling Yvonne all about the lovely lunch she'd had with her cousin. Then Charlotte's friend Ryan got on, obviously just finished work, briefcase in hand.

Laura's plan to subtly drop innocent-seeming questions on Yvonne all the way back to the Bay, just the two of them in the van like this morning, was now thwarted. Where had all these people come from, anyway? None of them were on the outbound journey this morning. Was Yvonne up to something?

This story was obviously getting to her more than she'd realised. When you started seeing things that weren't there, started questioning what didn't need questioning, you'd lost perspective. Or become completely paranoid. Neither of which was ideal.

It was time to regroup. Rule number seven – *know when to take a step back and return with fresh eyes.* She put her headphones in and selected some music on her phone.

They stayed stationary for another fifteen minutes, and Laura wondered why they weren't leaving. Then she saw him striding towards the van. Heath, in his hospital uniform.

'Thanks for waiting, Yvonne.' He leaned in to the driver's seat as he climbed aboard and kissed her on the cheek. 'I had some urgent bloods to get off.'

'No worries, love. We wouldn't leave you stranded, now, would we?' She patted his hand, which was resting on her shoulder.

Heath smiled at Laura as he took the seat next to her. 'Good day at the office?' He looked at the files in her hand.

'It was, actually. You?'

'A hard one today. We have a patient at the hospital. A kid. She's, well, she's not doing too well. It's always harder when it's a kid.' He rubbed his forehead.

Laura reached out her hand and squeezed his leg, pulling it straight back when she realised what she was doing. 'I'm sorry.'

He folded his arms across his chest. 'Unfortunately, life and death are indiscriminate. One thing I've learned is that there's no rhyme or reason as to who or how or when or why.' A look of sorrow crossed his face and hung there like a shadow.

'I guess working at the hospital brings all that into perspective,' Laura said softly.

'Mmm.' Heath stared ahead and then he looked back to her,

the shadow lifting. 'Tell me, Laura, what was the best part of your day?'

'Actually –' she reached down into the bag beside her – 'finding this.' She handed him the book she'd found in the bookshop. She'd had it gift-wrapped with yellow bumble bee wrapping paper and black ribbon. 'I thought of you and just had to get it.'

He carefully took the wrapping paper off and as he looked at the gift inside, his mouth dropped open. He ran his hands over the glossy picture adorning the hard cover.

'This is beautiful.' He looked at Laura, the blue of his eyes so pale, so captivating. 'Thank you.'

Laura couldn't answer, held silent by his intense gaze.

He looked back at the book and opened the pages, studying each picture and paragraph of text. 'This is so brilliant, Laura.' He reached across and held her hand.

She stayed silent and still. Afraid to say anything in case the catch in her throat betrayed her feelings; afraid to move in case he withdrew his touch. His gentle touch.

'Are you doing anything tomorrow afternoon?' Heath's voice was low.

'No.' The word barely came forth.

'Would you like to come for a surf? It has a different feel to the mornings.'

'Isn't that when the sharks are out? I read that somewhere, I think.'

Heath chuckled. 'I've been surfing this stretch of coast since I was a boy, and I've never had an encounter. And we'll be early enough to avoid feeding time.'

'I'd like that. A lot.' Most definitely not a lie, except for the casual mention of feeding time.

Heath took his hand back, hesitating as he did so. Laura looked straight ahead and caught Yvonne watching her – them – in the rear-view mirror. And she was most definitely not smiling.

Back in the Bay, Laura decided to take a punt that Ian would be home. Asking to see his photos would constitute looking at things with fresh eyes, wouldn't it? As she wound her way through town she came across him standing in his garage, the roller door open.

'Hey there, Laura.'

She waved. Behind him the walls were covered with photographs and she craned her neck slightly to get a better view.

'Do you want to take a peek?' he asked.

'You don't mind?'

'Not at all. Though you've already seen some of my work in the holiday house. Yvonne, God bless, likes to show off my pictures.'

All those pictures on the sideboard. But she was only half listening because the collection of Ian Holland photos was spellbinding. There were black-and-white and colour shots, big and small, close-up portraits and sweeping landscapes. There were pictures of the ocean, of surfers, of the town, of sunsets.

Laura worked her way along the walls. Some of them really should have been in a museum. Actually, many of them should have been in a museum – a beautiful pictorial record of Banksia Bay's history.

'These ones here –' Ian pointed towards to a series of shots taken at a bonfire – 'are some of my favourites.'

They were just like the one in the holiday house. Laura slipped her hands into her jeans pockets to stop them from shaking. Everywhere she looked, she saw Lillian. So many pictures of her and Gigi together.

'What do you think?' Ian asked

Unable to talk, she focused on one picture in particular. It was a close-up shot of Lillian, eyes averted down, next to Richard. Yes. It was him. She hadn't seen too many pictures of her grandfather, but she had no doubt.

She drew in a sharp breath.

'Are you okay, love?' Ian asked. 'Someone you know?' He stepped up next to her.

Laura pulled her gaze away and looked at him. 'Oh, what? Sorry?' She fumbled her words. She had to get out of there.

Laura thanked Ian for his time and ran out into the street.

When she got back to the holiday house, she splashed her face with water. That was close. What had she seen in his eyes? Was he keeping secrets too? Okay. This was getting worse, suspecting everyone, being paranoid about every little look or comment.

She was asking herself questions she'd already answered or ruled out as irrelevant. She was imagining people tampering with her files at the library. And the ink on the paper as she read her notes kept blurring. When you started questioning absolutely everything, you couldn't see the answers.

It was most definitely time to put rule seven into play and step away, get some sorely needed perspective. She'd have to take a break for at least twenty-four hours. That's what she did when she was missing perspective on a story.

Then, hopefully, she could focus on the questions and people that really mattered.

Sixteen

Virginia paced the living room in Yvonne's small house, her hands sweating, her mouth dry.

'You saw it? With your own eyes?'

Yvonne nodded. 'She knows there are issues of The Bugle missing.'

Virginia stopped and turned. 'And you couldn't get anything out of her about the angle of her story?'

'Nope. Tight-lipped, she was.'

The two women moved into the kitchen and Yvonne started getting their dinner ready. Virginia got out two plates and set the table. Every Monday for far too many years to count, they'd eaten dinner together. Once Virginia's little boy had grown up and moved out, she was terribly lonely, and Yvonne had stepped in, filling the void.

'There's one other thing.' Yvonne wrung her hands in the tea towel she was holding.

'What?' Virginia turned to face her. What else could there possibly be?

Yvonne fidgeted with her sleeve.

'Out with it.'

'I think . . . I think maybe what's going on between her and Heath might be, well, more than . . . more than nothing.'

Virginia raised an eyebrow.

'I think they might actually like each other.'

No. Virginia couldn't let this happen. It was one thing if Miss City Hotshot Reporter was here to destroy her. But not Heath.

'Stop. I know what you're thinking.' Yvonne put her tea towel down and stood in front of Virginia. 'But this might be a good thing.'

'How? How on earth is that a good thing?'

'If there are real emotions involved, well, then it will be harder for her to expose the truth. If that's what she's here to do. And we still don't know for sure that she is.'

Yvonne had been there for Virginia through all of life's highs and lows. Especially the lows. And here she was again, trying to comfort Virginia, protect her. And she never asked for anything in return. What a terrible blow it had turned out for her, to be Virginia's friend.

Guilt was a gnawing pain that ate away at Virginia every damn day of her life. So many lives ruined by one single moment.

And the heaviest burden of all those ruined lives for Virginia to bear was Yvonne's.

She retrieved the red paper serviettes from the sideboard and folded them into little fans. The roast lamb Yvonne had cooked smelled delicious as she carried it to the table. Virginia had never told her how much the woody aroma of the oregano she used tore at her heart.

They sat down and Yvonne said a prayer as she always did. Virginia had given up on God sixty years ago, but she still bowed her head. There were times Virginia had no desire for their weekly meal together, but she had never let her friend down. How could she? Some debts were so great they could never be repaid. All Virginia could do was share with Yvonne the simple moments in life that made up a friendship; so desperately inadequate to atone for what had happened.

January 1963

There wasn't a lot of sweetness to the remainder of the summer holidays.

There were only two more days until Gigi had to say goodbye to Lily. And while she hadn't seen her much in the two weeks since her engagement to Richard – there were, apparently, so many details to attend to already, even though the wedding wouldn't be for another six months – saying goodbye would not be easy. This summer's end meant everything was about to change. She knew that. And she didn't like it. Not one bit.

Next week Gigi would be back at boring old school, but thankfully this would be her last year. Small blessings, she supposed.

At least there was no way Lily would miss the end-of-summer bonfire the surf boys always put on. They'd been going together every year since they'd met in 1956.

Gigi wandered her private banksia track till she got to the top of the hill, where she could see the beach stretched out below her. A couple of guys, she assumed Ian was among them, were already starting to gather wood for tomorrow night's party.

'Oh, sorry.' A voice made her jump.

She turned around to see Costas standing a few strides behind her.

'I didn't think anyone else knew about this spot.' Costas took off his hat. His dark eyes shone in the sunlight, his dark skin glistening with sweat.

'Me neither.' Gigi found her voice, despite the tightness in her throat. 'I was just looking at the view. Do you want to join me?'

'Yes.'

They sat on the edge of the cliff, just back from the grey rocks that stacked on top of each other down the hill.

'How did you find out about this spot?' she asked him.

'I was exploring one day, and just kind of stumbled upon it. It has the best seed pods.' He pulled a banksia seed pod out of his pocket.

Only it wasn't a banksia seed pod; usually big, rough, ugly-looking hunks of hairy wood. This had been carved and polished into a delicate mushroom. The holes from the parts of the seed pod, which Gigi always thought looked like eyes, allowed light to penetrate the carving, giving it an ethereal feel.

'Did you make this?' She took the mushroom and turned it around so it could catch the light from different angles.

Costas nodded.

'It's beautiful.' Gigi exhaled in wonder.

'It's yours.'

She looked up into his dark eyes and he gazed back at her. And she knew she wasn't wrong. He did have feelings for her. He couldn't look at her like that if he didn't.

'A piece of me to stay with you, even when I'm not there.'

Gigi struggled to draw breath. 'Luckily, with school starting up again next week, you'll be around a lot more,' she whispered.

Costas dropped his gaze.

'What?'

Staring out to the ocean, Costas spoke softly. 'I won't be at school this year.'

'Why?'

'Mama and Baba . . . they have decided I need to work. I have to be able to provide . . . because I will be . . . they have found me a job in Ocean Heights.'

What wasn't he telling her? She desperately wanted to ask, but she was afraid to know. All that came out of her mouth was a muffled 'Oh.'

'I will miss seeing you every day.' His voice cracked and Gigi dared to look his way. There was a sadness in his eyes and she swallowed deeply.

'Well, we can still go fishing in the mornings. And on weekends.' Gigi smiled.

He reached out and took her hand. Heat coursed through Gigi's veins.

'Thank you, Virginia. For always being so kind to me.'

She could see the tears that rimmed his eyes and he turned away. He wouldn't let her see him cry. She knew that.

'Well, it was kind of easy. I enjoy spending time with you.' Oh dear. Had those words actually come out of her mouth? She really was feeling the melancholy of the last days of summer holidays. It was making her all soppy. Making her forget propriety. Not that she usually cared about propriety.

Costas squeezed her hand and she gasped. He pulled away.

'Sorry. I should go.' He stood up and moved away. 'Sorry.'

'No.' Gigi jumped up after him. 'Please don't go.'

'It's all right, Virginia. I understand how the world works.' He cast his eyes down.

Now Gigi was plain old confused. He was pulling away again. 'What?' She had no idea what was going on.

'I'll leave you to your peace.' He turned and started to walk back down the track.

No. She didn't want him to leave. Up here, alone, with no judging eyes looking on, they could be themselves. Just like when they went to the rock pools and fished, or dug for crabs in the sand. It didn't matter that she was poor and wore boy's overalls and would rather fish than do her hair. It didn't matter that he was an outsider. They were just Gigi and Costas.

'Will you be at the bonfire tomorrow tonight?' She blurted out the question – anything to keep him there.

'I'm not sure I'd be welcome.' He looked over his shoulder to her.

'I'd like you to come.' What had come over her? She turned away, unable to face him after being so bold.

From behind her she could feel him step up close. She could hear his breath – fast, short.

She closed her eyes, anticipating his touch, how it would feel if he put his arm around her shoulder, kissed her neck. She drew in a deep breath and waited.

A cool breeze hit her back and she spun around.

Costas was gone.

She slumped into the grass and pulled her denim-clad legs tightly into her chest, resting her chin on her knees, and she watched the beach through salt-veiled eyes. In her hand she held tightly onto the carved mushroom Costas had given her.

Gigi trudged back to the caravan park, and as she dragged her feet along the long gravel driveway, she looked up and saw Dr Harper's car near reception. He didn't make too many house calls all the way from Ocean Heights. She started running.

'Mum? Dad?' she called out, her heart beating faster. There was no one in reception. Where were they?

As she rounded the common building she saw a small crowd gathered around Arthur's van.

She slowed to a walk.

As she got closer her steps became even shorter. She caught sight of her dad, and when his eyes found hers, he beckoned her over.

Arthur was in his chair, seemingly asleep, his face tilted towards the sun. He looked happy.

'It was his heart, love,' Dad said, putting his arm around Gigi's shoulder. 'It was quick. There was no pain.'

Dr Harper was packing up his medical bag and Mum was trying to disperse the crowd. Gigi sat down beside Arthur and stared at the ground.

Once everyone was gone, and the ambulance had taken Arthur to the hospital in Ocean Heights, Dad helped Gigi to her feet.

'He was all packed up, ready to head off. He'd come by reception not an hour ago to drop this off for you.' Dad handed her a small parcel tied with a blue ribbon. 'He said, "One last cuppa and then I'll be off." Shame. Such a nice fellow.' Dad patted her cheek. 'Someone will be by tomorrow to take care of his things. Come inside, hey, love?'

'In a minute.' She held up the parcel. Dad squeezed her shoulder and let her be.

Alone, Gigi opened the small box. Inside was the silver pendant with sapphire gems. Gigi held it to her chest. There was also a note.

Elaine always said the guardian angel chose who to look out for. I believe she's chosen you.

Gigi closed her eyes. *Thank you.*

The door to Arthur's van was open. That wasn't right. She should close it up. She folded down the camping table and chairs and lifted them into the van, placing them just inside the door. She put the lid on the shoebox of coins, the pieces now all divided into envelopes. As she backed out, she noticed Arthur's suitcase open, his clothes inside neatly folded and packed. She stepped in and closed the lid. Behind the suitcase his large map of Australia was laid out – all the places he never got to see.

A single tear fell down Gigi's cheek. It wasn't fair.

Possessed by a force she didn't understand, Gigi folded up the map and slipped it into the front pocket of her overalls. She knew it was wrong. It wasn't hers. She had no right to take it.

But whoever was coming tomorrow to pick up Arthur's things wouldn't understand how important the map was. They'd probably just throw it away. And she couldn't have that.

As night melted from deep blue to the hollow black that engulfed the sky just before dawn, Gigi lay in bed staring at the little makeshift shelf above her where she kept her most prized possessions.

Arthur's map now sat up against the wall, and Gigi had put Elaine's pendant in a small, tin jewellery box that had once belonged to her grandmother. Beside the jewellery box was the mushroom Costas had carved. Beside that, perched precariously on the edge, sat a scrapbook she'd been keeping since she was little – all the important moments in her life were inside. Also on the shelf was a ticket stub from Taronga Zoo – the only time Gigi had ever been to Sydney – and the white gloves from Lily that she would never wear. They were the most beautiful things she possessed.

Some might say it wasn't much of a collection, but to her it was everything, a handful of precious moments that made up her life.

———

In the morning Gigi rose before her parents and knocked over her chores faster than usual. She didn't want to be anywhere near the caravan park when Arthur's things were taken away.

Once Mum had checked her work and signed off on the list of jobs she'd set, Gigi took off into the hills. As far away as she could get.

She wandered the tracks, familiar to her since she was little – so many hours of her childhood spent here alone. And soon she'd be alone again. Arthur was gone. Lily was getting married. Costas wasn't returning to school. She loved her piece of paradise – the banksia-covered hills, the soft yellow sand older than time, the ocean so wild and peaceful – and couldn't imagine living anywhere else. But sometimes it could feel like the loneliest place on earth.

'What are you doing wandering around here, Gilbert?'

Gigi stopped and dropped her head. The last thing she needed this morning was to have to deal with Todd. She turned around to face him, standing in front of her with his hands on his hips.

'You're a bit far from home, aren't you?'

Gigi looked around. She had walked all the way over the headland, right to the outskirts of town.

'I was just walking. What are you doing here?'

'Richard and I came up here for some target practice.'

It was then that Gigi noticed the rifle very casually leaning against his leg.

Because he was the son of the local copper, Todd's knowledge of shooting wasn't a surprise to anyone. Once, in primary school, he'd even brought in one of his dad's pistols for show-and-tell. Miss Smith had nearly had a heart attack when he led the school outside and showed them what a good shot he was, knocking the tin cans he'd set up that morning off the fence posts. She'd had very stern words with Todd's dad that afternoon about perhaps not sending

a loaded gun to school next time Todd wanted show 'how proud
he was of his father', Todd's father had looked embarrassed, Todd
pleased with himself.

The sight of his rifle now made Gigi nervous. She'd seen plenty
of guns before. There were farms all around Banksia Bay, and
where there were farms, farmers had guns. She'd even fired one
once when she was twelve, on Grandpa Gilbert's farm. But this
was different.

'Where is Richard?' He might not have been her favourite person on the planet right now, taking away her best friend like he
was, but she would have felt a lot safer if he was there.

'Oh, he just rode back into town to get a few more of these.'
Todd bent over and picked up an empty beer bottle. 'What's up,
Gilbert? You've gone awfully pale.'

'Yes. I'm not feeling well. I think I should head back home.'

'Wait on just a moment.' Todd picked up the rifle and stepped
towards her. 'You're not going to go dob on me, are you?'

'Of course not.'

The son of the Bay's policeman being caught drunk in the
middle of the day would certainly cause a ruckus in town.

Mrs Andrews not only ran the ladies' guild, who believed
themselves to be the moral compass of the community, but also
printed The Bay Bugle once a month, the bakery giving her access
to all the best local gossip. It was full of half-truths and juicy tid-
bits that kept idle tongues wagging around town. This was exactly
the sort of story she'd print.

But Gigi had no plans to be part of any Bugle article.

'It's none of my business what you've been doing, Todd.'

'I've only had one. No one's going to care that I've only
had one.'

Gigi backed away very slowly.

The sound of a car pulling up made her turn and she breathed out in relief when she saw Richard get out.

'Hi, Gigi.' Richard smiled. 'Would you like to join us?' He held up four bottles of beer.

'No, thank you. I was just leaving.'

'Stay, Gilbert. We can have some fun,' Todd called out.

Gigi kept her eye on him but didn't respond.

'Can I offer you a lift back home?' Richard stepped between the two and Gigi followed him to his car.

Along the road back into town, Richard made excuses for Todd. It couldn't be easy being the only son of the only policeman in town. He really was a good guy.

Gigi listened without responding.

As they neared the caravan park, Richard slowed the car down.

'There's not going to be any trouble out of this, is there, Gigi?' He turned and looked at her, his eyes steely in warning.

'Not from me, there's not.'

Richard reached across the space between them and patted her on the leg. 'Good girl.'

A shiver ran up her spine and she scrambled out of the car.

'See you tonight,' Richard called out, and Gigi waved as she turned and ran home.

For the first time she could remember, Gigi wasn't looking forward to the end-of-summer bonfire. Todd would be there and so would Richard, neither of whom she really cared to see. But it was her last chance to spend time with Lily. Their last chance before everything changed. She wouldn't say anything to her friend about what had happened during the day. There was no point. Technically, nothing *had* happened. And Gigi was fairly sure that if she did bring it up, Lily would simply dismiss it as 'boys being boys'. Maybe Gigi was overreacting. Todd hadn't actually done anything wrong and Richard was, well, he was just making sure she wouldn't dob. She rubbed her leg where he'd pressed his hand. People did funny things when they were scared.

By the time she got down to the beach, after washing up the dinner plates and helping her mother fold the washing, the flames of the bonfire were stretching their orange tendrils up to the indigo sky. Ian and his surfing friends were there, the oldest of the revellers, and Ian was taking snaps of everyone – some posing seriously, some pulling funny expressions.

The last remaining kids staying in the caravan park were also there, their young faces staring in awe at the older guys drinking beer. Ian photographed them too.

Off to the side, Gigi saw Lily standing a little way back from the fire, Richard with his arm around her. She drew in a deep breath, forced a happy expression onto her face and walked towards them.

'Oh, Gigi.' Lily ran towards her, embracing her in a tight hug. 'You're here at last. I've been waiting for you.'

'Sorry. I had chores.'

They walked back to Richard.

'Hi, Gigi.' Richard looked happy to see her. 'Glad you could come. My girl here would have been a blubbering mess if you'd missed the summer send-off.'

'No chance.' Gigi smiled at him. *Not even you can take this away from us.* 'I have to make the most of our time before you knock her up and have her tied to the kitchen.' Gigi would have laughed if she hadn't been so worried it would actually come true.

'We're both really sorry you won't be able to make the wedding.' Richard touched her arm.

Gigi turned to Lily.

'Um. Well, nothing is finalised yet, but we'll probably get married in Perth, where Richard's frail grandparents are, so I was assuming it would be too far for you to come. Of course you're invited, though.'

Out of the corner of her eye, Gigi could have sworn she saw Richard flinch.

'You know there is nothing I'd like more than to have you share our big day.' Lily's eyes were wide.

'I know.' Gigi held back tears. 'But it is what it is, I suppose. Just make sure you come back and visit afterwards.'

'We'll honeymoon here, won't we, love.' Lily turned to Richard.

He touched her cheek. 'Of course. Anything my girl wants, she can have.'

Lily threw her arms around him, the great big diamond on her finger catching the orange light from the bonfire. Richard certainly hadn't picked that up from anywhere around here.

'It's Mrs Prescott's,' Lily said, catching Gigi staring at it. 'Isn't she generous? She's been so welcoming of me.'

I bet, thought Gigi. As much as Lily marrying a doctor was a good match, the advantages of Richard marrying into a senator's family would not be lost on Mrs Prescott.

Ian came towards them, camera in hand. He took at least two shots before Lily realised he was there and she berated him for not letting her pose properly.

'Oh, promise me you won't print those.'

Ian winked. 'Candid shots are usually much more interesting.' He walked back to the bonfire.

'I'll go have a chat with him over a beer.' Richard untangled himself from her hold and strode towards Ian's group of drinking friends.

The girls moved further away from the noise of the bonfire and sat down on the picnic blanket Gigi had brought with her. Lily adjusted her skirt and sat tall, laying her hands in her lap. Then she played with her hair, pushing the same strand behind her ear repeatedly. She adjusted her skirt again.

'Is something wrong?' Gigi asked.

'Oh, Gigi.' She reached out and grabbed her hand. 'What if I'm not good enough to be Mrs Prescott? What if I make a terrible wife? What if I don't fit in with his friends?'

Gigi looked deeply into her best friend's eyes. 'Lillian Woodhouse, if there's one thing I know beyond any doubt, it's how special and wonderful you are. Richard is lucky to have you, and I think he knows it too.' She pointed towards the men huddled by the fire. Richard was looking over to them, a lovesick smile across his face as he gazed at Lily.

'Really?'

'Really.'

'I do wish you could come to the wedding. I tried to convince them to have it in Sydney, but Richard's grandmother can't travel.'

'It's okay.'

Lily squeezed her hand. 'It won't be the same without you.' Her voice caught.

Gigi suspected marrying into the Prescott family was going to be a little lonely for her friend. She put her hand in her pocket and pulled out the angel wing pendant.

'Seeing as I won't be there in body, take this.' She handed Lily the wings. 'This was Arthur's.' Her voice caught in her throat as she said his name. 'It was his guardian angel and he left it to me.' She bit her bottom lip. 'It can be your something borrowed.'

Lily shoved it right back into Gigi's hands. 'No. I can't accept this. It obviously means a lot to you.'

'Not as much as you do. Sisters, remember? I want you to have it. If I can't be there when you get married, then a piece of me can be. Besides, when would I ever get the chance to wear it?'

'You never know.' Lily pressed it back into Gigi's hands. 'Please. I can't.'

Gigi looked into her friend's eyes. 'You can and you will. You can bring it back to me next summer when you visit.' She could feel the tears welling up.

'Oh, Gigi. You were the best friend I ever could have asked for.'

'Were? You make it sound like this is goodbye.'

'No.' Lily's voice was firm. 'It's never goodbye. Not between us.' Her expression softened. 'But we can't pretend things will ever be exactly the same again after tonight. I will come back. Every summer. But it will be . . . different. This,' she held up the pendant, 'will remind us of the summers of our childhood.'

'Before adulthood got in the way.' Gigi looked into her eyes.

Lily nodded.

'Okay. But we still have tonight, right? Do you want to go for one last childish night-time dip?'

'I don't have a swimming costume.'

'Neither do I.' Gigi pulled Lily to standing and dragged her down the beach.

They ran into the water, fully dressed, giggling and splashing each other. The ocean was warm and the waves small, breaking around their knees. A few of the younger kids by the bonfire saw them and joined in. Ian and his friends stood where the sea foam hugged the sand, pointing and laughing.

The moon cast light and shadow that bounced off the water and Gigi spun in circles with Lily, round and round. Together they fell into the water and Gigi lay back, letting the waves wash over her. Lily tried to stand. Losing her footing, she fell onto Gigi, sending her under.

'Oh my. Are you all right?' Lily reached down to lift her friend.

Gigi came up spluttering. 'Yes.' She laughed. 'I'm fine.'

They scrambled to the edge of the water and sat on the wet sand. Lily's skirt floated around her, in and out with each wave.

'Lillian?'

The girls turned to see Richard standing behind them, his arms folded across his chest. 'What is this?'

Lily jumped up and tried to straighten her skirt, but it clung to her legs in soggy patches. 'Sorry. It's just . . . We . . . I . . .'

'It's my fault.' Gigi stood and stepped to Lily's side. 'I dragged her in.'

Richard shot her a look. Gigi never knew anyone could express anger, revulsion and contempt in one look the way Richard just had. She swallowed the lump in her throat and took a step to the side.

'That's okay.' He regained his composure, confidence and charm returning. 'We should probably go now, though, darling.' He looked at Lily. 'It's a long trip back tomorrow.'

'Yes, dear.' Lily turned and hugged Gigi goodbye.

As Gigi watched them walk up the beach, she sucked on her bottom lip to stop the tears she could feel welling up.

'Are you okay?' Ian walked towards her.

Great. Just what she needed. 'I'm fine.'

'Are you sure, squirt?' He rubbed the top of her head so roughly she had to duck away. He always did that. She always hated it.

'Go away, you big buffoon.' She thrust her hands in her overall pockets and stormed up the sand.

Drying off by the bonfire, Gigi watched the flames dance as they made strange elegant shapes that crackled and popped. She stepped closer and reached out her hand.

'Hey.' Costas appeared beside her. Where had he come from?

She pulled her hand back and turned to face him. 'You came.'

'I did.'

'What's that wog doing here?' Todd swayed as he walked towards them.

'I invited him.' Gigi squared her shoulders and put her hands on her hips.

'It's okay,' Costas whispered. 'I'll go.'

'No. You're as welcome here as anyone else.'

Todd took a wobbly step forward. 'Is this why you've been giving me the cold shoulder?' He pushed Costas but kept his eyes on Gigi. 'Hanging out with this wog? Don't tell me you're sweet on him.'

Gigi stepped in front of Costas. 'I said he was welcome.'

'Virginia.' Costas touched her on the shoulder. 'It's okay. I'll just leave.'

'Oh.' Todd tapped his chest and spread out his arms. 'Wogboy's a poofter, too. Needs a little girl to stand up for him.'

Ian came around the bonfire and put his arm around Todd's shoulders. 'Come on, mate. Leave these two be. They're not worth your trouble.'

Todd twisted himself free. 'Not you too? Bloody wogs taking our jobs and our women. Are you going to let this scum take your pretend sister?' He pushed his sleeves up and centred his stance.

Gigi backed up a little. She'd need some space to duck and weave when he threw his first punch. And she'd need some leverage to counter-attack. Ian had taught her well. Hopefully she could put all those boxing lessons into practice.

Ian moved between them. At six feet tall with the broad shoulders of someone who'd spent his life working and playing in the ocean, he was much bigger than weedy Todd.

'Let's go get another drink, mate.' His voice was low, his hand on Todd's chest. Todd's stern expression faltered. 'Why don't you head home, squirt,' Ian said over his shoulder.

Gigi stood her ground. She wasn't going to let Todd intimidate her, despite her instinct to sit down and cry.

Costas touched her shoulder as he backed away from the bonfire. She stood there, just a moment longer, staring Todd down. His shoulders lost their tension. 'All right, mate. Let's have another beer.'

As soon as the older boys moved away, Gigi spun around and ran down the beach after Costas. He'd covered a fair distance in the short moments that had passed.

'Wait. Costas. Please.'

Costas stopped just as he reached the other side of the dunes.

'I don't need you to fight my battles for me, Virginia.' He spat the words at her.

Her eyes pricked with salt and, despite sucking on her bottom lip, the tears fell. 'That's not . . . not what I was doing.'

'I'm sorry.' He walked towards her. 'I know you were just trying to help. But really. There's no point. Not with a *malaka* like that.'

Gigi laughed. She always liked it when Costas spoke Greek. She didn't know what *malaka* meant, but she could tell it wasn't nice. And that was just fine by her. Todd, despite a momentary lapse into decency over the past few months, was undoubtedly a *malaka* at his core.

'Tonight really didn't go the way I was hoping.' Her bottom lip quivered. 'I didn't get to say goodbye to Lily properly. Richard wasn't very impressed with me dragging her in for a swim. Todd . . . was Todd. And now I've upset you.' She plonked herself onto the sand dune and hugged her legs.

Costas sat down beside her and bumped her shoulder with his. 'It'll be okay'.

'How do you do it?' Gigi looked into his dark eyes. 'Always find the positive? Put up with it? Them?' She pointed towards the bonfire.

He took in a deep breath. 'There's no point getting into it with them. You're never going to change the mind of a bigot like Todd. It would just end in a fight and then that confirms for them that I'm a bad guy. My yiayia, my grandmother, always said, "Don't fight against the hate, fight for the love."'

His gaze bore into Gigi and her cheeks burned. She tried to look away, but couldn't. His hand inched towards hers, brushing her fingers. She held her breath.

A loud bang came from the direction of the bonfire as one of the branches exploded and a cheer went up from the crowd. Costas stood and held out his hand. 'Come on, Virginia. I'll walk you home.'

She took his hand and he pulled her up. She stopped, an inch away from his face. She could feel his warm breath caress her forehead. 'Why do you do that?' she whispered.

'Do what?' He brushed her straggly fringe off her face.

'Call me Virginia. Why don't you ever call me Gigi?'

'Gigi is a child's name. And you're not a child. You're a woman. A beautiful woman.'

Gigi turned away. 'I'm a bait-catching, overall-wearing tomboy with curly straw for hair.'

He moved around and stood in front of her, no space between them. 'You are a kind, brave, spirited breath of fresh air, with the most beautiful blue eyes I've ever gazed into.'

Gigi tried to come up with a funny retort – how many eyes has he been gazing into; 'spirited' is just another word for wild – but her brain wouldn't send any messages to her mouth.

Costas stared into her and she had trouble breathing. She leaned in. She'd never kissed a boy before, but she was pretty sure leaning in helped. He put his hands on her shoulders and gently pushed her away.

'We cannot, Virginia. It's not how the world works.'

Costas turned and walked off into the night, leaving her behind to sink into the dune as tears streamed down her face.

Seventeen

For three afternoons in a row, Laura had met Heath by the ocean's edge and they'd surfed together. She was getting better. At least she thought she was. He did tell her so, but she assumed he would say that regardless.

She would never admit it to anyone, but the moments she was out in the waves with Heath were the most peaceful she could ever remember having. While paddling out, or waiting in the undulating swell, or riding a wave she'd managed to catch, she didn't think about Lillian or her mystery; she didn't think about work.

Even being dumped, which happened more often than she liked to own up to, was a welcome distraction. Despite the fact that every time she was being rolled and pummelled by the force of surging waves she thought she might not survive. Funny how something so terrifying could be such an integral part of something so gloriously serene.

On the fourth afternoon, Laura and Heath were joined by Yvonne and Ryan. Laura didn't mind whenever Heath saw her fall, or miss a wave, or come up spluttering unceremoniously after being nearly drowned. One person watching her fail – a person she'd grown to trust – was one thing. Having an audience of experienced surfers was another matter entirely.

After her second dumping in three waves, Laura called it quits and waded in to shore. As she sat on the sand watching the real surfers do their thing, a pang of jealousy hit her. Would she ever be that good? Of course not. They all had a lifetime of surfing experience behind them. Once she left Banksia Bay and headed back to her quiet inner-city life, everything she'd learned would be forgotten.

She dug her hand into the sand and grabbed a fistful of tiny yellow grains. She raised her hand up and let the grains sift between her fingers. Once she left Banksia Bay, what would her life be like? What truths, or not, would she be taking with her? Was her mother right, in some way at least? Clearly Lillian had secrets. Was it possible that she'd kept them apart, especially if she knew Donna had the photo? It was looking more and more likely that the seemingly innocent picture of two young girls in the sand was carrying more meaning than Laura had imagined.

Out of the corner of her eye she saw two figures walking up the beach. Well, one was walking, one was running, a small board under his arm.

Charlotte waved to Laura as she neared and Aiden stood at the edge of the water, waiting for his mum's okay to go in. Ryan came in out of the surf and spoke with Charlotte for a moment. He reached out his hand and touched her shoulder briefly, which Laura most certainly noticed, and then Aiden was off with him, to join in the surfing fun.

Charlotte sat herself on the sand beside Laura. 'Have you given up?'

'Embarrassing myself in front of my teacher is bad enough.

With everyone else watching on . . .' She pointed to the water. 'And now Aiden is out there. Being shown up by a seven-year-old is not exactly my idea of fun.'

'I know what you mean,' Charlotte said. 'I did try it, growing up. It's kind of hard with a brother like that –' she pointed to Heath, who'd just caught a wave – 'not to at least give it a go. But I wasn't very good. Even Ian, the master of all surfing gurus, couldn't manage to bring out my natural surfer.'

Heath finished his ride and ran up the sand, shaking his head when he got to them, spraying them with sea water.

'Thank you, brother mine.' Charlotte frowned. 'That never gets old.'

Heath hugged her as she tried to squirm free.

'How old are you?' she squealed.

'Never too old to do that.' His grin was wide. 'Are you done, Laura?'

'I think for today, yes. But you keep going.'

He hesitated, only for a moment, and when she shooed him away with a flick of her hands, he ran back into the ocean.

Aiden and Ryan rode the next wave together, Ryan waving to Charlotte as he fell off the back of the wave, and Charlotte went red.

'Is there something going on between you two?' Laura asked.

Charlotte's cheeks burned even brighter. 'We're just friends.'

'Uh-huh.'

'Like you and Heath.' Charlotte looked her in the eye.

Touché. Time to change the subject. 'How's work been?'

Charlotte gave her a wry look. 'Not too bad. How's your project going?'

Damn. She'd walked into that. 'It's coming along.' Both truth and lie. She'd certainly learned more, put some pieces together. But the picture was still not whole.

'And now you have a wealth of information and experience you can include about surfing.'

'Wealth might be exaggerating it a little.'

'Maybe. But more than me.'

Heath caught another wave in and then plonked himself beside them.

'Are you okay?' Charlotte's face was a picture of concern and Heath shot her a look. 'I mean, it's not like you to come in early.' She stumbled over her words.

'I was just a bit worried about what you two might be saying about me.' He flashed her a grin.

'Contrary to what your over-inflated sense of self and charm would have you believe, dear brother, we weren't discussing you at all.'

Heath looked at Laura.

'Nope,' she concurred.

He put his hand to chest. 'I'm wounded.'

'Don't be.' Charlotte's voice was mocking, but her expression still showed worry.

What was Laura missing?

One by one all the gang came in, Aiden rather reluctantly.

'Uncle Heath.' Aiden stood in front of Heath, his hands balled into fists at his side. 'Can we go fishing? Please?' His little hands started shaking.

Heath took in a long, slow breath. 'Oh, buddy. I'm not sure they're biting today.'

Charlotte looked at her brother, but he refused to make eye contact with her. She turned to her son. 'Maybe another day, hey?'

Aiden pouted.

A look passed between Yvonne and Charlotte. 'I can take you, Aiden,' the old lady offered. 'I can show you my secret spot.'

Aiden looked back and forth between Heath and Yvonne, clearly struggling to weigh up the situation – beg his favourite uncle to take him, or find out where Yvonne's secret spot was.

In the end, the lure of learning a secret won out.

The two headed off down the beach, as Yvonne called behind her, 'I'll bring him home when we're done.'

Charlotte turned to her brother. 'Why don't we head off then, Heath?'

He didn't move. 'I was thinking of catching the sunset.'

'Heath?' Her inflection rose.

He smiled at his sister, but his voice was stern. 'Charlotte.'

She pursed her lips but said nothing.

'Hey, Ryan.' Heath turned to their friend. 'Weren't you saying you wanted to try out the new schnitty at the pub? Might be worth doing while Aiden isn't there to pick all the food off your plate. You know what he's like.'

Ryan laughed. 'What do you say, Charlotte? You don't get to eat in peace much these days.'

An expression of resignation, mixed with a little excitement, came over Charlotte's face. 'Um, okay, I guess.'

The look of joy in Ryan's eyes told Laura everything she needed to know about the 'just friends' declaration.

Charlotte got up and leaned over her brother. 'Don't overdo it,' she whispered.

He reached up and squeezed her hand. 'Promise.'

Alone on the sand, Laura and Heath watched the waves.

'Was that about me?' Laura broke the silence. 'Charlotte wanting you to go home?'

'No. It was about me. She's just being a big sister. Don't give her another thought.' He turned and looked her in the eye and all thoughts left her mind.

The sun began to set behind the hills, casting deep shadows across the rippling water. Across the sand Heath's hand inched, until it was nearly touching hers. He left it there, moved no closer.

Laura's heart was racing. With a sense of daring that came from who knows where, she stretched out her fingers and interlaced them with his. His thumb traced circles over her hand.

Rule number ten was at direct odds with rule number three: *don't get personally involved in a story* versus *trust your gut*. Laura was inclined to go with rule number three.

Her heart thumped in her chest.

Heath twisted his body towards her. In the fading light, his eyes locked onto hers. He reached out and brushed the still-damp hair from her face, running his fingers along her jaw. She breathed in. He took that as the sign she was hoping he would and closed the distance between them, his lips touching hers.

They tasted of salt as he kissed her, drawing her to him. His hand caressed the back of her neck, sending a shiver down her spine.

She leaned in closer to him, pressing against him. His other hand reached down her back, holding her tight. A quiet moan escaped her lips.

'I'm sorry.' He pulled back, cradling her chin in his hand.

She swallowed the catch in her throat. 'Don't be.'

'I didn't mean to just spring that on you like that.'

'I didn't mind.'

He kissed her again, leaning her back to lie down in the sand. Her hands roamed down his spine and stopped just above his hips.

Pushing himself up onto his elbows, his face raised just above hers, he breathed out. 'I think maybe we should . . .' He rolled over and stood, reaching out a hand to help her up.

'Yes. We probably should.' She cleared her throat.

'Sorry.' He started brushing sand off her back. It was caked into her hair as well.

'It certainly looks a lot more romantic, less . . . sandy in the movies.' She tried to flick her hair clean.

'Sorry. Romance is not really my thing.'

'Oh, no. I didn't mean . . . that was really . . .' She fanned herself with her hand, her cheeks burning, both from desire and now embarrassment.

'Hot, but sandy?'

She giggled. 'Yes. Definitely. Both.' The truest statement she'd made since arriving in Banksia Bay.

He wrapped his arms around her and she lay her head against his chest. Right there in his strong embrace, right then as the sun disappeared below the banksia trees behind them, she couldn't imagine it was possible to feel any happier.

And it scared her to death.

She pushed away.

'I should probably get you home, before I do something rather ungentlemanly.' He let her go and a surge of loss rushed over her.

Hand in hand they walked back to the holiday house. On the verandah they stood outside the front door facing each other, not going in. Heath ran his hands up Laura's arms.

'I really should go. Surf tomorrow?'

'Sure.'

He kissed her, slow, deep. As he pulled away, she leaned into him, wanting just a little more, and he kissed her again.

'Okay. I'm going. Now.' He stepped back, holding on to her hand, squeezing it before they separated.

Laura watched him walk down the steps and away from her along the path. He turned and ran back to her, leapt onto the verandah, and kissed her again. 'Sorry. Couldn't help it.'

He didn't turn back as he headed down the road and once he was gone Laura went inside. She closed the door behind her and slid down it until she was sitting on the floor, her knees pulled in to her chest.

'What are you doing?' she said aloud. How was it possible to want something so badly with your heart, but not want it at all with your head?

She sat there a while, composing her thoughts, slowing her breathing. When she got up she moved to the sofa where her notes lay across the cushions.

The evidence of her lies and deceit. Guilt ripped through her. She had to tell him.

But how?

Eighteen

Virginia left the cover of the sand dunes and trudged back to the shack, her head hanging low. Seeing Heath and Laura on the beach together had filled her with dread. It was bad enough that Laura was here to destroy her. That Heath was now caught up in it too . . . That was too much.

'Hey, squirt.' Ian's deep, gravelly voice came from behind as she dragged her feet through the sand. 'Penny for your thoughts.'

'Find me a penny and I'll give them to you.' She had no energy to shoo her old friend away.

'Squirt?' Ian reached out and took her hand. 'You know, if there's something wrong, you can tell me.'

Virginia stopped and turned to face him. 'What on earth are you talking about?'

He shook his head. 'Have you forgotten how long I've known you, Virginia? I know you better than you think. Ever since Laura turned up in town, something's not been sitting right with you.'

For the briefest of moments Virginia's eyes flashed before she regained her composure. 'I'm just not sure I like her hanging out with Heath so much.' Which was the truth, but only part of it.

Ian brushed her cheek with thick weathered fingers. 'Squirt, I'm here for you. Always. Talk to me. Whenever you're ready.' He turned and walked away, and a faint echo of Virginia's past danced around the edges of her memory.

She shrugged off the feeling of deja vu. There was no time for that. She had to act.

Everything she'd done, every secret she'd kept, had been to protect those she loved. And now Laura Prescott was here, determined to uncover a terrible truth. A truth that would hurt those Virginia held most dear.

That just wasn't fair.

Not that life was fair. If it was, well, how many things would be different? How much pain and guilt could have been avoided? Often in her dreams she imagined how very different her life could have been, if it had taken an alternative turn all those years ago. They were good dreams. Agonising dreams. Because life wasn't different. And it never could be.

Virginia had no idea if fate and destiny were real, or if it was all just some sort of random mess. She was inclined to think the latter. Because how could something preordained be so cruel? But then, how could chance explain the arrival of Laura, here in the Bay, staying in the holiday house, getting close to her family? No. There was nothing random about that.

Upstairs she unlocked the cupboard under the kitchen sink. All these years she'd told people she locked it out of habit, from when the kids were little, the cleaning chemicals safely out of the way. What a silly lie.

She pulled out the old shoebox and poured herself a stiff whisky.

Sitting on the sofa with her history in her lap, she drank a large gulp of scotch, hoping to find courage in the burning liquid.

She hadn't looked inside her box of memories for nearly sixty years.

Running her fingers over its dusty surface, she drew in a deep breath. Whether it was fate or chance at work, it didn't matter. Her past was back. And she was going to have to deal with it – to protect her family.

The lid tore slightly as she lifted it off and she placed it beside her on the sofa.

'Well, old girl. Time is up.' She looked up and took a deep breath.

On top of all the other items in the box – the zoo ticket, Arthur's map, the carved banksia seed pods – was an old blue envelope. Inside was the picture of Gigi and Lily, the day of Lily's first fry-up, and a broken silver pendant. The other half of Laura's necklace. She held it tightly in her hand, a symbol that had once held hope and promise, now a reminder of all that was lost.

Tears streamed down her face and she let them fall. There was no point now trying to hold them back.

She didn't know what to do about Laura – how to protect Heath and Charlotte and Yvonne. If she confronted her, then the truth would have to come out. If she did nothing, would Laura discover it anyway? She had to put a stop to her. Somehow.

In life there were some truths that had to remain buried. In death, some lies that had to be maintained.

March 1963

A dark cloud hung over Gigi as the school year plodded along. She hadn't seen Costas since the bonfire, despite her attempts to accidently bump into him. Granted, that night had ended awkwardly, more than awkwardly, and she had no idea what had gone wrong, but knowing Costas wouldn't be at school at all left Gigi less than excited to start studying again. This was supposed to be the best year yet – get her leaving certificate and be the first in her family to ever have the chance to go to university – and yet all she felt was a pervasive sadness that seeped out of her every pore.

She trudged through the day, answering questions when called upon by the teacher, helping the younger students with their work when they got stuck, but even that couldn't lift her spirits.

Lumbering over to sit in her usual spot for lunch, she caught sight of something nestled between the roots of the gum tree. As she got closer, she could see what it was.

A small apple carved out of a banksia seed pod.

She looked around, desperate to catch a glimpse of him. It hadn't been there at recess; he had to be nearby.

Over by the swing set one of the younger girls stood, hanging onto the pole with one arm, swaying back and forth, watching Gigi closely through a smoothed-down fringe.

Gigi beckoned her over.

'Do you know something about this, Yvonne?' Gigi asked her. Yvonne Beaumont was three years younger than Gigi and her dad ran the pub. She was always on the periphery of the older kids, hoping they'd invite her in, but they never did.

'Well?' Gigi prompted her.

She shrugged.

'You saw him? You saw him drop this off?' Gigi kept her voice low.

The last thing she needed was to draw attention to herself. Todd was now the oldest one at school and he was making sure everyone knew it. Ever since the bonfire, whenever Todd was in a group all semblance of niceness had disappeared. He'd pushed three first formers over before the first bell and had taken a kid's recess last break. He was blustering around the playground now, just waiting for another opportunity to prove he was on top.

'Yvonne?'

The girl said nothing.

'Did he tell you not to say anything?'

Yvonne didn't move.

'Did he give this to you? To put here?'

The girl cast her eyes down.

It was clear Yvonne was going to keep her promise not to say anything, which for the strange little girl wouldn't be hard. Gigi couldn't remember ever hearing her say a word, except when asked a direct question by Miss Smith.

But why would Costas give the carved apple to her to leave here? Wait. A memory. Halfway through last year there had been an accident. Yvonne fell out of the tree outside her house, four doors up from the Tinellises'. She was hurt pretty badly, if the stories were true.

And it was Mr Tinellis who helped her before the ambulance arrived. Yvonne had followed Costas around school every day for a month after she returned. At the time, Gigi just thought it was her usual attempt to get in with the older students. Now she realised it was more than that.

'Are you two friends?' Gigi asked.

She nodded.

'Can you thank him for me? Next time you see him.'

Yvonne turned to walk away.

'Wait.' Gigi pulled out her notebook and pencil and scribbled a quick message before tearing the page out. 'Can you give him this?'

As she handed the note to Yvonne, Todd strode towards them. 'What's this, then?'

He took the note out of Yvonne's hand.

'Seriously, Gilbert? You're still pining over that greasy loser?' He tore the note into tiny little pieces and scattered them in the dirt.

His posse of followers formed a semicircle around her. She pushed Yvonne back, but the little girl had more courage than Gigi gave her credit for. She stepped closer to Gigi and took her hand.

'Are none of us good enough for you, Gilbert?' Todd closed the gap between them. 'Are none of us Aussies your flavour? Probably just as well, hey, lads?' He turned to his mates and they slapped each other on the back. 'None of us would have you, anyway. Even if you threw yourself at us.'

Gigi took in a deep breath. 'Is that what this is about, Todd? That I rejected you over summer?'

Todd sniggered. 'You? Rejected me? What a joke, fellas.'

The posse all laughed.

'She's lost her mind. No way would I be the least bit interested in a reject like you.'

'Well, then.' Gigi stepped forward and pulled herself up tall. 'If you're not the least bit interested in me, what are you doing wasting your breath even talking to me?'

Todd looked confused. Maybe Gigi had used too many words.

'Yeah, Todd,' one of the boys piped up. 'Don't waste your breath.'

Todd stepped up so close to Gigi, she could smell the ham on his breath from his lunch. 'This isn't over, Gilbert,' he whispered, and he grabbed the carved apple out of her hands and threw it across the road.

The posse moved away and Gigi took in large breaths. One more year of this and then she'd be free of Todd.

She hadn't noticed Yvonne let go of her hand, and when she realised, she spun around looking for the brave kid. When she spotted her, she gasped. Yvonne had jumped over the fence and run across the road to pick up the apple. Gigi looked around, hoping Miss Smith wouldn't see her out of bounds.

Fast as lightning, Yvonne returned and gave Gigi the apple, a small chunk taken out of its side.

'Thank you,' Gigi said, and she hugged her before Yvonne went back to playing on the pole of the swing set.

As Gigi walked home in the afternoon, she knew it was going to be a long year. A very long year. Even the anticipated joy of summer wouldn't be able to sustain her like it usually did. Truth be told, she was less looking forward to summer, and more dreading it. Would Lily really come? What would it be like with her married? All Gigi knew was that it wasn't going to be the same. And if today was anything to go by, school was going to be a real drag.

She got back to the caravan park and checked if Mum had any chores for her. Bring the washing in. That was all. Dad and Ian were out at sea, so it would be just the two of them for dinner, and Mum was throwing together something simple. That was fine by Gigi. After the day she'd had, simple was welcome.

As she was doing the washing-up, there was a knock on the cabin door. Mum answered it and greeted Todd. *Todd?*

'Evening, Mrs Gilbert. I was wondering if I might have a word with Gigi?'

'Of course.'

Mum motioned that Gigi could speak with Todd outside, ignoring the look of horror on her daughter's face.

Gigi stepped out of the cabin. 'What do you want, Todd?' She stood with her hands on her hips.

'To apologise, actually.' He looked at his feet in the dirt. 'I shouldn't have said what I said today, done what I did.'

'No, you shouldn't have.'

'It's just . . .' He stepped towards her and she could smell the faint hint of alcohol on his breath. 'Dad's making me go into the force. You don't understand the pressure. And the fellas were egging me on. I just . . . I'm sorry.'

Gigi looked at the little boy in front of her, scared and confused, and believed his apology was genuine. In his mind at least.

'That's no excuse, Todd.'

'I know. I'm sorry. I'll go now. Just tell me one thing, though, Gilbert. You're not really keen on that wog, are you?'

Gigi refused to answer. It was none of his business. She stared at him in silence.

'Are you kidding me?' He tried to keep his voice low. 'Damn it, girl.' He threw his hands in the air. 'People round here won't take too kindly to you fraternising with a dirty wog, you know.'

'Goodnight, Todd.' Gigi turned and headed back into the cabin.

Inside, Mum was getting ready for bed. A chill in the air blew through the open windows of the cabin. Autumn was definitely here.

Gigi slipped a cardigan over her overalls, assured Mum she had no homework and that she'd be back before it was too late, then headed up the headland to her secret spot. The beach was deserted below, not a fisherman or surfer in sight.

She lay back in the long grass and looked up as the first stars began to poke through the evening sky.

'Virginia?'

She sat up. Costas was standing over her.

'I was hoping you'd come by tonight.'

Her skin tingled at the sight of him. She wanted to throw herself into his arms, but the last time she'd seen him, he'd pushed her away. 'Hi. Thank you for the apple today.'

'I heard there was a bit of trouble.' From his pocket he pulled out the tattered pieces of the note she'd written, stuck back together.

'Where did you get that?' Gigi asked.

'Yvonne.'

Gigi whistled long and slow. The girl had picked up as many pieces as she could and reassembled about half of Gigi's note. 'Isn't she a little surprise?'

'She's a good kid,' Costas said. 'I'm sorry. About what happened.' He looked at the ground.

'You are not responsible for Todd's pathetic behaviour.'

'No. But I put you in that position, and I'm sorry for that.' He reached out and brushed her hair behind her ear, and her breath caught in her throat. 'You don't deserve that, Virginia.'

'No one deserves anything Todd dishes out.' She grabbed his hand before he could pull it away. Everything was changing and she wanted to hang on to the one thing she knew to be true.

'Virginia.' He raised her hand to his lips and kissed her palm.

Her cheeks burned, her stomach churned. But she didn't let go.

'Virginia, we cannot. It's not . . .'

'It's not how the world works. You keep saying that. But the world can work any way we want it to. Surely. Todd is a mosquito. He'll be gone at the end of the year. You and I, we have something, I know we do. And I'll be damned if I let small-mindedness get in the way.'

Costas held her hand to his cheek. 'My sweet Virginia. It isn't just that. Though that is a hurdle bigger than you realise. It's also . . .'

'What?'

'My family. They have . . . plans. For me.'

'Plans that don't include me? They don't even know me. If they took the time . . .'

'Shh.' He kissed her palm again. 'If there was any way . . . I would make it happen.'

'What are you saying? We can't be together? Even though we both want it? End of story?'

He closed his eyes.

'Then maybe you're not the man I thought you were, Costas Tinellis.'

Gigi jumped up and ran down the headland. She didn't turn back when she heard Costas calling her name, and she didn't stop until she was back home.

On her bunk she buried her face into her pillow and cried silent tears until she had none left.

Gigi plodded through the next few months as best she could – doing chores for Mum, staying on top of her schoolwork, avoiding a certain street any time she had to go through town. Her withdrawal had the surprising effect of removing her from Todd's radar, and she was at least thankful for that. He too had shifted away from the crowd, even ignoring his posse. Rumour had it he'd stood up to his father about not wanting to go into the force and Sergeant Broadbent had expressed his disappointment physically.

At school Yvonne had taken to sitting next to Gigi for lunch. At first Gigi tried to shoo her away, but the girl was persistent and in the end Gigi gave up. Eventually, she grew to appreciate the quiet company. Then in the last week of July, Gigi received the post she'd been both anticipating and dreading.

A letter from Lily. But not just a letter, photos of the wedding, too. Lily looked stunning, as Gigi had expected. And she looked happy. Her white dress was simple with long elegant sleeves and her veil tumbled down her shoulders from beneath a pillbox hat. Around her neck hung the sapphire and silver angel wings Gigi had given her. Richard looked tall and terribly proud beside her.

Gigi pored over Lily's letter, drinking in every word, every detail of the wedding and life as the new Mrs Prescott.

'I have also sent back to you your guardian angel. Thank you ever so much for loaning her to me. She definitely helped me manage the few months leading up to the wedding. I am so deliriously happy now, though, I cannot possibly have need for her. And you sounded sad in your last letter. Perhaps you need her more than I right now. She is returned to you. I cannot wait to see you in the summer, my dearest friend. Until then, kisses from me, Lily.'

Gigi opened the tissue paper that held the pendant safely inside. She didn't like to admit it, but she could use a bit of guardian angel magic in her life these days.

In August Yvonne turned fourteen and invited Gigi to a barbecue to celebrate. Gigi didn't get invited to many birthdays, and certainly never to one of someone so young. But Yvonne's mum, who'd given her the invitation, assured her it was just family and a few friends, so Gigi let her guard down and agreed to go. With Costas missing from her world, and all contact with Lily revolving around married life, Yvonne, despite her shyness, was the closest thing to a friend Gigi had.

Gigi wrapped up a present – a book she'd picked up last time she and Mum went into Ocean Heights – and then picked a rose from the bush outside the cabin to make the present look a little more appealing. Mum would be mad if she found out Gigi had taken it; she didn't have the greenest thumb and getting anything to bloom was a real feat for her.

Oh well. Too late now.

Gigi walked through town, the warm spring air blowing lightly through the tree-lined streets. There was never much activity in town on Saturday mornings – a few customers at the bakery, some teenagers at the milk bar, the paper boy returning his little yellow cart to the newsagent after his delivery round.

She knocked on Yvonne's door, hoping someone would let her in quickly. The longer she was out the front, the more chance that Costas, if he was home, would see her.

The door swung open.

And standing there in the hallway was Costas himself.

'Oh. Hello,' she said, hoping her cheeks weren't as red as they felt.

'Hello. Come in. Everyone is out the back.' He stepped aside and let her pass.

Okay. So we're going to act as if nothing happened. At least she knew where she stood. It seemed the older she got, the less she understood boys.

In the backyard Yvonne sat on a picnic blanket, surrounded by a family of kittens. Mr Beaumont was at the barbecue turning over the steak, the aroma of which was mouth-watering. Not surprising, given he owned the local pub. Mrs Beaumont was at the salad table, pouring Mr Tinellis a drink. Mrs Tinellis stood behind him, saying nothing. When she saw Gigi enter the yard, her face hardened.

'Oh, Gigi, you came!' Yvonne jumped up and gave her a quick hug.

'And you do have a voice.' Gigi smiled at her.

Yvonne cast her eyes down. 'Yes. At home. Among friends. I . . . I get . . . nervous in public.' She cast her eyes downwards.

Yvonne introduced her to the partygoers, unnecessarily so, as Gigi knew everyone there except for the young boy trying to pull one of the kitten's tails. 'This is my cousin, Nick. Feel free to ignore him.'

'Nico!' Nick shouted without looking up. Gigi guessed he was around eight.

'His grandmother, his other grandmother, is Greek, and he's her favourite. She calls him Nico. It makes him feel special.' She leaned closer to her cousin. 'Even though he's not.'

Nick picked up a handful of dirt and threw it at Yvonne.

Mrs Tinellis barked something at Nick in Greek. He looked at her, suitably chastised, and then poked his tongue out at Yvonne.

'The Tinellis family know Nick's grandmother's family, distant cousins or something like that.' Yvonne shrugged. 'I don't know how it all works.' She ran to the table and got some fruit punch for Gigi.

'Thank you, Yvonne.'

Gigi couldn't believe this was the same quiet girl from school who never said boo. It was nice, though. Her energy was happy and fun, and everyone seemed to be infected by it. Except Mrs Tinellis.

Yvonne's dad served up lunch and everyone devoured the steak. The salad that was served with lunch was fairly average, but everyone ate it. Except Nick. There was some sort of pie that was also served on the plate and it was the most delicious food Gigi had ever tasted.

'What's this?' She turned to Yvonne.

'Oh, that's spanakopita.'

'Spana . . .'

'. . . kopita. Mrs Tinellis makes it. Isn't it divine?'

Gigi looked at Costas' mum. 'Can I have seconds?'

For the first time since they'd met, Mrs Tinellis smiled back at Gigi. And hope filled Gigi's heart.

As the party wound down, the ladies cleared away the plates of leftover food, and the men put away the barbecue. Nick continued to tease the kittens, who'd taken to hiding behind the rubbish bin to try to get away from him.

Mrs Tinellis wrapped four serves of spanakopita in foil and handed the parcel to Gigi, saying something in Greek.

'For me?'

She pushed the parcel into Gigi's arms.

'Really? Thank you. Um . . . ef . . . cha . . . ristó.' She really hoped she was saying the word she'd learned from Costas correctly.

'Nai.' Mrs Tinellis nodded. 'Efcharistó.'

A second smile.

While the two families were busy saying goodbye, Gigi caught Costas alone, outside the back door. He'd kept his distance during the party, staying as far away from Gigi as he could without being outright rude.

She lowered her voice. 'Do you know where the old cheese factory is?'

'Yes.'

'Meet me there this afternoon. Four o'clock.'

She turned and went inside to take her leave of Yvonne and her family before he had a chance to say anything.

'Thank you, Yvonne.' She hugged her new friend. 'It was a great party.'

'I knew it would be.' She winked at Gigi and then turned her gaze to Costas.

Gigi turned and got out of there as fast as she could.

———

Four o'clock took forever to arrive. Gigi had been at the cheese factory for half an hour already, just to make sure she wasn't late. She sat up in the old rafters, waiting. Every sound made her jump and look around. Every sound disappointed her.

The sun began its slow descent and Gigi's heart sank with it. Costas was half an hour late. He wasn't coming.

Well, she had her answer now.

As she started to climb down the wooden support, she heard a rustling coming from outside. She clambered to the ground and turned around.

'Virginia? Are you here?' Costas stepped through the debris.

'Here.'

He looked at her with an expression she found hard to read. She motioned towards the broken cart and they sat down together. A mouse ran over her leg, disturbed from its hiding spot.

'Yuck. I'm not a huge fan of mice.'

'They are simply misunderstood. Something we have in common.'

'I didn't think you were coming.'

'I'm sorry. I know I've been avoiding you lately. It's just so complicated.'

'Does it have to be?' In her mind it was all so simple.

Costas bowed his head. 'It is what it is. We cannot change the world.'

'We can change our part of it.'

Silence fell between them and they held each other's gaze.

'Oh, Virginia.' Costas took her hand in his. 'We could be so happy together.' He dropped her hand and dragged himself off the cart.

'So,' Gigi said, as she followed him, 'let's be together, then. I don't care what people say.'

'I know you don't. It's one of the reasons I . . . but this isn't just about any old people.' He ran his hand through his thick black hair. 'My parents . . . they . . .'

'I know your mum doesn't exactly like me.' She stood in front of him, her hand on his chest, her pulse thudding in her veins. 'But today, at Yvonne's, I felt there was a shift in her.'

Costas put his hand over hers. 'Sweet Virginia. Ma recognises how wonderful you are. But it isn't enough.'

'Doesn't she want you to be happy?'

He turned around, stepped back and then forward again. 'She does. It's just her idea of my happiness . . . it isn't . . . oh God, why is this so hard? There was a reason we went away last summer. A reason I had to leave school and get a job.'

Gigi took hold of his shaking hands.

'My parents have plans for me to marry the daughter of a family friend. She's Greek.'

'An arranged marriage?' Gigi dropped his hand and stepped back.

'Not exactly. Sort of. We both have to agree.'

'Then don't agree.' She didn't understand why this was so difficult.

'I couldn't do that to them. My parents. They've been through so much already.' He bowed his head.

She lowered her voice. 'Do you . . . want to be with me?' She couldn't look him in the eye as he answered.

His voice was soft, cracking. 'More than anything.'

That was all she needed to know.

In her pocket she squeezed the pendant that was always with her and made a wish. She took Costas' hand and smiled up at him. 'Where there's breath, there's hope.' She stood up on her tiptoes and kissed him, her lips brushing his briefly.

He put one arm around her waist and pulled her in tight. He

wrapped his other hand around her neck and kissed her, the want in him obvious, her own desire meeting his.

They kissed and held each other and it was perfect.

Gently, he pulled away.

'Virginia,' he said, through heavy breath. 'What are we going to do?'

She lay her head on his chest, unbothered by the obstacles in their path. 'We'll figure it out.'

Hand in hand, they walked back towards town. As the shops came into sight they let each other go and simply walked side by side, no words needed.

'Well, well, well.' A familiar voice came from behind.

They turned around to see Todd standing there with his hands on his hips.

'What have you two been up to, then?' He swayed slightly.

'Nothing, Todd. Leave us alone.' Gigi's voice was weary.

'Looks to me like you've been up to no good, those silly grins on your faces. Don't tell me . . .' He glared at Gigi and she knew the redness in her cheeks was giving her away. 'Oh, disgusting. You have, haven't you? You've been necking this dirty wog.'

Costas stepped in front of Gigi, his large frame between her and Todd.

'Oh really, Wog-boy? You want a piece?' Todd slurred his words and raised his fists.

Gigi put her hand on Costas' back. 'Let's go,' she whispered.

To Gigi's relief, Costas began to turn away.

'That's right. Take your filthy whore home, you dirty . . .'

In one quick movement Costas spun and decked Todd so hard he fell to the road. He tried to get up, but his legs gave way.

Gigi stared at the scene before her, unable to move. Todd was bleeding from his eye. Costas' shoulders were raised, ready to strike again. She touched his hand and he spun round. She shook her head.

The tension from Costas' torso released, and they backed away from Todd, who was now sitting in the gutter holding his head with dirt-stained hands.

In silence they walked towards the caravan park.

'This won't go unpunished,' Gigi whispered, Costas' face an inch from hers.

'I know. I won't have you part of it, though. Lay low for a few days.'

She walked into the park, not daring to look back lest she throw herself into his arms.

An hour later Gigi heard the sirens. She snuck up the road and hid at the end of the street. Sergeant Broadbent's police car was parked out the front of the Tinellises' house. The lights were on inside and Gigi could hear raised voices, though she couldn't make out what was being said.

A crunch of gravel made Gigi spin around.

'Yvonne, go home.'

The girl laced her fingers with Gigi's.

They crouched down behind a bush and watched on.

A few minutes later, Sergeant Broadbent led Costas out of his house, hands cuffed behind his back.

Gigi gasped and stood up, but Yvonne pulled her back down.

At the front door, Mr Tinellis put on his coat and hat and followed Costas and the Sergeant out. Mrs Tinellis slumped against the doorframe and howled.

Tears fell down Gigi's face as Yvonne put her arms around her.

Nineteen

*L*aura woke on the sofa in the living room of the holiday house and ignored the message from Maher asking her to call back. If it was important, he'd ring again. Right now she had to figure out how to talk to Heath about why she was really in Banksia Bay.

She hauled herself off the soft cushions and stretched, trying to release the tension in her shoulders and back. It must have been around five in the morning when she'd finally given in to exhaustion. She paced the living room floor, all her notes and photocopied articles spread out on the coffee table. All night she'd been poring over them, getting it straight in her head: what she knew, what she still had to discover; organising her thoughts so that when Heath asked questions about what she'd been doing here the whole time – and he would undoubtedly have questions when she revealed the truth – she could answer him. Honestly.

For the last few weeks she'd been justifying her decision to keep the secret of why she was really here – that it was the only way to uncover the truth. But she was wrong. Selfish. Finding out about

Lillian's past wasn't just about her, as she'd told herself it was. She might not yet know what had happened all those years ago, but the secrets her grandmother had obviously kept, the missing pages of The Bugle, the clues she'd found in Virginia's possession, all meant that whatever it was, it was significant. And that meant it was about everyone. It affected everyone. Virginia, Yvonne, Heath. There were real people involved. Real feelings now.

Very real feelings.

And those people deserved to know the truth of why she was really here.

She thought about going to Virginia first. After all, despite the holes in the story, Laura knew in her gut that this was where the truth would be found. But after last night, she had to speak to Heath. He would probably hate her, and the thought of that pained her more than she thought it would. Really, they'd only flirted a little, kissed a bit – a lot. But less than twenty-four hours ago. It wasn't as if they had a real relationship.

Except it felt real. And the pain of losing him felt real too.

Yes. She had to talk to him. Today. Instead of meeting him for a surf, she'd take him for a walk along the beach and confess. Then she'd face Virginia and hopefully get the answers she'd come here for – with a clear conscience.

She pulled on her running tights and tank top and slipped on her trainers. A long jog around the hills was exactly what she needed.

Standing on the top of the hill looking over Banksia Bay sleeping beneath her, Laura drew in deep breaths. There were no cars on the main street yet, a sprinkling of lights were blinking on where early risers were starting their day, and the waking sun bathed the entire town in a soft golden glow. The roof of the bakery was speckled where the rust was eating away the corrugated ridges of iron. The lilly pilly hedge in the beer garden of the pub rippled in the morning breeze.

In three short weeks she had grown accustomed to the gentle ebb and flow of this small town. She would miss it when she left. Just one more week till she was due to head home. Assuming, of course, they didn't run her out of town once her deception was revealed.

Laura stretched her legs and turned her back on the view, running further, harder, than usual. She ran until her chest hurt, and kept on running.

As she rounded the next crest she stopped with a jolt. Before her was the old cheese factory. She turned around, looking back at where she'd come from. It didn't feel like she'd run so far.

Scanning the now familiar coast, she realised the cheese factory wasn't as far out of town as she'd thought. Running in a relatively straight line was a much quicker way to get there than the winding country road she had taken with Heath.

She stepped through the gap in the stone walls and walked around the space, imagining Heath's vision, still so very clear in her mind. She had no idea whether his dream was possible, but it was a nice dream.

Lowering herself onto the broken cart, legs over the edge, she let out a long breath. 'If these walls could talk,' Mrs Duncan used to say. Laura wondered what these old walls would whisper to her.

The tattered old blanket she sat on was gnawed around the edges, mice perhaps, and covered with decades of dust. Actually, sitting here didn't seem like such a good idea after all.

She pushed herself off and slipped, falling to the ground with a thud. She lay in the dirt for a moment, mentally checking that she hadn't hurt anything vital. No. Just her pride. Thankfully no one was here to witness her clumsiness.

As she pushed up on her arms she caught a glimpse of something under the cart. Oh God, a mouse.

She screamed and jumped up, stamping her feet to scare the dirty critter away. Bending down, she checked to see if it had gone. But it was still there. She picked up a splinter of wood and threw it at the creature. It still didn't move. Gross – was it dead?

With a longer piece of wood she poked it. To her surprise it was hard rather than squishy. She hooked the piece of wood behind the mouse and dragged it out. As it came into the light, she realised it wasn't a mouse at all.

Well, actually it was. But not the kind that ate cheese and gnawed on old blankets and scared her witless. It was a knick-knack. A figurine. Covered in dust and dirt.

She brushed away the grime as best she could with the bottom edge of her tank top. Intricately carved out of some sort of wood, the mouse was delicate, with a tiny little turned-up mouth that, for some reason, made Laura feel sad. How long had he been lying under there, abandoned? Was it a child's favoured toy lost one day in a game of hide-and-seek?

Laura decided to keep it, clean it up. Maybe Aiden would like it, though he was probably too old for that sort of thing. Or she could give it to one of Maher's grandkids when she got home. Perhaps she would keep it, a reminder of her time in the Bay.

Tucking it into the pocket of her tights, she headed back to the holiday house.

Laura splashed her face with cold water. Confronting Heath wasn't going to be easy. But she had to do it.

She sat down and the mouse she'd forgotten all about stuck into her leg. She got up and wet a flannel and, with tiny concentric circles, wiped the mouse clean. There was a gloss to it where the polish hadn't been worn away by time, and the wood was covered in irregular oval holes, giving it a texture she found fascinating.

She set the clean mouse in the middle of the table. If she could polish it up, even it out, it would look quite sweet. Maybe Heath would know what it was made from, what she could polish it with.

Heath.

Facing him would be hard.

A hot shower now, then she'd tidy her notes and wait till the time came to confess her sins.

An urgent knock on the door startled her.

'Laura? Are you home?'

Her heart beat faster at the sound of Heath's voice. She hurried to the door and opened it, Heath standing there with a big grin on his face.

'Hey. I'm glad you've dropped by. There's actually something I want to talk to you about.' She steeled herself.

'Okay, but first, I have the best news.'

'What?'

He wrapped his arms around her waist and lifted her, spinning her around. 'I went to the bank this morning.' He put her down. 'They've pre-approved my loan to buy the cheese factory.' He picked her up again and hugged her tightly.

'That's brilliant.' She kissed him on the cheek and he turned his head, catching her lips.

It was a long, slow kiss, full of want. She knew she should pull away, but she couldn't.

He lowered her to the verandah.

'Tell me all about it.' She smiled.

Heath launched into an animated story about the dealings with the bank, how he'd been talking to the owners of the property, that a contract of sale was being drawn up, how long it would take, especially to get the money.

'I can't believe it's finally going to happen.' He paused for breath.

'I can. You are a force, Heath Gilbert. An inspiration. I can't wait to see what you do with the place.'

'Do you want to see? I have the plans here.' He grabbed the blueprints he'd leaned against the wall.

'Of course I want to see. Come in.' She stepped aside and he slipped past her, turning around to look at her as she followed him inside.

'You know, this is partly because of you.' He walked backwards into the living room, his eyes not leaving hers.

'Me? How?'

'Well, after our visit there together, you were so encouraging. It gave me the last little push I needed to move forward. The architect has been working on these for a while. Yesterday I finalised them with her. I love Charlotte to death, but she hasn't exactly been supportive of this crazy idea of mine. I wasn't sure I could do it. If I *should* do it. Until you said you believed in the dream.'

'Maybe Charlotte just doesn't want to see you risk your money. Any small business is a gamble.'

He turned around to lay the plans out on the coffee table.

Shit. Her notes.

'It isn't that,' he said. 'She's worried about . . . What's this?' He looked at Laura and then back to her notes.

'That's what I wanted to talk to you about.'

He dropped his plans on the floor beside the sofa, knelt down and sifted through the pages on the coffee table.

'Heath, let me explain.'

He turned over articles, read through her notes. 'This is about Gran.' He stood up. 'It's all about Gran. And Yvonne. And not about holidaying in Banksia Bay at all.' He stared at her, confusion and anger flashing in his eyes. 'You're not a travel writer, are you?'

'No.'

'Who's Lillian?'

'My grandmother.' She let out a long breath, relieved to finally be telling him the truth.

'You've been lying to me? To all of us?'

Laura's throat tightened. 'I didn't mean to. I was looking for something and I thought I might have better luck finding it if I . . .'

'Deceived us?' He stepped away from the evidence of her lies. 'How could you do this? To me? To us? We trusted you. We welcomed you.'

'Heath, just let me explain.' She clasped her hands in front of her chest.

He shook his head. 'Except Charlotte. She said when you first got here that something didn't add up.' He turned back to the files. 'There's so much here about Gran. What are you up to? If you're here to hurt her, then you're in serious trouble.' His voice was low.

'No. That's not what this is. I just wanted to find out what happened in the sixties. Between her and my grandmother.' She stepped forward and grabbed his arm. 'There's no malice. I swear.'

'Then why didn't you just come straight out and ask?'

'My gut was telling me it was something significant. I wasn't sure that if I asked, anyone would tell me. You said yourself small towns could rewrite their history.' All her excuses, so certain in her mind, seemed so feeble now as she said them out loud.

Heath yanked his arm free of her hold and paced the floor.

She rocked back and forth. It wasn't supposed to go like this. Finally coming clean was meant to be liberating. She wasn't doing it right. She had to make him see, convince him she meant no harm. 'I think I was right, Heath. I think everyone's hiding something. Something big. If you look here –' she ran towards the coffee table and picked up her copied pages of The Bugle, waving them in front of her – 'you'll see . . .'

'I'm not interested in hearing any of this. I can't believe you lied to me.' The sadness in his eyes bored right into her heart. 'This was all an act, wasn't it? To get close to my family. You used me.'

'No, Heath. No, that's not true.' She dropped the pages and stepped towards him. He backed away and she wrapped her arms around herself.

'None of this was real.' He waved his hands between them.

Tears fell down Laura's cheeks. 'It was real. It is. What's happened between us . . . I've never felt anything so real in my life.'

'And I'm supposed to believe you. After you've lied to me this whole time. Damn it, Laura.' He shook his head. 'I can't . . .' His voice was low, laboured. 'I'm not in a position to waste . . . damn it.' With heavy steps he walked towards the door.

'Don't go, Heath. Please.' She moved towards him, reaching out her hand, almost touching his back, but she faltered. 'I . . . I know I've done the wrong thing. But if you just hear me out . . .'

He bowed his head, his back to her. 'Stop.' His raspy word filled the space between them and his shoulders fell. He opened the door and trudged down the path, not once looking back.

Laura doubled over, sank to the verandah and watched him leave through salty tears. She'd known he'd be upset, but she wasn't expecting the air of defeat that had come over him. And she wasn't expecting her heart to shatter as he left. But it did.

Into a million painful pieces.

Her phone buzzed in her pocket and she pulled it out, hoping, expecting it to be Heath.

But it was Maher.

She sent him to voicemail, unable to face anything other than her own feelings crumbling inside her.

Twenty

Virginia sat at her dining table, Heath opposite her, silent, brooding. He'd stormed up the stairs of the shack fifteen minutes ago, but had said nothing. Virginia waited, rather impatiently.

But she knew her grandson well. He had never been very good at hiding his feelings, and when he was this agitated the best thing to do was let him spill his troubles when he was ready. If she asked him what was wrong, he'd bluster about a bit but say nothing. If she fussed about all worried, he'd brush her aside and say everything was fine.

She held her teacup in her hands, not daring to take a sip in case the movement made him startle and head off, revealing nothing.

So she waited.

Heath stared at the small dining table, breathing heavily. He looked up. There was pain in his eyes. Confusion, too.

He drew in a deep breath and his words came forth, low and slow. 'Laura isn't who she said she is. She's not writing a travel piece about the Bay at all.'

Virginia said nothing and had to concentrate on keeping her hands from shaking.

'She has all these files. About the past.' He looked her in the eye. 'About you. Why does she have files on you?'

With forced calmness Virginia spoke. 'I don't know.' Rubbish. She might not know for sure, but she had a pretty good idea. 'Did you ask her?'

'Yes. No. Maybe. I don't remember.' He rubbed his forehead. 'She said something about you and her grandmother and the past. I think.'

So maybe she hadn't uncovered the truth yet. If she had, and had said something to Heath, he most certainly would have remembered. You don't forget something like that. Ever.

Maybe there was still time to fix this. To throw Laura off the scent. To protect herself, her family, Yvonne.

'Gran?' He stood up, rising to his full height. 'Did you know her grandmother? What aren't you telling me?'

Virginia rose slowly and stepped towards him. 'Love. Sit back down.'

'No. What's going on? I really like this woman, Gran. *Really*. And now I find out she's lying to me, and somehow you're involved.'

Involved? Involved didn't even begin to cover it.

'Gran?'

'I don't know. I'll have to speak to her myself.'

Heath sat back down, then jumped up again. 'Hang on. You don't seem very surprised by this – that she's not here to do what she said she was doing, that she has a file on you. In fact, you don't seem surprised at all.' He furrowed his brow even deeper.

'Heath, I'm not sure what to tell you.'

He stepped back. 'How about the truth? It seems to be in short supply at the moment.'

Virginia turned away. She couldn't tell him. She just couldn't.

Walking to the door, Heath paused, his voice barely above a whisper.

'One thing you promised me, Gran, was that we'd always be honest with each other. That day in the hospital. Remember? No matter what. Right or wrong, happy or sad. Life or death. You promised.'

He walked out of the loft above the shack and Virginia pushed her hands into her knees to stop herself from collapsing. *Breathe, old girl.*

She righted herself and grabbed the photo of her and Lily from her shoebox and slipped it into the pocket of her overalls. She had to know how much damage had been done, how much had been discovered. And she had to know now.

With the weight of her past heavy around her heart, she walked out of the shack.

August 1963

Costas spent three nights locked up in the tiny police cell in Ocean Heights. Yvonne's dad, Mr Beaumont, brought reports home every day, making sure he visited with the Tinellises during the ordeal, and Gigi made sure she stopped by every afternoon for the news. Yvonne didn't say much, even when it was just the two of them. Gigi couldn't blame her. Most days she didn't feel much like talking either.

At school, Todd sported an ugly black eye and told everyone he had been minding his own business when he was set upon by Costas, who was crazy with rage, he didn't know why.

Gigi tried to set the record the straight, but every time she opened her mouth, Todd shut her down. On the second afternoon he bailed her up outside the schoolhouse, forcing her against the wall, his arm barring her escape.

He looked at the ground then back at her. 'Why did you force me into this?'

'What? How is this my fault?'

'I don't want to be that guy, Gilbert. I want to be a good man. Protect my friends. But you backed me into a corner.'

'If you want to be a good man, Todd, be one.'

She saw tears in his eyes.

'Everything is so simple with you, isn't it? But life isn't simple.' He closed his eyes and Gigi ducked under his arm and ran away.

A day later, Yvonne came running into the caravan park after supper. Gigi was outside the cabin, airing some blankets in the evening breeze, when her friend skidded in front of her and put her hands on her knees to catch her breath.

'Slow down, Yvonne. What is it?'

'Costas. He's out. He's up at the cheese factory . . .'

Before Yvonne could finish her message, Gigi was already running out of the caravan park.

'Gigi. Wait!' Yvonne called out and caught up to her.

Gigi turned around.

'You have to be . . . something happened. In gaol. It isn't pretty.'

Gigi ran. As fast as she could.

With moonlight shining through the holes in the stone walls of the cheese factory, Gigi picked her way over the debris strewn across the floor.

'Costas?' she whispered.

Out from a shadow he stepped and held up his hand. 'Don't come closer.'

'Like hell.' Gigi hurried to him.

His face was swollen and blue, his arm in a makeshift sling.

'What did he do to you?' She held back tears.

Costas didn't meet her gaze. 'It wasn't Todd. Though I imagine he was behind it. There were two other men locked up with me. Apparently they don't like dirty foreigners either.'

'Oh, Costas.' She reached her hand out to his face, but was too afraid to touch him. 'Didn't anyone intervene?'

Costas simply looked at her.

'I'm so sorry.'

He pulled her into a tight hug as she sobbed into his chest and they stayed like that, stopped in time, until Gigi's tears subsided.

When they parted, Costas held her hand, his thumb caressing her palm.

'What do we do now?' she asked, afraid of the answer.

'Where there's breath, there's hope, right?' He brushed her hair behind her ears.

'But we have to be smart about this,' she said.

Yes. They would have to be very careful. Together they laid out a plan. Gigi would finish school. They wouldn't see each other unless they could do it safely. Costas would accept his parents' decision and marry the girl they'd chosen for him, but he'd delay the wedding until the end of summer. Until he could save up enough money, like a good husband should. Then he and Gigi would run away, taking the money he'd saved, and start a new life somewhere else.

There was no other way.

'Virginia.' He cupped her chin in his hand. 'Are you sure?'

She nodded.

'I love you.' He pressed a carved seed pod heart into her hands and took off into the night.

'I love you too,' she whispered into the dark.

———

The next day after Gigi finished her chores, she strolled through the hills surrounding Banksia Bay. She was at peace with her decision to run away with Costas at the end of summer, even though it would destroy her parents. But it was the only way.

As she walked to her favourite spot on the headland, she noticed a rock tucked beneath the long grass. She knew every inch of these hills and that rock was never there before.

She knelt down and brushed the swaying blades of grass aside. In tiny letters carved into the rock were the initials V.G. and C.T. and a roughly hewn heart shape in the middle.

Gigi gasped and looked around. Was he here?

No. Her heart sank.

She touched the rock, drew in a deep breath and covered it back up with grass.

Staring at the beach below, the only place she'd ever called home, she held back tears. She had to leave and never return. Melancholy seeped into her soul.

A small group of surfers gathered on the sand below and stood in a line, their boards behind them. Ian's unmistakable figure stood in front of them, his arm waving about, giving instructions Gigi wasn't sure were being followed.

The group remained still for a few seconds as Ian pulled out his camera, before they broke off and headed into the sea. Ian stayed on shore a little longer, facing the waves.

Maybe Gigi could take a few of his photos with her when she left. Small reminders of home.

She would miss this place.

The last few months of the school year dragged by in a haze of lessons and self-imposed seclusion. Gigi worked harder than she ever had, and when her parents asked why there had been such a turnaround in her attitude to school, she brushed it aside, saying she wanted to make sure she had options at the end. After all, wasn't it a very modern thing for women to have options nowadays?

Dad accepted the explanation. Mum raised an eyebrow. Ian shook his head as he laughed. 'Good one, squirt.'

She didn't dare say a word about her true motive. Once she and Costas ran away, they'd both need to get jobs. And if she was to have any hope of getting something that paid more than cleaning, she needed to get a half-decent leaving certificate.

Twice she'd met Costas in the forlorn months that ensued, which wasn't nearly enough, but Todd was watching her closely. All the time.

Yvonne, God bless her, had delivered a note one day from Costas to meet him at the cheese factory and had played decoy that afternoon, pretending to injure herself as they were all leaving school, falling down in front of Todd and hanging on to his leg, crying. She'd winked at Gigi between tears and Gigi had slipped past the commotion, running into the hills.

The second time they'd met was in the dead of night, quite unplanned. So many evenings Gigi had stared up at her shelf of precious memories, willing sleep to come. So often slumber had evaded her. One night she'd given up altogether and wandered the beach barefoot under the stars. And Costas had come.

They'd held each other without words, waves lapping their ankles, until the chill blowing off the water forced them to move further up the sand. They'd sat on the highest dune looking out to sea, their words barely above a whisper.

'Are you okay? Really?' Costas had asked. 'I hate not seeing you every day.'

It killed Gigi that he was forced to maintain the charade of his impending wedding. 'Will she be crushed?' His future non-bride an innocent victim in all this.

He closed his eyes. Gigi knew the guilt was eating at him.

That night he'd left Gigi with a carved rose. She'd placed it in the box she kept hidden in the drawer under her clothes.

Gigi desperately wanted to write to Lily about her plans to elope. But she knew Lily wouldn't understand. She'd never warmed to Costas to begin with, and now that she was the pregnant wife of the well-to-do Dr Prescott, she would not approve of Gigi's lack of propriety.

The days ticked by.

Summer approached.

School finally ended.

And that brought welcome distraction – tourists and loads of chores around the caravan park.

Lily was due to arrive just before New Year's.

Gigi didn't know how she was going to maintain a façade of contentment, hiding her true feelings from her best friend. But she knew she had to.

At least now it was only weeks till it was all over.

After finishing her chores Gigi took a walk along the beach. Ian, back from his last fishing trip with Dad, was teaching a group of tourists how to surf. Every year more and more beachgoers flocked to their tiny town. Every year Ian took on more surfing students between trips out to sea, his camera always at hand to document his students' disasters and triumphs.

Finding a quiet spot to sit and think was quite impossible during summer now. Though maybe that wasn't a bad thing. Alone with one's thoughts, one's mind could wander to all sorts of places it shouldn't.

With her fishing rod in one hand and a bucket of bait in another, Gigi headed to the northern rock pools. The place she and Lily had first become friends. She knew she wouldn't catch anything. It was the wrong time of day and, with so many people about, most of the sea creatures would be taking cover. But standing on the edge of the rocks, casting her line into the ocean, over and over again, was calm and relaxing. She could switch off from everything else around her and just fish.

A familiar figure walked up the beach towards her and she nearly dropped her rod.

He waved, and she waved back, packing up her gear.

'Hi, Gigi. So good to see you.' Richard clasped her hand and squeezed it firmly.

'I didn't think you were arriving till tonight. Where's Lily?' Gigi looked around.

'It's okay. She's here. Travelling in her delicate condition takes a bit out of her is all. She sent me on a mission to find you and invite you over for dinner tonight.'

Gigi clapped her hands. 'Of course, I'd love to come. Thank you.'

Richard leaned in. 'She'll be thrilled.' He kissed her on the cheek, lingering a fraction too long. 'You've grown up this year, Gigi. Real nice.' He bowed his head and strode off down the beach.

She'd been hearing that all summer from the regulars who came to the caravan park each year. She'd grown up 'nice'. She was no longer a child. She'd come into her looks – whatever that meant. Even Ian had made a comment over dinner last week. And she'd thrown her fork at him for it.

Why, then, when Richard made note, did it feel different? Wrong?

As far as she was concerned, she was still the same old tomboy Gigi that no one took much notice of. And that was just as well, if she and Costas were to pull off their disappearing act. No one would notice she was gone. No one would notice wherever they ended up.

She raced home and got ready, far too early, for her dinner with Lily and Richard. She even brushed her hair and put on a floral blouse to wear under her overalls. Then she watched the clock, waiting till she could leave.

When five-thirty ticked by, Gigi took off from the caravan park and headed to the holiday house. This year it would be just Lily and Richard, their families heading elsewhere for the summer.

She walked up the path. This would be the first meal she'd had in the house, in her house, since they'd moved to the caravan park, so many years ago now. Her stomach tightened as she raised her hand to knock on the door.

Lily swung the door open, her belly pushing the fabric of her full blouse out, just below the tucks that ringed the jewelled neckline of her maternity top.

'Gigi.' She embraced her tightly. 'It is ever so good to see you.'

Once they hugged, Gigi didn't want to let go. She wanted to cry onto Lily's shoulder. She wanted to tell her everything that had happened these past few months. She wanted to spend the whole night talking to her best friend.

'Okay, give the baby some room.' Lily disentangled herself from Gigi's embrace.

'Sorry. How is it? Being pregnant?' She reached out and touched Lily's stomach.

'Tiring. But it will be worth it once he arrives.'

'He?'

'Well, we're only guessing, of course. But he feels like a he. And Richard would so love to have an heir to carry on the Prescott name.'

There was a sadness in Lily's eyes that betrayed her happy countenance. Perhaps Gigi wasn't the only one who could do with a good chinwag with an old friend. Gigi would make excuses after dinner, get rid of Richard somehow, and the two of them could catch up properly.

'Where are my manners? Come in.' Lily stepped back and invited Gigi in with a sweep of her arm. 'The gentlemen are waiting for us in the dining room.'

Gentlemen? Plural? As far as Gigi knew, neither Dr Prescott nor Senator Woodhouse had come for the summer.

She stepped into the dining room behind Lily and stopped dead. There, drinking a glass of whisky with Richard, was Todd.

'Good evening, Virginia.' Todd stood up.

'Three seemed like such an awkward number for dinner.' Lily waltzed in and stood next to her husband, who remained seated. 'So I invited Todd as well. It isn't long now till he starts his training as a police officer. I thought he might like a lovely social night out with friends.'

Gigi nearly choked when Lily said 'friends'. Todd was the exact opposite of her friend.

He sat back down next to Richard and the two of them ignored Lily and Gigi until dinner was served. By a maid.

Lily hadn't said anything in any of her letters about having a maid.

'Thank you, Mrs Duncan,' Lily said, as the roast lamb with all the trimmings was laid on the table.

The conversation wasn't the light banter Gigi had been hoping for. Lily sat rather quietly while Richard and Todd talked about Sydney and Perth and the differences in the cities – as if Todd would even know. He'd never been further than Sydney, as far as Gigi knew.

Every time Gigi tried to turn the talk to something more

interesting, like the upcoming surfing contest Ian was entering, the drop in the price of fish, the grand reopening of the pub after the Beaumonts' massive renovation, which they would all have to go to, the entire town was going to be there tomorrow night – Richard politely steered the conversation away from whatever she brought up. Even when she raised the topic of the escalating tension in Vietnam, she was met with a condescending smile and told that perhaps she should leave talk of such things to the men, who knew something about the situation. Todd averted his eyes. Gigi knew he wouldn't say anything that would contradict Richard. Lily remained quiet, the perfect picture of a supportive wife.

Gigi's heart ached as the night wore on – so very different to what she'd been hoping for.

Mrs Duncan served them silently, and each time Gigi thanked her, she simply nodded. Not once did Lily or Richard or Todd acknowledge her presence until Lily dismissed her after dessert was served. The men then retired to the living room for another glass of single malt, and Gigi helped Lily clear away the dishes.

She didn't even know where to begin. 'A maid, Lily? You never said you had a maid.'

At least she had the decency to look sheepish. 'I wasn't sure how you'd react.'

'A bit like this.' She pulled a face and Lily laughed, genuinely, for the first time that evening.

'Oh, I've missed you, old friend.' She put her arm around Gigi. 'So much. Mrs Duncan has actually been with us since I was ten. She came here that first holiday we had in Banksia Bay, actually.'

Gigi had never laid eyes on her before. The invisible help, she guessed.

'Mother would have had her here every summer, but Daddy said she needed a holiday too. Now with this one on the way –' she rubbed her tummy – 'she's going to be helping me. I think I'll probably need her, too.' She sighed.

But very quickly she straightened herself up and went back to making sure the kitchen was immaculate.

When they were done, they tiptoed out to the verandah, so as not to disturb the men, and they sat on the white wire chairs and looked up to the stars.

Lily asked about Gigi's plans now that she was finished school, and Gigi spoke around the question with nonsense about a part-time job to save up and hopefully go to university in another year.

'An admirable plan,' Lily said. 'You know what else is admirable? Marriage. A family. Todd's looking rather handsome tonight, isn't he?'

Gigi was glad the light from the bulb on the wall above them was not so bright that Lily could see her roll her eyes. If only Lily knew the truth about that wretch. Time to change the subject. She blurted out the first thing that came into her head.

'Are you happy, Lily?'

The pause said it all.

'Of course. And once baby Prescott arrives, everything will be perfect.'

Gigi didn't push any further. Even if Richard wasn't on the other side of the wall, she doubted Lily would have confessed to being unhappy. Not yet. They needed to reconnect first.

'Why don't you come fishing with me tomorrow morning? Just like old times.'

'Just like old times.' Lily sighed. 'I would love to, Gigi. Really. I just don't think I could climb those rocks in my current state.' She rubbed her stomach.

'We could fish off the jetty.'

The men came outside.

'I know.' Lily pushed her heavy frame out of the chair. 'Why

don't you go with Richard? You'd love that, wouldn't you, darling? An early morning-fish. He looks after me so well, he deserves
to have a morning where he doesn't have to wait on me.'

Gigi suspected Mrs Duncan did all the waiting on Lily, while
Richard was oblivious to her, if tonight was any indication.

'That would be fun. What time do I need to be ready?'

With the morning engagement settled, Gigi took her leave.

'I'll walk you home, Virginia,' Todd offered.

'That's not necessary. Thank you.'

Lily pushed both her and Todd towards the path. 'Nonsense.
Just let him be chivalrous, Gigi.'

As soon as they were out of sight of the holiday house, Gigi
turned to Todd. 'I think I can manage from here.'

'You do look lovely tonight, Gilbert. I'm sorry things have been
strained between us.'

'Strained?' She nearly shouted the word.

'You don't understand. There are expectations, pressures.' He
rocked back and forth.

'I think I understand more than you realise.' She almost felt
sorry for him standing in front of her, his face full of conflict. The
rumours about his father hadn't let up. Neither had the gossip
about Todd's drinking. It couldn't be easy trying to be who others
expected you to be when you didn't even know yourself. Especially
when you were weak. A boy trapped in a man's life.

But he'd been cruel and she couldn't forgive him for that.

He'd be gone soon, though, and maybe police training would
help him finally grow up.

'I'm glad you're not hanging around with that wog anymore,'
he said. 'Maybe we can be friends.'

No. Todd would never change. 'Goodnight,' she said and
turned on her heel.

Twenty-one

As the sun passed its highest point in the sky, Laura packed away all her notes and put them in the bedroom. She placed the tiny wooden mouse in the pocket of her coat and sat on the bed staring at the mess she'd created.

There was a knock on the door and she jumped up and ran to the front of the house, hoping Heath had returned. As she swung the front door open, standing before her was Virginia.

'May I come in?' The old lady looked frail.

'Please. Sit down.'

'It would appear we have a few things that perhaps we need to talk about.' Virginia lowered herself onto the sofa.

'I guess Heath's been to see you?'

'You guess correctly.'

'I never meant to hurt him. To hurt anyone. I was just trying to find out about my grandmother.'

Virginia sat perfectly still.

'Her name was Lillian Woodhouse-Prescott. I think perhaps

you might have known her.' She played with the pendant that hung around her neck.

Across the coffee table, Virginia slid over a familiar photo, but said nothing.

'You're Gigi, aren't you?' Laura asked.

'Yes. And that's Lily. I did know your grandmother. We were friends.'

Laura got up and paced the room. How much should she ask? How hard should she push?

'Were you close?'

'Very. We were like sisters.'

Laura handed her the same photo, 'Sisters of Summer', and Virginia's head snapped up.

'She kept it?' A tear fell down the deep lines of Virginia's left cheek.

The two photos lay on the coffee table, side by side.

Laura sat back down. Rule number eight, *start at the beginning*, *start simple*.

'What happened?'

A strange sound escaped Virginia's lips. A sad sound. 'We . . . grew apart.' She cast her eyes down.

It may well have been the truth, but Laura knew it wasn't the entire truth.

'That's it?'

Virginia lifted her gaze. 'Perhaps you can tell me. You haven't exactly been completely truthful and upfront with us, have you, dear?'

Touché. Was there even such a thing as complete truth? A tiny detail left out here, an insignificant fragment forgotten there. Maybe the truth wasn't just the first casualty of war. Perhaps it was the first casualty of life.

'I know something happened in the summer of sixty-three, sixty-four. I know it involved you. Possibly Yvonne. I know that was the summer my grandfather died. I know Lillian never came back here again after that.'

The colour drained from Virginia's face. 'Maybe that's all you need to know,' she whispered.

'I need to know the truth.' Laura leaned forward.

Virginia let out a huff. 'And what will you do with it, if you have it? Write your next award-winning article? I looked you up, Miss Prescott.'

Laura sat back, her mouth open, staring at Virginia. How long had she known Laura's true identity? In her mind she scrambled to find the right words to justify her deception. Yet again. But there were no words, no excuses left. She drew in a long breath and squared her shoulders.

'I promise you that's not why I'm here. I just want to know about my grandmother. She never spoke of the past. I just want to find out about her. And the people close to her back then.'

'And have you asked her?'

Laura closed her eyes. 'She passed away last month.'

Silence filled the space between them; another tear fell down Virginia's cheek.

'What if you don't like what you find?' she whispered. 'What if what you uncover isn't pleasant and paints people in a different light to what you believe to be true? What then?'

Laura hadn't thought about that. It hadn't even crossed her mind. She was so focused on uncovering the truth, she hadn't once considered what she'd do if that truth was ugly, or painful, or . . . worse.

She leaned back in the armchair opposite the sofa. 'I don't know. I think . . . I think maybe I'd still like to know.'

Virginia hauled herself to standing. She ambled around the room, touching the furniture, rearranging the photos on the sideboard.

'How do I know I can trust you?'

It was a fair question. And one Laura wasn't sure how to answer. 'I guess you can't know. Not for sure. I can promise you I'm not here to do anyone harm. But I understand my promise might not mean much.'

It meant nothing. She knew that. Not after she'd lied to everyone Virginia cared about. She also knew that whatever had happened all those years ago had power. Real power. And sharing it meant a level of trust Virginia probably couldn't give her.

But she knew it was the only way she could find out the truth. She had to make Virginia trust her. Somehow.

'Wait,' she said, and ran into the bedroom. There was only one way she could think of to convince Virginia that she was not here to hurt anyone.

She came back into the living room carrying her files, and placed them on the coffee table.

'This is everything I've learned, all the questions I've been asking. Take it. Take it all. I don't want a story. I just want to know more about Lillian and Richard.'

Virginia sat back down and looked at the files and then back to Laura. 'That's the thing, dear. It isn't just about Lily and Richard. Or me. There are other factors involved here. Other people.'

Laura crouched down beside her. 'Take them.' She placed the files in Virginia's lap and covered the old lady's hands with hers. 'Do whatever you want with them. And if you can find it in your heart to tell me anything more, I'll be forever grateful.'

She knew it was a gamble, but she had to take it.

She helped Virginia to her feet and walked her to the door.

'I don't know, Laura. I just don't know.'

The pain and conflict fighting within Virginia were clearly etched in the lines of her face. She stepped out onto the verandah, steadying herself with the railing that led down the steps.

'Virginia?' Laura called out to her, and the old woman turned around slowly. 'I know I have no right to ask, but do you think maybe you could let Heath know I'm sorry? Ask him to forgive me?'

'I'll be asking him for forgiveness myself,' Virginia said as she turned away, and Laura wondered if she'd heard her correctly.

The temperature dropped as the sun disappeared behind a cloud.

∽

Virginia knocked on Yvonne's door.

'Hey, Vir— what's wrong? You look terrible.' Yvonne let her in and they bustled into the kitchen.

Virginia handed over the files. She hadn't looked at them yet. She was too frightened. This was something they had to do together.

They spread the papers across the dining table and skimmed over each one.

By the time they'd got through them all, Virginia's hands were shaking and Yvonne's skin was pale.

'She's got all the pieces except one.' Yvonne stood up and opened the kitchen window. The light breeze was bitterly cold; the afternoon sky was turning grey. 'What is she planning on doing with all this?'

That was Virginia's worry. 'She says nothing, that she's just trying to find out about Lily's past. She said I can have the files, do whatever I want with them. She only asks that I tell her what I can about Lily.'

'Do you believe her?'

That was the question, wasn't it? Was she really just a grand-daughter trying to find out about her family, or was she a hard-hitting journalist looking for her next story?

In the end, the answer didn't really matter, Virginia supposed. Once the truth was out there, there was no hiding it away again, no matter if Laura wrote a story or kept it to herself. That was the thing about the truth. It had a life of its own once released.

'Are you going to fill in the blanks for her?' Yvonne asked.

'No. I can't. I can't do that to you.'

'To me? This isn't about me. It's about you.'

Was that what Yvonne really thought? That Virginia had kept their secret all these years for her own selfish reasons? She had, of course. But not only that. If the secret came out and an investiga-tion took place, Yvonne would be implicated too. She might not be punished. But her reputation would be ruined. Conspiracy, acces-sory, whatever it was called. Yvonne's life would be ruined too.

Small towns like Banksia Bay were quick to judge and slow to forgive.

And what would it do to Charlotte and Heath when they learned that their beloved grandmother wasn't who they thought she was?

'It's about both of us. All of us. She doesn't need to know. Maybe I can tell her about the early years when Lily visited. Nothing about that summer.'

'She'll ask more questions.'

Yes, she probably would. Virginia would have to make up something plausible about how it all ended. She could do that. Most of her life had been a lie, after all.

Yvonne left the room for a moment and came back with a manila folder inside a ziplock bag.

'You should probably have these.' She handed Virginia the folder. Inside were the missing pages of The Bugle.

'I thought you destroyed these years ago.' She looked at Yvonne, fear turning her cold.

'I know I was supposed to. But I couldn't. I guess I felt like I didn't deserve to be let off.'

'Let off? For what? You did nothing wrong.'

Yvonne wrung her hands. 'Maybe, maybe if I'd said something that night, if I'd stayed quiet that day . . . It's my fault, Virginia. I didn't deserve to erase what happened so easily.'

'Yvonne. Nothing that happened was your fault. Nothing.' Tears pricked Virginia's eyes and she embraced her old friend. All these years Yvonne had been carrying around a guilt she never should have borne.

Distant thunder rumbled through the air.

New Year's Eve 1963

As the sun began to rise, Gigi pulled herself out of her bunk and got dressed. At least it was fishing, she supposed, even if it was with Richard and not Lily. New Year's Eve was always slow around the caravan park and Mum never minded much if Gigi did her chores later in the day.

Outside the cabin, leaning up against the wall where she'd left them last night, were Gigi's rod and bucket. She picked them up and felt a weight to the bucket that surprised her.

She looked inside and saw a banksia seed pod carved into the shape of a little bird. Quickly she picked it up, held it to her chest for just a moment, and then hid it in her pocket.

It wasn't long now till they would be free to be together.

She wandered over to the beach, in no particular hurry. Richard would be there, or he wouldn't. Regardless, she would enjoy the morning fish, tasting the salt air, the cool breeze sailing over her skin.

With no sign of company yet, she threaded the bait onto her hook, breathing in deeply, exhaling slowly, and she cast her line. After ten minutes the genuine surfers began to arrive, ready to catch the first waves of the day. They wouldn't pay attention to her on the jetty. The tourists and pseudo-surfers wouldn't show up for a while yet. These first few hours of daylight, before the earth woke up properly, were her favourite of any summer day.

Eventually Richard arrived and apologised for his tardiness. Lily had had an uncomfortable night, which meant he hadn't had much sleep.

'But I see you've done just fine without me.' He pointed at her bucket, now filled with three good-sized leatherjackets.

'It's all in how you bait the hook.' She lifted her rod.

'Show me?'

Richard was most definitely a better fisher than his wife. With his first cast, he hooked a silver fish and reeled it in. He got so excited by his victory over nature that, as he was unhooking the fish's mouth, he lost his grip and juggled it for a moment before it fell back into the sea below.

Gigi doubled over, giggling.

'Picking on the beginner?' Richard moved closer to her and reached out his hand and touched her cheek. 'You have the most infectious laugh, Gigi. Lily doesn't laugh anymore.' He moved his hand so his fingers ran over her lips.

'Richard?' She stepped back.

He followed her and grabbed her shoulder. 'You are such a pretty thing. Why do you dress like a boy?' His hand moved to her neck. 'Your skin is so soft. It's been so long since she let me . . .'

Gigi slapped him. Across the face. Hard. 'What do you think you're doing?'

His face turned red. 'I'm sorry, Gigi. Please forgive me. I don't know what came over me. Please. Please don't tell her.'

'I think it's time you went home to your wife.' She emphasised the last word.

He bowed his head and mumbled some sort of goodbye.

Gigi packed up her gear and headed home as quickly as she could.

Back at the caravan park, Gigi completed her chores and then asked for more. She needed to keep busy. She didn't know what had possessed Richard that morning, and she didn't like one bit how it made her feel. Should she tell Lily? No. Richard would deny anything had happened. And technically it hadn't. Not really.

No. Best just to put it out of her mind. She would see Lily and Richard tonight at the reopening of the pub. There would be a crowd of people there, and she could act as if everything was normal.

Because it was.

Besides, there were bigger things to worry about tonight. Like whether Costas would be there. He was barely seen around town after the incident with Todd, certainly not at social events. But it was a big night for the Beaumonts, and the two families were close. She hadn't wanted to ask Yvonne, afraid the answer would be no.

An hour before they were all due at the pub, Yvonne knocked on the cabin door. In her arms was the basket of linen Mum had sent over to have mended. Mrs Beaumont was the best seamstress in town.

'Mum said no charge, Mrs Gilbert. Thanks for helping her clean all the dust out of the pub yesterday.' Yvonne handed over the basket to Gigi's mum.

It was good to see Yvonne happy again. It had taken so long after Costas' stint in gaol for her to come back out of her shell. Gigi wondered if Costas had told Yvonne about their plans. She doubted it. Although Costas and Yvonne were as close as siblings, the risk was too great.

Before she left, Yvonne turned to Gigi and winked. 'Here's the ribbon you asked to borrow.' She handed over a soft red bow. 'It will look great with your dress.'

Gigi hadn't asked for a ribbon. Message received loud and clear. Thank you, Yvonne. Costas would be there. Her heart started to race.

'Are you going to wear a dress, love?' Mum raised an eyebrow.

Gigi squirmed a little inside, hoping her mum wouldn't see through her ruse. 'It is a special occasion.'

She knew it was silly, getting all dolled up. Costas didn't care about that sort of thing. But the moments they managed to steal together here and there were always rushed, usually in the dark. He was going to be looking at her tonight. Properly looking at her. And she wanted to look nice for him.

She slipped on her red dress, brushed her hair and tied Yvonne's ribbon in her ponytail. Around her neck she hung the guardian angel pendant.

Together Gigi and her parents walked to the pub, and as they approached they could hear the joy of light conversation and music floating on the air. All of the locals were there. And some of the tourists. Even Mrs Duncan.

Mr Beaumont was sweating in the kitchen, trying to keep the patrons happily fed. Mrs Beaumont was out the front, playing hostess, and doing a fine job of it, as far as Gigi could tell. Yvonne sat in the corner on her own, watching, listening – still not great with crowds.

Gigi spotted Lily and Richard through the masses; they were sitting in the booth at the far end of the pub. Lily beckoned her over. If she didn't go and say hello, Lily would be upset. And worse, suspect something was wrong.

'You look simply gorgeous,' Lily said as she struggled to get up and hug Gigi. She pulled away and held her at arm's length so she could inspect her properly. 'Stunning. I always knew you had it in you. Todd will be impressed.'

'Beautiful,' Richard said. 'Really. Can I get you a drink?' He held up his whisky glass.

'Just a lemonade. Thank you.'

Gigi sat down next to Lily, who was rabbiting on about something that sounded so terribly urgent and dull at the same time. But Gigi wasn't really listening.

Over by the bar, just off to the left, away from the bulk of the crowd, stood Mr Tinellis. And Costas.

And he was looking straight at her.

Heat rose all over her skin. Richard couldn't come back with her drink fast enough.

Lily droned on. Gigi blocked out the noise.

When Richard returned, Gigi broke eye contact with Costas, afraid Richard would notice. Afraid she would give herself away.

She stole glances over to Costas when she could, every inch of her aching to go to him.

Todd made his way over to them and whistled when he saw Gigi in her dress. 'Wow-ee, do you scrub up all right.' His words carried the evidence of a few beers already drunk.

'Sit, Todd. Join us,' Lily's voice lilted sweetly.

Gigi remained polite. With Todd and Costas under the same

roof, she knew she had to be careful. Not cause a scene. She would smile, listen, and wait for the opportunity to remove herself from Todd's presence.

People mingled. And ate. And drank.

Gigi waited.

Todd went to the bar to get the next round of drinks and Gigi saw her chance. She whispered to Lily that she was going to the bathroom and slipped out of the booth.

On her way out of the pub, she made sure she walked past Costas and flashed him the briefest of glances, hoping he would know what it meant.

Once outside, she hurried to the beach, throwing off her shoes as she passed the fishing shack. The south end of the beach was protected from the strong wind that had stirred late in the day, and she sat in the sand dunes and waited.

It wasn't long before she heard a scuttling along the sand. Her heart beat faster. Her mouth went dry.

'I hoped you'd follow me out here,' she said to the figure walking towards her.

'Aren't I a lucky fellow, then?' Richard replied, the grating timbre of his voice turning her blood cold.

He stood before Gigi, his eyes glassy, his head tilted.

'I knew you wanted me as much as I want you.' He stumbled forwards.

'I wasn't . . . it wasn't you . . . Richard, go back inside.' She drew her shoulders up, stood tall.

With one hand he reached out and tugged at the ribbon in her hair. With the other he grabbed her waist. 'You look so pretty tonight.'

'Thank you.' She squirmed but he held her tight. 'Why don't you go back to the pub and tell your wife how pretty she is?'

He turned around, his back to her. She took a step back.

'She is pretty. And perfect. Boringly perfect. You? You've got spunk.' He spun around and grabbed her arm. 'She hasn't let me anywhere near her in months.' His hand moved up her arm and she tried to wriggle free, but his grip was tight.

'Richard, you're hurting me. Please stop.'

'I'm not going to hurt you, Gigi. I'd never hurt you.' His words were hot on her neck. 'I'm just lonely. You don't want me to be lonely, do you?' He kissed her cheek.

She shoved him backwards. 'Richard, go back inside and remember your manners.'

He lurched towards her. 'Manners?' He grabbed her behind the head. 'Who are you to talk about manners? Giving yourself to a wog?'

Gigi let out a little yelp.

'Todd told me all about your dalliance with that disgusting foreigner. You'll give it up for him, but not me? I don't think so, Gigi.'

He pushed her to the sand. She tried to scramble away, but he grabbed her leg.

'Richard, you're drunk. Stop. Please.'

He slapped her across the face.

'I'm not that drunk. A used whore like you shouldn't be so fussy.' He forced her legs open.

'Stop!' she screamed, her shrill cry echoing through the night, and he covered her mouth with one hand.

Beneath him Gigi writhed and bucked but he was too heavy. She kicked her legs to no avail. Panic and fear coursed through her.

'Don't fight, Gigi.' Hate dripped from his voice as he said her name. 'It will hurt less if you don't fight.'

Like hell she wouldn't fight.

She balled her fists and started punching him in the back. Still covering her mouth, he used his other hand to pin her arms above her head.

She felt a rock beneath her hand. Thrusting her hips up, she knocked him off balance. He adjusted his grip, just enough for her to get one hand free. The hand closest to the rock.

As she lifted it up, she heard a shout coming from down the beach. Richard groaned as he pushed her legs further apart, his knee digging into her groin. Pain shot through her.

With all the force she could muster, she thrust the rock down. *Crack.*

Richard's hand fell from her face.

She screamed. As loud as she could. Again and again.

He went limp on top of her.

Warm liquid pooled beside her.

Someone fell down next to her. 'Virginia. What have you done?'

Costas rolled Richard's body off her.

'Are you all right?'

She stared at him.

She looked at Richard's lifeless body next to her.

Her hands began to tremble. She dropped the rock and shrieked.

'Shh,' Costas whispered. 'They'll hear you.'

Gigi looked at Richard, darkness oozing out of him. 'No!' she screeched.

A commotion came over the sand dune. Todd's voice called out.

Costas picked up the rock and shoved Gigi aside.

'No!' she called out, her voice barely a whisper.

Todd rounded the dune first.

'No!' she yelled, loudly, hoarsely.

'What have you done, you no-good wog?' Todd threw Costas aside. 'You've killed him.'

Mr Beaumont ran to them. Ian followed. He fell to Gigi's side and wrapped his arms around her. Sergeant Broadbent strode forwards.

Lily scrambled towards them, helped by Mrs Duncan. A guttural screech escaped her throat as she collapsed into her maid's arms.

'I saw him.' Todd turned to his father. 'He hit Prescott with that rock. He killed him.'

No. Gigi protested, but the word was silent.

Todd punched Costas in the face and he fell backwards, but didn't fight back.

The scene played out before Gigi as if she were at the cinema. People rushing here and there, tending to Richard, restraining Costas, asking her questions she couldn't quite understand. She was there, but not part of it, simply watching it.

Sergeant Broadbent hauled Costas away, Todd spitting at him. Others joined in too, hurling their saliva at Costas, who simply bowed his head. Mrs Duncan cradled Lily in her arms. 'Don't cry, baby girl,' she whispered over and over. Mrs Beaumont helped them to their feet and pulled Lily away from the scene. Ian wiped Gigi's hands with his handkerchief. Why was he doing that? Why were her hands red? She looked up into his eyes.

'Shh,' he whispered and picked her up and carried her up the sand.

From behind another sand dune, a small figure ran through the gathered crowd and threw herself at Costas. He bent his head and whispered something in her ear. Broadbent jostled them apart and Yvonne fell to the sand, staring at Gigi.

Ian kept walking up the beach, carrying Gigi away.

Then everything went black.

Twenty-two

*L*aura went for a run, vacuumed the house, put some washing on, cleaned the bathroom. She changed the sheets on the bed, mopped the kitchen floor. Never in her life had she done so much housework. Never in her life had she been such a confused mess of guilt and sadness and despair.

She'd sent Heath a message. He hadn't replied.

All day she'd waited to hear from him, to hear from Virginia. All day there was silence. The clock ticked over four and the sky turned dark with clouds.

A knock on the door, and she rushed to open it.

Charlotte stood there with a stern look on her face and Laura let her in.

Refusing to sit, Charlotte stood in the middle of the living room, hands on hips.

'Do you remember that first day when you helped Gran out in the shack?' She turned and looked at Laura.

'Yes.'

'Do you remember what you promised me?'

'That I wasn't here to harm your family.'

'Care to explain, then?'

Where did she begin? Rule number eight – *at the beginning*. So she did. She told Charlotte about the photo that had led her here, the research she'd been doing. Virginia's visit that morning. As the whole story spilled out, relief washed over her. Charlotte listened to every word. Now everyone who mattered knew the truth. Now she could stop the lies.

'I never meant to hurt anyone.' Laura raised her hand to her chest. Charlotte had to believe her. 'Least of all Heath. I just wanted to know about Lillian's past.'

'I don't know anything about your grandmother.' Charlotte looked her in the eye. 'And I have no idea if Gran does. I do know –' she furrowed her brow – 'that sometimes people have a good reason to keep secrets.' She looked like she was about to say something else, but clearly changed her mind.

'I'm sorry, Charlotte. I really am.'

Charlotte looked tired. 'I only have one question for you, Laura. Are your feelings for Heath genuine?'

Laura reached out and grabbed Charlotte's hands. 'Yes.'

Lightning streaked across the sky. Charlotte nodded and headed home without another word.

Slumped over the dining table, Laura pushed her dinner around her plate, not eating any of it. Her phone rang.

Finally. Maybe Charlotte had spoken to Heath for her.

But it wasn't Heath.

'Hi, Maher.'

In all of the day's drama, Laura had forgotten to call him back.

'Laura, I've been trying to get a hold of you.'

'Sorry. It's been a bit of a day here.'

'I was just wondering if you're nearly done. A story has come up and you're the only one I want to put on it.'

Laura paused. 'Well, as it turns out, things might just be wrapping up here.'

'Great. Get home as soon as you can.' Maher hung up.

Was there any point hanging around now? Laura had upset everyone, and it was unlikely Virginia would open up to her. She'd pushed Heath away.

No. There wasn't much point at all. She pulled on her running gear.

As Laura opened the front door, a blast of icy wind hit her and she stepped out into the night. She opened the gate to the holiday house and ran towards the beach, thoughts, questions, doubts colliding in her mind.

Thunder boomed. Lightning flashed.

Heavy raindrops began to fall as Laura reached the south end of the beach. She ducked under the jetty and sucked in great gulps of air. The rain was getting heavier, the wind stronger.

With her back against one of the jetty pylons, she sank onto the damp sand. The cold seeped into Laura's skin and she felt it in her bones. But she didn't get up. She drew her knees up to her chest and hugged them tightly. What harm could a little rain do to her now?

A jagged flash of lightning streaked across the sky. She counted. One, two. A habit left over from her childhood. *Boom.* Less than a kilometre away.

She eyed the shack. Should she make a run for it?

Thunder bellowed, shaking the air.

'What are you doing out in this?' Heath darted in next to her.

She looked at him, unable to answer. *Where had he come from? Why was he here?*

Hope filled her, before it gave way to shame. She'd been so deceptive. Could he ever forgive her?

Surging waves crashed into the wooden pylons of the jetty.

'This is going to be a big one, and she's rolling in fast. Come on. We need to take shelter.' He reached out his hand and she took it. Together they ran through the storm to the shack.

'This will have to do.' He opened the side door to the shack and pulled Laura in with a jolt, yanking her arm so hard it hurt.

'What are you doing?' Laura stood with her hands on her hips.

'I'm sorry.' He briefly touched her shoulder before pulling back. 'It isn't safe out there.' Heath looked around for a blanket and threw it over Laura's shoulders. She realised then that she was shivering.

Lightning illuminated the sky, followed instantly by a loud crash of thunder. And another. And another. A barrage of light and sound, unrelenting, unending.

The shack vibrated with each boom.

Through the tiny square window in the side door, Laura watched the show.

Flash! Crash!

A tree just metres away lit up and burst into flame.

She jumped back and looked at Heath, terror coursing through her.

'It's okay. The rain will take care of the fire. But we might want to brace things. She's about to get worse.'

Worse?

'Grab some cushions,' he barked.

Laura stared at him. All day, all she'd wanted to do was talk to him, explain things. And now here he was, but the urgency in his voice, the sharpness of his movements, kept her silent.

Another crack of lightning and she jumped.

Heath picked up a cushion off the sofa and waved it at her. From beneath the sink, he grabbed some gaffer tape. He held the cushion up to one of the porthole windows. 'Like this,' he shouted, the wind howling so loudly outside Laura could barely hear him. He taped the cushion across the glass.

This was a Heath she'd never seen before. Beneath his gruff exterior she sensed something else. Fear? No. Not Heath. Then she remembered his story about how he'd got his scar. In a monster storm. Her hands began to shake.

'Now!' he yelled.

Laura grabbed another cushion and did as she was told. Once all the porthole windows were covered she stood in the middle of the shack, salty tears drying on her skin.

'They reckon there're going to be gale-force winds.'

She stared at him. 'Virginia?' She pointed to the loft above the shack.

'She's at Charlotte's. I've just come from there. But I'll go up and batten down her windows. Wait here.'

The wind outside screeched and wailed, relentless in its attack. Frightened, Laura started to head up the stairs.

'Stay in here.' Heath came bowling back down the stairs. 'We'll be safer.' He handed her a towel. 'You must be freezing. Dry yourself and get out of those wet clothes. You're soaked through.' He left a T-shirt and another blanket on the counter and turned his back.

Once she was dry and changed, Laura wrapped the fresh blanket around herself.

A loud crash came from nearby as something fell behind the shack. Laura gasped. The walls of the shack began to shake in the wind. The knick-knacks on the shelves rattled and toppled over. One of the cushions fell from a window.

Laura pulled the blanket tighter around herself, for what little good it did to quell her rising fear.

Another loud crack.

'Come here,' Heath said. In the middle of the room he'd placed the sofa upside down against the sturdy counter, creating what would, under other circumstances, have been a cute fort for a kid. He beckoned her to join him under the scant protection.

Sitting curled up tight on the floor, every crack of thunder made Laura jump. Every surge of air trying to force its way into the shack made her gasp.

Heath put his arm around her shoulders. 'We'll be okay. It'll pass over soon. We just have to wait it out. That's all you can do in a storm like this. They don't usually last long.'

Within Heath's embrace Laura remained perfectly still, afraid to move, to speak, to breathe too deeply. This stolen moment of closeness might be the last she'd ever have with him. If she moved, he might pull away. Fear and want fought within her.

She had no idea how much time passed before the wind eventually began to subside. It felt like hours one moment, the blink of an eye the next.

The wind no longer roared, but whistled through the cracks in the walls. The lightning had slowed. So had the thunder. But not the rain. The rain was heavier than before.

'I'm just going to check upstairs.' Heath climbed out from beneath their fort.

'No. Please. Don't leave me.' Laura followed him.

He held her hand and squeezed it gently. 'I'll be right back. We don't want that rain leaking in if there's any damage to the roof.'

Laura tiptoed to the cushion-less window. She couldn't see much in the dark. A distant flash of lightning lit up the beach for a moment. Tree branches and leaves and seaweed littered the sand.

And she counted. One, two . . . six, rumble. The storm was moving away.

'No damage upstairs.' Heath returned. 'Looks like there are a few trees down outside, though. One only just missed the shack. The rain hasn't eased up yet. We might be stuck here for a little while.'

Laura looked back out the window into the blackness. She couldn't bear to look at Heath, knowing she'd hurt him, lost him.

'Thank you,' she whispered.

She could feel him move behind her. So close she could hear his breath, feel the heat radiating from his body.

His arm reached around her waist, his lips moved beside her ear. 'I'm sorry I didn't give you a chance to explain.'

She turned around in his arms. 'I'm the one who should be sorry.'

He leaned down, his face stopping an inch from hers.

'I have no idea what this is, Laura. Or what else is going on. But I know life is short, and I know I want you.'

She lifted her head, ever so slightly, and Heath didn't hesitate, kissing her forehead, her nose, her cheek. Her lips.

The blanket fell from her shoulders and Heath lifted her, carrying her back to their fort.

෴

Virginia sat with Aiden in his room, listening to him read from his schoolbook. Trying to block out the storm.

She'd put her two cents' worth in earlier with Heath, and the fact she and Charlotte were on the same page had been enough of a shock to convince him to give Laura a chance to explain herself. He'd gone off to see her just as the storm rolled in. She hoped they were both safe.

Aiden's voice sang as he read out loud. Charlotte came in and they huddled together as the lightning and thunder burst around them. Virginia closed her eyes. She could feel her strength waning with every crack in the sky. So many burdens carried for so long. All she wanted to do now was rest and stop the old memories from haunting her.

January 1964

Gigi woke in Ocean Heights Hospital. She ached all over, particularly her legs. Beside the hospital bed her parents sat quietly. When they noticed she was awake, they rushed to her side.

'Did he hurt you?' Mum asked. 'Did Costas hurt you?'

'What? No.' Her head was foggy.

'It's all right now, love. He's in custody.' Dad patted her on the shoulder.

She tried to sit up. 'No. You don't understand.' Tears streamed down her face. 'Richard . . .'

'He's gone. So tragic. He was just trying to save you from that monster.' Mum wiped away a tear.

'No!' Gigi screamed.

'I'll go get the doctor.'

'No. You don't understand.' She tried to throw her legs over the bed, but they wouldn't move. And Dad held her down. 'Stop. Let me go.'

A doctor hurried into the room, a needle poised in his hand. 'Shock can be a terrible thing.' His voice was calm, stern. 'This will help.'

He injected something into her arm and she drifted off into a haze.

When she woke again it was dark. She pulled herself up and let her eyes adjust to the lack of light. In the corner sat Yvonne, her legs pulled up to her chest.

She put her finger to her lips and beckoned Gigi to follow.

Together they tiptoed through the hospital corridors. Down the hall and around two bends, a police officer sat outside a room, sleeping with his head on his chest.

Yvonne indicated the need for silence again and pointed to the room.

Gigi slipped past the officer and Yvonne stayed outside.

Costas was lying in the bed, a mess of dried blood and bruises.

She went to his side and touched his hand gently.

He stirred.

With bleary eyes he looked at her, his swollen lips turning up.

'Virginia? You're okay?'

Her voice caught in her throat at the sight of him.

'Good.'

'I don't understand what's happening. Why are you under guard?' she whispered.

'It's the only way.' His words were soft, slow. 'The only way to protect you.'

He was making no sense.

'I confessed. To killing Richard.'

Gigi covered her mouth so she wouldn't scream.

'It will ruin your life, Virginia. Do you have any idea how powerful Woodhouse is? His son-in-law is dead. Someone is going to have to pay. I won't let it be you.'

'No. You can't do this for me. It isn't right. I . . . I think . . . I don't really remember. It's all a bit foggy.' Snippets of the night came back to her in flashes – Richard forcing himself on her, his head hitting a rock. Had she pushed him? Had he fallen? A rock in her hand. *Oh no*. Costas picking up the rock. She tried to fight through the fog.

Costas stroked her hand. 'They won't believe you. Todd has already corroborated my story. He said he saw the whole thing. That you were trying to kiss Richard and he pushed you away. That I saw it and flew into a jealous rage. That I tried to take you for myself and Richard tried to stop me, and that's when I hit him with the rock.'

Gigi's stomach tightened. 'But they have to believe the truth.'

'Whose truth, Virginia? The honourable son of the local copper, or the girl who's been throwing herself at the greasy wog for the last few months? That's what they'll say. Can you even remember the details?'

'Not all of them. But enough.'

'My confession is all they need.'

Gigi couldn't believe what she was hearing. Surely if she told the truth, they would see it. They had to. This couldn't happen.

'No. I'll tell them now.' She turned, but Costas grabbed her arm and pulled her back.

'Virginia. You'll go to gaol. They'll lock you away forever.'

She yanked her arm free. 'But you can't ruin your life for me.'

'If you were sent to gaol, I'd have no life. Virginia, listen to me carefully. This is only a taste of what happens in gaol.' He pointed to his injuries. 'I will not let this happen to you. I couldn't protect you from Richard. I'm so sorry. Let me protect you now.'

'No. Costas, you can't.' Tears streamed down her face.

'I already have.' He squeezed her hand. 'Go. Before they find you here.'

'No!' she screamed. A nurse came running in, followed by the police officer, and they dragged Gigi from the room. Someone injected her with another sedative and Gigi was taken by the haze once more.

Twenty-three

In the early hours of the morning, the rain finally began to ease. Laura lay in Heath's arms, naked beneath the blanket that covered them. She reached up and touched his cheek, running her finger along his scar. He stirred but didn't wake.

She'd drifted in and out of sleep for the last hour or so, soothed by the rhythmic sound of soft snoring beside her.

She unwrapped herself from Heath's arms and stood by the window facing the ocean. The first rays of light were reaching out from the horizon, casting a soft light over the debris that covered the sand.

'We're in for a mighty big clean-up today.' Heath's sleepy voice floated across the shack.

She turned around to see him stretching as he rose, his bare muscles tightening and relaxing. He pulled on his jeans and walked towards her.

'Good morning.' He kissed her forehead and hugged her. 'I'll fix us a caffeine hit and then we should probably go and check everyone's all right. The phones are out.' He waved his mobile in the air.

Together they sat on the sofa drinking their coffee.

'Laura? Can I ask you what you were doing under the jetty last night?'

'I . . . went for a run, to clear my head. You were angry with me . . . Rightly so,' she added when he started to protest. 'And Virginia had come by, and then Charlotte. And the whole situation is a complete mess, one that I've created myself. I thought you were never going to speak to me again. Then my boss rang and he wants me home. I just needed to think. I didn't even realise it was raining at first.'

'Rough day, huh?' He smiled.

'Yep.' She leaned her head on his shoulder. 'It got better, though.'

'That's life. Always twisting and turning,' Heath whispered into her ear.

'Do you think Virginia and Charlotte will forgive me? For lying about why I was here?'

'I think they already have. They both told me to come see you.'

Laura tilted her head.

'Gran's pretty shaken up, though, about whatever the big secret is. Do you have any idea?'

She pushed herself up and swivelled around on the sofa to face him. 'I have plenty of ideas. From a secret affair to an alien invasion.'

Heath's lips turned ever so slightly upwards.

'But nothing concrete. I told Virginia I'd leave it in her hands if she wants to tell me, or not.'

'That can't have been easy.'

Laura shook her head. 'It wasn't. I've never let a story go before. I'm desperate to know about my nan, and Virginia has the answers.

But I think I've caused enough pain already. And something Charlotte said makes sense.'

'Curse her, she is often the voice of reason.' He chuckled.

'She said that sometimes people have good reasons to keep secrets.'

Heath coughed and shifted his body weight.

'I've been thinking about that most of the night.' Laura stood up. 'And I think she's right. I mean, I don't think it's good that we do. Look what happened here. But I think she's spot-on that people often believe they're doing the right thing by keeping secrets. Does that make sense?'

Heath joined her in the middle of the shack. 'It does. A lot, actually.' He looked at the floor. 'Laura, I have to tell you . . .'

His phone trilled loudly.

'Back on, I guess.' He answered. 'Yes. I'm fine. You guys? Yes, she's fine too. No. Wait for us. We'll be there in a minute.'

He put his phone in his pocket. 'How quickly can you get dressed? That was Charlotte. She needs some help.'

The destruction the storm had wreaked was devastating and indiscriminate. Heath and Laura picked their way over the fallen trees and branches strewn across the main road as they headed to Charlotte's house. The roof of the bakery lay in the middle of the street and the windows of the post office had shattered, thousands of tiny pieces of glass that looked like hail littering the footpath. But the pub appeared unscathed, as did the grocer's, other than the flapping awning which had come loose in one corner.

As they stepped their way through the debris, other people started to emerge to inspect the damage. The houses off the main road had fared much the same. Some had pieces of roof missing, some cars had windscreens smashed in. Others were seemingly untouched, the pools of water in the front yards the only indication that there had even been a storm.

They waved to Trish and Ian, who stood in their dressing gowns looking up at the holes in their pergola. The old surfer waved back, no words exchanged. Laura hoped Ian's studio had survived.

When they arrived at Charlotte's they were confronted by the sight of a fallen tree right through the centre of Charlotte's car.

Heath broke into a run. 'Charlotte?'

Charlotte came running out of the house, followed closely by Aiden.

Heath threw his arms around both of them. 'Are you okay? Are you both okay?'

'Yes. We're fine.' Charlotte kissed her brother.

'And Gran?'

'I'm fine too.' Virginia emerged. 'Luckily it missed the house.'

Laura watched on, relief flooding through her. Charlotte untangled herself from Heath's embrace and hugged her. 'And you're all right?'

Laura held her tightly. 'Heath helped me shelter.'

'Good.' Charlotte squeezed her hand.

Aiden was telling Heath all about how brave he had been, helping Mummy tape up the windows and reading to Gran so she wouldn't be so scared.

'You did a great job, buddy.' Heath gave him a high five, and Aiden grabbed onto his hand.

They started to head inside when Virginia stopped. 'Heath, would you mind walking with me to Yvonne's? She's not answering her phone and I just want to make sure she's okay.'

'Of course.' Heath began to move, but Aiden refused to let go. 'It's not far, why don't we all go?' Heath suggested, and Aiden nodded emphatically.

Yvonne's house was only a block away and they walked in silence, nodding at neighbours as they passed. The thick black clouds that had brought so much destruction were beginning to break up, and the morning's light burst through them with a happiness that seemed out of place. An eerie quiet hung over the streets.

From the corner they could see the Bodhi Bus parked in Yvonne's driveway, a couple of tarps and blankets crumpled across the roof and sliding down the side.

Virginia picked up her pace and the others followed. As they came round to the other side of the driveway they saw Yvonne.

Lying beside the Bodhi Bus.

Hands clutching a blanket.

Chest not moving, blood staining her forehead.

'No!' Virginia screamed, running to her friend's side. She wiped the blood from Yvonne's face with her bare hands.

Charlotte knelt beside her. 'There's a pulse, but it's weak.' She looked up to Heath. 'We need to get her help, but the paramedics are going to have a tough time getting through. There's so much debris on the roads.'

Laura struggled to breathe. Yvonne didn't look good. At all. And they were completely isolated. What should she do? Yvonne was in trouble. The whole town was in trouble.

'I'm on it.' Heath grabbed Laura's hand and dragged her a few houses away to Ryan's place, where a motorbike sat under a carport, unscathed by the storm.

'Mate, we need to borrow that,' Heath barked as Ryan came outside. On Heath's instructions Ryan collected ropes and a broom and a wheelbarrow, and Laura ran off to get Ian and Trish, her heart racing.

With only one road in and out of Banksia Bay, all they had to do was clear a path wide enough along the main street for an ambulance to get through. Other people came to help once they saw what was happening.

Laura could hear sirens as she swept small tree branches to the side of the road and Ryan and Heath towed the larger debris – huge branches, torn-up roof panels – out of the way with the bike.

Eventually the ambulance arrived and the paramedics started work on Yvonne.

Virginia, all colour drained from her face, tried to climb into the back of the ambulance when they moved Yvonne from the driveway.

'Sorry, Virginia.' The older of the two paramedics put his hand on her shoulder. 'We're going to have to transport more than one patient.'

Around the corner two men carried another who was seriously hurt, his khaki chinos covered in blood.

'Hop on, Gran,' Heath said, patting the motorbike seat behind him, and Virginia didn't hesitate.

They followed the ambulance out of town, and Laura wrapped her arm around Charlotte's shoulders as they watched them disappear.

It didn't take long for people to gather at the pub. Rosters were being drawn up with the most urgent jobs listed first, and people were assigning themselves to groups to get started.

Gary, a Bay fireman attached to the Ocean Heights brigade and the local State Emergency Services coordinator, was in charge. He was efficient and calm, and everyone did as he said. There was a group tasked with clearing the side streets, so that services could get in and out. A couple of farmers from the district had offered up their trucks to help haul out the larger debris. Tradies, both local and from Ocean Heights, were dropping in to the pub and being assigned tasks – fixing leaks in residential homes, repairing powerlines.

Charlotte was put in charge of attending to minor wounds – mostly scrapes and cuts, a few bruises, one broken leg; those with more serious injuries were slowly being ferried to the hospital in Ocean Heights. Ian was asked to coordinate crews to start tarping damaged roofs.

Heath strode into the pub.

'How is she?' Charlotte asked, and everyone turned to face him.

'Touch and go. Gran's with her. I thought I'd be more useful here.'

He and Ryan were assigned to one of the repair crews.

Laura felt useless standing there watching everyone swing into action. What good were her investigative skills in a situation like this? She looked around, wondering where she could be the most help.

'Have you ever used tools?' Heath came up to her as he wrapped a tool belt around his waist.

'No.' How hard could it be?

'Our team is going to start at the bakery.' He handed her a hammer. 'I'll show you how.'

As evening rolled around and darkness settled in, the crew at the bakery stopped work. They could only do a patch-up job. Until supplies could be brought in and the insurance companies had made their assessments, all they could do was make things safe, hopefully watertight, and return some basic amenities.

Heath put his arm around Laura's shoulders as they headed back to the pub. It was one of the buildings that had suffered little damage and everyone was heading back there for a hot feed.

'You did good today. You worked as hard as the seasoned tradies.'

What else could she do? This was home to these people. Not only were they physically distressed, but their hearts were hurting. If they could tough it out and work, then so could she.

'It doesn't seem enough.'

'It'll be weeks before the clean-up is complete. Some things will take months. But the sooner we can get the businesses up and running, the better. With winter around the corner, it's going to be tough for some of them to survive till the tourists come in summer.'

The hint of an idea started to form in Laura's mind. Perhaps she *could* use her skills to help.

At the pub, where the back-up generator was whirring, the sweet smell of onions and snags cooking on the barbecue was a welcome tonic. Hot chips and vinegar were also being served, and beer was on the house. Laura stuck to water, but tucked into a sausage sandwich like she hadn't eaten for a week.

Ian sat in the corner ticking off a long list of tasks that had been accomplished and making an even longer one for tomorrow.

Laura took him a schooner.

'Thanks, love. I heard you did us proud today.' He raised his glass to her in salute and then took a long gulp, downing half the amber liquid. 'Ahh.'

'I have an idea, Ian, which you might be able to help me with.' She sat down and outlined the very sketchy plan she'd come up with. It would need tweaking, but it had merit and they agreed to meet in the morning just before dawn.

Carrying a sleeping Aiden in his arms, Heath walked Charlotte home and then went with Laura to check out the damage to the holiday house. There was one smashed window, a little water damage, some plants flattened by the storm. Heath nailed a tarp across the broken window and helped Laura mop up the water covering the floor.

They sunk into the sofa with a mug of hot chocolate each, extra marshmallows, but neither one of them finished their drink before they fell asleep propped up against each other.

In the morning, Laura's vibrating phone alarm woke her just before sunrise. She slipped off the sofa, pulled the crocheted blanket over Heath, left him a note on the sideboard and went out. She picked her way to the jetty through the trees and seaweed that covered the beach and waited for Ian.

When he arrived, he had five young men and women with him. Laura had seen them before, surfing. They had rakes and gloves with them.

'This lot are going to make a start on that.' Ian waved his hand at the debris covering the sand. 'And Chad here will bring his bobcat down later to help out. Now, love. Shall we get started?' He pulled his camera out of his backpack.

Laura had no idea if this would work, but she could try. For an hour she and Ian walked around town, him taking photos, her taking notes. She still hadn't thought the whole thing through yet, but the more she considered it, the more she hoped it would work.

As the people of Banksia Bay started to stir, Laura and Ian headed to the shack. It was open, and Heath and Charlotte were having a coffee on the deck.

'Morning.' Heath waved. 'You planning on running off with my girl, you old salty?' He slapped Ian on the back and embraced Laura. She held back a giggle at the 'old salty' reference.

'I'm pretty sure this one's only got eyes for you, mate. I'm going to go see if these guys need a hand.' He pointed down the beach to the clean-up team working on the sand. 'See you at midday?' He looked at Laura.

'See you then.'

'So, what's this plan you've cooked up together?' Heath asked.

'Well, something you said yesterday kind of hit me. About the businesses rebuilding and sustaining themselves till summer. I was thinking maybe, if the town agrees, of doing a story. Encourage people to visit in winter. It might help?'

The look of warmth Heath gave her was all she needed to know that it wasn't a ridiculous idea.

At midday Laura met Ian and they took more photos of the volunteers working tirelessly to clean up and rebuild. In every photo, the people had smiles on their faces. Sometimes exhausted smiles, but grins nevertheless. As Ian snapped away, Laura wrote down her observations – details of the work being done, the names of the people doing the work, the feelings swirling inside her as she documented what was happening: despair and hope, fear and pride, sadness and awe.

She'd never done a story like this before. Never written a piece that fell under the 'human interest' umbrella. And she'd never had a story so completely wrapped around her heart.

She liked how it felt.

She'd have to head home soon, back to her real job, but she'd do this story in two parts. The disaster and the immediate aftermath now, and then she'd return in a few weeks and capture how Banksia Bay was rebuilding itself. She still had to pitch the story to Maher and it would mean more time off but, surprisingly, she didn't mind that thought so much.

Twenty-four

Virginia sat beside Yvonne's bed, gently holding her cold hand. The doctors had done all they could – something about a trauma to the head, a coma, waiting. The endless waiting. Over twenty-four hours now and still no change.

'This isn't fair,' she sobbed. 'You don't deserve this. You didn't deserve any of this. I'm so sorry.' She sucked in great gulps of air. 'I know I've asked so much of you already. Too much. But please don't leave me now.'

She raised her head and looked up at the ceiling. It had been sixty years since she'd spoken to God. He probably wasn't listening anymore, but for Yvonne she had to try, and she said a quiet prayer.

'Hey, squirt.' Ian entered the hospital room and put his hand on Virginia's shoulder. 'How is she?'

'No change.' Virginia's voice waivered.

'She's tough.'

'Tougher than you know.'

Ian walked over to the sink and wet some paper towel.

'How did you get here?' Virginia asked.

'Heath dropped me off.' He sat in front of her and started wiping the blood from her hands. She'd forgotten all about the dried red blotches covering her palms.

An echo of a memory pushed its way into Virginia's mind and she stared at him with wide eyes.

'The two of you have been so strong for so long. Maybe now Laura's here it's time to put the past to rest.'

Virginia pushed her chair back and it screeched as it dragged across the vinyl flooring. 'You know?'

'The moment she arrived.'

Looking at the blood-stained towel in Ian's lap, a flash, a moment in the night so long ago, danced before her eyes. Ian next to her in the sand, wiping Richard's blood from her hands.

'And you knew. Back then. The truth?'

'Yes.'

'All these years? And you've never said.' Her words were barely audible. 'You could have saved my Costas from . . .'

Ian stood and put his arms round her. 'But I would have lost you. Unfairly so. No one would have believed it was self-defence, even if I'd said something. You're family, squirt. And then when Todd . . . well, later it didn't seem to matter anymore. But maybe now, with Laura here, it's time to let the burden of truth go.'

'Oh, Ian.' Virginia collapsed into his arms and cried into his chest as memories swallowed her.

January 1964

They let Gigi out of the hospital the next day, once she'd gone more than a few hours without any 'hysterical outbursts'. She'd tried to see Costas again, but they'd moved him to the district hospital to await trial.

The entire town was abuzz with the heroics of Richard, the pathetic fall of Gigi and the evil Costas. The story grew, the rumours rife, The Bugle fuelling the fire against Costas. And there was not a word of truth to any of it.

Gigi had to go and see Lily. The Woodhouses had arrived overnight to take her back home with them, but Gigi had to see her before she left. Maybe if she could get Lily on side, convince her of the truth, they could figure out a way to save Costas.

She knocked on the door of the holiday house.

Mrs Duncan answered, her face drawn and pale. She left Gigi waiting on the verandah.

Lily, dressed in black, walked down the hall towards her, her hand over her bulging belly.

'What are you doing here?' Her voice was tight, her eyes red.

'I needed to see you. To talk to you.'

A strange gurgling sound escaped her lips. 'Oh, that's rich. You seduce my husband, then your feral foreign boyfriend kills him.'

'Lily, you cannot believe I would do that to you. I'd never seduce Richard. Costas didn't . . .'

'You do not get to say his name,' she spat. 'How can you spout lies to me?'

'I'm not lying. The truth is . . . The truth . . .'

'The truth? Out with it, then.'

Gigi stared at her as Lily rubbed her stomach. The truth – so simple, so painful. How could she tell her? Even just a small part of it? No. To tell her the truth would be to tell her that her beloved husband, the father of her unborn baby, had tried to rape her best friend.

She lowered her eyes.

To save Costas, she would have to destroy Lily, her memories, her soul.

'That's what I thought.' Lily broke the silence. 'Richard told me, you know. About how you tried to kiss him when you went fishing together. Is that why you rejected Todd? Richard said it was nothing to worry about. Just a silly little crush. He was wrong, though, wasn't he? Well, now you have taken everything away from me. I hope you're happy.'

She turned to go back into the house.

'Wait.' Gigi reached out. 'Wait. I brought this. For the baby. You should take it with you.' She handed Lily the guardian angel pendant, wrapped in a crisp white handkerchief.

Lily opened it, her eyes flaring. She threw the pendant onto the floor with such force that it broke in two, one half spinning across the verandah, the other half ricocheting into the house.

'You were wearing that. The night you seduced my husband. The night he was killed because of you.' She spat out her words. 'Get out of here, you evil little wench. I never want to see you again.'

Mrs Duncan appeared and wrapped Lily in her arms. 'You need to leave.' She shut the door in Gigi's face and Gigi ran as fast as she could away from there.

Sitting in her special spot among the banksias above the town, one hand on the rock hidden beneath the grass, Gigi let her tears flow.

She'd lost Costas and Lily. She'd lost hope. She might as well have been in gaol. What kind of life could she have now?

'Damn you, Richard,' she cursed out loud.

She drew her legs to her chest and sobbed into her knees.

A cough from behind roused her from her melancholy. She turned around. Yvonne was standing there, a piece of paper in her hands. She held it out and Gigi took it. The writing was scribbled, the paper scrap.

'My dearest Virginia. I write this in haste and no words will be adequate. But I could not leave without saying goodbye. I will not go to gaol. There I will surely die. I will run. Hide. Know this, always. I love you. You accepted me when no one else would. You are the light in my life. I would die a thousand deaths if it meant protecting you. I would do it all again. Stay safe. Live your life, for both of us. C.'

Gigi stared up at Yvonne. 'He gave you this? When?'

No answer.

'I have to go to him.' Gigi stepped past her, but Yvonne grabbed Gigi's arm.

'He's already gone?'

She nodded.

'Yvonne, please. Talk to me. Tell me something, anything.'

Yvonne pressed her lips together.

A memory, a snippet, flashed into Gigi's mind – a figure hidden in the dunes. 'You were there, weren't you? That night . . . You saw everything?'

Tears fell down her cheeks.

'Oh, God. Yvonne . . .' Gigi backed up, bile rising in her throat. She turned, doubled over and vomited. 'I'm so sorry. I'm so sorry.' She sobbed into the earth and Yvonne put her arm around her.

'You know the truth? But you haven't said anything?'

Yvonne pointed to the note. 'He made me promise.'

'He asked you to keep this secret? Yvonne, no. It's too much. You cannot keep my lie for me.'

Yvonne touched Gigi on the cheek and together they walked back to town in silence.

———

Every day for the rest of summer Gigi visited with Yvonne. Every day Yvonne refused to speak – to her, to her family.

Yvonne's parents pieced together that she must have seen something that night. For her to regress so completely into silence, it must have been horrific. They called a doctor, but he said it wasn't uncommon for someone to withdraw after a trauma.

Gigi took Yvonne fishing every Sunday. No words. She asked Ian to teach Yvonne to surf, hoping that it would break the silence. No words, but a lightness to her eyes, which was at least something.

So many lives ruined by one single moment.

Guilt hung heavily around Gigi's heart.

When summer ended she stayed at the caravan park and worked, taking as much of the load from her mother as she could.

She put off cleaning the holiday house for weeks, easy to do with no one else booked in till April. But eventually she returned, memories of the last time she'd seen Lily there assaulting her mind.

She washed the floors and dusted the surfaces. She made the beds and scrubbed the bathroom. When she was done she pulled the door closed behind her. The midday sun beat down on the verandah and a sparkle beneath the deck caught her eye. On her hands and knees she got down to take a closer look.

It was the guardian angel – half of it, at least. She couldn't reach it from there, so she climbed under the deck.

The wing was covered with dirt and Gigi wiped it clean. She hadn't seen the other half when she was cleaning. Was it down here too?

After an hour digging in the earth, Gigi finally gave up and trudged home, the broken pendant in her pocket.

She passed the Tinellises' house, boarded up and defaced with red paint that had dried in dripping slashes across its front.

So many lives ruined by one single moment.

Once Costas became a fugitive, the hostility in town had been too much for them. Mrs Beaumont told Gigi they'd moved to their cousin's. 'Sad,' she'd said.

Sad. Such an inadequate word.

Gigi trudged down to the jetty and hung her legs over the edge as she sat, ghostly echoes of joy and water splashing haunting the quiet afternoon air. Footsteps behind her, a shadow.

'Hey, squirt.' Ian lowered himself down beside her. 'Are you okay?'

There were no words to describe how she felt.

'Do you want to talk about what happened?'

Her shoulders dropped. Talking was the last thing she felt like doing.

'Well, if you ever need me, I'm here for you. Whenever you're ready.' He hugged her, for just a few moments, before leaving her there with her thoughts.

Lying in her bunk that night, Gigi stared at her keepsakes, the broken pendant now sitting next to the photo of her and Lily on the beach. The next morning she wrote to Lily, a simple letter asking how she was. She sent it off in a blue envelope, the nicest one her mother had tucked away in the kitchen drawer. Every week for a year Gigi sent Lily a letter. Each one went unanswered.

Just before Christmas she sent a postcard, the simple words 'Forgive me', written on the back in her best handwriting.

There was no response.

Twenty-five

After the storm the entire town fell into a routine that saw the most phenomenal amount of work get done. After three days the beach was completely clear, and the roads showed no sign of there having been a storm at all. The bakery was fixed. The windows in the post office too. There were still many homes and buildings that needed repair, and makeshift solutions – tarps, and sheets of plastic, and generators borrowed from farms for public buildings that still had no electricity – were in place all over town.

But the scars were slowly healing.

At the end of each long day, Heath walked Laura back to the holiday house. Tonight they sat on the verandah, legs entwined on the bench seat, looking up at the night sky. It was the clearest, cleanest night since the storm, and a thousand diamonds blinked above.

'I don't think I've ever seen a sky quite like this before,' Laura whispered.

'It's not the same view you get in the city, that's for sure.' Heath's fingers traced shapes across her thigh. 'I'm sorry you have to leave soon.'

'Me too. But I have to return or Maher will have my job. I will come back, though. I spoke with him this afternoon.'

'Really? What did he say?'

Laura stood up and leaned with her back against the balustrade. 'He likes it. He's not thrilled about me going off brand, but I think he knows I need to do this. You know, reset myself, so to speak.'

'He sounds like a wise man.' Heath got up and held his hand out. Laura took it and they went back inside.

'Before I forget.' Laura reached behind the sideboard where she'd put Heath's plans for the cheese factory. 'You dropped these on the day of the storm. I've been meaning to give it back, but, well, it's been a bit hectic.'

Heath took the papers, his hand brushing hers. 'Thank you. I went up there today. Not much left of the old building now. With everything else going on at the moment, maybe I should put this on the back burner.' He rolled the plans up.

Laura put her hands on her hips.

'Heath Gilbert, if you even think for a second of delaying this dream of yours, there'll be hell to pay.' She took the papers out of his hands and grabbed his shoulders. 'This is exactly what everyone needs right now, and your dream is brilliant. That day you took me up there and shared your vision with me, I was blown away. I could see it, feel it. Please. You have to follow it through.'

Heath kissed her, long, hard. When he pulled back for air he brushed her cheek with his finger. 'This is why I love you.'

He kissed her again before she could respond and carried her into the bedroom. Slowly he undressed her, caressing her bare skin.

He kissed her shoulders, her neck, her breasts. She groaned as he lifted her onto the bed, want flowing through her.

In the middle of the night Laura lay awake, naked in Heath's arms, staring out the window at the liquid night sky. Never before had she felt so content. Never before had she known such happiness.

Never before had she been so scared.

She nuzzled into Heath's shoulder and he rolled slightly, his other arm wrapping around her.

'I love you too,' she said, her voice soft, muffled.

ces

As the moon shone through the hospital window, Virginia changed the water in the four vases of flowers that cluttered the small bed-side table.

'Are they for me?'

Virginia spun round towards the croaky voice behind her. 'Yvonne?' She rushed to her side, tears streaming down her cheeks.

'What's going on?' Yvonne tried to sit up, but slumped back down again.

Virginia called for a doctor.

'You're a lucky woman,' the doctor declared after he'd given her a thorough check. The specialist would be by in the morning and she had a long road of physical therapy ahead of her, but she'd be all right.

After Virginia saw the doctor out, she sat beside her old friend and told her everything that had happened since the storm.

'Ian knew all along?' Yvonne drew in a sharp breath. 'So what are you going to do? About Laura?'

'I don't know. I have to protect you, and Ian.'

With a weak wave of her hand, Yvonne hushed her. 'You don't need to protect us. You never did. Why do you think we've kept quiet all this time?'

Virginia shrugged.

'You silly old girl. To protect you. This isn't about us. What did Ian say?'

'It was time to unburden myself.' Virginia ran her fingers through her short grey hair.

'Set the truth free. Set Gigi free.' Yvonne looked Virginia in the eye. 'I always said Ian was wise.'

When the sun rose, Virginia returned to Banksia Bay to share the good news about Yvonne. Down at the shack she found her friends, and many people were at the beach, taking a welcome break from the clean-up.

The late autumn morning was crisp and fresh, hinting at the cold weather just around the corner, while allowing the memory of warm blue summer skies to linger just a little longer.

Surfers gathered near the jetty, Ian, Ryan and Heath among them. Aiden had his board ready too. Virginia set up the deck with jugs of cold water and small cakes. Trish and Charlotte sat on the jetty, their legs dangling over the edge, their faces lifted to the sun.

Laura waxed her board, the one Heath had given her, readying herself to go in.

Virginia had heard about Laura's efforts the past few days. The girl had certainly pulled her weight. It would have been easy for her to simply pack up and go after the storm, but she'd hung around. And not only that, she'd pitched in and helped as much as anyone else.

Even her story was something Virginia could get on board with. Long after the clean-up was done, the effects of the storm would still be felt. If Laura's story could bring business to their community, then it was worth it.

She watched her now with Heath as they headed into the water. There was genuine affection there, she had no doubt. There was also no doubt how happy Heath was lately. That Laura was the cause of that happiness was enough for her.

Was Yvonne right? Ian? Was it time to let the past go?

Too long she'd borne the weight of guilt.

Too long she'd gone unpunished.

The cool water rushed over Laura as she dived beneath the waves. Emerging into the warm autumn sun shine, she lifted her face towards the sky.

Ryan and Aiden caught the first wave, and Aiden waved at Heath, who was sitting beyond the break.

Filled with confidence, or adrenaline, or perhaps madness, Laura set herself up to catch the next wave. She watched the swell, she picked her ride, she paddled and popped. Up she stood, balancing on her board, cutting through the wave.

Ian cheered her on. Ryan gave her a clap. And she went back in for another.

She rode four waves successfully and couldn't help but be a little proud of herself.

As she paddled out the back again, she realised Heath hadn't caught a single wave; he was just sitting there bobbing in the deep blue.

'Waiting for the perfect ride?' She paddled towards him.

'Something like that.' He reached out and took her hand.

They sat in the water together, watching the others surf.

'I wish we could stay out here forever,' Laura said, linking her leg around Heath's under the water. It was so calm, so peaceful, so far from reality.

So perfect.

'Me too.' Heath rubbed her thigh. 'Although I've been thinking all morning about what I'd like to do with you tonight, and I'm not sure we could manage it out here. But I would be willing to give it a try.'

Laura leaned across her board and kissed him. He wrapped his hand behind her neck and held her there, leaving her in no doubt where his mind was. She pulled away.

'I could be convinced.' She breathed heavily.

Heath groaned and slumped forward.

'Heath? Are you okay?'

He started to slip off the board.

'Heath!'

She held him above the water, his head in her lap. She looked around, panicked, not knowing what to do. She screamed for Ryan.

He paddled towards them.

'Help me,' she called.

Ryan put Heath on his board and turned towards the shore. Laura followed.

They dragged Heath's body up the sand and everyone rushed to their side.

'He just sort of fell forward.' Laura was breathing heavily.

'Heath!' Charlotte shouted, running to her brother. 'Not now. Please, no.' She knelt beside him.

Laura stood there, unable to move. Ian and Trish hugged each other in the circle that formed around Heath's wet, limp body. Virginia slowed down as she stepped towards her grandson. Aiden joined his mother, nestling into her lap.

Ryan pulled his phone out of the folds of his towel, which lay on the sand with his thongs.

Why wasn't anyone doing anything? Performing CPR or something?

Laura stepped forward. Someone had to take charge.

'Move out of the way.' She barked the order at no one in particular and pushed forward. 'Is he breathing?' She turned to Charlotte.

Charlotte was checking Heath's pulse, his airway. 'Laura,' she said in a low, calm voice. 'I think it might be his meningioma.'

'His what?' *What is that? Why isn't anyone doing anything?*

'His brain tumour. I think he's had a bleed. Come here.'

She held out her hand and Laura took it, kneeling beside Heath in the sand.

'He won't have long.'

What? What is Charlotte going on about?

'Laura.' Heath's voice was ever so soft. She took his hand. His skin was clammy, pale.

'It's my time.' His voice rasped. 'Thank you.' He closed his eyes.

Charlotte let out a howl and Ryan scooped her into his arms. Virginia started to sob and Ian knelt down beside her, holding her to his chest. Aiden lay himself down next to Heath, his head on his uncle's shoulder.

Heath's hand went soft in Laura's.

'Heath?' she whispered, her throat so tight that the sound was little more than a squeak. She started CPR.

———

When the ambulance finally arrived, Laura was still working on Heath's chest. They pulled her away and checked him over. Then they took his body without words or fuss. Virginia would ride to the hospital with them. Ryan would follow in the car with Charlotte and Aiden.

'I should go too.' Laura turned to Ian and Trish. 'I should be there when he wakes up.'

Trish hugged her tightly.

Laura knew he wasn't breathing. She knew there was no pulse. But they hadn't put a sheet over him. Didn't they always put sheets over dead people? He wasn't dead. He couldn't be. She hadn't stopped CPR. They would perform some sort of surgery at the hospital and he'd be okay.

'Shh.' Trish smoothed Laura's hair.

Did she say those thoughts out loud?

'He's at peace now,' Trish whispered, through sobs.

At peace. No. That meant he was gone.

'Walk with me.' Trish's voice was calm, full of love.

To the hospital? It's a long way to walk.

Trish led her back to the shack and they sat at one of the tables.

This wasn't the hospital. Why weren't they going to the hospital?

'It was his tumour, love. There was always a chance this could happen.'

Laura stared at her, trying to comprehend her words. 'What do you mean?' She tried to listen to Trish's response. He was diagnosed three years ago with a brain tumour, a meningioma. It was benign, but because of where it was, they couldn't operate. With these things there's always the risk of a bleed.

But the woman's words jumbled and made no sense. Meningi-what? Heath didn't have a brain tumour. He was a fit young man.

'He's gone.' Trish's words were soft, absurd. 'But we can take comfort that it happened while he was surfing. Doing what he so loved.'

Gone. He was gone. *No. He wasn't.*

'And you brought him so much joy these last few weeks. I've never seen him so happy as when he looked at you.'

Looked. Past tense. He would never look upon her again. *No.*

'We were all so lucky to have him in our lives. God bless his soul. And he was lucky to have you come into his. As short a time as it was.'

God bless his soul. His soul.

'He's gone?' Laura tilted her head as she looked at Trish.

The woman in the blue kaftan looked at Laura with sad eyes. 'Yes, love.'

Laura doubled over, gasping for air. Tears burst forth in a flood and she wept into her hands.

Wandering from room to room around the holiday house, Laura felt numb. She was sure she would wake up any moment now and the whole horrible day would turn out to be a dream.

She'd assured Trish and Ian she would be fine and they'd left her alone with the kettle boiling. She'd boiled it three times since and still hadn't made a cuppa.

After all, she wouldn't be able to drink it once she woke up.

But the minutes ticked by. The hours. And she didn't wake.

There was a light tap on the door. Charlotte stood on the verandah, her puffy eyes rimmed red.

This wasn't a dream at all.

Laura opened the door. 'Come in.'

She poured two cups of tea and sat opposite Charlotte at the dining table, waiting for her to break the silence. She had no words to start their conversation.

Charlotte stirred sugar into her cup, but didn't take a sip.

'He made me promise not to tell you.' She kept her eyes on the table. 'At first I didn't think it would matter. You would breeze out of town as easily as you'd breezed in and you would never give any of us a second thought. Then you two got close. I spoke to him. A couple of times. But I couldn't convince him to tell you.'

She looked up and Laura held her gaze. So many secrets.

'Was he always going to die?'

Charlotte gulped. 'No. But it was a possibility.'

He's not like other guys . . . more fragile than most. Charlotte's words of warning took on a whole other meaning.

'I suppose you figured I didn't deserve to know, seeing as I kept my own secrets from you all.' Laura pushed her teacup away.

Charlotte jumped up and came round to Laura's side of the table. 'No. It wasn't like that at all. As I said, at first I didn't think it mattered. When I realised it did, I tried to get him to tell you. But . . .'

'But what?'

Charlotte closed her eyes, and when she opened them again they were wet with tears. 'He didn't want you to treat him differently. Or worse, fall for him out of pity. He'd fallen for you. So completely.' She sniffled. 'He wanted to see if you felt the same way, without his tumour in the way.'

Laura held back tears and walked around the room.

Would she have treated him differently, pitied him if she'd known? Maybe. Possibly.

'I did, you know.' She turned and looked at Charlotte. 'Feel the same way.' The tears she'd been holding back pricked her eyes.

'I know,' Charlotte said. 'And if it's any consolation, he knew too.'

Laura frowned. *He hadn't heard her say she loved him last night. Had he?*

'He told me at the shack before you all went out today . . . well, he said he was going to take you up to the cheese factory and tell you about his condition tomorrow. He wouldn't have been willing to tell you if he wasn't certain about how you felt. He said that the night of the storm made everything clear.'

Laura closed her eyes. Sadness and anger and regret and understanding and grief and love all fought inside her.

'I should go,' Charlotte said. 'Aiden's devastated. I need to be with him.'

'Of course. Of course. Poor little tyke. I can't imagine how he's feeling. Give him a hug from me?' She threw her arms around Charlotte before she left. 'Thank you.' Knowing Heath had known how she felt was indeed some small consolation.

The next day, Laura didn't leave the holiday house until just before sunset. She figured no one would miss her as they dealt with their own grief and, to be honest, she didn't think she could face anyone. As the sun began to sink in the sky, she pulled on her tights and sneakers and went for a run.

She ran and ran, through the hills surrounding the Bay, back and forth until her chest ached. In the dark she returned to the house and there was a note pushed into the screen door.

When afternoon rolled around the following day, Laura picked her surfboard up off the verandah and headed down to the beach. The note had said half-past four.

As Laura walked along the sand she could see people gathering at the shack from all directions. Everyone was wearing a wetsuit, even Virginia. And there were surfboards lined up three deep along the shore.

From the deck of the shack all the way to the water, a line

of lanterns hung from iron hooks half a metre high. Inside the lanterns candles were burning. Between each lantern, flower petals of pink and orange and yellow had been scattered.

Laura greeted Virginia with a hug. Charlotte too.

Yvonne sat in a wheelchair, a blanket tucked tightly around her legs. Laura bent down and embraced her.

'They let me out for the day for this,' the frail woman whispered, tears in her eyes.

'We're glad you came.' Charlotte squeezed Laura's hand. She turned around and picked up a wreath made of banksias from the table behind her. She walked along the lantern path and Ian joined Virginia, surfboard under his arm; Ryan joined Charlotte, with his surfboard too. Aiden followed, so did Laura. Yvonne waved to them from the beach.

A long line of people walked behind and when they got to the water, everyone got on their boards and paddled out through the calm blue. They formed a circle, holding hands.

Virginia, supported by Ian, nodded at Charlotte. Helped by Aiden on the board next to her, she pushed her wreath into the middle of the circle. Ian called at the top of his voice so the whole circle could hear, 'For Heath.'

Everyone raised their arms, holding onto the hand of the person next to them.

'For Heath,' the group echoed, and dropped their arms and splashed the water towards the wreath bobbing in the gentle swell. They splashed until Ian raised his arm and the circle joined hands once again. Then there was a long quiet as everyone said their own silent goodbye.

Ian turned his board first, Virginia atop with her head held high. Then, one by one, the surfers peeled off the circle and caught waves back to shore. Laura waited till she was the last one left and gave Ian a thumbs up as he turned back to make sure she was okay.

She put her fingers to her lips, kissed them and then trailed them in the water, tears streaming down her cheeks.

'Thank you, Heath. I love you.'

Back at the shack everyone mingled in quiet chatter. Some people had gone home to change after the paddle out, while some had just stripped off their wetsuits on the sand and thrown on some warm clothes.

Laura had gone back to the holiday house, unsure if she could face any more sadness, but Aiden had followed her and begged her to come back. She'd changed quickly and they'd walked back down the beach hand in hand.

A bonfire was alight between the shack and the jetty, and the lanterns dotted soft pools of yellow light across the sand.

Ian was handing out cans of drink. Virginia and Trish were passing around plates of finger food that just seemed to keep on coming.

Some people sat on the deck, talking quietly with Yvonne, others sat around the bonfire where Ryan played muted tunes on a guitar. Laura sat herself down next to Charlotte and Aiden climbed into her lap.

'He's taken it hard,' Charlotte whispered, looking at her son nestled against Laura.

'Hasn't everyone?' Laura reached out and held her hand. 'For what it's worth, he knew how much you loved him.' Laura knew how comforting those words could be.

'It's worth everything.'

Soft conversation drifted on the night air as they talked of their friend, their brother, their light.

Laura looked around for Virginia but couldn't see her. She lifted Aiden, who'd fallen asleep, and handed him to Charlotte. She picked her way past small pockets of people, exchanging those looks of sympathy people shared when they didn't know what else to say.

At the back of the shack Virginia sat in the armchair, a patch-work blanket pulled tightly around her.

'Can I get you anything?' Laura bent down next to her, placing her hand on the arm of the chair.

'No. Thank you. It's funny, you know. You get to my age and death is not a stranger. But it's never easy. Especially when he takes those you love too soon.'

'I'm so sorry, Virginia. I can't image your pain.'

'We are all hurting, my dear.' She patted Laura's hand. 'There is one thing you can do for me.'

'Anything.'

'Meet me here tomorrow morning.'

Laura agreed. If it helped Virginia in any way, then of course she would.

One by one friends started heading home, embracing Virginia as they left, kissing Charlotte.

Ian and Trish sandwiched Laura in a bear hug and said good-night, before taking Yvonne back to the hospital as promised.

Laura trudged back up the beach to the holiday house.

Alone.

In all her life this was the most alone she'd ever felt.

The sun shone brightly the next morning, cruel in its happy continuation, taunting Laura with the promise of a warm day, while refusing to deliver. She pulled on her coat and kept her word, meeting Virginia at the shack.

'Ryan has let us borrow his car. Would you mind driving?' Virginia threw her the keys.

They pulled up at the end of the gravel road that led to the old cheese factory. Reminders of the storm were scattered across the headland – fallen trees and branches, parts of the old roof.

Virginia held on to Laura's arm as they walked towards the site of Heath's dream.

'Why are we here?' Laura asked, her stomach tightening.

'Seems fitting.' Virginia stepped carefully over the debris strewn across the ground. 'I know what it meant to Heath, and this is where it all ended.'

'Where what ended?'

An old beam lay across the doorway to the factory and Virginia groaned as she lowered herself down. Laura sat beside her.

'My life,' Virginia said. 'Where one part of it ended and another began, to be more accurate. You deserve to know what happened all those years ago.' She sighed. 'I've been doing some soul-searching these past few days – Yvonne's accident, Heath. Life is so unpredictable. So fragile. You have a right to know what I did to your family.'

'What you did to my family?' Laura stared at her. This was it. The moment of truth. The moment she'd been wanting since before she'd arrived.

Was she ready? Did it even matter now? Yvonne, Heath – what did any of it matter anymore?

From inside her overall pocket, Virginia pulled out a broken angel wing and handed it to her.

Laura gasped and her doubts melted away. Yes. She needed the truth.

'I saw the other half around your neck. You have a right to know what it is, what it means, how it got broken.'

Laura reached beneath her shirt and unhooked the half-pendant from around her neck, laying the two pieces side by side on the bench. She raised her gaze to meet Virginia's. 'My governess, Mrs Duncan, had it.'

'She was there the night it happened.' Virginia nodded. 'You are very much like your grandmother, you know. When I look at you, I see Lily's eyes, her face. It's uncanny.' She let out a long breath. 'Are you ready to hear the truth? It won't be an easy burden to bear.'

Yes. Of course. It was what she'd come here for, after all. *No. Wait.* Whatever this was, it couldn't possibly be good. A secret kept so long, shrouded in mystery, couldn't be.

Would the truth hurt her? Possibly. She breathed deeply. Her heart was so heavy now, she figured it couldn't possibly hurt any more. And maybe, just maybe, even if it was really bad, finding out the truth would give some meaning to this whole tragic situation.

'I want to know.' She looked Virginia in the eye.

Laura listened to every word Virginia wove together. Not as a journalist, her story finally coming into focus. But as a granddaughter, a friend. As family.

Virginia's voice was steady as she recalled when she'd first met Lily, and Laura was transported in time. Year after year, the story unfolded, Virginia remembering events with vivid clarity.

Tears ran down her cheeks as Virginia detailed the night on the beach that Richard died.

'I'm so sorry, my dear. It was me. I killed your grandfather.'

Laura stood up and stepped away from Virginia, her brain trying to decipher the words. Virginia had killed her grandfather. Her grandfather, who'd forced himself on her. None of it made any sense. She paced back and forth.

Of all the scenarios Laura had imagined, this was so much worse. Virginia had warned her. *What if what you uncover isn't pleasant and paints people in a different light to what you believe to be true?*

'If you can bear to hear more, there's just a little to go.' Virginia looked so weary.

Laura hesitated. She didn't know if she could hear any more. She didn't know if she wanted to. But what was a story without an ending? She had to know. 'Go on.'

Virginia continued. 'A year is a long time in the memory of a small town. Stories get twisted, truths become warped. History is rewritten. But now you know what happened. And this is how the story ends.'

January 1965

No one spoke of the events twelve months ago. No one uttered the Tinellis name. Todd had returned from training, a junior police officer, but mostly stayed out of Gigi's way.

On the surface, you'd never know that night one year before had even happened.

But scars run so much deeper than that.

Gigi had accepted her life helping her mum run the caravan park. Dad had tried to bring up the idea of going to college, but Gigi couldn't bear the thought of it. Guilt and loss and shame ate away at her every day. She didn't deserve a life outside of Banksia Bay. She didn't deserve a future. Not after what she'd done. Not after Costas had given up his future for her.

It was one of those special mornings in late summer that Gigi had always loved. The tourists had all gone home, the days were still long, the beach was quiet.

Barefoot, she walked along the sand, skipping small stones across the water. It had taken her a while to be able to come down here again and not be overwhelmed with fear, but now it was her place of solace, the tide of the ocean renewing each day.

From the north end of the beach, Yvonne came running towards her, something in her hand.

'Gigi,' she called. 'Gigi.' Yvonne stopped in front of her, trying to catch her breath. 'I don't know what this means, but I'm guessing it's for you.'

She held out a little mouse, carved from the seed pod of a banksia tree.

Gigi took the carved mouse and ran up the beach, through town and over the banksia-covered hills.

Puffing, she slowed down as she reached the old cheese factory. She dared not call out his name. Dared not hope.

She picked her way through the ruins. 'It's me. Are you here?' she whispered.

Out of the shadows Costas came towards her. She threw herself into his arms and sobbed into his chest.

'Shh.' He stroked her hair. 'It's all right.' He held her tightly.

When her tears subsided, Gigi stepped back, taking in the sight before her. Costas was thin, terribly thin, and his face was gaunt. A thick black beard covered his chin.

'I know. I'm a mess,' he apologised. 'But I had to see you. See if you were okay.'

She cradled his face in her hands, and with that gentle touch, his bravado faltered and tears streaked a path under his eyes. They slid to the floor and Gigi held his shaking body. She couldn't imagine what he'd been through in the last year. She didn't want to.

She held him till his breathing returned to normal.

'I wasn't sure you'd understand my message.' His fingers trailed over her arms, sending a shiver down her spine. 'Or that you would come. I couldn't risk going to the caravan park.'

'I knew instantly what the mouse meant.'

'How have you been?' He looked deeply into her eyes.

'Me? What about you?'

'I manage.'

'How long can you stay?'

'A few hours. Then I'll have to move on.'

Gigi understood. Him being here at all was a miracle. She would be happy with whatever time she could steal.

'Wait here.'

'No. Don't leave.' His voice cracked.

'I'll be right back.' She kissed him and held his gaze. 'I promise.' She ran off into the bright day.

When she returned, she had with her a knapsack. Inside was a change of clothes – Ian's, which she'd lifted from Mum's washing pile; a wet towel and a bar of soap; a paper bag full of food.

'I made sure no one saw me. I wasn't followed.'

Costas moved back into the shadows and emerged a few moments later, his face washed, clothes changed.

'Thank you.'

They sat together on the old cart and Gigi pulled out the selection of bread, cold meat and fruit she'd brought with her. Costas shoved the bread into his mouth and then smelled the banana before devouring it.

He belched. 'Sorry.'

'It's fine.' She giggled. 'You have no idea how good it is to see you.'

Tears filled his eyes once more, but he held them back.

She kissed his forehead. Then each eye.

'It's okay,' she whispered.

She kissed his nose, then each cheek.

'It's okay.'

Dropping the mouse she'd been clinging to, she took his hands in hers and kissed them.

He pulled her towards him and pressed his lips against hers. He kissed her hard. She let him.

Throwing her arms around his neck, she lifted herself onto him. He grabbed her hips and pulled her closer.

The afternoon sun filtered through the holes in the stone walls, bathing them in dappled light. With clothes half on, half off, they lay in each other's arms.

It certainly wasn't the way she'd imagined losing her virginity, but it was with the man she'd dreamed of, and that was all that mattered.

'It will be even harder for me to leave you now, Virginia.' He kissed the top of her head.

'Then let me come with you.' She sat up.

'This is no life for you. It wouldn't be fair.'

'What about any of this is fair?' Her bottom lip began to tremble.

He ran a finger over her mouth and she nipped it.

'I shouldn't have come back. I've made life so much harder for you.'

'No. I'm glad you're here. I'm glad we . . .' She lowered her eyes. 'Now I know you're still alive and that is the greatest gift of all. Where there's breath, there's hope, remember.'

He wrapped his arms around her and kissed her again. Long and hard.

When they pulled themselves apart, Costas started to get dressed. 'It isn't right, I know. To make love to you and leave. I'm so sorry. But I should get going.'

'I understand.' She stepped into his arms. 'I do. I will never regret what we shared today.'

They finished dressing in silence and held each other's gaze. Watching Costas leave would quite possibly tear Gigi's heart from her chest, but she knew he couldn't stay. He'd already been here too long.

A sound from outside made them both jump.

A voice. Calling.

'Gigi!'

It was Yvonne. Fear and panic in her tone.

'Gigi!'

Gigi ran outside.

Yvonne was being dragged across the clearing by Todd, dressed in his police uniform.

Gigi turned and shouted, 'Run!'

Todd threw Yvonne to the ground and ran towards the cheese factory. Gigi tried to block his way, but he shoved her aside.

'Where is he? Where is that no-good murderer?' He burst into the old building.

Yvonne came running towards Gigi. There was blood trickling down her neck from her ear. Her lip was swollen. 'I'm sorry. He saw you running through town. I tried to keep my mouth shut.'

Gigi could see a lump forming above Yvonne's eye. That bastard. She ran into the factory and straight into Todd.

'Stop, Todd. Please.'

A crash from the other side of the building echoed through the empty space.

Todd pushed Gigi out of the way and spun around the corner.

Gigi and Yvonne scrambled to catch up to him.

On the north side of the building, Costas was running towards the trees.

'Stop! Fugitive!' Todd called, and pulled out his pistol.

Bang. The deafening shot echoed through the trees.

'No!' Gigi screamed as Costas dropped to the ground. He didn't get up. She ran towards him, but her legs gave out just feet away. She collapsed into the long grass. Yvonne knelt beside her, tears streaming down her cheeks.

'I'm so sorry, Gigi,' she sobbed. 'Gigi?'

Virginia Gilbert stared ahead, her eyes dry, her heart numb. The man she loved lay before her. The man who'd shot him stood over him, trying to make contact with the station on his walkie-talkie.

There was no breath. There was no hope.

Her soul leached out of her body.

'Gigi?' Yvonne shook her. 'Gigi?'

But Gigi was gone.

And the parched yellow grass in front of her ran red with Costas' blood.

Twenty-six

'I went away after that. For a year.' Virginia wiped away her tears as Laura stared at her. 'I was pregnant, you see. I went to stay with my aunt and uncle in Brisbane. When I came back, we told everyone the infant I had with me was my cousin's and he and his wife had been killed in a car accident. I doubt anyone truly believed our story. My baby, Steve, Heath and Charlotte's dad, had olive skin, just like Costas. It wouldn't have been hard to put two and two together.'

History is rewritten, thought Laura. She wanted to be angry at Virginia, at Richard, even a little at Lillian. But it was all too tragic for any kind of concrete emotion. She just felt numb.

'I will understand if you want to take this story . . . well, wherever you take such things. I have lived with this too long now.' Virginia stood on wobbly legs.

Laura had no idea what to do with all she'd just been told; what to think, how to feel about it.

In silence she drove Virginia back to the Bay, and took her to the shack.

'Laura, I know I have no right to ask anything of you, but please, before you tell the world, just let me know. So I can prepare Charlotte.'

Laura agreed.

Virginia handed her a tub of pages and photos. 'Your notes. And a few added in from me. Whatever happens now, I'll accept my fate.'

Laura dropped the tub at the holiday house and changed into her running gear.

She ran across the hills and stopped when she came to the look-out. She glanced down at the rock with Gigi and Costas' initials carved into it as she passed, and let out a long breath. The burden of truth was hers now. Lillian had never known. Virginia and Yvonne had carried it for so long. It was her turn now. But what did she do with it? What did it all mean?

In her mind she sifted through the facts, the images, the secrets, the lies, unsure how she was supposed to feel about any of it. About Richard, Lillian, Virginia. She wasn't sure she ever would.

At the top of the headland she stood, looking down at the Bay below her. She imagined Heath surfing in the waves and smiled through the tears.

From this distance you could see no evidence of the storm that had torn through the place a week ago. It was the picture of a perfect piece of paradise.

But there was no such thing. Nothing was ever perfect. Not if you looked closely enough.

The next morning, Laura packed up her things. There was nothing here for her now. And she needed some distance. Some time and space to think about everything that had happened – in these past few weeks; sixty years ago – and try to make sense of it all.

Tomorrow she'd catch the bus back to Sydney, resume her life, her career. It was best to keep moving forward.

As she packed the last of her clothes into her suitcase, she folded her coat and felt a bulge in the pocket. She reached in and pulled out the little wooden mouse.

Gigi's little mouse.

Walking towards the shack, wetsuit on, board under her arm, Laura counted her breaths in her head. She sat her surfboard on the sand and stepped up onto the deck.

'Hello,' Virginia greeted her. 'I'm glad you stopped by. I heard you were leaving tomorrow.'

'I thought I'd go for one last surf.'

'Sounds perfect.'

'I found this.' Laura held out the mouse and Virginia's eyes went impossibly wide. 'A while back. I didn't know what it was until you told me your story. I thought maybe you'd like it back.'

Virginia held the memento in shaking hands. 'Does this mean . . .'

'I don't know what it means. If I write your story, what would that achieve?'

'Justice?' Virginia cast her gaze down.

Laura hadn't slept all night, turning over and over in her mind what to do with the knowledge she now had. She'd played out different scenarios, each one of them leading to pain – for her, for Virginia, for Yvonne, for Charlotte and Aiden. For someone. Pain no matter what she did.

'What is justice?' she asked. 'The way you describe it, it was self-defence. Costas' parents are long gone, there's no justice for them. My father died when I was young. Richard's only living descendant is me. I came here to find out the truth. And now I know. Maybe that's enough. Maybe it's not.' She shrugged. She had no idea.

Virginia looked her in the eye. 'The truth can be a terrible burden to bear.'

'Seems so.'

'Before you go, I want you to have this.' Virginia gave her the pendant, repaired, in one piece on a long silver chain. 'I got Ian to solder it back together. He's no jeweller, but it will do.'

Laura ran her fingers over the ridge where the wings had been joined.

Nothing was perfect if you looked closely enough.

'Thank you.' She fastened the necklace around her neck. 'I . . . I'm going to go.'

Laura turned her back and walked up the beach, sucking in deep breaths as she went.

She stood in the white wash, board under her arm, watching the waves rise and break. She stood and watched, her feet sinking deeper into the sand with every ebb and flow.

'Are you going in?' Aiden came up beside her and took her hand. 'I could go home and get my board and we could go in together.' He looked up at her, his tiny face full of hope.

'I don't seem to be able to take the next step.' She looked down at him. 'Maybe my surfing days are done.' The thought filled her with sorrow.

'You're leaving tomorrow, aren't you?'

'Yes.'

'Why don't you stay? Is it because you're too sad?'

Laura's heart ached at his simple question. All the conflicting emotions and thoughts she'd had over the last few days, and a seven-year-old boy summed it up so easily.

'Yes. I'm too sad.'

'I'm too sad, too.'

Guilt surged through Laura, knowing she was going to leave Aiden and Charlotte and Virginia to fight their grief alone.

'It's more than that, buddy. I just . . . I don't belong here.'

Aiden dropped her hand. 'I'll miss you.' With slumped shoulders he started up the beach and she watched him go, her heart breaking all over again.

As he reached the dunes he turned around. 'I know it's not polite to say this, but you're wrong.'

'About what?'

'You do belong here.'

Twenty-seven

*L*aura sat by Mrs Duncan's bed and watched her sleep. In hushed tones she told her everything she'd learned in Banksia Bay.

'What am I supposed to do?' she whispered. 'What good is the truth to anyone now?'

Could a case be built? Would Virginia go to gaol? Did she deserve to? Wasn't she a victim in this too?

Laura's head hurt.

She kissed Mrs Duncan on the forehead and headed home.

Under lamplight in Lillian's dining room, Laura opened the other folder she'd brought back with her – the one with Ian's photos for the story she was supposed to write. There was a picture of Heath on the roof of the bakery, one of the surfers cleaning up the beach, one of Trish in her flowing blue kaftan feeding a group of weary-looking volunteers, one of Charlotte tending to a cut forehead.

Photo after photo of the aftermath of the storm. There were also photos of the Banksia Bee Festival and one of the paddle out. She held that one to her chest. Laura had no idea who'd taken it, but she was grateful someone had.

It was a pity she couldn't finish the story, but a happy ending was beyond her now.

The last photo in the pile was of her and Heath, taken when they were on the beach watching Aiden on the festival climbing wall. Tears fell down her cheeks as she touched Heath's face.

All she could do was keep moving forward, focus on her work. Maher was certainly happy to have her back.

Weeks passed. A month. And another.

Every Sunday Laura went to Bondi Beach and stood where the water met the sand. But she never went in – simply closed her eyes and breathed in the salt air. She found no peace, though. Perhaps it was because, even in the depths of winter, this stretch of coast was always busy – an army of wetsuit-clad surfers, the odd swimmer brave enough to endure the cold, people walking, people jogging. A never-ending tide of humanity bustling about their lives. Or perhaps it was because she saw an echo of Heath in the waves every time she stared too long at the undulating sea.

Perhaps it was because the burden of all she now knew would not allow her to find peace.

At work, Maher finally put her on the story he'd told her about, the leads now giving them something concrete to go on.

On a wet day in early September, she pushed her way through the crowded grey streets to get to her undercover assignment. Knocked and shoved and jostled, she said sorry to those she passed. No one said it back.

Sitting in the lunch room of the minister's office, Laura adjusted the collar of her white shirt. Plain white shirt, grey skirt suit. Nothing that would draw attention to her. Securing the position as a junior copywriter had been relatively easy, and she had her backstory memorised – nothing that strayed too far from the truth. Rule number two. This would be a walk in the park.

All she had to do was make friends with these lower-level staffers, gain their trust, and then figure out who was the most likely to turn on their employer.

All she had to do was lie. Her chest tightened.

A young man sat next to her and pulled out a Caesar salad for lunch. 'Hey, newbie. I'm Kyle.'

'Lara.' Not too far from the truth. 'Nice to meet you.'

'And you. What brings you to this sacred playground of political intrigue?'

'A job to make ends meet, like everyone.' She forced lightness into her voice.

'And what did you do before joining us?'

All she had to do was lie.

Except she couldn't. Looking into Kyle's happy, innocent eyes, she couldn't lie to him. If he was twenty, she'd have been surprised. So young. So not fair to lie to him.

Lies and secrets led to pain. Someone always got hurt, even if the intention of the person telling the lie was justified. Secrets and lies always ended in pain. She touched the pendant hanging around her neck.

'Excuse me, Kyle. I'm not feeling well.' She stood up and ran out of the office, texting Maher as she went.

Back at Lillian's house, Laura waited for Maher to turn up. He'd never been to her place before and she ran around making sure everything was tidy.

When he arrived she offered him a coffee, which he refused. 'Out with it, Prescott. You didn't get me to come over to infuse me with caffeine.'

'I . . .' She took in a deep breath. 'I don't know if I can do this.'

'The story? Is it too much for you?'

'No. It's more than that.'

'You were close to that Heath fellow, weren't you?'

She nodded. But it wasn't that either. It was everything. 'I think . . . I think it might be time for me to move on. From work.'

Maher sat up straighter and raised his bushy eyebrows.

'I'm not sure if I can be the reporter I was. To go undercover, to lie, and dig into people's lives. I just . . . my heart isn't in it. I don't . . . I don't want to be that person anymore.'

He furrowed his brow and Laura waited for him to respond.

And she waited.

When he spoke, it was with a low voice. A kind voice. 'You haven't quite been yourself since you got back, have you?' He raised his hand, letting her know he wasn't actually expecting an answer. 'There's one rule I've never taught you, Laura. And that's rule X. It's best learned firsthand, but sometimes people need a little push to get there.'

'Rule X?'

He stood up, put his hand on her shoulder and leaned in close to her ear. '*Always be true to yourself.* Maybe you need to figure out what that is.' He kissed her on the top of her head. 'I love you like one of my own children, Prescott.' He smiled. 'Go and find yourself.'

After Maher left, she made a hot chocolate with extra marshmallows and turned his question over in her mind.

What was her truth now?

Alone. Sad.

The next morning she rang her mother and arranged to meet for coffee. It would take time for them to build any kind of relationship, and she wasn't sure if they ever truly could, but one thing her time in Banksia Bay had taught her was how important family was. It was worth a try, at least.

'You seem sad,' Donna said, once they'd exhausted all the small talk. She reached across the café table and patted Laura's hand. 'When was the last time you were truly happy?'

The answer to that was easy, and Laura's heart ached for the quiet stretch of beach that haunted her dreams.

She looked into Donna's eyes. Should she tell her what had happened in Banksia Bay? Would it perhaps help her understand Lillian? Would it make a difference? She hesitated. Was it even her story to tell?

The moment passed and she didn't mention a word about Virginia, or the history she was now custodian of.

Back at Lillian's house that night, Laura sifted through all the questions and doubts and quandaries that had plagued her since coming home. She opened the kitchen cupboard and pulled out the box of files she had on Lily and Gigi. She took out the photo of Gigi and Lily on the beach and placed it in a photo frame on the mantelpiece.

She skimmed through her notes, the copied articles, the pages of The Bugle. So many people had lost so much, paid so much.

Perhaps sometimes it was better to let the truth fade into the dark.

She flicked through the files again and stopped. The missing pages of The Bugle were in her hand. She hadn't noticed them before. As she scanned the articles, each word of Richard's death, of Costas', made her stomach churn. So embellished, nothing more than tawdry gossip to fuel hate and scandal. Laura placed the files in the kitchen sink and lit a match. Rule number three, *trust your instincts*. Truth always lost its battle with gossip, people being far more eager to believe the latter. And in turn, gossip became truth. That Laura knew what had happened was enough now. Watching the past burn, she let the last of the tears she had inside her flow.

Sunshine filtered through the trees as Laura waited on the stump in the middle of the clearing, breathing in the fresh air. She hadn't told anyone she was coming. When she booked the holiday house, she'd used a pseudonym. One last lie.

As the Bodhi Bus came round the corner, she stood up and her heart swelled with joy when she saw Trish behind the wheel.

'Well, bless your soul.' Trish billowed out of the van, her blue kaftan a cloud around her. 'Why didn't you tell us you were coming?' She embraced Laura, squeezing the air from her.

'I was afraid I'd chicken out at the last minute and then I'd let everyone down.'

'Nonsense. But why don't we have a little fun with it?' Trish giggled and came up with a plan.

The holiday house was exactly as Laura remembered, even her surfboard on the verandah resting up against the wall of the house where she'd left it. She ran her fingers over it before heading inside.

She unpacked her things, spreading Ian's photos across the dining table. She was going to finish the story. A little late, she knew, but hopefully it would still help. She'd decided to go freelance while she figured everything out, and she was going to start with her story about Banksia Bay.

The money Lillian had left her was substantial. She'd be able to pick and choose her stories, and the freedom filled her with excitement.

At three o'clock, just as Trish had instructed her, she headed down the beach towards the shack.

As she came around the sand dune she made out familiar figures gathered on the deck of the old fishing shack.

Aiden was the first to see her and he ran towards her, throwing himself into her arms. He'd grown so much in the months since she'd seen him.

Ian saw her next and stared at her as she neared the shack. He coughed. Loudly. Everyone looked at him and he pointed in her direction. They followed his gaze and Laura could hear the collective gasp.

Ryan waved and Charlotte let go of his other hand to step forward and hug Laura. 'Welcome back.'

Trish winked at her and Ian caught the exchange. 'You knew?' He frowned at his partner. She simply smiled sweetly at him.

There were balloons in bright colours on the tables and food and drink for everyone.

From inside the shack a voice rang out. 'Why has it gone quiet out there?' Virginia walked outside, helping Yvonne manoeuvre her Zimmer frame. When she saw Laura, Virginia gasped. 'Is it really you?'

'Someone told me there was a birthday.' Laura beamed.

Yvonne, looking smaller than Laura remembered, paler, wiped tears from her eyes.

As the afternoon grew cold, Laura talked to Ian about finishing their story. He was excited to help. Even more excited when he learned his name would be included in the by-line. They put their heads down and started to make a plan for what photos to take and how they should structure the story.

'All right, you two. You can continue this tomorrow. She's here for a while, Ian.' Trish grabbed his hands. 'It's time for us to go home. Not as young as we used to be.'

People started to take their leave, hugging and kissing each other goodbye.

Aiden stole another piece of cake as Charlotte packed up his bag of toys. Ryan saw him but said nothing, and Aiden grinned at him.

'It's so good to see you again, Laura.' Charlotte gave her a quick hug. 'Can we catch up properly tomorrow?'

'Of course.'

'Can I get a lift home?' Yvonne called out and Ryan helped her navigate her walker over the sand. 'It's so good to have you home.' She clasped Laura's hands on the way.

Laura stayed back to help with the last few dishes that had been missed in the tidy-up.

'How long are you staying?' Virginia lowered herself onto the sofa.

'I don't know. Depends on the story. I don't have a schedule.'

There it was again, that sense of freedom.

'And after that?'

Laura could see the question in Virginia's eyes.

'I burned my files, Virginia. There's nothing left.'

The old woman's chest rose and fell with a deep breath. She got up and walked over to Laura, reaching out and squeezing her hand. 'You head home. I'll finish these off.'

The next morning Laura sat on the sofa tying up her sneakers. The angel wing pendant slipped from her neck and she reached down to pick it up. Under the sofa she felt something solid. She pulled out a long cylinder. Heath's blueprints. She spread them across the coffee table.

As she looked over them, an idea began to form in her mind.

Taking the familiar route over the banksia-covered hills, she passed the lookout and a sense of peace washed over her.

She continued running north until she reached the headland where the cheese factory lay forlorn. The morning clouds hadn't yet lifted and the scene was veiled in mist.

Picking her way over the ruins, she made her way to the centre of the site. So much had happened here. A life had been created, one had been taken. Dreams had been made, shared and shattered. So much joy, so much tragedy.

As the clouds began to burn off, sunlight filtered through the holes in what was left of the roof and she pulled the blueprints out of her backpack. She spread them over one of the broken tables and looked around the space. Heath's vision came to life in her mind.

The copper kettle, polished and laden with jars of honey; Heath's sculptures hanging from one of the restored beams; the cart repurposed and propped up just so, heavy with sourdough and nut loaves and bowls of olives, all sitting on a red polka-dot picnic blanket; artworks by local artists hanging on that wall over there. She could see the back wall transformed into glass French doors opening out onto a brand-new deck, a café full of people enjoying meals made from local produce. They'd call it 'Heath's'.

She walked out to the edge of the headland and looked at the view before her, unable to contain her excitement.

She pulled out her phone. 'Charlotte, do you think you can meet me at the old cheese factory? I think I have an idea.'

Back at the holiday house, Laura changed into her wetsuit. Charlotte had been almost as excited as she was at the thought of bringing Heath's vision to life. It would take some work, but she knew they could pull it off.

She headed to the beach and stood at the edge of the water, her surfboard under her arm. She closed her eyes, searching for the courage to go in. When she opened them again, she could see Heath sitting on his board, bobbing in the swell behind the waves. So many times since he'd passed, she'd seen his echo in the water. This time, though, she felt him pulling her in.

She reached beneath her wetsuit and held the angel wings that hung around her neck. Heath's silhouette shimmered, then disappeared, and Laura ran into the white wash.

'I'm back,' she whispered to him as she sat beyond the breakers. She could feel him next to her. Sadness mixed with joy, for what they'd had, for what could never be. Close to him now, she knew she was home.

Acknowledgements

I ran a competition for anyone who donated to my family's JDRF One Walk fundraiser to go into the draw to win a character named after them in *The Banksia Bay Shack*. Thank you everyone who donated, and a special thank you to the winners, Sarah Mercer, who asked me to use her daughter Charlotte's name, and Yvonne Trunley. I hope you both love your characters as much as I do.

A very special thank you to Mishell Currie, who reads anything I send her, no matter how long I give her to do it, and who came on tour with me for *The Cottage at Rosella Cove*. She kept me in good company over long stretches of country roads where we survived the scariest petrol station on earth and battled the elusive Ebor panther.

To my amazing critique partner, Léonie Kelsall, who is a whiz with feedback and the fastest reader I know: thank you, Lee, for always being there for me. Thank you also to Jennifer Johnson for your eagle eye and amazing cheerleading.

As always, thank you to Dianne Blacklock, my mentor, for continuing to share your knowledge and wisdom with me and reassuring me when I message you in a panic.

Michael Denner, thank you for sharing your surfing knowledge with me. You are a beautiful soul and I'm lucky to have known you most of my life. Thank you to Joanna Nell for your insight and knowledge regarding Heath's medical condition. You were invaluable in bringing his story together.

Claudine and Steve, thank you for helping me with Costas' story, for allowing me to use a family name, and for sharing your insights into immigrant struggles in the sixties.

To my 'Wednesday Writing Buddies', Michelle, Claudine, Georgie and Cassie, thank you for our fortnightly writing sessions. Your support and enthusiasm are a lifeline I couldn't do without.

Thank you to the ladies at Park Beach Bowling Club for the amazing support you have shown me since my first book hit the shelves. You are all so very special to me. There's a book in there somewhere, I'm sure. I'm just not sure I'm brave enough to write about you crazy lot!

Ali, my publisher; Elena and Fay, my editors; Emily and Sophia, my publicists; Laura, my cover designer: thank you all for your care, insight and support, and for helping turn the jumble of words inside my head into this beautiful book.

To my friends and family, for your continued support, thank you.

Mum, three books in, thank you for continuing to recruit readers and introduce people to my little stories about small towns.

To my sister, Karen, you have believed in my writing since this journey began. Thank you for being such an amazing support, often when I've been at my loneliest.

Chris, you had no idea what you were getting into when we met twenty-five years ago, but you have stuck by me through the many ups and some pretty horrendous downs, and none of this would be possible without you.

My daughter, Emily: life threw you yet another curve ball while I was writing *Banksia Bay* and you took it in your stride with characteristic strength, determination and humour. You are the might that I infuse into my characters, the resolve behind every word I write, the laughter that keeps me going.

And to all the readers, reviewers, libraries and booksellers, thank you for giving my words life.

Book Club Questions

1. Gigi and Lily form a very strong bond, despite the differences in their upbringings. What is it that draws them together?

2. What is Lily's motivation for trying to push Todd and Gigi together?

3. Gigi doesn't tell Lily the truth about the night Richard dies. Do you understand her motivation? How would life have been different for Gigi and Lily and Costas if she had?

4. Yvonne shows incredible loyalty to Virginia. Where does this loyalty come from? Is it justified?

5. How does prejudice influence the events in *The Banksia Bay Beach Shack* and the characters' behaviour?

6. Discuss the ways in which the events of the novel are indicative of the era. How might things play out differently today?

7. 'Where there's breath, there's hope.' Discuss the importance of hope for both Gigi and Heath.

8. Laura applies her rules of journalism to her time in Banksia Bay. Do you think the rules help or hinder her in her search for the truth?

9. Heath is worried his condition will change the way Laura feels about him. Is it ever right to keep something from someone you care about?

10. 'Maybe the truth wasn't just the first casualty of war. Perhaps it was the first casualty of life.' What does this statement mean?

LOST

Nicole has left her city life for the sleepy town of Rosella Cove, renting the old cottage by the water. She plans to keep to herself – but when she uncovers a hidden box of wartime love letters, she realises she's not the first person living in this cottage to hide secrets and pain.

FOUND

Ivy's quiet life in Rosella Cove is tainted by the events of World War II, with ramifications felt for many years to come. But one night a drifter appears and changes everything. Perhaps his is the soul she's meant to save.

FORGOTTEN

Charlie is afraid of his past. He knows he must make amends for his tragic deeds long ago, but he can't do it alone. Maybe the new tenant in the cottage will help him fulfil a promise and find the redemption he isn't sure he deserves.

Welcome to the cottage at Rosella Cove, where three damaged souls meet and have the chance to rewrite their futures.

'The best of the best of heart-wrenching yarns . . .'
Woman's Day

the kooka-burra creek café

THE PAST

For Hattie, the café has been her refuge for the last fifty years – her second chance at a happy ending after her dreams of being a star were shattered. But will the ghosts of her past succeed in destroying everything she's worked so hard to build?

THE PRESENT

For Alice, the café is her livelihood. After Hattie took her in as a teenager, Alice has slowly forged a quiet life as the café's manager (and chief cupcake baker). But with so many tragedies behind her, is it too late for Alice's story to have a happy ending?

THE FUTURE

For Becca, a teenager in trouble, the café could be the new start she yearns for. That is, if she can be persuaded to stop running from her secrets. Can Becca find a way to believe in the kindness of strangers, and accept that this small town could be the place where she finally belongs?

One small town. Three lost women. And a lifetime of secrets.

'Docker soars from the absolute heart, as she rebuilds all our lost souls in a café to call home.'
Australian Women's Weekly

Discover a
new favourite

Visit **penguin.com.au/readmore**